ITP:
Future Hope

By David Gelber

Ruffian Press
150 FM 1959
Houston, TX 77034
www.ruffianpress.com
www.itpfuturehope.com

Library of Congress Catalog Number: 2008937014

ISBN-13: 978-0-9820763-0-9
ISBN-10: 0-9820763-0-4

First Edition – 2009

Typesetting/Book Layout Design:
Gianna Rocha
www.brighteyes.org

Cover Design:
Samantha Wall
www.samwall.com

Printed in the United States of America.

Acknowledgements

I wish to thank Patricia Hadad, Gianna Rocha, and Samantha Wall for their invaluable help in preparing the novel for publication.

This novel is dedicated to my loving wife of twenty three years, Laura, and our three children Courtney, Chelsea, and Joshua.

ITP:
Future Hope

You may surely eat of every tree of the garden, but of the tree of knowledge of good and evil you shall not eat, for in the day that you eat of it you shall surely die.

-God

You will not surely die. For God knows that when you eat of it your eyes will be opened, and you will be like God.

-Satan

I. PRESENTATION

GENERAL MOOSEWOOD FUMBLED WITH THE SWITCHES AT THE PODIUM as he stood before the assembled band of political bureaucrats, preparing to start his annual report to the Joint Congressional Committee on Interplanetary Travel and Commerce. The group of senators and representatives sat and waited impatiently. Every year since the start of the program the general had the unenviable task of going before this group of officials to justify the funding for the Interdimensional Transport Protocol or ITP. It wouldn't have been so unpleasant if any of his audience had even the slightest idea or comprehension of anything that he reported to them. The general was correct when he assumed that the only reason he was forced to go through this annual exercise was to allow the politicians the chance to demonstrate their "fiscal responsibility" and concern for the "little guy." The vital importance of the program always seemed to be secondary. These thoughts ran through his mind as the general finished fiddling with all the switches and knobs and started his presentation.

"Good afternoon, ladies and gentleman. For those of you that are new to these committees, I am General Justin Moosewood, Chairman of the ITP Committee. It is my task to brief you on the nature and progress of our work. You all received our information packets prior to today, so you should be familiar with the basics." As the general spoke, a large hologram of a clown materialized above the podium. He heard the muffled laughter from the audience, looked up, shook his head, and bent down to fiddle with the apparatus again. The clown faded away. "I hope that's set properly, now." He took a deep breath and continued. "Today, I will run through the highlights for you, detail our progress, and inform you of our future plans. There will be time for questions afterwards.

"The Interdimensional Transport Protocol was developed following the pioneering theoretical research by Dr. Deborah Tennyson." A hologram of Dr. Tennyson materialized above the podium. "As an undergraduate student at Stanford University she built upon the theories of Einstein, Nguyen, Cooper, and Teacher with a very simple model proving the existence of multiple dimensions." Dr. Tennyson faded away and a series of colored spheres appeared connected by beams of white light. "These dimensions exist simultaneously within time and space. The model also predicted interdimensional corridors and portals. These portals and corridors connect these multiple dimensions, acting as points of intersection between them. The implications of this theory were staggering and opened up the real possibility of not only interstellar, but also intergalactic and possibly interdimensional travel." The spheres and connections disappeared.

"As you know we are currently limited to interplanetary travel within our solar system. Our most modern astroplanes reach speeds of .32c. This has made interplanetary travel routine and has allowed natural resources from our neighboring planets and moons to replace consumption of many of the Earth's resources, preserving the Earth from eventual extinction." The solar system appeared with miniature astroplanes zipping from one planet to another.

"The ITP, however, opens endless possibilities for our future. The greatest is the exploration of countless other solar systems and the ultimate goal of finding intelligent life elsewhere in our universe. The obvious economic potential is also an important consideration.

"We have completed all the preliminary phases of our protocol and are now preparing to launch the first manned expedition through the interdimensional portal. The initial probe was sent to the nearest portal which is just outside Jupiter." The hologram zeroed in on Jupiter and a large gray veil appeared across open space near the largest planet. "Measurements from the portal allowed us to calculate the parameters necessary to enter the portal. A combination of velocity and high frequency vibration allows the vehicle to pass through the portal and enter what we call the interdimensional plane. From the interdimensional plane one can leave through a nearly infinite number of portals and emerge at a point light years away. We have determined that vibratory frequency variations lead to navigation to different points in the galaxy. The mathematical equations predict the destinations with remarkable accuracy. Thus, we have constructed an intergalactic vehicle that can enter through a nearby interdimensional portal and emerge at a distant site intact and undamaged." The black ITP vessel was shown approaching the gray portal accelerating and disappearing as it passed through.

"The design of this vehicle combines an outer titanium, aluminum, carbon alloy shell that will withstand up to 5.2 x 10 to the eight vibrations/second with an inner carrier also made of the same titanium/aluminum/carbon alloy. Anything contained within the outer vehicle will be carried through the portal and into the interdimensional plane. Unfortunately, we have found that computer recording of conditions within this interdimensional plane have not been possible. The time spent outside our dimension is a black box, devoid of information. However all of our tests have succeeded perfectly. We have sent unmanned probes through the portal and then back through the same portal without mishap. We have sent a probe through the portal, emerging at our colony at Alpha Base One about three light years away. A probe was sent to Alpha Base One and then back through the portal, also perfectly. Live animals have been transported totally unscathed. First, a white mouse as a passive passenger and then Little Bit, the famous, intrepid West Highland White Terrier. You are all probably familiar with his exploits as they were widely reported in all the usual news media." A hologram of the dog, in full uniform, appeared as the portal faded away.

"Now, ladies and gentleman, we are ready for the most important phase of our project. A manned ITP vehicle will be sent to Alpha Base One and back. This will be the vital step that will lead to widespread interstellar and intergalactic travel.

"We spent many months looking for the right astropilot for this assignment. The ITP Committee has chosen Major David Sanders as our first ITP pilot." His image appeared alongside Little Bit's. "Some of you may know of him and his reputation. He has consistently been evaluated as our most skilled and accomplished pilot. He has ranked number one in the rigorous pilot reflex and response test. He may be somewhat of a hotdogger but he is best qualified to take on this vitally important mission.

"Our backup pilot is Major Anthony Sorino." His image also appeared. "He has been second ranked in most of our testing behind Major Sanders. He is not as flashy, but is just as capable. If anything happens to Major Sanders, he will be prepared to step in.

"Major Sanders has been training for the last six months and we are scheduled for the first manned ITP flight thirty days from now. If you have any questions, I will answer them now." The holograms faded away, leaving only the ITP logo.

There was murmuring among the audience; Senator Adrian Leavitt stood up. "A very impressive circus act, General. However, could you explain the safety precautions that have been taken to ensure that not only Major Sanders, but the ITP vessel returns intact?"

General Moosewood replied, "We've done all that we can to ensure the safety of our pilot. The ITP vessel has the most sophisticated computer ever developed. It is capable of responding to any command within five nanoseconds. Furthermore, it will be synchronized with Major Sanders' thought pattern so that any sudden actions that require rapid execution can occur almost instantly. The vessel can withstand temperatures ranging from just above absolute zero to 5000° C, pressures of 3000G and vibrations as previously stated. Of course, it will be equipped with all the standard safety equipment found on any astroplane. This includes medical diagnostics and therapeutics, immediate autopilot activation to provide some protection for a disabled pilot, and planetary probe, which quickly scans for inhabitable planets within 15 billion kilometers should a rapid landing be necessary. I believe all precautions have been taken."

Representative Ross McCauley: "Once our pilot enters the interdimensional plane, how long will it take for him to arrive at Alpha Base One?"

"The pilot emerges almost immediately from the exit portal; the actual time within the interdimensional plane is about eight minutes. He then will arrive at our base about one hour later. You can see a flight that normally would take greater than fifty years will take only about four hours."

Senator Gump asked, "Why is all this needed? Why subject a valuable pilot to such potential danger?"

"The dream of exploring the entire universe has been with us for centuries. This is our first opportunity on a large scale to step outside the limited confines of our solar system. Also, to be honest, Senator, this planet needs new territory. We are using up the Earth's resources as well as those of our neighboring planets and moons. Interstellar travel with our current technology is not feasible. The ITP is the most exciting new technology to appear in decades. It will open up the entire universe to us."

A few other congressmen asked questions, mostly inconsequential, primarily trying to get free publicity.

General Moosewood closed the briefing. "We are scheduled to take off from the lunar launch point in thirty days. I thank you, ladies and gentleman, for your time. Good afternoon."

The general left the briefing relieved that no serious objections had been raised. On paper everything seemed perfect and he could not think of any possibility that had not been considered. Still, sending a man into such unexplored territory was unsettling to say the least. He was sure that this project was nothing short of mankind's only hope for the future. He hoped the congressional committees agreed. Despite his optimistic presentation he knew that the Earth was in trouble. Technology was doing its best to maintain its 60 billion inhabitants, but resources were limited and the population continued to grow, despite the rigorous regulation of new births. The ITP and interstellar and intergalactic travel, allowing identification and colonization of suitable planets, was the last hope. He was positive the religious fanatics were not correct when they preached that God had created the universe solely for the Earth's existence and there was nowhere else to go. Science predicted thousands of habitable planets. He hoped that at least one could be found.

The drive from the congressional hearing chamber in Washington to the ITP complex in Wildwood, New Jersey, took about an hour. The huge buildings in Washington faded into the background as he settled in for the trip. The car was on automatic; he put his home destination in the navigation system and took a nap as the car negotiated the roads home.

The media reports of his congressional presentation were varied. The media were everywhere, reporting on every detail of every trivial event from lost puppies to interstellar travel. The ITP was always big news, always pulling in big ratings. Chaunce Edwards of the IBS network always had the largest audience for his reports:

"This is Chaunce Edwards coming to you live from the steps of the senate hearing chamber. Today, General Justin Moosewood, the Chairman of the ITP or Interdimensional Transport Protocol Committee, gave his annual briefing to the Joint Congressional Interplanetary Committee. As always it was a hopeful presentation designed to impress the politicians and keep the program funded. This reporter has been to these briefings for the last five years and as the ITP inches forward I can tell you that it is poised to take a huge step backwards. General Moosewood announced today that Major David Sanders will be the lead pilot on the first manned ITP flight. I have followed the career of this astropilot since he was a collegiate athlete and I can say with 100 percent confidence that this man will guarantee that the ITP goes down in flames. He has filled his career with unnecessary dangerous stunts, recklessness, and disregard for his fellow astropilots. I can tell you that not one of these astropilots would drive down to the corner store for this man. Just what were Dr. Tennyson and the rest of the ITP Committee thinking when they chose this egotistical show-off?"

The report went on with a nonstop tirade against Major Sanders, something that Chaunce Edwards had used to build his career, attacking Major

Sanders at every opportunity. It was not known why such venomous words were reserved for the major, but it made for good ratings and Major Sanders had never denied, expressed any anger, or even responded, at least publicly, to anything Edwards had said.

II. SPACE TRAVEL

WITH THE DISCOVERY OF THE HYPERDRIVE PROPULSION SYSTEM, INterplanetary travel had become routine. Commercial installations on planets and moons within the solar system, with the purpose of mining any available natural resources, became possible and profitable. Spacecraft velocity was measured on the sublight scale. The number represented a fraction of light speed, 1.0c equaling the speed of light. Therefore, .32c was thirty-two hundredths of the speed of light. Most interplanetary vessels traveled at speeds up to .22c maximum, with the huge space freighters barely reaching .025c. The fastest astroplanes could reach .32c. The record for sustained interplanetary velocity was .342c, achieved by Major David Sanders flying the XJ 240 in the year 2155. Interplanetary travel was primarily commercial, as none of the outlying planets offered any sort of recreational or colonization opportunity. There was considerable commercial activity, however, with huge freighters transporting natural resources that had been mined from the various planets and moons back to Earth. The Astropilot Corps had been born of the need to provide safe escort for these freighters. Interplanetary travel gave birth to interplanetary pirates. The Astropilot Corps, equipped with the most advanced and sophisticated space vessels, worked diligently to keep the solar system secure.

III. MAJOR DAVID SANDERS

MAJOR DAVID SANDERS ROLLED OUT OF BED, FALLING TO THE FLOOR with a loud thud. A thousand tiny drums seemed to bang simultaneously as he held his head as if to keep it from bursting. He dragged himself to the bathroom where a haggard man and a pair of bloodshot eyes stared back at him from the mirror. "Gelustat," he said as his medicine chest sprang open and a round green and white tablet and a glass of water appeared. He took the pill with the water, lay down, and waited for the pounding to fade away.

He had gone to the "free races" the night before as a spectator. These races were run on the outskirts of the city, offering free admission, and freedom from rules, regulations, and government interference. The main event was a twelve car race, two laps around the 200-kilometer course. All the participants drove identically equipped souped-up Mustangs. Although he had planned to remain only a spectator, one of the scheduled drivers failed to arrive (apparently he was stopped for speeding and reckless driving on the way to the event) and this opened the way for one of the spectators to participate. As soon as the unofficial judges realized that there was an astropilot in the crowd and that it was Major Sanders, they chose him to be the replacement. Of course Sanders could not resist the challenge, which he figured would be a stroll in the park compared to flying around the solar system. The fact that he was scheduled to take-off on his historic ITP flight in two days didn't deter the major from showing his mettle on the race course.

The air was heavy with the smell of rocket fuel and exhaust as he took his seat behind the wheel of the super charged auto. He took note of the power system, guidance and hazard sensors all of which made the car capable of driving itself around the course, if necessary. Each driver could have as much or as little control as he deemed necessary. Each system that was engaged, however, took power away from the main drive train and lowered the maximum attainable speed. Most of the drivers retained the hazard sensors, but implemented manual velocity control and guidance. Sanders put all the systems on manual, which meant he would have to respond to each of the many obstacles using only visual recognition and his own responses. He would be able to reach higher speeds, but at the cost of increased danger. He wasn't worried.

As he sat behind the wheel of his racing machine he turned and saw the competitor next to him stand up on the hood of his car and address the crowd. The man was dressed in black and his car was black. He appeared to be in his fifties, had a wild look in his eyes, and was unshaven with long hair. The girl who had been servicing Sanders' auto whispered to him that the man in black was named Fyodor and he had won the previous thirteen free race events. He would preamble each race with a short speech to the crowd and his fellow drivers. The attendant, whose name was Mary, said Fyodor was crazy, always going on about God, and Sanders would do well just to ignore the deranged man.

Fyodor screamed, "Repent, for the Kingdom of God is at hand. Prepare ye the way of the Lord. Repent from your sinful ways and trust in God. He is coming and ye all will be judged. Repent all ye sinners, the Lord is merciful and he will forgive you if you trust in Him and repent of your evil ways." When he finished, he strapped himself in for the race. His words had been broadcast to the entire crowd as well as his fellow racers. Each driver was equipped with a broadcast communicator so that anything said during the race could be heard by the entire crowd as well as by fellow competitors. Sanders heard these words which came from Fyodor, "Major David Sanders, you are about to embark on a journey to a new place that will bring you to a destiny that most of us only dream about. Now is the time for you to give up your sinful ways and remember that no matter what happens, trust in God." For reasons unknown, David was the only one to hear these words.

The words ran in and out of David's mind as he prepared for the start. He turned to the driver on his opposite side and smiled; an obscene gesture was returned, setting the proper tone for the race. The race started down a long straightaway for two kilometers, the course then suddenly narrowed to allow only three cars to pass at a time. The race was two laps around the 200-kilometer course that included hairpin turns and various shifting hazards. At the start, David and Fyodor shot ahead of the rest of the cars and through the first hazard as the others were caught up in the bottleneck. The two raced as a team as the other ten competitors were left behind to fight for third place. David and Fyodor were caught up in a match race as the course was suddenly blocked by a burned-out bus. Each driver was forced to alter course to steer around the hazard. When they came together on the other side, David had a slight lead. David heard Fyodor over the communicator, "You have God in your corner. I can clearly see that you were made for this."

David wasn't sure what he meant by "this" as they careened around the course dodging hazards with the man in black providing a steady commentary aimed only at David. They finished the first lap with David in the lead by about one car length. As they entered the second and final lap, Fyodor took a dangerous inside turn and emerged with a clear lead. At this point there was a loud crack of thunder and a heavy rain started to pelt the race course. Despite this new disturbance, David shut off all safety mechanisms to boost his speed and pulled alongside his rival. The other drivers were far behind. As they reached the halfway point on the final lap a new hazard appeared, a series of trucks. David saw that there was space for one car to go beneath one of the trucks, while the other driver would have to go around. David slowly eased his race car to the right and nudged Fyodor away from the path to this open space. As they approached David shot ahead and sped beneath the truck, shearing off his roof in the process. He looked back to see Fyodor run up a ramp and fly through the air with the rain and lightning illuminating the flying car, which struck a metal pole and burst into flames. As this was happening, he heard the old man's voice, "Good-bye, Major Sanders, you will come to know great sorrow and even greater joy.....Father, into your hands I commend..." And Fyodor's voice was silent.

David continued around the course at breakneck speed, the rain drenching him through the open roof. He finished the race in record time as the crowd, which hadn't budged from their seats, wildly cheered his victory. David felt a little uneasy when he heard that Fyodor had not survived the crash, but soon forgot all about it as he claimed his prize, a plastic trophy with his name written on the side and his choice of any two of the auto detailers, his for the night, for his own pleasure. David chose Mary and another buxom blonde lady named Esther. The three left together, headed for David's home.

David had a wild night, filled with wine, women, and every other stimulant one could imagine. He still was troubled by the words of Fyodor and asked Mary about him. "Why did he do it, race that is?" he asked.

Mary was silent for a moment and then said, "I think he had a message to tell and this was his way to get noticed. I know that when he won, he never did anything to any of us, except talk. He would go on about God and sin and repentance. We all just thought he was crazy. It was easy time; all we had to do was listen. But, some listened more than others. There was the other Mary. She went home with him after his eighth victory and never came back. I heard that she joined some freaky religious group and is living in a mountain cabin somewhere."

David found all this interesting, but not very enlightening. At about 4 A.M. he tired of the girls' company and kicked them out.

All these thoughts of the night before raced through his head as he waited for the Gelustat to kick in and his head to clear.

Major David Sanders was a tall, tanned man with thick black hair and perfect chiseled features, reminiscent of an old time movie star. He had been an astropilot for five years and had demonstrated, over and over, remarkable skill under the most difficult and arduous conditions. He was well known for his ability to push the existing astroplanes to their limit, routinely reaching speeds of .325c. He had flown manually through the asteroid belt when his navigation computer failed, something no other pilot had ever accomplished unscathed. There was no better pilot for the potentially dangerous assignment he was preparing to embark upon.

Despite his obvious skill, there were those who questioned his fitness for the ITP. Many considered him reckless and too much of a daredevil. His reputation for wild living caused some of the members of the ITP committee to question his dedication. They thought Major Sorino, who seemed much more level-headed, would have made a better, safer choice. In the end Dr. Tennyson had made the final decision. She had her own reasons for choosing Major Sanders, his obvious skills being foremost, but there were also other, more personal, reasons.

For now, the principal ITP pilot had cured his hangover. "A fine hope for the future of mankind," he said to himself. In two days he was to take the historic trip that would bring him the fame he so craved. The Gelustat finished working its wonders and in ten minutes his head was completely clear. "Breakfast #4," he mumbled and the kitchen snapped to work. In less than five minutes a half grapefruit, a bowl of raisin bran, orange juice, and coffee appeared on the kitchen table. The monitor came to life broadcasting the previous day's news and the coming day's schedule.

Major Sanders lived in a Quad home. These were five-room town homes with a central media center and four rooms projecting out of the center like spokes on a wheel. There was an eating area with computer controlled food synthesizing center, a living area, a bedroom with large computerized bathroom, and a fourth auxiliary room where Major Sanders kept his exercise equipment. The walls were undecorated and the furnishings were Spartan. Only the bedroom was lavish, to help the major impress his frequent guests. The bedroom had a large circular automated bed in the middle, which was designed to respond and conform to the slightest movement, lighting that automatically adjusted to any activity and an entertainment system suspended from the ceiling that was equally responsive to the occupant's movements. The room had a slight scent of old sweat, which was always present despite the efforts of the automated cleaning system.

As the major was eating, he heard the voice of Chaunce Edwards come over the monitor, "In a new low, Major David Sanders was caught on video at the scene of illegal 'free races...'" He quickly changed the channel.

Little Bit quietly walked into the kitchen from his bed in Major Sanders' bedroom. He barked at the computer monitor and a variety of dog food and treats appeared on the screen that was close to the floor. He pushed his nose against the screen and his breakfast appeared, a mix of chicken and cheddar cheese, fresh water, and a few choice treats. Little Bit was a West Highland White Terrier, currently the most famous dog on the planet. He had been the first being to utilize the ITP protocol to travel through the interdimensional zone. He had piloted the ITP vessel through the interdimensional plane and returned from Alpha Base One unscathed. His image had appeared all over the world. Of course he took the whole media thing in stride being happy to spend his days now dreaming of chasing rats and other vermin. He had suffered no ill effects from his journey. Major Sanders had noticed that his coat seemed a little whiter and he seemed slightly less rambunctious. He and all the scientists had decided that this was an inconsequential effect of interdimensional travel. There had been no measurable changes in any objective physiological, neurological, or behavioral parameters.

Little Bit finished his breakfast and jumped onto the major's lap, licking his face. Previously, the two seemed to have some affection for each other, but this had grown into a much more obvious devotion since the dog's flight. Major Sanders was crazy about the feisty little dog and the feeling was apparently mutual. Deborah Tennyson suggested that Little Bit knew that Major Sanders was preparing to try the ITP and was somehow empathizing with him. Of course she wasn't serious; after all, Little Bit was just a dog.

Major Sanders was the quintessential All-World male. He was 6' 4" tall, solidly built with a face and physique that made women swoon. He had graduated first in his class from Bush Memorial High School where he had starred in cross country, basketball, and track. He had won state championships in cross country and the 5,000 and 10,000 meters in track. He had also been the soloist in the school choral presentation, winning accolades for his powerful baritone voice. He attended Stanford University on scholarship, majoring in mechanical and extraterrestrial engineering, graduating with honors and eventually completing his Ph.D. At age twenty-two, he briefly came to national prominence while in college. He had taken up maximum marathon running and had won the world championship while a junior, running the 100 kilometer race in five hours forty-eight minutes, winning by more than twenty-six minutes. The effort had nearly killed him and he spent three days in the hospital afterwards. Understandably, he retired after this effort.

He had achieved additional minor fame at the age of twenty when he had skydived from a record 38,000 meters without any equipment save a parachute. He had blacked out during the free fall for about twenty-five seconds before he recovered and successfully landed; remarkably only five meters from his landing target. The record stands to this day as nobody since has shown the reckless determination to attempt such a foolhardy task. Major Sanders himself never attempted another skydive. He always said that he had reached the pinnacle and had nothing else to prove.

He developed an interest in interplanetary travel and joined the military, becoming their top astropilot. He helped design and test the XJ 240 Solar Fighter, piloting it to a record velocity of .342c, a feat unmatched to this day. This should have been enough to win him the coveted ITP pilot spot. However, he wanted to guarantee his selection, which led to his intimate relationship with the lead scientist for the entire ITP mission. The fact that he harbored no true feelings for Dr. Tennyson was of no concern as he was perfectly justified in using all available means to further his ambitions. Besides, nobody had been hurt and he was sure the fair doctor had enjoyed herself.

Their relationship was ongoing and he looked forward to a midday rendezvous. "Call Dr. Tennyson," the computer silently carried out his command and, as she answered, her holographic image appeared to be seated next to him. "Good morning, Deborah." "Good morning, David," replied the image.

"Can I meet you for lunch?"

"I don't know, I'm awfully busy with your preflight checklist."

"Just thirty minutes. I'll meet you at Buddies. I need to see you before I leave tomorrow."

"What about dinner tonight?"

"I'm dining with Joshua."

Deborah was quiet for a moment. "Do you have to, I don't like him; I think he's strange."

"Well, you're right he is strange, a very strange, peculiar man, but he has such a unique way of looking at things. I really want to get his opinion about this whole ITP. I know it won't change anything, but it certainly will make me feel better if he doesn't foresee any potential hazards."

"What if he does?" she interjected.

"That would mean one more thing to worry about, I guess."

Deborah thought for a minute. She really did need to see him as she had some important news for him. "OK, lunch at Buddies it is. I have something to tell you. I'll meet you at 11:30. See you then. Bye."

What news could she possibly have after months of midday meetings followed by intimate dinners? Probably some new fuel figures, he thought. He went to exercise and didn't give it another thought.

IV. DR. DEBORAH TENNYSON

DEBORAH TENNYSON CLICKED OFF THE TELEPHONE AND RETURNED to her ITP computer. She was a petite woman, twenty-nine years old. She had long brown hair which she invariably wore tied back in a bun, and wore thick glasses with large black rims. After the call from Sanders, she sat down at her computer, reviewing the same figures and computations she had been reviewing for the past three weeks. She went through every measurement, equation, and valuation one more time and one more time came up with all the same numbers. She had worried over every detail of every ITP flight, but this one especially. Major Sanders would be totally dependent on the accuracy of these measurements and calculations. A human life would be at stake for the first time, one that was very dear to her.

She sat down to her breakfast which consisted of computer synthesized grapefruit, wheat toast, and coffee. She lived in a simple three-room apartment decorated with fake floral arrangements and some horrible paintings on the walls which had come with the apartment. She had the most basic home computer system which fixed the simplest of meals and kept the apartment clean. She had a second, very powerful computer which she used for her work. This was linked to the Astro Monitoring and Measurement Center, providing her with the latest measurements from ITP portals throughout the galaxy. Her one great luxury was a huge fully automated computer chair which allowed her to sit for hours and never get fatigued. There were no books in the apartment, everything being on computer and modified to accommodate the reading disability that she never would outgrow.

After breakfast she reviewed her figures one more time and then went for her morning walk. She reflected on all that had happened recently.

The last three months had been the most exciting, wonderful, and stimulating she had ever experienced in her twenty-nine years. Seeing the ITP project through to its anticipated climax, coupled with her relationship with Major Sanders, was more than she had ever dreamed.

She certainly had not been a typical child. Her in utero genetic screening had been mishandled, resulting in a baby girl who turned out to have the uncorrected genes for myopia and dyslexia. Her mother had died giving birth and her father disappeared shortly afterwards leaving her to be raised by the state. Her disabilities had been discovered during her early schooling, forcing her to wear glasses and to be labeled mentally slow by her "teacher." She suffered unmerciful ridicule from schoolmates as she struggled to master the most simple sentence. She seemed destined to settle into the lowest levels of society until one day, while she was cleaning a classroom after school, she saw her teacher preparing a lesson for an elite math class. Deborah looked at the complex equations the teacher was copying and quietly mumbled, "They're wrong." The teacher was startled, looked up and shook her head. "They are wrong," repeated Deborah, this time emphatically. The teacher humored her and asked "What's wrong?" Deborah proceeded to go through the equations step by step, demonstrating where an incorrect assumption had led to a totally erroneous answer. The teacher was fascinated by this supposedly "slow" ten-year-old girl dissecting a college level math problem after only a quick glance.

A series of exams followed and the little girl with the thick glasses who had been destined for oblivion was found to have a math IQ of 225. She still had great difficulty with reading which led to repeated frustration, but she dazzled mathematicians with her brilliant insight into the most complex problems. She graduated high school at age sixteen, also attended Stanford University, and also received her P.h.D at age twenty-two. The last seven years had been devoted to sending a man across the galaxy and back. Her personal life had always suffered. She went from being the social outcast, ridiculed by classmates, to the intensely brilliant student and academician with no time for frivolous activities. That is, until Major David Sanders stepped into her life. He had been just another astropilot, but there was something in him that stood out. He certainly was handsome, but so were the others; he was intelligent, as were the others. It was something else, hard to explain, but very obvious. Whatever it was, she had fallen for it and was hopelessly in love. This explained her obsession with the current measurements and calculations. She wanted him home, safely and intact.

She looked forward to lunch at Buddies. This would probably be her last time to see him alone before the launch and she had very important news. She had hoped he would want to spend the evening together, but lunch was better than nothing. She finished her walk and returned to her computer.

V. BUDDIES

BUDDIES WAS A THROWBACK TO AN EARLIER TIME. THE FOOD WAS freshly prepared without any computer assistance, using real ingredients. Everything seemed to be fried, drowning in butter, totally unhealthy and wonderfully delicious. Buddies had been in the same spot for 200 years, owned by the Broening family, passed from father to son or daughter. Local health officials frowned on the establishment, but their many attempts to shutter the place had all failed. The kitchen was immaculate, the lines were long and the fare never failed to satisfy. The Broening family grew their own vegetables, raised their own livestock and caught their own fish. In a world where the food was synthesized rather than grown, Buddies was an oasis.

Deborah and David sat down and perused the day's selections. The menu varied by the season and by what Chef Richard had in his pantry.

"What looks good?" Deborah asked the waiter who was standing by. "It's all as good as it gets. Everything as fresh as possible," he replied. "Fried catfish lunch special," said David. "Grilled chicken Caesar salad," from Deborah.

"You look awfully relaxed for someone who is about to go off into the great unknown," Deborah said as she handed her menu to the waiter.

"I have the greatest confidence in my ground team, particularly their leader," Sanders replied.

"I can't help but worry; it's my nature I guess," Deborah said.

"I have the best team that has ever been assembled, every test has been perfect and I know I'm the best pilot ever to fly the solar system, nothing is going to go wrong."

"You have enough confidence for both of us. You really are carrying our hopes for the future. Maybe it would be safer to probe the interface more or try to find a way to actually monitor the interdimensional plane so that we really know what you're getting into."

"Maybe you can teach Little Bit to talk and then we would know what's out there. Deborah, I have the greatest confidence in you, in my spacecraft, and in my ability to get out of the stickiest situation. Stop worrying."

"I guess you're right." She paused for a moment and looked down at the glass of water in her hand. "I do have some other news to tell you. I was going to wait until you returned, but I think it's better to tell you now."

"What's that?"

"I'm pregnant."

"Is that all? Just take the pill and that will solve the problem."

"I can't do that. I'm three months along so the pill isn't safe. I think I'll just keep it."

Sanders seemed a little annoyed. "But, you know this is an unsanctioned baby and will lose most of its rights. You'll just have to see the doctor to fix everything."

"I don't want it fixed. I think I want to keep it. I can take care of it and if the government won't teach it, I'll just have it school at home. I hear that used to be very popular 150 years ago."

"Of course you might have some difficulty teaching it to read."

That was a low blow and Deborah started to cry. "I'm sorry, I shouldn't have said that," David said and he put his arm around her. "Let's discuss this when I get back in a few days, after I've made history."

David dried Deborah's tears as their lunch arrived. He knew he would be able to convince her that it was a bad time to have a child and he had no intention of signing any marriage contract now that he was about to become the most famous man on the planet.

"Will you fly with me to the moon tomorrow?" he asked.

"I just found out that I need to be there tonight, so I'm taking the three o'clock shuttle," she replied.

"Too bad. I was hoping you would go to the beach with me." David always spent the afternoon before an important event running for several hours along the New Jersey shore. It was his time to reflect upon the upcoming mission.

"Sorry; I'm sure I'll see you before you take off."

They finished lunch and shared a quick good-bye kiss. "See you on the moon," he said.

VI. 2156

THE YEAR OF THIS HISTORIC LAUNCH WAS 2156. THE WORLD POPULATION was now over 60 billion. The large population had strained the Earth's resources to the limit, but science had managed to find ways to provide for the people. The development of the computerized food synthesizer allowed basic food components to be processed into almost anything. An added benefit was that the nutritional value could be controlled, so that everyone got high quality, palatable food that was equally high in nutrition.

The United Nations Food Act of 2125 had guaranteed food via synthesizer to all the population of the Earth. The synthesized food was inexpensive and the basic components could be produced on a massive scale. As a result, hunger became a thing of the past. However, thirty-one years later the population had doubled and even synthesized food was threatening to be in short supply. Although there was an adequate supply at present, if population growth continued unchecked, significant food shortages would result.

Population growth was the most serious challenge that the planet was facing. The United Nations Population Growth Act of 2140 was designed to limit the rapid population expansion that had been the norm over the previous 150 years. The law made it necessary to receive government sanction for all pregnancies that were to be carried to term. Unsanctioned pregnancies were certainly permissible, but those women were denied government services such as mandatory prenatal genetic screening and therapy, and the unsanctioned child was deprived the right to basic education and the guarantee of future employment. The government encouraged termination of all unsanctioned pregnancies. Most women took the monthly pill. This pill evacuated uterine contents, essentially a mini abortion. It was safe and painless and caused little interference with everyday life. However, it could not be safely taken after the second month of pregnancy. At that point surgical abortion was necessary. After five months the pregnancy was mandated to progress to term.

The Education Reform Act of 2056 had been enacted to provide a uniform educational experience across all nations. The war on terror had dragged on for years, draining society of precious resources and limiting financial and technological development. The United Nations Conference on Terrorism had determined that there were two factors fomenting this terrorist activity. These were lack of proper education and religious fanaticism. The United Nations initiated an international effort to bring educational reform to all the nations. The concepts of tolerance and acceptance of differences were emphasized. Religion was taught to be the source of hatred and all religions that believed in exclusivity were downplayed and eventually ridiculed. After about 20 years of this intensive educational effort the sources for terrorists dried up and the War on Terror ended due to attrition of the terrorist ranks.

The massive education program led to a great reduction of religious influence in the world. All dogmatic religions diminished, including Islam, Christianity, Hinduism, Judaism, Buddhism, and many smaller religions. Gradually all religions faded away from public exhibition. There always were small groups of fanatics who insisted that there was a God, but they were generally well outside mainstream society. Those that preached their religious dogma were shunned as if they were lepers. In addition, a host of archaeological discoveries had all but proven Darwin's theories to be true, at least as it was presented by the media. The discovery of an ape-like skull with a pelvic and vertebral structure that mandated upright posture and walking and the discovery of links between amphibians and birds had been touted as absolute proof that Darwin was correct and all life had evolved from lower forms. The conclusion was that there was no need for God and no need for religion.

The discovery of the detailed genetic code for a large variety of species also proved, in the minds of most biologists, that evolution was correct and all other theories pertaining to the origin of species were invalid. Genetic mapping demonstrated only minor variations in the genetic makeup of widely disparate species suggesting that minor genetic alterations were adequate to account for all the known species. Most could easily be explained by isolated mutations as predicted by Darwin. These findings had also contributed to the demise of religion.

Incredible advances in medical science also helped prove that mankind was free from any deity. Prenatal and In Utero genetic screening prevented all congenital defects, inherited diseases, and a whole host of other imperfections. In Utero genetic therapy made it possible to choose a variety of traits for prospective children. The need for corrective lenses was eliminated with a very simple genetic manipulation. If a parent had the financial resources their child could almost be tailor made to their specifications. All genetically inherited diseases could now be corrected in utero.

Beyond prenatal and perinatal care, medicine now could cure most diseases. Cancers were routinely discovered in their earliest stages and immunologically attacked and destroyed with a minimum of discomfort to the patient. Acquired diseases such as atherosclerosis or obstructive lung disease were effectively cured with the current therapy. The computerized food synthesizer eliminated most harmful nutrients which helped eliminate many infirmities that were related to diet. Surgery was very uncommon as most diseases were prevented or cured with non-operative therapy. Surgery was usually only needed for trauma and most surgical repairs involved only minimally invasive procedures.

The unmasking of the genetic code had shed new light on aging, leading to a variety of treatments that retarded the aging process. However, the aging process still was incompletely understood and cellular weakening and death still occurred.

All of these medical advances led to increased longevity, with the average lifespan now approaching 130 years. Sometimes this increased longevity had disastrous consequences as a body lived on with a brain that had more or less died. There were countless nursing homes full of these aged individuals who required round the clock assistance. Medical research was actively pursuing this area to try to eliminate the feeble-minded elderly as they were called.

The United Nations had become the principal governing body of the Earth in 2076, ironically coinciding with 300th birthday of the United States. The nations of the world maintained their autonomy, but were obliged to honor laws as passed by the UN. The problems facing the Earth were global in nature and only a global forum could properly find the solutions. There was a single global currency, the dollar, and finances were funneled through international exchanges. All human rights were granted on an equal basis to all the people of member nations. Only a few insignificant developing nations were not members in the UN. The UN guaranteed that every individual would have medical care, food, education, and housing. Each member nation delivered these in the way it thought best. Members that did not comply with UN mandates suffered harsh sanctions, which ranged from financial penalties to loss of UN charter. Such a loss would leave the nation essentially orphaned, socially and economically, which would result in that weakened nation being annexed by a more powerful nation, akin to a hostile takeover in the corporate world. Such takeovers were usually nonviolent and considered necessary by the UN governing bodies.

Energy concerns had been eliminated in 2091. The completion of the Lunar Solar Project allowed inexpensive energy to be available for the entire planet. Ninety percent of the lunar surface had been converted to solar collecting panels which were eighty-five percent efficient in converting solar energy to heat and electricity. This was coupled with individual solar collecting panels on homes or vehicles, providing all the energy needs of the planet. The Earth was free from the effects of combustible energy sources, eliminating pollution and the potential for global warming. All the population received a set allotment of heat and electricity. Amounts above the standard allotment were purchased on a progressive fee schedule. Therefore, if one had extraordinary energy needs one was forced to pay extraordinary prices. Overall, however, energy was inexpensive and abundant and was a major factor in the prosperity that was enjoyed in the years following the completion of the Lunar Solar Project.

The exploding population had put a strain on the housing industry. Finding acceptable shelter for a population of over 60 billion had presented a huge problem. The solution was the quad home complex. Each massive building complex contained approximately 10,000 individual quad home units. Families often were allowed two units, which were modified as necessary. The huge buildings were energy efficient with solar collectors that provided a majority of the needed power, recreational facilities were on site, and transportation to other parts of the city was always available. The huge complexes usually were grouped together in one part of the city, separate from the industrial complexes, casino recreational districts, and waste management centers. Ninety five percent of the population lived in one of these complexes. Only the very rich and powerful could afford individual homes with individual yards. A very tiny percentage of the global population lived outside of government-provided housing, underground, on the fringes of society. These were the mentally unsound, criminal element or the religious fanatics; people that refused to be productive members of society.

VII. DINNER WITH JOSHUA

MAJOR SANDERS SPENT THE AFTERNOON RUNNING ALONG THE

white sandy beach that was outside his backdoor. The day was warm and sunny, a perfect June afternoon. As he ran, he flew the upcoming mission over and over in his head, trying to anticipate every possibility. Of course this mission was unique as he truly was going where no man had gone before, entering a complete black box. Despite the uncertainty, he still had the same cockiness that he felt before every important flight, along with his ever present indifference towards danger.

After his long run, he showered and drove into town to meet Joshua for dinner. They were meeting at the Regency Palace Casino, which was the major's favorite nightspot, one he frequented often. He walked past the large casino, the all male bar with its deep purple lights, the open bar filled with scantily clad men and women looking for an evening of companionship, and the exercise room that overflowed with sweaty man and women in tight fitting clothes pumping iron and running to nowhere.

The casino was one of thousands that had been built around the world. As the UN mandated social net, guaranteeing food, shelter, basic necessities, and work, was put into effect, the average work week diminished to three and a half days. The casinos arose to provide an outlet for all this leisure time. In addition to gambling, restaurants, shopping, rooms for rent, and games to play of all types, the typical casino contained a number of clubs, each filling a different need; one for single men and women under twenty-five, one for those between twenty-five and thirty-five, thirty-five, fifty, and over fifty. There would be similar clubs for men only and for women only. Typically those going to one of these clubs dressed provocatively, usually in the heat and hormonally sensitive dating apparel. This clothing gradually seemed to disappear as two people hooked up. As their interest increased the clothing decreased, eliminating the usual awkwardness that inhibited successful interaction. Everyone hoped to meet a willing partner and avoid an evening of solitude. This mating ritual was sadly repeated night after night. The "meeting clubs," as they were called, served a variety of stimulants to enhance the experience. After downing a few of the available drinks and pills everyone looked good and everyone seemed to hook up. There was never any worry about commitment and all the dreaded diseases had long been eradicated. The sentiment of the day, as with most things, was nobody gets hurt, everyone is responsible, so no need to worry.

He arrived at Duncan's Steakhouse and found Joshua waiting out front. "You're late," stated Joshua.

"I know, story of my life," replied David, who asked, "How did you do today?" Joshua answered, "I won a little."

"As always," muttered David.

Joshua spent almost every day at the racetrack. That's where the two men met, at Bar #23 on the second floor of the clubhouse. Joshua was somewhat of an enigma. He was sandy haired with a slight build, always clean shaven and neatly dressed. His most remarkable feature was his deep, piercing blue eyes. David knew that Joshua made his living betting on horses and that he was very successful. Although he couldn't be sure, it seemed that Joshua cashed a ticket after almost every race that he bet. Joshua never really would say. David did know that Joshua had a way of looking at a situation that was totally different from other people. He seemed to know what was important and what was inconsequential. This explained his horse playing success (Joshua never called it gambling).

David was anxious to get Joshua's opinion on his upcoming mission. The scientists and engineers had done all they could to insure the mission's safety, but Joshua would surely have a unique perspective.

The two sat down at a table away from the bustle of the main dining room. "Scotch and soda," David told the waiter. "Ginger Ale," said Joshua. David started, "What do you think of my upcoming trip?"

Joshua replied, "A few minutes riding in a huge blender, what's the big deal?"

"Do you really think it's much ado about nothing?"

"I don't know why you're asking me; I'm no scientist. What do I know about outer space and other dimensions? I have enough trouble with the daily double at Monmouth. You should be asking that sweet Deborah."

"I've already asked her and it's going to make her crazy before it's all over. I want to know what you think. I realize you are not an astrophysicist, and that you've never left this dear planet, but you've read the reports and I know you've studied the published accounts of the protocol outcome and you've even met Little Bit; so tell me what do you think?"

"OK, OK, I'll tell you." He paused for a moment and then stared into David's eyes. "To me, something is not quite right. You know what bothers me: Little Bit. Before he left he was your typical rambunctious Westie. Even though he is very intelligent, he still tore things up, dug holes in the back yard, and always tried to escape, just like any other Westie. But, since he's come back, something is different. He seems reserved, I know he still runs around and tries to dig up the yard, but not like before. His coat stays white no matter what he does and he looks at you with an expression that is either pity or envy. I'm sure you've noticed the change."

"You're right. I have noticed a change but it all seems very minor to me. Poor Little Bit has been poked and prodded and examined up and down, front and back more than any beast deserves. In every way that can be measured he is totally unchanged."

"I don't think you really believe that. You know something is different, otherwise you wouldn't have asked. Now I'm not sure these little changes merit canceling what may be the most important happening in the history of the world. But, you did ask my opinion. Besides, this is your big chance to be famous for all time, which is all you've ever wanted. Even the prospect of having a child doesn't compare."

"How did you know about that? Even I just found out about it."

"I watch the news. I can see that Dr. Tennyson has gained a few pounds and I know that she is not one to put on weight unless there is a good reason. Knowing you as I do, and knowing how spacey she can be, it doesn't surprise me she would allow herself to not only get pregnant but also to allow it to progress."

"You amaze me; you have to be the most observant person in the universe. I guess that is why you win all the time. Well then, what would you do if you were me?"

Their drinks arrived as David asked this question.

"This is good Ginger Ale," Joshua said.

"Don't evade the question. Tell me, what would you do?"

"I truly believe that you should go. First, the planet Earth needs this. We are in an unsustainable situation. Although technology has kept us safe from our excesses, it is only a matter of time until we overwhelm our ability to provide for the people of this planet. The population keeps increasing, medical science is keeping us alive longer and longer and we are slowly consuming and destroying all the resources the Earth and the solar system have to offer. A safe and practical way to locate other inhabitable worlds is the only solution. There is no way that current interplanetary travel can provide what is needed. Even at the speed of light it would take eons of time to find suitable places to relocate. So, this is the utilitarian thing to do. Second, even though there may be something that causes some change in you, I can't say that this would be bad. Although Little Bit is somewhat altered..."

"Don't say altered."

"You know what I mean. Anyway, I don't know that it is something bad. He's still a Westie, just a little more refined. You'll probably come back as a perfect English gentleman of old; chivalrous with a black derby and umbrella with impeccable manners, not the selfish womanizer you are now. If that's the case we can send the rest of the population through the ITP and make the world a respectable place."

"Dream on."

"Finally, you have been given the opportunity to possibly experience something wonderful and special. What do you think is waiting for you outside our confines of space and probably time. You may get in there and never want to come back. I can't help but think that there may be something of mythological proportions that you are going to be part of, and not just to observe but to actually participate in. A lot of the mythology of old talks about places too wonderful to describe or else too terrible for words. If such a place did exist I believe it would be outside space and time. I would speculate that it's not bad, however, because Little Bit came back in one piece. Of course, he's just a dog and the monsters in there may be fishing for something with more meat.... just kidding."

"You really know how to make a guy feel better. I'm expecting that it will be the most boring ten minutes of my life. I'll just be a passenger inside the giant mixer, as you called it. I'm going to let the computer do all the work while I admire the scenery. Let's order dinner."

"Do you have anything fresh?" Joshua asked the waiter. Joshua hated computer synthesized food. He preferred freshly prepared real food. It was one of the few luxuries he allowed himself and he did not mind paying the extra money. The waiter replied, "Today we have fresh oysters at $209 a dozen and we have a garden salad with real egg for $259." Of course the price was exorbitant. At home, Joshua usually prepared his own food, cooking it the old fashioned way. "I'll have one order of each," he said. "I've had a good week," he told David.

David ordered an eighteen ounce strip steak with salad and baked potato, this for a much more reasonable $32. "I can't tell fresh from canned. Now, what were we talking about? Oh yeah, passively riding along to fame. I'm not expecting to have to do anything. This whole ITP thing is extremely complicated, but also completely automated. The ship does have a manual override if I get into a jam, but I don't intend to use it. I can't see anything going wrong."

"Just keep telling yourself that and you'll be fine. When are you leaving for the take-off?"

"I'm jetting up to the moon tomorrow morning. Deborah left on the lunar shuttle today. Sorino is already there, I think. I guess they want him available if I crash on the way to the launch. He could just step in like a good little understudy, just like in a Broadway show. Anyway, I'm waiting until tomorrow to fly up there. I want to sleep in my own bed, preferably with some willing female companionship."

"What about Deborah? Doesn't she mind your extracurricular activity?"

"I don't even think she is aware. She has been so tied up in this project that when we are not together she is stuck to her computer figuring and calculating. Besides, I don't have any marriage contract with her. She knows I have no obligation, even if she is pregnant. She should have stopped the whole thing early on like any other woman would have done. I'll just deal with that when I get back. What about you are you going to watch history in the making tomorrow?"

"I'll watch the recording. There's a filly in the seventh race tomorrow I've got to see in person. She has been working like she's the second coming." Joshua had been waiting for years for a horse that could match the legendary Ruffian. Even though she had raced nearly two hundred years ago, there had never been another that approached her level of perfection. David had always thought it odd that someone so intelligent could be so obsessed with searching for the perfect horse.

"What's the filly's name?" David asked.

"Ruth Rising," he replied. "She's only run once. She worked in 55.4 prior to her first race. She broke her maiden by 22 lengths, running 1:00.35 for five and half furlongs. She's running in a non-winner of an allowance. She won't be worth a wager, but I want to see how she runs."

"I hope for your sake she is what you are searching for; then you can finally die in peace."

"Maybe history will be made on several fronts tomorrow."

Dinner arrived and the waiter laid their plates down. "Would either care for anything else?" he inquired.

"I'll have another scotch and soda," said David.

"I'm fine," said Joshua, who added, "Shouldn't you keep a clear head about you."

"I'll be OK," he replied. "That's the great thing about modern medicine. You can live the hedonistic lifestyle and never suffer any consequences. All you have to do is look around you." It was true. Everywhere in this and countless similar casinos were people, young and old, looking for a night of thrills or excitement. They came to find sex, intoxication, a gambler's rush or a myriad of other amusements to pass the time. And it was also true that medical science had removed the risks of disease or bodily damage that could be associated with such excesses. Consequently, David could spend the night indulging himself and still be able to fly across the galaxy the next day. Still there were limits. Science had never found a way to eliminate the need for sleep and the pills could eventually lose their effectiveness. This didn't stop David from depending on them to keep his head clear at flight time.

"What music will you be playing on your flight?" Joshua asked. They were both connoisseurs of classical music.

David answered, "Bach for the trip to the interface, Orff as I pass through the portal, and Beethoven once I'm interdimensional. I haven't decided about the trip home, probably just reverse them."

"I'm listening to Berlioz now. His music is quite unique in many ways."

David looked around the room.

"Are you bored?" Joshua asked.

"Just checking out the room," he answered. "Look at those two at the table over there." David pointed to two attractive women seated across the room. He called the waiter and sent a bottle of real champagne to their table with a hologram asking them to join him. "Now where were we?"

"Discussing music. You need to worry less about below your belt and think about tomorrow. You are about to become famous. Your name will go alongside the Wright brothers, Lindbergh, Armstrong, Walton, and Strasser. You'll be the most famous astropilot on the planet. You'll be the one to lead the people out of the wilderness and into the Promised Land. I know it's what you've always wanted, to be famous and go down in history. Well, the whole world will be watching you. You'll be so well known that you'll have to beat the women off with a stick. Now, you should go home, take a hot bath, and go to bed. Saving the world requires a good night's sleep."

"Oh, I'll be fine. A couple of Gelustat and I'll be ready to fly anywhere."

"You can't live on that stuff. Eventually it will catch up with you."

"Thank you, almost a doctor, perhaps you're right, but I don't think eventually is tomorrow."

The two ladies giggling to each other came over. "Hello ladies," David greeted them. "Have a seat. I'm David and this is Joshua." "

"Hello," Joshua said quietly. He had no interest in mingling with the young ladies, but he would mind his manners and try to be pleasant.

"I'm Briana and this is Tawny," replied the blonde. Tawny had reddish brown hair. Both had the typical appearance that was popular with young women, thin with long hair and prominent chest. Joshua caught the scent of the latest pheromone-based perfume. The two ladies sat down and the next hour was spent talking about nothing. Both were properly awed by David and equally bored by Joshua. Finally, David suggested that they leave together. "Perhaps we can go to my apartment," he suggested.

"That sounds great," they both replied.

"You coming, Joshua?"

"Maybe," he answered.

The waiter brought the check and Joshua treated them. The four walked to the parking lot where David had his S-280 parked and fully charged. As they approached the car six young men brandishing the latest laser knives jumped out from the shadows. They grabbed the four and held their knives to their necks. "Let's see how you did at the casino tonight," said one of them. Before the words were out of his mouth a fist struck one of the assailants on the side of the head and he crumpled to the ground. The other would-be muggers tried to react, but a flurry of fists and feet left them beaten and bloody on the pavement. David stood over them taunting them as Joshua notified the police. The six would-be assailants were afraid to even move. Never had any of them seen such a violent and rapid reaction. David's martial arts training came in handy. His military instructors had noted that he had the fastest reflexes and keenest perception of any trainee they had ever encountered. David seemed exhilarated after the very one-sided fight. However, he no longer craved female company and sent Tawny and Briana home in a cab.

Gangs of marauding youths frequently terrorized the casino district. The dangers these groups posed were widely reported in the media. Normally the police kept them away, but this group had apparently eluded the usual surveillance. David couldn't understand what they wanted. Everyone was given all the necessities, shelter, food, work, medical care, and even luxuries like cars. Why go around attacking innocent people. It made no sense, but there was a lot in this world that made no sense, he thought, as the police arrived. He gave a statement to the authorities and they wished him luck on his upcoming launch. As he was leaving he called to Joshua, "Look in on Little Bit for me while I'm gone, will you?"

"OK, have a safe flight."

David hopped into his S-280 and sped home. He knew that Joshua preferred to walk and didn't offer him a lift home.

Joshua reached his apartment in about thirty minutes. He chose to walk the two flights of stairs to the two-room apartment. The rooms were clean but stark. There was a truly functional kitchen with a real refrigerator, stove, and oven. There were shelves filled with books. There was a solitary, simple computer on a table. In the second room were a bed, nightstand, and dresser. A small bathroom opened off the bedroom. A simple but refined music system sat on the table next to the computer and a separate videophone was on a smaller table between two chairs. All in all a functional apartment for someone who spent most of his time studying racing charts or watching horses compete.

Joshua turned on the computer. The next days past performances appeared on the screen and he sat down to study them once again, always looking for the little clues that said that this was the day for that horse. He had learned to read between the rows of figures. Among his friends at the track he was regarded as a legend, he was that successful. Still, it required some work. He stared at the monitor looking at the charts, but without comprehension. Something about dinner that evening bothered him. He lay down and thought about David and Deborah and Little Bit and the whole ITP. If David's mission were a horse race, he wouldn't consider betting on it. There were too many unknowns. Sure, he could see the beginning and the outcome, but it was like a horse race on a foggy day. It was impossible to see what happened in the middle. He hoped David would be OK, but he still felt uneasy as he dozed off.

David arrived home and looked at his messages. Deborah had called saying everything was ready for tomorrow and that she missed him. She really loves me, he said to himself. I like being with her, he thought, but he didn't think he could ever really love another person.

Little Bit jumped on the couch and lay down next to him. There were several messages from friends and acquaintances wishing him luck and a safe voyage. "Bach," he spoke to the computer and the vibrant strains of a Brandenburg Concerto filled the room. He tried to relax, but the night's events played back in his head. The fight with the now incarcerated muggers had left him tired, but also restless. What if he had been injured or killed, what if Joshua or the girls had been hurt; that would have ended his chance to be famous. Sorino would take over and David would have become a footnote in future history lessons. He felt fortunate that it all had turned out alright. He took it as a good omen. Perhaps the powers that be were looking out for him. Little Bit stretched and put his paw on David's arm. "I wish you could talk," David said as he stroked Little Bit's rough fur. "You could tell me what to expect." Little Bit barked as if he understood every word David had said. The sweet melody of Bach filled the room and David and Little Bit drifted off to sleep together.

VIII. PRELAUNCH

DEBORAH SAT UP LOOKING AT HER MONITOR, REVIEWING FIGURES, checking measurements and sometimes getting up and going to the window to stare out at the lunar sky. "Everything's perfect. Stop worrying," she said to herself. She lay down on her bed, but she couldn't sleep. She knew that she wouldn't relax until David was safely home. She lay in the dark staring up at the ceiling as numbers swirled around her brain. "I wish he were here now," she thought as she got up and went back to her computer.

Major Sorino had arrived earlier that day. As backup he was given the duty of checking the ITP Vessel, dubbed the Falcon, prior to Major Sanders arrival the following the day. With the computer tablet in hand he went through the checklist with Scully, the senior mechanical engineer. "Everything checks out, Scully. I want to run a scan on the trans-ionic coating, make sure that there are not any defective areas. Could you get the molecular scanner?"

The trans-ionic coating was the outer shell of the ITP vessel. When charged it would provide the vibration that would allow the ship to pass through the portal into the interdimensional plane. The coating was bonded to the titanium aluminum alloy and had to be perfectly uniform and intact. A scan had been run earlier in the day, but Sorino wanted to be sure.

They went to the monitoring center and brought down the scanning probes. A white light enveloped the ship. "100 percent perfect, of course," said Scully. "I never doubted for a moment," came the response. "Let's lock this down and get some rest. She's as ready as she'll ever be."

Major Sorino returned to his quarters and sat down at the computer console. He looked at the solar clock. New Jersey time was 11:30. "Call home," he said and Jessie appeared on the screen looking radiant in her nightgown. "Hello beautiful," he began and he proceeded to tell her about all the day's events.

Major Anthony Sorino had only one thing in common with David Sanders. They were extraordinary astropilots. Sorino did not indulge in any of the excesses that filled Sander's life. He had a lifetime marriage contract with Jessie which was most unusual. Most married couples opted for the far more flexible one-year renewable marriage contracts. This allowed for easy separation at the end of the contract without requiring any complicated and messy divorce proceedings. Even the eighteen year child-raising contract was more common. A lifetime contract was generally not recommended by the legal counsel because the commitment was thought too great for any man or woman to make.

That Major Sorino was alive to be any sort of pilot was miraculous. He had been a disturbed child, indifferent to school, in and out of trouble until the age of twelve. Shortly after his twelfth birthday, he was riding a three-wheeled motorized vehicle, enjoying the wind in his face beneath the clear blue sky, when he struck a rock on the side of the road, lost control, struck a retaining wall, and was hurled through the air, landing with a thud thirty meters from the wall. Luckily, he was wearing his helmet, but he sustained severe injuries, with fractures to twelve ribs, punctured lung, fractured pelvis, lacerated liver and right kidney. He was found within minutes as his implanted transponder signal alarmed and life support crews were immediately dispatched. He arrived at the hospital with no obtainable blood pressure. The Trauma crew worked feverishly to save him, but all vital signs were lost for nearly ten minutes. The Trauma chief called it quits and the crew left to go on to the next victim. The morgue attendant, however, saw him take a breath and the monitors that had not been removed revealed both a heart rhythm and blood pressure. The crew returned and was able to bring him back to life and stabilize him. Three weeks later, he walked out of the hospital. Afterwards, he seemed different. The aimless, troubled youth was replaced by a determined young man with a strong sense of purpose. He decided early on to become a pilot, taking what was considered average talent and turning it into extraordinary skill. Through intensely hard work he reached the level of number two in the Astropilot Corps and was selected backup to Major Sanders for the ITP. Although he was disappointed that he was not first choice, he accepted the number two role, confident that he would be on the second manned ITP flight.

The Sorinos lived in a nondescript three-bedroom home with Mary, Jason, and Angelica, their three children, and Malcolm, their calico cat. Their home was filled with a vibrancy that was only found between people totally devoted to one another. The home had only the most basic conveniences, computerized food synthesizer, self cleaning, basic communications, and such. They had disabled the adult entertainment access found on all the new home computer systems. Most of the computerized functions were automated and could not be disabled. Jessie wished there wasn't any computer, but it was impossible to find a house without computerized services these days. A frequent game for her was trying to beat the computerized cleaning system. She would race the computer to clean any mess that her kids made and she always said she did a much better job.

Jessie recounted her day's events, the trouble the kids had caused, what she had for dinner and all the other mundane occurrences that were part of a young mother's day. "I miss you so much; I hate it when you are gone even for one day." "So do I," he replied, "but you never know what to expect when Major Sanders is involved. He's not even here yet."

"You don't think he'll miss this mission do you?"

"I'm sure he'll be here. After tomorrow he'll be famous, probably be featured on talk shows, write a book, and retire to a life of leisure on some distant planet where he's the only man among a population of eager women. I shouldn't say such things. He is an excellent pilot and probably the best qualified."

"Except for one other pilot that I know pretty well."

"I think you're maybe a little bit biased. Anyway if anything were to happen at least he's not married and has no family."

"Except Dr. Tennyson. He's sleeping with her."

"We don't know that for sure and even if that's true I don't think the committee would let that influence such an important decision. He has set solar speed records and scored highest on all of the preflight evaluation. I do wish it was me, though. I think the ITP is the start of something extraordinary, something that will do much more for mankind than find new worlds to inhabit. Eventually I think it will allow us to answer questions that we've has been asking for thousands of years, who we are, why we're here and is there any more to life than the meaninglessness that we live with now."

"How is a ten-minute flight through nothingness going to do all that?"

"You need to see the big picture. Stepping out of the confines of space and possibly time opens endless possibilities. Maybe we can find God."

"Be careful what you say, someone may be listening."

"I don't care. What if there is more than a huge void out there, perhaps infinite other dimensions, making past and future times all accessible to us. I just hate to see it wasted on Major Sanders. I know I shouldn't be bitter and I will stand by him as any backup pilot would. I guess I'm just jealous. I know you're happy that it's not me and I can't blame you. This is a dangerous mission."

"You're right. I am happy it's not you. I want you to stay right here with me, where we can grow old together. I love you so much."

"I know. I love you, too. I'll see you tomorrow. Kiss the kids for me and the cat. Good night."

IX. MORE HISTORY

THE MARRIAGE ACT WAS PASSED IN 2070. OVER THE YEARS, THE worldwide divorce rate had incessantly climbed, reaching over 80 percent. Marriage as an institution had lost its value. Individuals were unable to commit to another person for a prolonged period of time. The Worldwide Council on the Family convened in 2069 to try to define the value of marriage to society and determine what role marriage would continue to play in the rapidly evolving, computerized, automated society that existed. The council reviewed all available studies on marriage and the family. It concluded that marriage had some value in providing stability for individuals and a safety net for children that government could not adequately provide. At the same time, the very high divorce rate suggested that there was a fundamental flaw in marriage design. The conclusions of the council led to the Marriage Act. The act stipulated that marriage was allowed between any two persons over the age of fifteen years. The two individuals would sign a contract for a specified period of time, ranging from one year to lifetime. The contracts could be automatically renewed after the initial contracted period. Persons under the age of eighteen required parental or judicial consent to enter into an initial marriage contract. Special provisions were made for childrearing with safeguards for the any parent who gave up a career to provide childcare.

Divorce became more difficult for any individual under contract. There were steep penalties for anyone trying to unilaterally dissolve the contract. As a result, most couples opted for the one year renewable marriage contract. This allowed any mismatched couples to walk away from their bad marriage after only one year, saving the pain and hassle of a divorce. Marriages were performed by judges and the contracts were readily available without need for legal counsel, unless special provisions were necessary.

The Marriage Act had nearly eliminated divorce. It was considered one of the most effective pieces of legislation of the twenty-first century.

A secondary provision of the Marriage Act was the Child Protection Amendment. The very high divorce rate prior to passage of the Marriage Act led to frequent abductions of children by estranged parents. Often the parent would disappear with the child for years, denying the other parent and the child of their rights. The Child Protection Amendment mandated that all properly sanctioned newborns be injected with a Nanochip that would allow for locating the child anywhere on Earth. Every newborn also had a DNA sample taken and recorded in a global database, to help insure proper identification of any individual even if external appearance had been drastically altered. In addition all newborns were assigned legal counsel to oversee the child's development and insure that the child's rights were not infringed upon in anyway. Everyone born after the year 2070 could be monitored anywhere on the planet and their upbringing was subject to repeated legal scrutiny until they were independent of their parents. The nanochip was supposed to degenerate after twenty years, but many remained functional for over 100 years. The over abundance of lawyers had plenty of work and were handsomely paid for their new and very important role.

Automobiles had evolved considerably over the years. The development of the regenerative solar engine had eliminated the need for any fossil fuels. The cars of modern times were sleek, fast, and perfectly safe. All the cars were equipped with a high efficiency solar collector that charged the electric motor. The construction was of high grade titanium and carbon alloy that was very light, durable, and nearly indestructible. All vehicles were equipped with highly sensitive motion and speed sensors that constantly scanned the surrounding area and the projected vehicle path for any potential hazards. Even the roads had built in sensors that helped the cars navigate safely. The great benefit was that a motor vehicle accident was now avoided before it had a chance to happen. Rarely, when an accident actually did occur, then the passive restraint mechanism built into all vehicles automatically deployed. The passengers were enveloped in a protective cushion that absorbed all impact. The automobiles structure was so strong and resilient that the outer shell was almost never significantly damaged. The solar engines were not flammable as there was no fuel to combust, therefore car fires or explosions never occurred. The other important feature of the automobiles was the universal application of Global Positioning Systems. These systems, along with sensors built into the roads, had achieved such a level of refinement that all the driver had to do was input his destination, push start, and the car would drive on its own. The driver became a passenger, free to talk, read, or sleep without any worries.

The automobiles that were available could easily achieve top speeds of 400 kilometers per hour. The S-280 that Major Sanders drove was one of the fastest on the market and he routinely reached speeds of 560 kilometers per hour. He also had disconnected the automobile sensor system. He believed it inhibited the car's performance. He knew that he didn't need any help avoiding accidents; he was more than capable of staying out of trouble.

The computerized food synthesizer was considered the single greatest achievement of the twenty-second century. As the world entered the twenty-second century impending widespread food shortages were facing the UN and the World Hunger Organization. A team of farm managers, life scientists, nutritionists, and bioengineers was commissioned by the UN to study and to find a solution to the problem. This elite team came up with the ingenious concept of rapid food synthesis from basic food building blocks. The idea that natural products could be artificially synthesized was nothing new. Synthetic gemstones had been the norm for decades. The previous twenty years had seen an explosion of products that could be synthesized in the lab, with greater purity than the naturally occurring material. Wood, stone, medicine, and many other products were routinely manufactured. Applying the same principles, scientists and engineers developed the computerized food synthesizer. Using basic building blocks, such as alcohol, water, carbon dioxide, oxygen, and ammonia, along with a host of trace materials, palatable food was economically and efficiently produced using a tabletop system. An added bonus was that the nutritional value could also be controlled, guaranteeing that the vast population that utilized the food synthesizer would not only have abundant food, but also optimum nutrition. Widespread testing proved that 99.99% of the population found the synthesized (not synthetic) food indistinguishable from the naturally occurring product. The small proportion of the population that actually noticed the difference was considered inconsequential.

The food service industry had adapted to the change as the highest quality synthesizers were capable of producing higher quality food. Chefs also embellished the food with "secret" flavorings, so that restaurants still flourished. Many of the restaurants still offered natural foods, but at considerably higher prices.

X. ON THE MOON

MAJOR SANDERS GOT UP EARLY ON FLIGHT DAY. HE WAS SCHEDULED to take off from the lunar base at 3:00 P.M. that day. He was jetting up to the moon at 10:00 A.M. He took two Gelustat and ate breakfast with Little Bit. He packed his overnight bag with a few essentials and strapped on his vintage wristwatch. He had an antique rose gold automatic watch made in the year 2005 by Roger Dubuis. It was about the only thing he owned that was not fully computerized. He had found the watch at an antique shop in New York. The watch was able to tell time, date, day, month, year, and phase of the moon. He had managed to find an old jeweler who understood the mechanism and restored it to perfect working order. He thought it was very stylish, it kept accurate time and he was sure it brought him luck.

He checked the computer to be sure that it was set to leave food for Little Bit and that the little dog could not help himself for too many treats. He hopped into his S-280 and sped off to the spaceport. His shuttle was warmed up and ready to go. He threw his bag into the back and took off uneventfully. An hour later he safely landed at the lunar launch site. The media were all present to record his arrival. He was greeted by Major Sorino, Deborah, and General Moosewood.

"It's about time you got here, damn it," greeted the general.

"You know I have to make an entrance," Sanders replied.

"Damn astropilots," muttered the general.

"Everything's checked top and bottom," said Sorino. "Here's the check-list if you want to go over it yourself."

"Thank you, Major, I'll do that shortly. Hello, doctor," David said to Deborah.

"Hello, Major; all the final figures are here for you to review before take-off."

"I'm sure they're perfect if they come from you, but I'll check them anyway."

Major Sanders walked into the space hangar and looked at the ITP vessel. It was pure black about fifty meters long and shaped like an elongated football. He quickly went through the checklist and reviewed the figures that Deborah had given him. Everything was in perfect order, as expected.

"I'll answer a few questions from the media before I takeoff." He walked to the conference room and sat down with Deborah, General Moosewood and Major Sorino. There were about seventy-five reporters present.

"Why did you wait until the last minute before flying up here for the launch? Were you trying to be sure you made a grand entrance?"

"I wanted to spend my last night sleeping in my own bed. I am going into a totally unknown place, and although all possible precautions have been taken, the bottom line is the ITP is still a great mystery. If I am leaving and never come back, I at least wanted to spend my last day on the good old Earth."

"Do you think going out to a casino and getting attacked by a gang of muggers was the best thing to do with your last night on Earth?"

"I see nothing wrong with enjoying myself. Besides, I was only having dinner with a friend. I certainly couldn't predict that a group of ragamuffins was going to appear. Anyway, the assailants got what they deserved."

"If you hadn't been so lucky you wouldn't be here and we'd be asking Major Sorino these questions."

"Luck had nothing to do with it. I could never be in any real danger from punks like those that attacked me. Next question."

"What do you think you'll find in between dimensions?"

"That's a question for our eminent physicist to answer. Dr. Tennyson, I defer to your greater wisdom," he said with a touch of sarcasm.

Dr. Tennyson answered, "That question should be answered in about twelve hours when David, I mean Major Sanders, returns."

"The ITP has been touted as the salvation for mankind. Would you agree with this assessment?"

General Moosewood answered, "The human race has made great advances over the last 250 years. From the first time the Wright brothers took off at Kitty Hawk to the invention of the computer to the endless possibilities of genetic engineering we have made great technological advances. The ITP should be the greatest advance of all. It will open up the entire universe to us. Who knows what new worlds and life forms are waiting for us to find. All of the problems of overcrowding and limited planetary and interplanetary resources that we now face will become history. We will be able to safely and efficiently expand the Earth's influence out into the entire galaxy. The ITP truly will be the salvation for all mankind. We have time for one more question."

"Major Sanders, you will really be making two trips through the interdimensional plane; isn't that correct?"

"That's right. I'll land on Alpha Base One and then return after the ITP vessel has been inspected."

"Thank you all very much," said General Moosewood, "Now we've got a ship to launch."

After the news conference, Chaunce Edwards made his report: "I'm reporting to you live from the lunar lift-off site awaiting the impending historic flight of Major David Sanders into the great unknown. Of course I am referring to the much touted ITP, the great hope for the, quote, salvation of mankind, unquote. And...what do you think the lead pilot was doing the night before this important historic flight? I have it on the excellent authority that he was out at the casinos, looking for cheap women and starting fights. I ask you, is this the type of man that we should pin all of our hopes upon? I think the ITP Committee has made a grave error and if this flight ends in disaster, remember, you heard it here first....This is Chaunce Edwards reporting from the moon."

XI. THE LAUNCH

MAJORS SANDERS AND SORINO WALKED TOGETHER TO THE READY room. Major Sanders went over the launch checklist one more time. Everything was in order. He put a telemetry probe on his finger. This would allow continuous monitoring of his vital signs and all life energy functions as long as he was within radio range. He loaded his survival suit and classical music into his pack, to be stowed aboard the vessel. The two walked together to the ITP vessel. The name Falcon was neatly printed on its nose.

They entered together and went over each of the ship's systems. Everything checked out perfectly. "You've done a good job as always, Anthony. I can't foresee any problems," Major Sanders said.

Major Sorino replied, "I have to pretend it is me going. But, I'm glad I'm not the one making this maiden voyage. I think I'll let you work out all the bugs before I start romping around the universe."

"I'm sure the lovely Dr. Tennyson has made sure there are no bugs, kinks, or T's left uncrossed."

"For someone you've been dating, you don't seem to like her very much."

"Oh, I like her well enough. She's just a little intense for me and rigid in her thinking. She'll probably relax once I'm safely home. Let's run through the computer checklist."

The two finished all the preflight checks. There was a final meeting with the lunar control crew and Major Sanders then boarded the Falcon. Unlike launches from the early space program, the lower gravity on the lunar surface allowed for safe and gentle lift-off. Major Sanders eased the Falcon off the ground and the computer took over, guiding the ship into space on a course for ITP portal one.

XII. THE ENTRANCE

MAJOR SANDERS SAT COMFORTABLY IN THE FALCON'S PILOT CHAIR, the earth fading into the background. The console showed his velocity, energy readings at the ITP portal, and results of astroprobes of the space within one million kilometers of the portal. Any object moving through space was important as it could, theoretically, change energy levels at the portal, physically block the portal, or somehow change the speed or vibration necessary to enter the portal. There were no signs of any comets or meteors, and energy readings at the portal entrance remained constant. His speed gradually accelerated. He was at .005c on his way to the .18c necessary to pass through the portal. The computer projection for time until portal arrival was displayed. The outer shell vibration would reach the required level about ten minutes after activation. The projected time until initiation of the activation sequence was 243 minutes. He was in constant communication with the lunar control center, but there was nothing to report. The mission was going exactly as it had in hundreds of simulations.

In the background a Mozart piano Concerto played as Major Sanders closed his eyes and relaxed. He set the computer to notify him in 225 minutes to make the final preparation to enter the portal and he fell asleep. Major Sanders had the uncanny ability to sleep under the most trying circumstances and to awake totally refreshed. This had serve him well during long solar flights which involved periods of intense flying around planets and asteroids interrupted by long, uneventful stretches in deep space. He was in deep space now and took advantage of the time to get some rest.

His sleep was intruded upon by a dream, a rare occurrence for him. He saw himself standing in front of a large crowd. Most appeared angry and were jeering at him. A few appeared to be listening intently to his words with looks of contentment. The major himself appeared to be sad as he addressed the throng. He could not make out the words, but as he spoke, the crowd became angrier and started to rush towards the stage. He continued to speak as the throng of people enveloped him.

A loud siren sounded and Major Sanders was immediately roused from his sleep. The dream immediately faded into the dark recesses of his memory as he returned to the console. He started the activation of the outer shell, checked his velocity and ran another probe of the surrounding space. All was well, the velocity was .18c. He switched to the computer-generated image of the portal. It appeared to be a vast circular, gray curtain across the emptiness of space. He realized it was only the computer graphically demonstrating the energy variation across the portal but it still was a striking image. The outer shell vibration started. The increasing level appeared on the console. The value to pass through the portal was 2,156,000 vibrations per second. The console simultaneously showed the vibration with the ETA at the portal. If there were no disturbances he would hit the portal at exactly the right level of vibration.

ETA was now eight minutes. This is as exciting as a merry-go-round, Major Sanders thought. I guess it's better than the alternative. Besides, the fun would start after he passed through the portal. Bach was winding up in the background. "Three minutes to interface," came a voice from the computer. Outer shell vibration was now at 1,760,000 and everything still was perfect. The vibrations steadily climbed as Bach finished and O Fortuna started up. The portal loomed large on the auxiliary console, vibrations raced past 2,000,000 and Orff began to grow louder and louder. The countdown started at thirty seconds...twenty-nine...twenty-eight... twenty-seven...velocity was steady at .18c, vibrations were at 2,080,000, and the ship was humming along in perfect silence. Twenty...nineteen... eighteen... Velocity was maintained and vibrations passed 2,100,000. Hull temperature remained well within the safety zone, everything was perfect. "Good luck," said Deborah softly. Ten...nine...eight... Vibrations passed 2.148,000...five...four...three...two...one.

When the image reached the moon, the crew at the lunar control center saw the ship simply vanish. Everyone cheered loudly. The vibration level reached 2,156,000 at the precise moment the portal was reached and the ship ceased to exist. Portal energy readings remained constant. If all went as planned he would emerge light years away at the Alpha One portal in about fifteen minutes. The ship would automatically release an ITP transmission as it exited the interdimensional plane which would inform the control center that the flight had progressed as planned. The lunar crew waited nervously.

Major Sanders sat at his control console staring in wonder. All energy readings were blank, the outer shell computer clock was blank, and all outside sensors read zero suggesting that he had entered a huge vacuum suspended in time. The inner mechanisms were functioning and he saw that the charging system was functional so the computer would reactivate the outer shell as programmed after the requisite 400 seconds after entering the interdimensional plane. Everything by the book so far, he thought. O Fortuna had finished and Beethoven's Ninth Symphony started as he began to relax, feeling confident and secure.

With 360 seconds until outer shell reactivation the control console and the inner ship went dark. Power readings went to zero. He activated the emergency back-up system, but nothing happened. He checked power reserves, but there was no reading. He found himself sitting in absolute darkness, completely helpless with no idea of what to do. He looked at his watch. There was a faint luminescence from the dial and the seconds dial continued to work. At least I can tell the time for what that's worth, he thought.

Back at the lunar control center the ITP team continued to monitor the portal. The ITP transmission was expected within about twenty minutes of entry. The team anxiously awaited its emergence. From their perspective, everything was proceeding as planned with no surprises.

On Earth, Joshua Smith anxiously watched as Ruth Rising entered the starting gate. He had read historical accounts of Ruffian and her tragic end. There had never been a horse since that had matched her total dominance. Perhaps this was the one. As the starting gate opened he was oblivious to the news monitor carrying reports on the first manned interdimensional space voyage. He had won two large bets that day and he had the feeling that this horse was what he had dreamed of ever since he had discovered that horses could run and that he could actually get paid for something that seemed so simple as picking the fastest.

The starting gate opened. "They're off!" cried the announcer with a Fred Capposela nasal twang. "Ruth Rising quickly takes the early lead." One minute and five seconds later it was over. Ruth Rising had run away from the field, winning by eighteen lengths and breaking the track record by half a second. Joshua finished the day on this successful note and left the track. He briefly wondered if David had made it home safely. *I'll have to check the news reports as soon as I get home.* Ruth Rising was the big news to him, as she looked like the real thing.

Major Sanders sat in totally pitch black solitude, Beethoven was dead, and the only sound was his pounding heart and his rapid breathing. He had punched the large emergency startup button immediately with no response. He had tried to activate emergency battery power with no response. *I'm dead,* he thought. The seconds ticked away on his watch as 400 seconds came and went. He knew that the control center would know there was a problem as soon as the ITP transmission was missed, which would be in about fifteen minutes. He considered putting on his survival suit, but decided there wasn't any point. *If I'm a goner then let it happen quickly. Even if the suit works, why prolong the agony?*

He looked at his watch. One thousand seconds gone. At that moment, blinding reddish light filled the cabin. His sense of trepidation turned to intense fear and a sense of impending, immediate death. All he could think about was getting away. He felt he was being pushed through the back of his chair as the light pierced him like a dagger. He heard a loud cracking sound and felt intense pain in his legs and chest. The light disappeared as quickly as it had appeared. The power resumed, but he remained enveloped by blackness and unable to move. Major Sanders knew he had to get out without delay, anywhere but here. With supreme effort, he blindly hit the outer shell activation simultaneously with the escape switch. The ship accelerated to .007c slamming Major Sanders back into his chair with incredible force. He felt the pain in his chest intensify; he heard another snap and then felt more searing pain in his legs. The ship shot out through a portal somewhere in the universe, racing out of control.

Per standard protocol, all space vessels were equipped with planetary sensors as a safety feature. In the event a pilot became disabled the sensors searched for a safe place to land. They automatically probed any planets within cruising range for appropriate gravity and atmosphere and would land the vessel and emit a universal homing signal.

Major Sanders was still blinded, badly injured, and unable to navigate. The ship sensed this and began searching for a suitable place to land. All planets within 300 million kilometers were probed. A suitable planet was found only 7.5 million kilometers away and the ship automatically set off at .07c. Per standard protocol, the ship computer announced the planned destination and astro coordinates relative to the zero reference point which, in this case, was the ITP portal that the ship had exited.

Major Sanders remained blinded and barely able to move. He felt intense pain in his chest and both legs. He asked the computer for its location relative to Earth. The computer responded with "insufficient data." This meant that he was in a totally unknown part of the universe, which meant very little hope of ever being found. "I guess I finally pushed it too far," he thought. "Well, I'm not dead yet," was his final thought just before he passed out.

At the Lunar Control Center the ITP transmission was finally received. The committee expected to receive a message reporting that the ship had emerged at the Alpha One Portal and that all was well. The received transmission was much different. There was no message from Major Sanders, just a notification of emergency activation of the outer shell and emergency escape mechanism. The energy reading at the escape portal also was recorded. In theory this would allow them to find where Sanders had emerged. In practicality, it would be the equivalent of looking for a needle in a haystack, with the kicker being that the needle may not even be in the haystack they would be searching. There were millions of portals within their own galaxy and even with their high speed computers it would take months to measure the energy level at each. There were millions of galaxies outside the Milky Way; identifying and measuring the ITP portals in each would be nearly impossible.

Dr. Tennyson sat at her console, speechless and unable to move. She went over every number and measurement in her head trying to find the flaw that allowed this disaster to happen. She pulled up the records of all the previous ITP missions looking for something she had overlooked. Every test had been perfectly flawless. What had happened? There must be an answer, she thought. The magnitude of the problem facing her overwhelmed, for the moment, her personal sense of loss.

Theoretically, the ITP team could build a new ship and send it through the portal and follow Major Sanders to his exit portal. They then could follow his path and locate him. The residual radiation path would remain in space unless it was disturbed by a passing comet or meteor, an unlikely event. Outfitting a second ITP vessel would take several weeks. The Committee would have to weigh the risks and benefits of sending a second astropilot on such a rescue mission.

General Moosewood moved to the front of the control room. "Ladies and gentlemen, this appears to be a great tragedy. Major Sanders has been lost. We do not know where he is, or even if he is alive. As I'm sure you all know he made an emergency exit from the interdimensional plane at a portal with an energy reading of 2,081,200 joules. At this point we will begin immediate scanning for this portal. I am also convening an ITP Committee meeting to study the problem and to determine the feasibility of outfitting a second ITP vessel to follow Major Sanders and, hopefully, find him and return him safely. The meeting will commence in twenty minutes in the lunar conference room.

XIII. LOST AND INJURED

MAJOR SANDERS CAME TO. THE INTENSE SEARING PAIN IN HIS LEGS and chest was worse. "Medical scan," he said. The computer began its scan of him which lasted about ninety seconds. The results were announced as well as appearing on the monitor. Comminuted fracture of left tibia and fibula with extensive crush to muscle and nerve; comminuted fracture of right femur; laceration left lung with left hemopneumothorax; multiple contusions, temporary bilateral loss of vision. "Treat injuries," he said. "Medical therapeutics not functional," the machine replied. "Repair," he said. "System damage beyond repair," replied the computer. "Just great," he thought. "I need Joshua here," he thought. "At least he had three and half years of medical school." He felt helpless as he sat at the console. "Arriving at acceptable planet," announced the navigation computer. "Landing in 120 seconds."

"Ship status," he asked the computer. "All functions operational except medical therapeutics, and ITP portal sensor. Outer shell is damaged, but is salvageable and can be regenerated. Fuel reserves at 62%, maximum attainable velocity .19c, life support fully functional."

"Just perfect," he thought, "injured and stuck." The ship scanned the planet's surface.

Atmosphere 21%
Oxygen, 76%
Nitrogen 2%
Other, no toxins
32% land
68% water (2% fresh)
Average equatorial daytime temperature thirty-two degrees.
Average polar daytime temperature minus twelve degrees.
Abundant life forms detected.

"Seems suitable," he thought. "Best landing site," he said. The computer picked out a subtropical region with abundant plant life and fresh water. "Maximum caution," said Major Sanders, in a weak raspy voice. This told the computer to try to evade detection and land in an area where the ship would not be detected.

The computer eased the ship into the planet's atmosphere and it landed uneventfully in the middle of a lush, warm forest. "Outside temperature thirty degrees, nearest fresh water twenty meters, animal life detected, no artificial energy sources detected," droned the computer. "Sounds perfectly lovely," thought the major. "Now, how do I get out there?" With medical therapeutics not available he could not get a motorized chair or even crutches. The two things he needed most were not operational. He could not treat his injuries and he could not return home. Well, first things first. He activated the ships outside viewer. He was surrounded by a jungle filled with abundant, vibrantly colored vegetation. A stream was running nearby. He saw trees laden with fruit. "Joshua would love all this fresh food," he thought. He saw two rabbits scurry away and several birds flying among the trees. A tiny bird hovered right next to the camera seemingly staring into the lens before it zoomed away. "That was a hummingbird," he said to himself. He had never seen a real hummingbird; they were extinct back on Earth.

He decided that there may be some type of intelligent life on this planet. With any luck they would be able to help him, as he did not seem to be able to help himself. He tried to get up and pain shot through his body. With the greatest difficulty he dragged himself to the door which automatically opened. He hobbled down the ramp to the soft grass. In the distance he made out the form of what appeared to be a human. The pain in his chest intensified and he fainted.

XIV. COMMITTEE MEETING

GENERAL MOOSEWOOD STOOD BEFORE THE COMMITTEE. HE HAD A grave look on his face. The conference room was equipped with the latest audio-visual holographic presentation equipment, which now flashed all the latest data on the large screen. The general addressed the committee, "Ladies and gentleman, you all know what has happened. What we need now is a plan of rescue. As I see it we have two ways to tackle this problem. The first has already commenced. We are scanning all ITP portals for 2,081,200 joules. As you know, even our fastest computers can only map about 800 portals per day. Since there are probably billions of portals in this universe, we are not optimistic. We also cannot even be sure that he is within our universe. The ITP protocol predicts other dimensions within theoretical parallel universes. Major Sanders could easily be in one of these. The second approach is to outfit a second ITP ship and go after him.

This will take several weeks at best. I have already contacted our suppliers and work has begun, but the interdimensional vessel requires a great deal of preflight testing before it can be safely utilized. I am open to any other suggestions, ideas, or discussion."

Dr. Robert Burkitt stood up. "General Moosewood, with all due respect, I think these extreme efforts to recover one astropilot, who was well aware of the great risks he faced in venturing into this noble, but ultimately fool-hardy scheme, are a colossal waste of resources. We all have known that the ITP was a shot in the dark. It now is obvious that our current knowledge of interdimensional dynamics is woefully inadequate. To suggest that a second valuable ITP vessel and astropilot be sacrificed is, in my opinion, the height of incompetence. Of course I feel sorry that Major Sanders has been lost, but such are the fortunes of our times. I truly believe that our efforts should be directed to attacking this planet's problems by some other means rather than squandering our precious energy on a maverick and expendable astropilot."

"What a windbag," whispered Major Sorino, who then stood up. "Members of the Committee, our current dilemma hits very close to home. It could very easily have been me up there. I cannot believe that anyone would suggest that we completely abandon our best pilot. If it were me lost out there, I certainly would expect that attempts would be made to bring me home safely and Major Sanders deserves nothing less. As far as wasting resources, whatever we do to find Major Sanders will surely add to our existing knowledge of the ITP and interdimensional travel. I concur with General Moosewood's plan and am willing to begin immediate work on outfitting a new ITP vessel and preparing for the flight. Perhaps our head physicist can comment. Dr. Tennyson?"

Deborah had been silent since the ITP transmission had been received. She kept her personal feelings to herself. She had gone over the possibilities again and again in her mind. An image of a giant sea monster filled her thoughts, pushing scientific calculations to the side. She stood up and the rest of the committee became silent. "I believe there is something about the interdimensional plane that is beyond our ability to predict. Exhaustive preflight testing and calculation suggested that travel through the interdimensional plane would be rapid and safe. The only unknown was what would be found between dimensions. The assumption has always been that there was nothing there, that the interdimensional plane was an empty corridor. Our current situation screams that we have been wrong. There must be something within that arena that disrupted this mission. I believe that until this question is answered a second manned ITP mission will be doomed to suffer a similar fate. We have only one living being that has actually gone through the ITP and safely returned. I suggest that we reexamine all the records from Little Bit's test mission and we also re-examine Little Bit. Maybe, if we ask the right questions, we can get the right answers. I also think we should continue to scan for Major Sanders' exit portal, although, unless it is very close, which we know is not the case, it will be of little value. There would not be any way to send a rescue team that could arrive in any timely manner. However, no matter what is finally done, and despite my misgiving, I have no doubt that a second ITP vessel will eventually be necessary."

"Thank you, Dr. Tennyson. Your points are well taken," the general said. "Any more thoughts from the committee?" There was some grumbling and murmurs from the other members, but no one had anything constructive to add. "OK," said the general, "we all have work to do. Let's get going."

XV. LOST SURVIVOR

MAJOR SANDERS FELT SOMETHING STANDING OVER HIM AND SENSED he was being examined. He lay still, hoping not to arouse any suspicion. He felt some soft hairs brush against his face and body. His examiner finished, Major Sanders heard him run away quietly. He opened his eyes just in time to see a huge male lion disappear into the foliage. "I guess I'm not good enough for lunch," he said to himself. He tried to pull himself up, but intense, searing pain shot through his legs. He had a terrible headache and it hurt to take a breath. He could hear water running in a stream to his right. He realized how thirsty he was and started to crawl toward the stream. He attempted to stand but the pain in his legs was too great. Gradually, he reached the stream. He put a drop of water into his portable analyzer. 99.99% pure water came the reading, no hazards. He reached his hands down into the stream and brought out a cupful of the water and drank it down. He took some more and splashed his face and he began to feel better. Overhead was a tree laden with what looked to be oranges. "That would really hit the spot," he thought. There was a fallen branch next to him by the stream. He hoisted it up and struck the branch several times and several oranges fell, one striking him on the head. "Sir Isaac Newton all over again," he said out loud. He looked at the orange; he sniffed it and poked it. Looks real enough to me, he thought. He peeled off the skin and took a bite. Seems OK, he thought and he devoured the orange, and then another and another. He felt a little better, but was so weak he couldn't move.

He heard some rustling in the bushes and a man and a woman emerged. They were both naked, with deep olive complexions and perfectly proportioned bodies. The woman was elderly, but strikingly beautiful with long dark brown, with a hint of gray, not only on her head but also in areas that the major was used to seeing hairless. The man had white hair, nearly shoulder length, with a neat beard and moustache. "Be careful," said the man. "He is badly injured. We are asked to take him to a safe place and care for him. Both his legs are broken and he has an injury to his left lung. It will be difficult to heal him."

"Won't the Creator come and heal him as he would us?" asked the woman.

"We have been asked to treat him as we would one of our other inhabitants. The Creator is unable to help him."

"But he is a man, similar to us. Why won't the Creator help him?"

"Enough, Sarah, we will talk of this later. We must get him to safety now."

With great speed they built a stretcher from two branches and some long leaves and, with surprising ease, gently lifted him and placed him upon it. As they were carrying him, he passed out again.

XVI. LITTLE BIT

JOSHUA SMITH OPENED THE DOOR TO MAJOR Sanders' APARTMENT. The day had been profitable for him. He had promised to look in on Little Bit while the major was jetting around the universe. He was completely unaware of all that had occurred, although all the media outlets had been following the story closely with as many grisly details and possibilities as could be conjectured. He found Little Bit staring at the one of the monitors as the day's events were recounted.

"Astropilot Major David Sanders is lost in space ... somewhere in the universe...2,081,200 joules.... Unknown if he has survived.... Entire ITP program thrown into chaos...."

"Well, that's interesting," Joshua considered the possibilities. "If I know David, he managed to survive and he'll find some way to get back." Little Bit stared forlornly at the monitor. Joshua walked over and sat down on the floor next to him. "You know what's going on, don't you little fella. It's too bad you can't talk; you probably know more about this than anyone. Let's go for a walk outside where we both can think more clearly."

Little Bit jumped up and ran to the door and the two went out to the street together. As they walked towards the small park, a government van pulled up, six men in dark suits jumped out and tried to grab Little Bit, who scampered away. One of the men stopped to talk to Joshua. "We're from the ITP project. We need the dog for some tests." He quickly flashed a government ID badge. His name was Agent O'Connor.

The other five men ran about trying to catch the little Westie, who zipped from one bush to another, leaving the men in suits grasping at air as he easily evaded them. Joshua snapped his fingers and Little Bit ran up to him and sat down. "You need to go with these men." Joshua spoke to Little Bit. "They need you to help find David and bring him home safely." Little Bit wagged his tail and jumped into the front seat of the van with his front paws resting on the steering wheel. "You can sit in front, but you can't drive," O'Connor said. The other agents had a different idea and they grabbed the little dog and put him in the back inside a small cage. Joshua walked away, wondering about the meaning of it all.

XVII. A BIG PROBLEM

DR. TENNYSON SAT STARING AT THE FIGURES ON HER MONITOR. Something did not make sense. The nearest ITP portal had always had an energy value that was constant at 8,052,234 joules. The reading now was 8,200,334 joules and was unstable. Fluctuating energy values at portals would make ITP travel much more difficult. The fluctuation also seemed to be random, which would make entering the portal nearly impossible with the present technology. It was necessary for the ITP vessel to reach the precise level of vibration to enter the portal and it took a few minutes to reach that level. If the energy values were varying every few seconds, the precise value to enter through the portal could never be achieved.

She called General Moosewood. "We have a problem," she stated. "I've just seen the figures," he replied.

"General, I need a continuous reading on the energy levels from our entry portal if we are ever to hope to reinstitute ITP travel."

"I've put a team on it. Data should be forthcoming within the hour. It will be immediately entered into your database. Do you need any assistance?"

"No, something like this I work much better alone. I just hope there is a definable pattern or else the ITP is doomed." She stared at the numbers on the monitor. What could it mean? Was there some cosmic joker playing games with the universe? Was the fabric of the universe being suddenly altered? She knew that this sudden change would make it almost impossible to find Major Sanders. After all, what used to be 2,081,200 probably was now changed. They were now searching for a needle in a haystack, but the needle was no longer a needle and they did not know what they were looking for. Unless this was merely a temporary aberration and things were to return to their previous state, then Major Sanders was truly on his own. She felt a weak kick inside her. "I guess we'll be on our own, too," she said to her unborn child.

XVIII. SANDERS' NURSE

MAJOR SANDERS OPENED HIS EYES TO A DARK NIGHT ILLUMINATED by a bright moon and thousands of stars. Soft grass caressed his back and he was covered by what seemed to be huge leaves that reminded him of pictures of elephant ears he had seen as a child. His flight uniform had been removed and his legs had less throbbing, braced by tree branches that had been expertly fashioned to provide support and traction for his fractures. His chest had been covered with some sort of leaves and roots which seemed to provide some relief from the pain he had felt earlier. No people were in sight. He figured he had somehow found his way to some primitive culture; at least it was one that was very good at first aid. Next to him was a pile of fruit, oranges, bananas, pineapple, and grapes. There was a small pile of what looked like white feathers and another leaf-like object that had been fashioned into a cup that was filled with water. He took a drink, emptying the makeshift cup, and ate a few grapes.

In the moonlight he saw the silhouette of a woman approaching him. She was not the same woman he had seen earlier. She kneeled down next to him. "Hello," he said in a raspy voice. "Do not speak," she replied. "You must save your strength. You have suffered very severe injuries."

"You speak English?" he asked.

"That is a gift from our Creator. We understand many forms of communication. This allows us to be good stewards over all that has been created."

"Where am I?"

"You are in the garden, what we call Eden."

Major Sanders first thought was that either he was dreaming or he had died and this was heaven. He had read of the mythical Eden as part of one of his high school courses. In what was called Bible mythology, Eden was created by God. Man lived there, in harmony with God and nature, until he sinned and was forced out. "I must be dreaming." he thought. He took a deep breath and felt a sharp pain in his chest. "How long have I been here?" he asked.

"We found you two days ago, badly injured, only barely alive. But you seem strong and we will try to help you."

"What planet is this?"

"You must rest now. We will answer your questions when you are stronger." He watched her as she mixed some leaves with what looked like white feathers. She stirred them together for a few minutes then gave it to him.

"What is this?" he asked.

"It will help you feel stronger and give you some nourishment." She responded, "It has what you would probably call manna along with herbal teas. It will help your pain. After you drink it you will be able to rest and your body will continue to heal."

"OK, I'll try it; just don't take advantage of me while I'm sleeping."

Major Sanders did feel exhausted and the pain he felt in his chest and legs seemed to be worsening. He also noticed a new twinge of pain in his right side. He drank the entire concoction. "Good to the last drop," he quipped. He closed his eyes and fell asleep again. The woman stayed at his side watching him as he slept, studying him intently with each labored movement of his chest.

XIX. JOSHUA AND DEBORAH

JOSHUA WALKED UP THE BRICK SIDEWALK TO HIS APARTMENT. DR. Tennyson was sitting on the steps as he approached.

"What a pleasant surprise, Doctor. I never expected to find you waiting for me, but I am truly happy to see you again. David is always talking about you." Joshua greeted her, a hint of sarcasm in his voice.

"We can dispense with the platitudes, Mr. Smith."

"Call me Joshua."

"Mr. Smith, I've come to ask for your opinion. David has told me you have some special powers that make you almost clairvoyant. Well, David is in big trouble and I thought you might be able to help. I imagine that you have heard what happened?"

"I get the news reports and a group of very rude men have just carted Little Bit away. David is lost in space and you don't have a clue where he might have disappeared; what can I possibly do?"

"David always tells me how smart you are, how you are never wrong. The greatest minds on this planet are stumped. I thought a fresh perspective might be helpful. Or are you too busy gambling your life away to help a friend?"

"I am not an astrophysicist. I am not anyone that could be of help to you. I know nothing about ITP, space travel, or the man in the moon. You're right. I spend my time waiting for the next race. I don't think I can be of any help to you or David."

"Wait, I'm sorry. I shouldn't be so rude. Let me tell you what's happened then you can decide if you can help. Maybe we can go inside?"

"After you, Doctor."

The two rode up the automated stairs to Joshua's apartment on the second floor.

"Can I offer you something to drink? Let's see... I have water, lemon water, strawberry water, and power punch."

"Plain water will be fine." She sat down on the chair, which immediately conformed to her body. "This chair is very comfortable," she said.

"It's one of the few modern conveniences I own. It automatically scans your body and provides padding and support to make it so you never want to get up. It does have a special feature, however, that keeps you from spending too much time seated there. Try pushing that button on the armrest."

She pushed it and immediately heard a clock ticking, counting down from thirty. At zero the chair suddenly stiffened and she felt a gentle push and she immediately stood up.

"I custom ordered that feature to give unwanted guests a hint that they may have overstayed their welcome. Please, tell me what has happened to David and what you think I may be able to do to help him."

Dr. Tennyson recounted all the events from the time Major Sanders had arrived at the lunar launch center until they had received the final ITP transmission. She also told of the recent changes in portal energy measurements with all of the implications.

Joshua listened carefully and sat silently for what seemed to be hours to Dr. Tennyson, but was in reality only about fifteen minutes. Finally, he replied.

Joshua started, "As I'm sure you are aware, there are two separate issues facing you, both are probably related. First is the nature of the interdimensional plane as it is called. Second is this suddenly changing nature of ITP portal energy levels. I suspect that if we could figure out the first we would then have the answer to the second. I know that collecting any information about what happens inside the interdimensional plane has been impossible. I gather that's the reason poor Little Bit is being tortured, I mean examined again, as he is the only living creature that has actually been through interdimensional space and is still living. It is too bad that he can't talk as I bet he could tell us a great deal. You are aware of the few noticeable changes in him since he returned?"

"Not really," she replied. "The physiologic scans were all unchanged."

"That's true, but if you spent any time with Little Bit you'd realize that he has become a little less rambunctious and seems to stay cleaner than he used to. He has a brightness to his white fur that never seems to go away. David said that Little Bit would follow him and sit with him as if the dog knew that he was about to share something extraordinary, something that the dog had already experienced. I had even joked to David that maybe the trip would bring him some refinement that he so desperately needed."

"I was not aware that there had been any noticeable change to the dog. However, your observations don't seem very helpful."

"Can you tell me all that you know about the interdimensional plane?"

"I wish I knew more. It is primarily a place whose properties exist in the realms of mathematics and physics. We have never been able to obtain any objective information about it. The best way I can describe what it would be like is for us to consider that we are in a book. Our universe has a beginning and presumably someday will have an ending. It exists confined by space and time, the pages of the book. Now, consider that there are innumerable books. Each one would be its own universe with a beginning and an ending. As long as one remains inside the book, one would be limited to living within its confines, following the rules of space and time that existed within that book. The interdimensional plane is outside the books. When inside the interdimensional plane, one would not be limited by space and time as they existed within the universe. What the ITP Committee had hoped was that we could use the keys we had discovered to briefly leave one part of the book and reappear in a distant part. The problem now is that we don't know where Major Sanders is in this vast book or if he is in our book or another one."

"Can I ask you another question?"

"Please do."

"Does your math allow for one to go to an earlier part of the book? That is, your description suggests that travel forward or back in time would be possible. Has this been considered?"

"Elapsed time is not a part of any of the equations. The assumption has always been that time is an exclusively forward vector. Of course you know that Einstein theorized that time is not constant, but because of the constraints made by the speed of light, time has always been a positive number. The actual measured times that we have made on the test flights were of very short duration. The observed elapsed times from entering the

ITP portal to exiting have been only a few minutes. Of course this is the remarkable thing. Space travel that normally would have taken years is accomplished in a matter of minutes."

"You are presenting a difficult problem to solve. We have a vast impenetrable black box that has absorbed David, probably spit him out somewhere, and now you have the impossible task of trying to find him. I don't know if I can be of any help, but give me some time to study the problem. I have an idea that may help more clearly define what has happened. But, if my hunch is true we will not be able to find him. It would help me if I could get a copy of the actual ITP, particularly the technical specifications and a copy of the ITP Committee presentation to members of Congress."

"You don't sound very encouraging, but I'll send those documents when I get home. David has great faith in you; I hope he's right."

"I'll do what I can, but don't have high hopes."

Deborah left, fighting back tears as she called for a taxi.

XX. JOSHUA'S SEARCH

JOSHUA HAD BEEN CONSIDERING THE INTERDIMENSIONAL PROBLEM long before Dr. Tennyson came to his apartment. The interdimensional plane existed outside of space and likely outside of time. Current scientific thought would be useless. Joshua thought that philosophy would provide the answer. There was a book that had been written about seventy-five years ago that was a wildly speculative treatise on the nature of time and space. It had not been well received in philosophic or scientific circles and its author had been discredited by academia. The book presented theories on the nature of God and his relationship to mankind and man's perspective within the universe and the space time continuum. Joshua turned on Berlioz and made himself comfortable as he started reading, "The Elements of Time," by Arthur Thurlsby.

"In observing the human condition one must be ever aware of the confining nature of space and time," the book began. "Man lives within a vast universe. One is compelled to ask, 'Are we alone? Is it possible that we exist merely for the amusement of an omnipotent, omniscient being who regards us as so many little white rats?'" Mr. Thurlsby starts with the bias that if God exists it is only for His own amusement that he created man and there is no true benevolence within Him. Joshua had read the book before. Once he got beyond the anti-God venom there were some insightful observations on historical events. Thurlsby starts with a premise that he borrowed from GK Chesterton; that the whole of human history centers around Jesus Christ. Everything that happened after Christ will bring mankind to the second coming and Armageddon. Joshua didn't believe a word of it. He was, however, fascinated by Thurlsby's theories on space and time.

"God exists in a state outside of all human thought and perception. If the stories of Jesus are true, then the extraordinary act of God coming to live among his subjects is something to be celebrated. That this could be true is, however, laughable. For if God chooses to take on human form and human frailty, he ceases to be God. The fact that Jesus could be put to death at all renders God less than omnipotent, thus subject to all the constraints of time and space as all men are. The only logical conclusion is that God either does not exist or that he exists totally outside time and space and must remain outside of time and space, or cease to be God."

This was the point Joshua was trying to recall. David had left the confines of time and space. The presumption had been that he had entered an empty corridor. The fact that something had gone terribly wrong suggested that the corridor was not empty or that the ship had suffered some unforeseeable malfunction. From what Joshua knew of the ship it had more sensors, safety features and backup systems than anything previously developed. Joshua was convinced that David had encountered something that had thrown him off course or had caused him to abort the mission. Joshua knew David well enough to know that he would never have abandoned his mission plan, except under the greatest duress. The theory, which certainly was not new, was that God, if He existed, lived outside of time and space, which would be within the interdimensional plane. The question then became: Why should God cause David to abandon the mission?

Unfortunately, Joshua, like 99.99% of the world population, knew very little about God. Where does one go to learn about what is now called a myth? He was all too familiar with mythology as taught to school children. The God in those stories had all attributes of deity stripped, leaving him an emasculated bystander observing human triumph. Joshua realized that he needed an unabridged Bible to learn the true nature of God. This posed quite a problem. All religion had been cited as the primary cause of global strife and although not made outright illegal, religions had been ridiculed in the media and in all properly sanctioned schools. The education system taught that religion was the single greatest source of evil in the world. Sales of religious writings had dwindled and publication of scriptures had ceased. Over the last fifty years there had been no publication of the Bible, Koran, Jewish prayer books, or any other religious scripture. Religious stories were relegated to myth and were taught as equivalent to Greek, Roman, and Norse mythology.

Joshua thought that the answers to the current crisis were to be found in the nature of God. The only proper place to learn about this was in the Bible. The problem now was finding one. Bible's had been systematically destroyed by governments desperate to remove religion from society. There were no stored records of accurate biblical text and actual Bibles were not easy to come by. People who might have copies were careful not to make it known, lest it mysteriously disappear one night. Joshua wasn't sure where to start. He had heard of groups of religious fanatics that lived on the fringes of the cities alongside violent gangs of disenfranchised young people. These gangs were a boil on the butt of what was supposed to be the perfect new order. Joshua remembered his first-hand experience with one of these groups on the night prior to David's launch. They had been easily dispatched by the brutish skills that David possessed; still there had been a sense of desperation about them that almost made Joshua pity them.

As Joshua recalled that night something else flashed in his mind. One of the would-be assailants had something around his neck that was very unusual for these times. If his memory was correct, the shortest of the attackers, the one with wispy brown hair had a gold chain around his neck with a cross dangling from it. No one in legitimate society would so blatantly display such a religious symbol, for fear of bringing a visit from the police. Joshua figured that only someone that truly believed the religious dogma would openly demonstrate that belief. Such a person may be in possession of a Bible. He realized it was a long shot, finding a person who likely lived underground, away from watchful government eyes, and even a longer shot to convince him to do something to help find a man who had recently beaten him to a pulp and sent him into police custody. It was unlikely that he was still in custody as the revolving door legal system rarely kept people off the streets for more than a few days. Still, he could search the police records and at least find a name, address, and phone number. He sat down at his computer and started his search.

XXI. EDEN

MAJOR SANDERS WOKE FEELING CONSIDERABLY BETTER. HE COULDN'T say refreshed, but the pain in his chest was much less and he was breathing with far greater ease. He looked up to see his beautiful naked nurse seated on the ground next to him. "How long have I been sleeping?" he asked.

"Almost a full day," she replied.

"Have you been here all that time?"

"Of course; I have been given the job of nursing you back to health. When you have healed you will be allowed to meet the rest of our group."

"Are there very many people living here?"

"You will find out when the time is right."

"What's your name?"

"Ruth."

"Well Ruth, you are doing a great job. I feel 100 percent better. I think I'm ready to run a marathon, that is, if I could stand." He pulled himself up to a sitting position, leaning against a tree trunk. "Of course, my legs still hurt and it still hurts when I breathe, but overall I think I'm well on the way to a complete recovery. Then I can figure out how to get back to Earth."

"What is Earth?" asked Ruth.

"It's the name of my home planet. It would be somewhere up in your night sky. Of course I have no idea where I am or where Earth is." He looked at his watch. He was surprised to see that it was still running. According to it, he had been gone for seven days. "Have you been with me since I crashed here?"

"As I said before, it is my task to bring you back to health."

David changed the subject. "This is a beautiful place you live in. You called it Eden. As in the Garden of Eden? If this is Eden, where are Adam and Eve? Where is the serpent?" Sanders remembered some of his high school mythology.

"We have talked enough. Your questions will be answered soon. Now you must eat and rest." She gave him some of the manna plus tea mixture along with a banana and grapes.

"I must be getting better; I've graduated from manna to fruit."

Ruth sat down next him and they ate and drank together.

Sanders thought that in the near future he really needed to get to know her better. For now he was happy to have her share the simple meal. Bananas and grapes had never tasted so good. Ruth knelt next to him silently enjoying her meal. David asked, "Don't you get cold? You don't wear any clothes, and although the weather is very nice here, it still gets cool at night." He had noticed that she did not cover herself with the large blanket-like leaves that he slept under.

Ruth answered, "The Creator provides for us, keeps us warm and safe. He is the one who sent me to you, to bring you back to health and, eventually, join our group and live here in Eden. Praise the Creator."

"Is your Creator, God?"

"His full name is God, the Creator. He made all that is here, the sky, the ground, the plants, animals, and all of the men and women. I'm sure that he made you, too."

"I beg to differ, but I was born from my mother and father, as they were, as all living things are."

"But where did the first living thing come from?"

David did not have an answer for this. "Enough of philosophy. Let's get down to more important matters; do you have a boyfriend?"

"I don't have a husband, if that is what you mean. When the time is right, the Creator will provide a helpmate."

"Maybe it will be me." David thought that he would love to be her "helpmate" at least until he could find his way back to Earth. And, if he were stranded here forever, he could be happy living with such a beautiful woman. Ruth was a beautiful woman, with perfectly developed features, smooth olive-colored skin, and she certainly seemed devoted to him. I guess it's only natural to fall for your nurse, he thought.

They finished dinner and David lay down next to Ruth. "Do you want to know about my world?" he asked.

"If it will help you recover, I will listen."

"The name of my planet is Earth. There are billions of people that live there. We have no place as pretty as this. There are people and buildings and machines everywhere; very few places with trees or grass. It seems that all we do is try to provide for all these people, food, energy, a place to live, pleasurable activities. Anything to help the people forget their meaningless existence. There I go talking philosophy again. Anyway, that is what brought me here. I was trying to find a way for my planet to spread out into the universe, maybe to ultimately free us all from our mundane, confined lives. We have machines that do everything for us, make our food, clean our house, bring us the latest news and trends, and keep us so occupied that we never realize that there is no point to any of it.

"The government provides all of this, just like your Creator provides for you. If I could find a way to bring this back to Earth, I would be not only famous, but rich also. The billions of people would give anything for a vacation in Eden. I guess if you think about it, the entire history of man has been an attempt to vacation in the Garden of Eden."

"Why did you ever leave Eden?"

"We didn't leave voluntarily. If I remember my mythology correctly, God kicked Adam and Eve out when they sinned. I guess it's been downhill for mankind ever since. There was the story about Jesus that supposedly was to lead all the chosen to salvation, but we proved that to be a bunch of hooey, strictly pabulum for the masses. I have to say that we have been building quite comfortable lives for all men. There has not been any war for decades and only the occasional criminal activity. Food, homes, work, and all our needs are provided."

"Why did you leave to come here?"

"I'm not here by choice. I was on a test flight when something went wrong and now I'm here talking philosophy with a beautiful naked lady when I should be trying to 'know' you to use the biblical vernacular."

"I don't think that will happen in your condition. You can barely sit up. As your nurse, I have seen you most intimately and you do have a certain charm, but the Creator has given me the job of nursing you and that is all that I shall do."

"Well, I can dream. But, I am tired, it's dark, it's time to get some rest." He lay down and quickly fell asleep.

Ruth got up to sit against the large tree to watch him, as she usually did when he slept. She thought about all that he had said and decided to lay down beside him. She lay on the soft grass, feeling the warmth spread from his muscular body and soon she was fast asleep.

She awoke suddenly as she felt his body shaking. Instead of the warmth she had felt earlier, he now seemed to be burning up. He was calling out incoherently, "Deborah... Little Bit... Joshua... ITP..." and other words she could not understand. His breathing was rapid and shallow and he had a horrid blue gray tint to his skin. She feared that she would lose him; even though she had done all that she knew to nurse him back to health. She realized that she needed help. She knelt down.

"Dear Creator, you brought this man here and asked me to stay and care for his injured body. Why are you taking him away? Please help me to know how to help him. Show me what to do to make him whole. You, Creator, can do anything. Use me to bring him back to health and if necessary take my life instead."

Ruth spent the night kneeling at David's foot imploring her Creator for assistance. David's body frequently suffered uncontrollable fits of shaking with rapid shallow breathing. She put her hand to his heart and felt it racing. He was flushed and calling out incoherently.

As the sun rose she saw a new plant had grown in the middle of the clearing. It looked like manna, but with yellow cotton-like flowers. Ruth immediately knew that this was God's answer to her prayers. She picked some of the flowers and mixed them with water and set them in the sun. The mixture quickly brewed into a bright yellow tea. She tried to get him to drink, but he was fighting her. She managed to get only a few drops into him before he pushed her away splattering the tea all over Ruth's chest.

The few drops seemed to help, however, as his breathing slowed and his body seemed to relax. She turned back to the plant and saw that the flowers had already grown to replace those that she had picked. She picked some more, crushed them into a fine powder and sprinkled it over his body and into his nose. His brightly flushed cheeks started to fade as his heart slowed and his breathing became regular and his delirious ranting stopped. Ruth turned to the plant and saw that there were no more flowers.

Seeing that David was out of danger, at least for the moment, she lay down beside him to rest.

It was dark when she awoke. David was awake, but seemed restless again. He spoke names that she had heard before; Deborah was repeated over and over again. Ruth wondered who she was and she made a mental note to ask him when he was better. She sat up and saw that the yellow flower had reappeared. She plucked the flower from its stem and mixed it with water as she had done before. This time she was able to get David to drink most of it. Once again, he became calm and he called her name. He pulled himself up to sitting and Ruth knelt beside him.

"Thank you," he said with a raspy voice. "Thank our Creator," she responded. "I am only the vehicle He uses. Healing the sick and injured is His work."

"Then I thank your Creator." The yellow flower had reappeared. This time David ate and drank, helping him to feel stronger. His legs also felt strong, almost to the point where he thought he might be able to stand. Ruth sensed what he wanted and she gently admonished him to be patient and allow healing to progress.

"You're a good doctor and, for once, I'll follow my doctor's advice."

XXII. AT THE LAB

THE AGENTS THAT HAD TAKEN LITTLE BIT THREW HIM INTO A CAGE IN the back of their car. Little Bit barked and growled loudly and continuously until they let him out. Little Bit jumped into the driver's seat with his feet on the steering wheel. "You can't drive," said O'Connor, as he picked up the little Westie and handed him to his companion in the back seat. Little Bit barked and squirmed and growled, freeing himself and jumping up front into the driver's seat. This went on for nearly thirty minutes until; finally, they had to let him ride up front in the driver's seat on the driver's lap with his paws on the steering wheel. People passing by were startled to see the large black vehicle being driven by a little white dog.

They arrived at the Institute for Animal Research where new tests were to be performed on Little Bit. There was a new universal translator that was being tested on various animals with promising results. If this new device worked as well on dogs as it had worked on other animals, then Little Bit might be able to tell them what had happened on his space voyage. There was also an upgraded brain scanner that might be able to pick up subtle changes in the dog's neurological activity.

He was carried into a bright room filled with blinking lights and stainless steel. "We'll start with the new translator. That will be our best bet to gather any new information." This new translator was the Institute's latest effort to talk to lower life forms. There had been some limited success communicating with dolphins and parrots, this would be the first attempt with a dog. The concept was that there are universal patterns of communication that transcend all creatures with any level of intelligence. Input receivers and computers had never been sensitive enough to interpret the data to provide any meaningful analysis. This latest model employed powerful picotechnology that could detect noise variations at the most minute level. The translator also recorded visual input that might be of importance. All this data was analyzed and converted into English. The machine was flawless with all variations in human speech and seemed to work with dolphins. Dogs had not been tested, but with the stakes being what they were, Little Bit was to be the first. He was a truly exceptional animal; at times it seemed like he already understood complex human speech.

A technician sat Little Bit on his lap, some earphones were fitted onto his head and a microphone and camera were focused on him. A series of stimulating holographic images were flashed: a cat, food, Major Sanders, the inside of the ITP vessel, recorded images from his flight. All of Little Bit's responses were recorded and immediately analyzed by the translator. A green light appeared and the translator announced that analysis was complete and questioning could begin.

"What is your name?"

A few low growls were heard. "Bark," said the translator. "I thought your name was Little Bit," asked the technician.

Two barks and a long growl came in response. "Bark. Bark. Bark."

"What happened on your space voyage?"

Along series of barks and whimpers followed. "Woof. Bark. Woof." "Did anything unusual happen?"

More barking. "Bark. Woof. Bark."

"Did anything happen when you left space?"

"Bark."

"Do you feel any different?"

Little Bit jumped out of the technician's lap, pulling the cords out of the machine and knocking the translator to the floor in a shower of sparks.

"Catch him!"

The little Westie raced around the room, overturning tables, damaging millions of dollars of delicate machinery. A government agent ran into the room and Little Bit raced out the door, down the stairs, and out of the building.

A parade of black-suited government officials, white-coated Institute technicians, and uniformed security guards raced after him. Little Bit should have been named White Lightning as he raced across the institute compound to the heavy chain link perimeter fence. In a flash he dug a hole under the fence and raced away to freedom. He knew how to find David; these stupid men with their stupid questions and stupid machines were clueless and he was tired of wasting time. He needed to find Joshua. He was the only one that might understand what had happened and that there was nothing to worry about. David would come home when it was time and everything would be OK.

XXIII. BACK TO EDEN

DAVID WAS HEALING RAPIDLY. HIS LEGS WERE NO LONGER PAINFUL and after four weeks he was able to stand. His breathing was normal and there was no pain in his chest. With Ruth's help he started to walk. It was quite a sight to see the uniformed astropilot being assisted by a beautiful, petite naked lady.

The weeks of recovery were filled with David telling about Earth. He talked about the growing population, the casinos, space travel, ITP, and anything else that popped into his head. Ruth would sit and listen, fascinated by his descriptions.

"Your Creator must be wonderful to give you such a world," she said one day.

"We have no Creator," David responded.

"Where did you come from, then?"

"We evolved from other animals."

"Where did they come from?"

"They came from other animals."

"Where did the first animal come from?"

"It grew out of the primordial soup. This was what was present when the world was developing. The world allowed for chemical reactions that created molecules that came together to form simple animals. These animals over a long period of time changed into more complicated animals until the ultimate animal appeared, mankind. I suppose we are still evolving, but human intelligence has allowed us to grow out into space and eventually to the entire universe. That's what brought me to this place."

"It sounds very complicated," answered Ruth. "It's much easier with a Creator."

David was strong enough to leave the sheltered glen that had been his home for the past several weeks. He felt stronger and his thoughts were clearer than they had been in years. He noticed some changes in his body. Although he seemed to eat only small amounts, he never felt hungry. Over the last week he noticed that he rarely needed to pee and did not need to poop. His sexual urges were diminished. He previously sought sexual partners at least daily. However, this had rarely crossed his mind since he had arrived in Eden. He figured it was due to his being seriously injured and that his normal desires would return. It was strange to him that leaning against a gorgeous naked woman did not arouse him. He hoped that Ruth was not offended.

"We can go for a short walk, but you must promise that you will rest afterwards," Ruth said.

"Of course I promise, you slave driver," came David's reply.

They emerged from the shaded, protected glen, to a sunny day, brightly colored with brilliant flowers. Vibrantly-hued birds flew overhead calling to each other. The grass under his feet was feather soft. He was surprised that there were not any insects flying about except for an occasional bee or butterfly. The trees varied in size from towering redwoods to short banana trees heavily laden with fruit. He saw every type of fruit and nut he could imagine and a large number of plants with fruit and berries that were completely alien to him.

Animals of all types walked about, some coming up to him sniffing him or holding on to his lower pant leg to hitch a free ride. A lion emerged from the trees and walked along a parallel path, but kept his distance. He had an extremely regal countenance about him, as is expected from the king of beasts. David wasn't completely sure, but he thought the lion had winked at him. "Is he friendly?" David asked, nervously. The lion roared and David said, "I think he should stay over there. On Earth we have parks and there are wild animals, but they are afraid of people and stay away. Of course I've seen lions in the zoo, but never walked with one. On Earth you'd worry about being eaten."

They walked along a wide stream, its edges teeming with vibrant, colorful flowers.

"I never thought something could be so beautiful," he said to Ruth.

Ruth replied, "It is natural for us to live together with all of Creation. We are part of this place and everything is made to be together."

"I'm getting tired. Let's sit down and rest."

Ruth and David sat by the stream and the lion disappeared among the trees. David said, "I really would like to take a bath. It's been weeks, I must smell like a garbage dump." Ruth answered. "This stream gets wider and deeper a little farther ahead. Why don't we walk a little more?"

The two walked to where the stream became almost a pond. Ruth helped David out of his uniform and he eased himself into the water with Ruth's help. She stayed with him as he was still weak. The water was cool and refreshing. David felt the grime and dust melt away. He was too weak to swim, content to sit in the water and feel it charge his broken body with new energy. "I feel great," he said. "I'm glad," Ruth said. "The water renews us and keeps us pure. Now you are ready to be part of Eden."

"Ruth, where are the other people that live here? I've been here for weeks and I've only seen you. There are other people here aren't there?"

"Yes, David, there are other people. Until now you have not been ready to meet them. You needed to be prepared to meet them. While your body has healed, your soul also has been healing. Bless our Creator; He has washed the hatred and the sin from your soul. You are finally ready to meet my companions. The lion has gone to tell them. Didn't you wonder why you weren't afraid? Don't you wonder why you feel the way you do about so many things? Our Creator has cleansed you. Look, here come the others."

David looked up to see a crowd of people, all naked, men, women, and children, coming towards them.

The man in front was tall, with deep olive skin and thick white hair with a white beard and mustache. Holding his arm was a beautiful woman, also with olive skin, which was smooth except for a few wrinkles around her eyes, and long brown hair with a touch of gray.

"Welcome to Eden," said the man. "I am Abraham and this is my wife Sarah. We were very worried about you, but I see that Ruth has done a magnificent job bringing you back to join the living. I know you have an abundance of questions, but let us go back to the clearing where we can celebrate your recovery. It is only a short walk from here and we have gathered all manner of food to welcome you into our fold."

David walked with them, once again being supported by Ruth. Many of the others greeted him as they walked. He heard many names: Noah, Jacob, Moses, Bithia, Rebecca, Rachel, Isaac, Samuel, Tomar, and on and on. He thought that he had heard them all before. He remembered that many of these names were in the biblical mythology along with Eden. He wondered if there was another David or a Joshua among them. "I think I can walk on my own," he said to Ruth. She seemed a little hurt as she let go of his arm, but he took her hand in his and she smiled as they approached the clearing.

There was quite a feast awaiting them. In the bright sun he saw piles of bananas, pineapple, grapes, and olives, nuts of all types, manna, various berries, nectarines, tomatoes, beans, carrots, oranges, grapefruit, and so many others he couldn't name. Joshua would love this, he said to himself.

Each person chose some food and everyone sat and ate.

Finally, David said, "I have so many questions. Tell me about Eden. How you came to be here? How long you've lived here? I am dying of curiosity."

One of the children shouted, "Let Moses tell the story, he tells it best." The other children also spoke up, "Yes, we want to hear Moses."

Abraham raised his hand and the children became quiet. "Very well. Moses, would you please come forward and tell David about Eden."

Moses was shorter than Abraham. He had curly black hair, the same olive complexion as Ruth and Abraham, but a shade darker and a full curly black beard. He seemed rather shy as he came forward.

He started to speak, "In the beginning, our Creator looked out into the void. 'Let there be light.' There was a sudden bright flash and a thunderous boom. The void was gone, now filled with billions of lights. Our Creator then spoke, 'Let there be a world to be filled.' And our world was created out of nothingness. Our Creator spoke once more, 'Let the light be separated by periods of darkness.' Thus day and night were created, the first day. And He saw that it was good. And He rested." Moses had a sweet pure voice that resonated with subtle power.

"Our Creator spoke again, 'Let there be heaven above the world and heaven was created. Let there be the sun to feed the world and the moon to guard the night. Thus, the sun and the moon were created. Our Creator saw that it was good and He rested, completing the second day.

"Our Creator spoke once again. 'Let there be great seas to cover the world and between the seas let there be dry land.' Thus, the world came to be covered with great areas of water separated by land. The Creator saw that it was good and He rested. The third day.

"The next morning our Creator spoke, 'Let there be plants to cover the lands.' All manner and type of plant sprang up, covering the lands with grasses and trees and flowers and every manner of plant life. The seas also brought forth plants. Our Creator looked out and saw the lush green world and he said, 'It is good.' And He rested, finishing the fourth day.

"On the fifth day He looked over the world and He spoke, 'Let there be animals to live in the land and in the trees and under the sea and in the air.' And all sorts of animals appeared, birds to fly through the air and rest in the trees, fish to swim in the sea, and animals to walk and crawl and climb on the land. The sun fed the plants and the plants fed the animals. Our Creator looked into the world and saw that it was good. And He rested, finishing the fifth day.

"The next day our Creator looked out into the world and He spoke, "Let us make man in our image to care for the world.' And out of the dust He fashioned man and He named him Adam. He put Adam into a garden which Adam named Eden. And Adam watched over Creation. But, our Creator saw that Adam had no companion. This was not good. He placed Adam into a deep sleep and took a portion of his rib. He sealed Adam's flesh and fashioned a helpmate for Adam. And when Adam awoke our Creator brought her to Adam. Adam said, 'This is Eve' and the two were together in the garden. And our Creator looked at them and said, 'It is very good'. And He rested, ending the sixth day.

"On the seventh day our Creator rested and all Creation rested with Him.

"Adam and Eve lived together in the garden. They were given the task of naming and caring for all Creation. The plants and the animals were studied by them. Each was named and Adam and Eve learned all they could about each living creature and plant. They even learned to communicate with the animals.

"The Creator visited with them every day. During the cool morning hours or the late afternoon He would walk with them. Each day Adam and Eve would tell the Creator what they had observed that day. He was very pleased with them and they were exceedingly happy.

"Within the garden the Creator had told Adam and Eve that they could eat of any food that was growing in the garden, except from the Tree of Knowledge of Good and Evil. If they should eat of its fruit they would surely die. For many seasons the two lived together content to obey their Creator.

"But, Satan hated the Creator and His Creation. He took the form of the serpent and entered the garden to tempt them. Satan had lived with the Creator in heaven. He had been the Creator's favorite of all the angels. Satan was given all he asked and he was loved by the Creator. Satan, however, was not content. He asked to be given the power to create, to be equal to our Creator. This could not be granted and Satan rebelled. There was a fierce battle in the heavens and Satan and his followers were defeated. They were cast out of heaven into the fiery pit. Satan, however, could not be held there indefinitely. Satan escaped into the world. 'If I cannot rule in heaven, then I shall rule over Your creation.'

"The serpent met Adam and Eve as they passed by the Tree of Knowledge. 'Has your Creator said that you may eat any food that is found in the garden?' he hissed.

"'We may eat anything except the fruit of the Tree of Knowledge of Good and Evil,' replied Adam. 'For, if we should eat its fruit we will surely die,' said Eve. The serpent replied, 'Has your Creator said that you would die or does He want to keep you from knowing all that He knows. Your Creator knows that if you eat from this Tree, you will then know what He knows and you will be like Him. The serpent picked the fruit from the tree and held it out to them. Eve took it into her hand and put it to her lips. Adam pulled her arm down and said to her, 'If we are to do this evil thing let me go first.' He took the fruit from her hand and was about to take a bite when Eve knocked it from his hand to the ground. He looked at her and then at the serpent. 'Be gone foul snake for we will not be tempted by you.' The serpent smoothly slithered away.

"Adam and Eve stared at each other. 'What have we done, what will the Creator think when he sees that the fruit has fallen to the ground? But He must know that we did not eat the fruit. We have not died and the garden is as always.'

"The two quickly left that spot and walked together to the other end of the garden. The Creator came into the garden and saw the fruit on the ground, but uneaten and He knew what had happened. He saw that Adam and Eve were at the opposite end of the garden and He went to walk with them.

"'I found this on the ground next to the Tree of Knowledge. What happened?'

"'Forgive us for we were tempted by the serpent. He told us evil lies and tried to trick us and make us eat the fruit, but Eve saved me,' Adam explained.

"'Is this true, Eve?'

"'Yes we were greatly tempted and I almost ate the fruit, but Adam stopped me as I was about to eat. He would not let me eat the fruit first. Before he could eat I knocked the fruit from his hands and we sent the evil serpent away.'

"'I am pleased that you have been obedient. Satan has come into the world and brought evil. You have shown great courage to resist him. You shall be rewarded for your obedience. But you must be careful. Satan will try to tempt you two more times. He lusts for power and to dominate the world. You and your children must always be wary, for he is cunning and will appear when least expected.'

"Adam looked confused. 'What are children?' he asked.

"They will be a gift from me to you. You and Eve will come to know each other in a new way. The result will be children, a creation that you two will make together. This challenge by Satan has shown me that you are worthy and together you will create miracles.'

"Adam was still confused, but he did not want to question the Creator further. Eve seemed to look at him in a different way, as the Creator left them alone.

"Eve took Adam's hand in hers and the two walked away together, each lost in their own thoughts, but content to be safe and together. Adam thought about how they narrowly avoided the fatal temptation, while Eve thought about Adam's sacrifice for her. She moved closer to him as they walked along. They stopped for some food and water, feeling more love and devotion towards each other than ever. As evening approached and the pale moon rose, they fell asleep together coming to know each other in a completely new way. Adam's confusion melted away with this wondrous love that he had discovered for Eve who he now looked on as a true mate; so much more than companion.

"The two spent endless, joyful days together, exploring the garden and learning all they could about each creature and plant that they discovered. The Creator continued to join them daily, walking with them in the cool of the morning or late afternoon. Each day Adam and Eve recounted their discoveries, a new plant with tasty fruit, an unusual animal with a pouch and a mouth similar to a duck, a colorful frog, each was studied closely and the tiniest characteristic committed to memory. Their days were filled with expanding their knowledge of the wonderful world that had been created for them.

"As the seasons changed Eve also noticed a change. She realized that she was going to have a baby. A boy, Abel, was born. Their days became filled even more as Adam and Eve watched Abel grow. Abel was followed by another son, Cain. The two boys grew up together. Everything that Adam and Eve had learned about the garden around them was taught to the boys. They learned where to find food, which animals ate which plants, how the days changed and seasons changed, they named the stars in the sky. As the two boys reached manhood, mates were created for each of them and the family lived together in perfect harmony.

"Cain was wed to Lilith. They did not have any children yet. While strolling through the garden they happened to pass by the Tree of Knowledge of Good and Evil. Cain had been warned repeatedly that Satan could one day appear to tempt him. Eating the fruit of the Tree of Knowledge was forbidden by the Creator. Cain had dutifully instructed Lilith about the danger that Satan posed.

"From within the tree they heard the call of the vulture. They stopped to look into the tree. The bird called to them. 'What has your Creator told you of this tree?' cried the vulture. Cain replied, 'If we eat of the fruit that grows on the Tree of Knowledge of Good and Evil we will surely die.' 'Has your Creator said this to you or were you told this by Adam and Eve?' The vulture responded. 'Adam knows that if you eat of the fruit from the Tree of Knowledge, then you will surpass him and become ruler of the garden and all the world. There is a great world outside the garden that has been kept from you. Your Creator keeps you in ignorance, while keeping the best for himself.'

"Cain and Lilith were greatly tempted by the deceiving words of the vulture. 'One tiny bite surely couldn't hurt,' said Lilith.

"'This bird is evil,' said Cain, 'I will not be a part of Satan's handiwork. All we could ever want is given to us by the Creator. Lilith, you are his work, fashioned by his own hands. I will not allow you to do this.' 'But, Lilith took the fruit and ran away among the trees, hiding from her husband. He chased after her, fearful of what she was contemplating. The vulture flew after her and landed on a branch above her hiding place. 'Now's your chance, take a bite and be free from the shackles put on you by your Creator and your husband. You will be greater than your Creator, with all His knowledge and power.'

"The words 'your Creator' burned deep into her mind and soul. She remembered Adam's words, 'You will love the Creator with all your heart, soul, and mind'. The Creator truly was benevolent and had given her everything. No, I cannot betray Him, she said to herself. The vulture practically read her mind. 'Has the Creator said that you would betray Him? Or, has Adam said this to keep himself as lord over the rest of you?'

"Lilith searched her mind. It was Adam and not the Creator that ruled over them. If I eat this fruit I will be closer to my Creator, perhaps be with Him at all times. This would be worth the risk. It is Adam's fault. He walks with my Creator and keeps Him from me. This will free me to be joined to Him for all time. She raised the fruit to her lips, but heard Cain call out, 'Lilith, stop, please let me come to you.'

"She lowered the fruit as she thought of her husband and the joyful times they had spent together, walking through the wooded areas, hand in hand, laughing over the antics of a monkey. She could not leave him behind and eternity with the Creator was something they could look forward to in the future, together. She dropped the fruit to the ground and ran to her husband and tightly embraced him. He saw the fruit on the ground and saw the vulture fly away as he held the sobbing Lilith tightly in his arms. 'You are a strong woman to fight off such powerful temptation. I am proud of you,' he said to her as the two walked off through the woods hand-in-hand.

"The Creator came into the woods and saw the fruit on the ground. He returned it to the Tree of Knowledge where it still hangs, a memorial to the strength of one woman who saved us all. Cain and Lilith reported to Adam all that had happened. The Creator came and told them that He was pleased with them, that men were proving to be very strong and loyal. He blessed them and told them that they must be very careful, because Satan was very devious and would try to tempt them one more time.

"The people of Eden flourished and their numbers grew to several hundred. Adam and Eve grew mature, and after several thousand seasons, they were taken to be with the Creator for all time. The people were busy learning of the world that had been created. They studied the animals and plants, the patterns of the seasons, night and day the wind and the stars. They learned to predict when the rain would fall, when the sun would shine, what food was eaten by which animals, all the while walking with the Creator each day and telling him all that they had learned. Like a proud father, the Creator encouraged them and watched over them. He kept them safe and sheltered.

"In this way, we have lived here for thousands of seasons, undisturbed until now. We have a visitor among us who has traveled a great distance to be with us. Welcome, David, we hope you will live a long and prosperous life among us."

David was astonished by the story which was so different from the Bible myth he had read as a student. Was this really the Garden of Eden? Man had never fallen and now lived every day with God, the Creator as they called Him. He was amazed and he could not wait to meet the Creator.

XXIV. JOSHUA SEARCHES

JOSHUA SMITH LEFT HIS APARTMENT TO SEARCH FOR HIS FORMER ASsailant. The police records of the arrest had yielded a name, Richard Cosby, and an address, 3231 Plainview. His locator pinpointed this on the outskirts of the city, a rundown part of town, made up of dilapidated buildings and abandoned souls. He would start there, although he doubted that Richard had stayed put after his arrest. The gangs were nomadic; their only constant was roaming the casino district for handouts and victims. It struck Joshua odd that someone who supposedly adhered to Biblical teaching could lead such a violent life. This was a paradox that he would have to ask Mr. Cosby to clarify.

He walked through the casino district towards the edge of the city. The casinos were quiet with only a few early birds coming and going. It was only eight in the morning. Joshua figured that his best chance of finding Richard would be in the early morning. Someone that made a living holding up innocent victims probably kept late hours and probably would be sleeping at this hour. As Joshua walked he heard a familiar noise. In the distance there was a faint yap, which steadily grew louder. He saw a white streak racing towards him and then there he was. Little Bit had tracked him down. The little Westie danced around Joshua on his hind legs and yapped with joy at Joshua's familiar face.

"Those government agents let you go?" Joshua asked, almost expecting Little Bit to answer him. "More likely you gave them the slip." Little Bit barked as if he were in agreement. "Well, I guess you're coming along. We're on our way to find a person that tried to kill me a few weeks ago, who, incidentally was almost killed by David, to see if this person will help me find something that will help me understand what happened to David. So, you are more than welcome to join me in what may be a complete folly."

Little Bit put his nose to the ground and started on ahead. They had passed all the mammoth buildings housing the casinos, strolled past some of the typical modular apartments and approached the outskirts of the city. Here there were only worn down and wrung out buildings, some with smoke coming from chimneys, others with fires blazing outside the entrance. Where to start? That was the question. He did not expect much help from the inhabitants.

The outskirts of the city were populated by the outcasts of society. Attempts had been made to integrate everyone into mainstream culture, providing all the basic necessities and many luxuries. To receive this basic government assistance one only had to live within the laws established by UN and federal legislators. Certain groups had rejected these laws and lived outside the usual acceptable society. These included the mentally ill (although most would say that they were all mentally challenged), those who clung to and espoused outdated, reactionary, untruthful religious dogma, criminals and gangs who chose to fight society rather than conform, and unsanctioned offspring who had reached adulthood and found no future waiting for them within acceptable society. The total number was not known, but out of a population of over sixty billion, it was estimated that no more than ten million lived in this underground culture.

It was into this world of outcasts that Joshua and Little Bit now ventured. There were very few people about at this time of day. He saw a disheveled old man sitting by an open fire and Joshua approached him. "Excuse me, sir, but I'm looking for someone," Joshua started. "You've found someone," the old man said. "You don't understand. I'm looking for Richard Cosby; do you know him?"

"Nope."

"Do you know any religious groups? I think that Mr. Cosby is a member."

"Nope."

Joshua saw that he was getting nowhere with the old man. "Come on Little Bit, we'll look somewhere else."

"Did you say Little Bit, *the* Little Bit, famous Astropilot, intergalactic Westie?"

"Yes, that's him."

"Just a moment." The old man put his wrist to his mouth whispering into it. "Forty-one hundred. Strawberry, in the basement." He went back to the fire.

"Where's Strawberry?" Joshua looked at his global locator, but no "Strawberry" was apparent. Stupid, he thought to himself. The old man only pointed down the street, but would not utter another syllable. Joshua started walking and Little Bit raced on ahead. The little dog stopped at the street corner. The signpost said Strawberry. He waited for Joshua then ran down the street, stopping at 4100. He started sniffing at the door as Joshua walked up and knocked on the door. As they stood there a huge woman came up from behind and wrapped a wire tightly around Joshua's neck. In a flash Little Bit jumped up and grabbed her wrist tightly in his jaws, loosening her grip and allowing Joshua to free himself. Joshua heard hands clapping as a man stepped out from an alley.

"Little Bit really is a remarkable dog," the man said.

"Richard Cosby, I presume," Joshua replied. The gold cross was prominently displayed around the man's neck.

"At your service. Although you look familiar I don't think I've formally had the pleasure?"

"My name is Joshua Smith. I'm a friend of David Sanders. I've been looking for you."

"So I've heard. Your coming was announced." The woman who had nearly decapitated Joshua stood by silently. She was about 6' 3" and probably over two hundred twenty pounds of solid muscle. "Don't worry about Ms. Jameson," Cosby said, pointing to the huge mass of woman. "She's really as gentle as a bunny, unless she sees that I might be in danger. Of course, she doesn't talk much. She had a run in with some government police and her tongue doesn't work properly anymore." Jameson stuck out her tongue, exposing a scarred stump that barely moved; certainly of little use for talking and barely serviceable for swallowing.

"I wasn't really worried. Little Bit is a match for anyone. I'll take him over the biggest man or woman any day." Joshua thought for a moment. "I guess the old man called you?"

"Just because we live in the slums doesn't mean we've never heard of communications. Of course we knew you were coming. You've got a lot to learn about sneaking up on people. It's obvious you are not with the police or Government Intelligence; that's an oxymoron if ever there was one."

"No we're just friends of David Sanders. We've been trying to figure out how to find him and bring him home and I thought you might be able to help."

"Well you thought wrong. You may take your little dog and just go back to your nice comfortable home. What makes you think I would raise my little finger for astropilot Major David Sanders? He almost knocked my teeth out last time we met. All I can say is that it's a good thing Jameson wasn't with me that night or your Major Sanders would have been doing his flying from the morgue. Now, you and your little dog can leave."

Joshua persisted. "You wear a cross. Only someone with a death wish or a true believer would openly display such a religious symbol. I don't think you have a death wish so I figure you must be a true Christian. This being so you will probably have something that I need to help me figure out what may have happened to Major Sanders. What I need is a Bible."

Richard stood silently after he heard Joshua say this. "Let's go inside," he said.

The room was spare and dimly lit. There was a large suitcase on a table, a chair and an air mattress on the floor with a sleeping bag. The walls were empty. There was a portable computer on the table. There was no kitchen and no food.

"Not much of a place," said Joshua.

"I need to stay mobile. The authorities are always after us. We try to stay a step ahead."

"Who is 'us?'" asked Joshua.

"The social outcasts, unsanctioned people, those considered defective because they don't conform to society's norms. Mainstream society pretends that we don't exist. The government hounds us and tries to bring us back into the fold by 're-education.' We just want the same rights that everyone else has. The right to be ourselves and believe what we want to believe, not what the government tells us." Richard opened the suitcase as he spoke. Inside was a change of clothes and a book. "This is my Bible," said Richard. It was a leather-bound book; the cover appeared worn. "Most books are available via computer. I have quite a library on mine, but an unabridged and unedited Bible cannot be found in any literary database. This was published more than seventy-five years ago. You may borrow it. First, however, you are in time to hear me speak. Come with me."

Joshua and Little Bit followed Cosby and Jameson into the next room. There were about thirty people, men, women, and children seated on some benches, a few seats, or on the floor. The room was stark, without decoration, save a cross hanging on the wall behind the podium, which was at the front of the room. Cosby moved to the front and stood at the podium and started to speak.

"My friends, the Lord welcomes you. We gather together to learn about our beloved God and what He wants from you and from me. This book." He held the Bible up. "God's word tells us how we are to act in this crazy world. The Lord does not want to keep you in poverty. He does not want you to be cold or outcast from society. No, He wants you to discover the person inside that will make you great. He knows that you did not choose to be here, to be sick or 'different.' If you listen to what I say and do God's work, you will find yourself freed from the abyss, happy and whole. God wants you to do His work, to follow his commandments. And…. you can pull yourself up with God's help. I've studied the good book and it says, love your neighbor as yourself, but also, good things come to those who do follow God's law. Remember, it has been written the Lord helps those who help themselves. As you follow me, you will learn what you can do to bring yourself out of the gutter." Cosby's voice rose and he shook his Bible. "Begin today to make the choice to discover the real victorious you… The man, woman or child that will set you free." Cosby pointed to a man in the front row. "You Samuel, it is not fair that you are sick and the government does not consider you a person. You are not responsible for the circumstances of your birth. You can't get the medicine or therapy that you need and are entitled to. The Lord says you have the right to take it. The other people have so much and what do they do? They spit on us. They run away, scared, they hide their children, they send the police to hound us, keep us out of sight and tell everyone what a great job their benevolent government is doing keeping society safe. It is time to do the Lord's work, to bring God back to the people. If you follow me I will show you the truth. God wants everyone to be healthy, happy, and safe. He wants to help everyone, not just those in a fancy 'Quad' home, not just Joshua, our guest here. No, He wants us all to be happy. So listen to God's word and be happy."

As Cosby spoke, Little Bit, who had been watching and listening quietly, started to bark loudly, disrupting the sermon. Joshua tried to quiet him, but he only barked louder and started to growl. "I'm sorry, I've never seen him act like this before," Joshua said and he carried the feisty little dog out of the room. Joshua felt uneasy that Little Bit would be so upset by words that seemed to be only of encouragement. The sermon, as a matter of fact, sounded like one of the weekly motivational speeches that the government sponsored to provide encouragement to the people. As Joshua thought more about it, he realized that if the word God or Lord were changed to government there really wouldn't be any difference at all. These thoughts raced through his head as he returned to the sermon, leaving Little Bit in the adjoining room.

"So... Love God and He will love you, do good works and you will find his favor. Amen."

Cosby finished as Joshua returned. "I'm sorry for the disruption," Joshua said.

"It's OK," Cosby replied. "Now, you needed a Bible. I want you take mine."

I'm surprised that you would just give it to me," Joshua said. "It must be very rare and valuable."

"If you read it and study it you will know why I'm giving it to you. Perhaps you will learn all that you need and more. Besides, I know where to get another."

Joshua flipped through the Bibles pages. The pages were crisp and clean. He put it into his pocket. "I need to ask you one question. I'm no religious scholar, but I'm also not completely ignorant. Why would a group of 'Christians' attack and steal from innocent people? It seems very un-Christ-like. I believe that He was known for turning the other cheek and loving thy neighbor. You need to let me know where in the New Testament it says to mug thy neighbor."

"Maybe you shouldn't believe everything that's reported in the media. Did you get hurt by us? As I recall it was quite the opposite. Do you know of anyone that has truly been hurt by a Christian mugger? It is true that we travel in groups, often within the casino districts and we will occasionally encounter people as they leave a casino; but next time take a closer look at our 'weapons.' Maybe you'll see that it is in the government's interest to keep the masses a little bit scared and a little bit dependent on government police force for protection. After all, if there were no criminals why would any police be necessary? Think about it. One other thing, don't try to copy the Bible. That will bring a knock upon your door and you may not be heard from again and Major Sanders would stay lost in space."

"Thank you," said Joshua. He and Little Bit left. Richard wondered what the Bible possibly could have in it that could help find a lost astropilot. A fool's errand, he thought.

XXV. DEBORAH

AFTER HER ENCOUNTER WITH JOSHUA SMITH, DEBORAH RETURNED to her apartment to study the sudden change in the interdimensional portals. The variability of portal energy readings had to have some pattern. She just could not believe that something that was such an integral part of the fabric of space and time could be so random. Also, this sudden change had to have a cause that math and science could decipher. Her life now became a routine of waking, eating, and studying readings from portals, looking for a pattern of change that would allow a pilot or probe to enter safely and search for Major Sanders. She also was becoming obviously pregnant and she did not want to be fodder for the tabloid media for carrying an unsanctioned child. She knew that the truth would eventually be revealed but for now she didn't need such aggravation.

She spent hours at a time staring at table after table of numbers and times trying to make some sense out of what appeared to be a random jumble. The most powerful Space Agency computers could not find any discernable pattern, but with her special gift for number and mathematics she was sure that she would find the answer. She had not heard anything from Joshua. This didn't surprise her; unlike David, she really didn't have much faith in him. She was sure that he was back at the track and not giving Major Sanders a second thought.

She turned to the monitor and looked at the latest data. She felt a strong kick that made her stop. "This baby is going to be a kickball star or a karate champ," she thought. It must be time to eat something. The baby always seemed to know when mealtime was. You'd think the food was going straight to its stomach, she thought. She had some bread and orange juice, wishing it was fried fish from Buddies. She lay down as numbers swirled around her brain.

She thought back to her first meeting with David. She was doing the preliminary work on the ITP protocol, meeting with other mathematicians and physicists, testing her theories and working with engineers on the space craft design. No definite plans had been developed as to how inter-dimensional travel was to be utilized, but rumors were that an astropilot was to be selected for a test flight. She was walking down the corridor of the Space agency en route to a meeting when she was suddenly slapped on the side of the head, which caused her glasses to go flying, leaving her nearly blind. The man who had accidentally struck her rushed to her side, apologizing profusely. He had found her glasses and handed them back to her. She put them on and saw a very handsome man with dark hair and smooth tanned skin standing over her.

"I am so sorry," he said. "I didn't see you coming." He smiled at her in a disarming way. Any anger she may have briefly felt melted away as she looked up at him.

"It's OK," she said. "No harm was done, not even my glasses are broken. Now excuse me but I'm late for a meeting." She tried to hurry away.

"Major Sanders, ma'am. Let me make it up to you; let me buy you dinner tonight."

She glanced back at him, but did not say a word. She made it to her meeting on time, but may as well have missed it completely as the image of the tall, handsome man stayed in her head. She didn't even know who Major Sanders was, but suspected he was a pilot of some sort. She wished she had responded to his invitation, but the thought of dining with a strange man was frightening, besides the mountains of work she had to do.

She hurried home after the meeting, her mind a muddled jumble of thoughts about this major, interdimensional portals, and mathematical equations. As she approached her door she saw a message floating across the entrance: Buddies at 7:00 P.M., DS. She looked at her watch, 6:27 P.M. It wouldn't be right, she thought. Definitely a pilot, he's probably got a dozen girlfriends, he really couldn't care about me, she thought, as she changed her clothes, hurrying to get ready. Of course if he really cares, he won't mind if I'm late.

I'll try out the chair, she thought. Her makeover chair had never been used; she'd never had the need. It had been advertised as the latest ultramodern tool, guaranteed to bring beauty, poise, and companionship or your money back. Just sit in the chair for five minutes and even the most repulsive person would be converted into a sultry, sexy, and sophisticated lady (or man). Deborah had bought it on a whim; she could never be sexy with her thick glasses and her slight frame. She thought, now or never. She sat down in the chair and pushed the blue button for extensive. The chair totally engulfed her, soothing music started to play as she felt herself being scanned. She heard a whirring noise and felt little jets of air cascade over her body. The whole process was very soothing. Before she knew it the whirring stopped and the chair opened up. She saw her before–and–after image projected as a hologram. Her wispy brown hair was fuller with streaks of black and magenta, her eyes were darker and deep blue, and her face was vibrantly made up. Her skin was smooth and silky and all unnecessary hair had been removed. Her fingernails and toenails were full and a deep, shiny red. Her breasts seemed fuller and rounder and butt felt firmer. Hanging next to the chair was a new outfit with the latest in see through undergarments made of fabricated silk. The dress was also the finest fabricated silk, ivory, and cut to reveal just enough to be enticing. There were even new glasses, shoes, and a handbag. She put on the clothes and admired her holographic projection. He probably won't recognize me, she thought. The entire transformation had taken only nine minutes.

She called for transport from her computer and a taxi appeared at the curb downstairs.

"Buddies," she said. The automated taxi sped away and she arrived at 6:57 P.M. It was a warm night and there was a line out front. She made inquiries, but Major Sanders had not arrived. She sat down and waited. Several minutes passed and still she sat. Several men walked past, but no Major Sanders. She felt silly and a little embarrassed as she decided to leave. She had waited over thirty minutes and she had plenty of work that needed to be done. She was about to summon a taxi when a bright blue sports car sped past and abruptly stopped in front of her. "There you are. It's about time you got here I've been waiting forever. "Get in." It was Major Sanders, but what did he mean he'd been waiting forever.

"Come on, if we hurry we can make it in time," he said. "Make what?" she mumbled, but before she could finish he grabbed her hand and pulled her into the car. He sped away and she felt like she had been kidnapped. Still, there was a sense of excitement. She noticed that he was doing all the steering and turning. Where's the navigation system? she thought. As if he could read her mind he said, "The computerized controls are too slow and it is much safer letting me navigate, don't worry."

"Where are we going?" she asked. "Siros, they have some fresh prime steak, but just for tonight. If we can get there by eight-thirty we can have some. Joshua is treating."

"I've never heard of Siros and I don't know any Joshua."

"Siros is in Saratoga and Joshua is a friend of mine. By the way, you look very pretty, but I like you better without the makeover chair. It looks too artificial and turns you into something out of a fashion show that isn't real. I like the real thing. But don't worry, by morning you'll be back to you. That's what I really prefer."

"I don't think you'll get to see the transformation. Oh, and isn't Saratoga over 500 kilometers away. I don't think we'll make it." She looked at his speedometer; it was in the red zone, which meant at least 450 k/hr. I'm driving with a crazy person, she thought. Just close your eyes and maybe it will all end.

"Don't worry, you're safe with me."

Don't worry, he says. That's the third time he has said that to me in less than two minutes. She should be worried, but something about him made her feel calm and safe. She sat back and watched as the scenery flew by. They were flying down a series of back roads with very little traffic. She couldn't see the speedometer, but she sensed they were going awfully fast. As they raced around sharp turns and up and down steep hills, all of a sudden they stopped. Before she could protest, David had jumped out of the car. She saw him bend down and pick something up and put it at the edge of a stream that was running along the road. "What was..." she started to ask. But, before she could finish, he said "Turtle... it was a turtle that was stuck in the road. I thought it needed to be rescued. I'll have to pick up the pace if we're going to make it in time." He zoomed back on to the road. What kind of man is this, she thought, as she sat back to enjoy the rest of the ride.

In what seemed like no time they pulled into the lot at Siros. David opened the door for her and held her hand as they walked in together. "Do you have a reservation?" the maitre d' asked. "I'm meeting a friend, Joshua Smith," David replied. "Ah, yes, he is expecting you, follow me."

He led them to table in the back of the dining room, in a dark and quiet corner.

Deborah saw a thin man with fine brown hair seated at the table. He stood up and greeted them. "Hello David, and you must be Deborah; hello, Dr. Tennyson, my name is Joshua... Joshua Smith."

"Very pleased to meet you," she said politely. "Do you live here in Saratoga?"

"Oh no, just visiting for the season."

"Which season is that?" she asked.

"Joshua makes his living at the racetrack. He means the racing season," David interjected.

"Really? Are you a jockey or a trainer?"

"Oh no," came Joshua's reply, "I just bet on the races,"

Deborah remembered the dinner as being very boring as the two men talked about horse racing, sports, and mostly ignored her. The steaks were fantastic, however, and she had a delightful conversation with the waiter, who was really a musician and only waiting on tables between gigs.

Joshua did finally address her asking what field of medicine she was in. She explained that she was a doctor of mathematics and physics. She was working on characteristics of space, time, and interdimensional connections.

"If interdimensional connections are real, then transgalactic and interdimensional space travel becomes a real possibility," Joshua concluded.

"That's very perceptive of you," Deborah responded. "How did you know that?"

"Just because I waste my life at racetracks doesn't mean I'm totally ignorant. I went to school and I can put two and two together and get five. It seems obvious that the current limitation to intergalactic as well as even interstellar travel is the constraint of the speed of light as well as space and time."

"You are correct. I've found a mathematical equation that predicts the existence of interdimensional portals and have developed a protocol for transport that is in the early phases of testing."

David listened closely to what she had said. The rumors were true. This date had become very worthwhile even if he didn't end up getting any action later. "I'm glad you two have found something to talk about," he said, but it is getting late and we have to get back. I have an early meeting tomorrow and I'm sure the fair doctor has to be up early. Joshua doesn't have any early obligation I'm sure, not until post time."

The drive home was relatively leisurely as David drove at only 300 km/hr. He asked a multitude of questions about her work and what the plans were for future interdimensional travel. She told him that they were a long way from any manned missions, but an astropilot would likely be the first human to fly such a mission. That was the information that David had wanted. He was on his way to becoming the first interdimensional pilot.

David parked in front of Deborah's apartment and walked her to the door. She thanked him for what had been an interesting evening. As she fumbled for her key, David asked if he would see her again. She said that of course she would be around the Space Center and they would probably run into each other from time to time. As she turned to unlock her door, she felt a hand on her shoulder; as she turned, he encircled her with his powerful arms and gave her a big kiss. She took a step back and the two fell to the floor through the open door. "I guess that's one way to get into your apartment," he said, as he gave her his hand and helped her up. She thanked him again, and as he tried to kiss her again, she turned her face and received a light kiss on her cheek. "Good night, Major Sanders," she firmly said. "Good night, Doctor, I'll call you."

Deborah turned back to her monitor and thought of everything that had happened since that night. They had continued to see each other discreetly, the ITP program progressed, and David was chosen as the first intergalactic pilot. Deborah had become pregnant with his unsanctioned child and David was either lost in space or dead. She turned back to the numbers on the monitor, trying, unsuccessfully, to put everything else out of her mind.

XXVI. SENATOR LEAVITT

SENATOR ADRIAN LEAVITT ENTERED HIS OFFICE THROUGH THE BACK door and locked the door behind him. The failure of the manned ITP mission was made to order for his plans. He activated a special communications program on his office computer. A second computer monitor came up out of his desk and a call was placed. Simultaneously, his office security measures were activated. This security system would thwart any attempts to eavesdrop or monitor his communication. It was the most expensive and advanced security system available, but very necessary for the kind of work he did and his partner required the tightest security possible. It was this partner the senator was calling on this rarely used secure line. The connection immediately went through and the hologram of Mr. Diblonski appeared. "Hello, Senator, how is our plan going?" "Better than we'd hoped for," Leavitt answered. "I'm sure you've heard of the disastrous manned ITP mission."

"Yes, I've seen the media reports. One never knows what is true and what is for the benefit of the public."

"The reports are essentially true. Major Sanders has been lost attempting the first manned Interdimensional space flight. Even better, however, is that there seems to have been a major shift in the portal energy output such that it is no longer constant so that any future attempts to utilize the ITP will be nearly impossible."

Mr. Diblonski replied, "This is better than I could have hoped. You have been very helpful in discrediting the ITP program. To put it to rest we must discredit it at the source. We must eliminate Dr. Tennyson as a viable scientist. She must be exposed for the charlatan that she is. I don't want her physically harmed, but she must be professionally ruined, rendered impotent so that she and the ITP are no longer a threat to our operations."

"What would you have me do?"

"You are a United States senator, Chairman of the Interplanetary Committee. It is your duty to investigate the miserable failure of the manned interdimensional mission and insure that such a disaster never happens again. Of course, you will be compensated in the usual way."

The image of Mr. Diblonski faded away and Senator Leavitt sat back in his leather chair. He opened a panel in one of the walls of his office which led to a room whose walls were elegantly adorned with paintings by some of the most famous old masters, Renoir, Monet, Van Gogh, Da Vinci, and Picasso, among others, that were part of a most impressive collection. He kept his collection secret, only allowing the occasional special guest to enter his private gallery. He wondered what would arrive next. Mr. Diblonski had never disappointed him.

He had met Diblonski years ago at an art auction. At the time, Senator Leavitt was an underpaid college physics professor. His passion for art had always burned, but it had mostly been vicarious, as he never could afford even the simplest of the old masters that he loved. He frequented art auctions and museums to view these masterpieces if only for a short time. He had seen Mr. Diblonski at several art auctions, never giving him much thought until the day that Mr. Diblonski had purchased Starry Night after a particularly heated bidding war. Afterwards, Leavitt found himself sharing an elevator alone with Mr. Diblonski.

"You are lucky to have that painting," he said to Diblonski. "Yes, it is quite beautiful. It will be a fine addition to my collection," Diblonski replied.

"Do you have a large art collection?"

"Yes, over 300 of the great masters."

"I would love to see such a collection. My name's Leavitt, Mr. Diblonski, Adrian Leavitt."

"Pleased to meet you; how do you know me?"

"Anyone serious about art knows the name Diblonski. Aaron Diblonski, industrialist, financier, and art collector. I've read of your collection in the art media."

"Would you like to see it firsthand?"

"Certainly," Leavitt said enthusiastically.

"Well then, you may come with me now and I shall be happy to give you a tour. My transportation is waiting just outside."

"Thank you, thank you very much."

Leavitt wasn't quite sure, but he thought this could open some doors for him, give him a way out of the limited prospects of teaching college physics, and bring him greater wealth and power. He knew that Aaron Diblonski was a powerful man with connections all the way up to the top senators and maybe into the highest echelons of the United Nations.

Diblonski was silent during the entire ride, which was only about fifteen minutes. The automobile pulled up in front of a palatial home surrounded by perfectly manicured green lawns and groves of tall trees. The house was red brick, surrounded by a small river, with a large fountain in front. Small bridges crossed the river at various points.

The two crossed one of the bridges and walked through the massive front door to enter a foyer that was larger than Leavitt's apartment. There was ornate marble flooring and intricately carved molding on the walls which was painted gold. There were twin mahogany staircases leading upstairs, which although antique in appearance, were also motorized. There was an elaborate fresco on the ceiling depicting men at war charging at each other on horseback, brandishing lances and broad swords.

"Very impressive, overwhelming, really," Leavitt observed. "You like my humble abode? It keeps the rain off my head," replied Diblonski. "Follow me and I'll show you my collection." They walked through double doors that were to the left into a smaller foyer. "My gallery is in there; let me turn off the security system." He waved his hand in front of a light and another light flashed across his face and the doors opened. Diblonski led Leavitt into another huge room, all the walls hung with paintings. "Enjoy yourself," Diblonski said, "I have some business to attend. I will be back in a few hours."

Leavitt felt giddy and lightheaded as he started to shuffle along the walls, longingly staring at each masterpiece. There were Rembrandts, Degas, Van Goghs, Matisses, Renoirs, Monets, Da Vincis, Rockwells, and on and on. As he viewed each painting it came alive as a miniature image of the artist appeared and gave a detailed discourse on the painting's creation. The observer could see an actual recreation of the steps the artist took to create each masterpiece. Of course it was all virtual, but of such high quality that Leavitt felt he could have a conversation with each artist. This must be heaven, even if no such place exists, he thought to himself. He inspected each painting, even using his pocket probe to verify that each was authentic. This must truly be the most valuable collection in the world, public or private, he thought. It was almost unheard of in this world of exact duplication to have the means to purchase what was probably billions of dollars worth of rare paintings. This Mr. Diblonski would be a good friend to have, one that might help to pull himself into the upper echelons of society and save him from spending the rest of his miserable life teaching physics to apathetic college students, whose only goal was to make it to the casinos for a night of hedonistic pleasures. Those college students didn't know true hedonism, he thought; this room was the ultimate in sensual pleasure. Such classic beauty could never be found in a casino or through the media or anywhere in this superficial, computer-generated world that man had created.

He had only gone about half way through the gallery when a door opened and Mr. Diblonski joined him. "I see you like my little collection," he said. "I am very impressed," Leavitt gushed. "This is pure joy, to see such beauty. I could easily die a happy man after spending a day with these masterpieces. It almost makes me believe that there is a God."

Diblonski's nostrils flared and there was a flash of anger in his eyes at the mention of a deity, but he quickly became calm. "Take your time, enjoy yourself, and then join me in the sitting room at the end of the gallery. It will be through the black double doors. I will wait for you there."

Leavitt took his time, savoring every moment as he studied each painting, admiring the exquisite detail and style of each artist. When he had finished viewing the collection he saw the double doors and went into the sitting room. The room was huge, dimly lit with a large fireplace that was blazing, more old masters on the walls, a number of statues and shelves filled with books. Diblonski was waiting for him. Leavitt had a strange feeling, as though he were somehow of great importance. Why should someone as rich and powerful as Aaron Diblonski care one bit about someone as insignificant as me, he asked himself.

"Come in, Professor Leavitt, come in. I hope you enjoyed my gallery."

"It was magnificent. I could spend the rest of my life in these halls."

Diblonski offered him a drink and the two sat down together.

"Would you like to own a collection like this one?" Diblonski asked.

"You know I would," Leavitt answered, "but I couldn't afford one of the frames, let alone any such paintings."

"I think I can help you, if you will let me," Diblonski said. "I am looking for someone to help me with various projects, certain things that I cannot do myself, because of my position. Nothing illegal, of course, just tasks that would draw too much attention to me or to one of my regular employees if we were to do them. If you agree to help me, you will be well compensated, including receiving one of these fine masterpieces upon successful completion of each task. What do you say; will you help me?"

Leavitt thought for a moment. This is too good to be true. To go to work for one of the greatest men in the world, to get away from the mundane life of a teacher and to receive just one of those fabulous paintings was a temptation too great to pass. "Of course I'm interested. What do I have to do?"

"Just wait, for now. Soon you will be presented with an opportunity that will start you on a new career path. You need not ask what it will be, as it will be obvious. You need only to make the decision to give up your present life and go on to much greater accomplishments. Now you may stay as long as you want, wander among the paintings for as long as you wish. Oh, there is one item of importance. As you make your way to greater wealth and power, you must never let it be known that I have assisted you or even know you. If our relationship does become known then all that you have been given will be lost. You must promise this."

"Yes, I promise, that is, as long as you keep up your end of the bargain."

"Thank you, we have a deal then. Good-bye."

Leavitt went back to his teaching, greatly anticipating the change that was to come. Days became weeks and then months and nothing happened. He even tried calling Mr. Diblonski, but never could get a response. After about seven months he received a letter asking him to participate in an advisory role on a government committee studying effects of interplanetary mining on solar energy. He had never been approached in this way previously. The assignment would include a trip to Washington DC and all expenses paid for a period of three months. This must be what Mr. Diblonski had planned for me and he quickly accepted.

He looked forward to his new career as he settled into life at the government's hub. The day before the first meeting he received a printed communication instructing him to ask one of the interplanetary engineers a question regarding the safety of certain mining procedures utilized on Mars. He thought it strange to receive an anonymous written note and the question seemed very innocent. This seemed harmless and indeed it was at the time. However, two months later the exact concern he had raised did occur and thirty-five men lost their lives. All of a sudden, he became important as the media portrayed him as a champion of the common worker. He was asked to chair the Interplanetary Safety Committee, where he performed splendidly. Shortly after this he received a painting, a Picasso, with a hand-written note saying, "Thank you, AD."

From there he moved into Congress first as a representative and finally as a Senator. Along the way he would receive similar anonymous notes, usually instructing him to ask a certain question or raise certain issues. Each one always led to doubts being raised about the respondent that would lead to in-depth media investigation and to the individual being discredited. The interests of Diblonski Ltd., were somehow promoted at the same time. Leavitt occasionally communicated directly with Diblonski as he had done with the ITP affair. This was always in the most secure manner, as the connection between the two, by necessity, had to be covert.

Diblonski Ltd., was a vast empire of manufacturing, media, interplanetary mining, and transportation. President, CEO, and Chairman of the Board was Aaron Diblonski. He seemed to have been leading the company forever, always appearing youthful, surrounded by an entourage of pretty women, gophers, and security. Through shrewd, almost mystical business decisions, impeccable timing, and luck his influence had come to encompass the entire solar system. He maintained his own fleet of security vessels and pilots, who often looked down with scorn on the military astropilots. Their purpose was the security of the various mining and power generation operations on the moon and other planets.

The ITP posed a great threat to his empire. Expansion of mankind's domain to include the entire universe would make the operations of Diblonski Ltd., very minor and of little value. Major Sanders' ill-fated voyage was everything he could have hoped for, as the ITP would, with the help of Senator Leavitt, become hopelessly stalled in the government bureaucracy. Senator Leavitt would guarantee that. Discrediting Dr. Tennyson would kill the program forever; Diblonski knew that she was the only scientist with the insight to solve the current dilemma and advance the program to the next, more practical level. He had made it clear to Leavitt that it was imperative to start congressional hearings on the ITP program to keep her distracted and away from her research.

XXVII. BACK TO EDEN

DAVID'S STRENGTH WAS RETURNING. HE WAS ABLE TO WALK UNASsisted, although Ruth stayed close to him in case he should have a relapse. David was getting to know the inhabitants of Eden. In particular one of the younger boys, Elijah, spent a great deal of time with David. Elijah introduced David to many of the animals who had seemed wary of the newcomer. He was particularly friendly with the tigers. They would spend hours together walking with the eldest tiger as David told Elijah of life on Earth and Elijah taught David about Eden. Ruth was always nearby, but she gave David the freedom to explore independently as he was no longer in need of constant nursing.

Elijah told David how the Creator had given them dominion over the world; their task was to learn all that they could of the world. The Creator always came daily and they were always anxious to report what had been observed that day. Elijah related how he had discovered a new type of frog living at the edge of a lake. He had studied it for hours, day after day. He described how it moved, where it found food, how it swam, every detail of its existence. David was impressed. "Is that what all of you do?" he asked. "That is what our Creator has commanded. We all study the world around us and then report to the entire group and to the Creator. This way, every-one learns all that can be known. The Creator is always bringing new life into Eden and often changes what is here," Elijah explained. "It makes the world interesting and keeps all of us very busy."

David was constantly surprised and amazed by Eden. The ground was covered in soft grass. Walking barefoot he never had to worry about step-ping on a thorn or being bitten by any sort of insect. As a matter of fact, the only insects he had seen were bees and butterflies. There were no mosquitoes, or fire ants or brown recluse spiders or any bugs that were harmful. He never saw any snakes, only what were called serpents, which had a snake's body, but with short legs, more like a very long lizard. There seemed to be food for all the animals, there was no such thing as one animal killing another for food. There were abundant flowers of the most vibrant, almost overwhelming colors, all with the finest fragrance that one could imagine.

Most surprising was the perfect cleanliness of this magnificent garden. There was no decaying plant life, no evident animal waste; any portions of food that were discarded seemed to disappear in a very short time. He noticed that he almost never had to urinate or move his bowels. The diet here must be perfectly digestible, he thought. The animals and the people knew exactly what was good to eat.

David came to know most of the Edenites. The eldest was Abraham. He had lived through over 4,000 seasons and was married to Sarah. There was Isaac married to Rebekah. He was the son of Abraham. Ishmael was his brother. Jacob was married to Rachel; their sons were Joseph and Benja-min. Their wives had been created for them. David learned that as the pop-ulation had grown, wives were born for each man instead of being created de novo. There was no leader per se, except for the Creator, but Abraham, as the eldest, was considered the wisest and most learned, so the others frequently came to him with questions. As the eldest, Abraham was given authority by the Creator to do certain tasks. He could perform marriages, he could choose songs to be sung or how the Creator was to be thanked. He was a tall rugged man with long white hair and beard. He was deeply tanned but did not appear old except for his white hair.

David spent hours talking with Abraham, usually with some of the other Edenites present, questioning him about the Creator. Abraham also questioned David about Earth. David learned that the Creator visited every day. He appeared as a man, with deep blue eyes that seemed to change color, and he was always clothed in bright white light such that his body could never be seen. He seemed to walk like any other man. He was never angry, always loving, kind, and generous. He asked only two things of the Edenites, that they learn all they could of the world he had created and that they not eat of the fruit of the Tree of Knowledge of Good and Evil. He had told them that if they should eat of its fruit they would surely die. The Edenites loved the Creator and praised him in song and with words. They held gatherings where they would sing of his greatness, love, and generosity. Before every meal they gave thanks for the life he had given and the food he had provided. David had ambiguous feelings about the Creator. He felt some admiration, but also distrust, like there was some catch to all this benevolence. He found it difficult to believe that any being could provide so much and expect nothing in return. Abraham had sensed his uneasiness.

Abraham explained, "You think it impossible for our Creator to give us so much, while we can never repay him. You are missing the greatest payment that one can ever provide. We give him our love and devotion. Maybe you have never so loved another person or been so loved. If you had then you would not question our Creator's motives."

"How did you know what I was thinking? Are you telepathic?" David asked.

"I have lived for thousands of seasons. I have learned a great deal of the world around me and the people that live within it. I could see the doubt in your eyes and knowing what I do of your world it was easy to surmise what was going through your mind."

"My life on Earth was very different. I spent my time moving from one thrill to another. It was a good life, never dull or boring. We had no Creator. Mankind had learned to look after itself. We learned the secrets of life and could manipulate them so that we were living longer and longer. My life on Earth was a never ending stream of fun and excitement."

Abraham interrupted, "Why?"

"Excuse me," stammered David.

"Why did you need to fill your life with thrills and excitement, to what purpose?"

"Does everything need a purpose? We had solved most of the problems that limited our existence. Diseases were all but eradicated, our lives were fulfilling and people were happy, just like you. We do not need a Creator, we don't want a Creator."

"You speak as if you are the voice for all the people of Earth. It sounds more like you are trying to convince yourself. It is not a point that can be argued. You are here with us and will probably be here for the rest of your days. I hope you will be able to find happiness in our boring, mundane garden."

The prospect of spending the rest of his life in Eden, studying tree frogs and singing a cappella to an as yet unseen Creator was becoming disturbing to David. The only bright spot he saw was Ruth of whom he was very fond. He also knew that she loved him. As he gained his strength he felt very attracted to her. His thoughts also turned to his ITP vessel. He knew it was somewhere in Eden. Once he found it, he hoped it could be repaired. He also hoped that Ruth would come with him when he left to go home.

XXVIII. JOSHUA'S STUDY

IN THE BEGINNING GOD...

Joshua started to read the Bible he had gone to such lengths to secure. He was careful to be in an area that was safe from any monitoring. If a Bible were discovered it would probably mysteriously disappear, as often happened with so-called subversive literature. He was convinced that the interdimensional travel had brought David into God's backyard, so to speak. Although mankind had effectively eliminated God from its collective consciousness, Joshua was convinced that the only explanation for all that had happened was God's intervention. In particular the subtle changes in Little Bit pointed him in this direction.

It was with this belief that Joshua started reading, trying to learn all that he could about the nature of this God. Joshua had a special talent that had always served him well throughout school and even now as a horse-player. He could read anything and immediately commit it to memory. The words entered his mind and stuck there, filed away for future use.

What he learned was totally unexpected. The Bible had become relegated to myth and the stories of God, Moses, David, Jesus and everything else had been watered down and placed alongside Perseus and Hercules and Thor. What he read was a historical treatise on God detailing His interaction with the stubborn, disobedient people of the world that He had created. He was fascinated and a little ashamed. The book was the story of mankind running away from God, who would then pursue them and reconcile, only to face rejection anew. As he turned each page, he noticed that each page was crisp, like brand new and untouched. This is very strange, he thought, for a personal Bible that had been read and studied for years. He continued to read.

Joshua came to the Book of Job and suddenly the tone changed. His interest piqued as the cosmic stakes were laid out between God and Satan. There was Satan given free reign to afflict Job, Job's steadfast devotion to God, and finally God humbling Job, but also restoring him. Joshua knew that David Sanders was no Job, but he also was not Satan. God's character shined throughout Job and made Joshua even more confident that his suspicions about interdimensional travel were true. He read on.

Ecclesiastes seemed like a summary of present times. Everything that was important to people of current times could be summed up as vanity. The pursuit of pleasure without substance resulted in feelings of emptiness and futility. Joshua saw this on the faces of people every day, never more so than at the casino the night before David's fateful flight. Joshua knew that his own life was nothing more than empty vanity. He, of course was the first to admit this was of his own choosing, having dropped out of any meaningful pursuits years ago.

Joshua continued on through the Prophets into the New Testament. The tone changed dramatically as God reconciled Himself to man's disobedience. The Jesus of the New Testament had very little in common with the mythological Jesus that was taught to schoolchildren these days. This Jesus was filled with fiery wisdom and loving compassion. Joshua understood why there were still people who clung to their belief in this man who seemed to transcend the ages even as the government tried to wipe Him away from society's collective consciousness. Joshua suspected that for every Richard Cosby that would openly acknowledge belief in Jesus there were probably ten people that secretly harbored some belief in the ancient Galilean carpenter. The philosophy of love and charity that Jesus preached was sorely lacking today. It would be fascinating if David had truly encountered Jesus.

Joshua raced through the Epistles and Revelation. When he closed the back cover, he lay down on his couch with a smile on his face and closed his eyes, tired but satisfied, like a successful day at the track. Nothing he had read would contradict his theory about David's fate. However, if Joshua was correct, it would be impossible to pursue him, but it was also likely that David was still alive. Joshua needed to call Deborah. After all, she had asked him to look into the problem and he was sure she would want to know his findings immediately. He looked at the clock: 2:38 A.M. It was very late (or early), but she was probably up. David said that she slept only three to four hours a night and was usually up until 3 or 4 A.M.

He pushed a button, "Call Dr. Tennyson." She appeared on the screen. "Good morning doctor. I have some news for you, good and bad. I need to explain it to you in person, for several reasons."

"We can meet tomorrow, just tell me where and when," she answered.

"Meet me at the track, Monmouth Park, Bar #23 on the second floor of the clubhouse before the first race," Joshua replied.

Joshua got up and fell on his bed and was asleep in two seconds with Little Bit curled up at his feet.

XXIX. WORRIES

DEBORAH TURNED BACK TO THE MONITOR. I HOPE IT IS GOOD NEWS, she said to herself. She looked at the array of numbers on the screen, the same numbers she had stared at and manipulated over and over for weeks. She could not accept that this essential part of the universe existed in a state of randomness. Science demanded that there be order. The thought that Joshua Smith had some news for her filled her mind, pushing all the numbers to the side. This is hopeless she said to herself for the thousandth time. "Save it," she said and the monitor went blank as the array of numbers was safely stored away into its own little niche deep within the computer's artificial brain.

What could Joshua have found, she thought. The greatest scientific minds on the planet were researching this problem and an insignificant nobody says he found something. Why does David have such confidence in him anyway? He knows almost nothing about astrophysics, space, time or anything that could possibly be helpful. Of course she was curious, and why was he being so secretive. I guess I'll try to sleep she thought knowing that it would be a futile effort. She lay down with thoughts of David and Joshua mixed with endless numbers dancing between the two men whirling through her brain. The numbers kept whirling until she finally passed into a fitful sleep.

She awoke in a state of panic. The sun was shining brightly through her window, the clock said 7:42 A.M. and she felt a wave of relief. For a moment she worried that she had slept right through first race and had missed her opportunity to meet Joshua. Plenty of time to get up, do some work, and find her way to the track by 1:00 P.M. She took a quick shower, ate a synthesized orange and muffin, and sat down at her console to work for a few hours.

"ITP portal data," she said and the monitor sprang to life with the familiar array of numbers. She had repeatedly stared at, manipulated, and juggled these numbers over the last several weeks, never finding any pattern or common thread. She had almost reached the point of concluding that there was no sequence pattern, that the array was truly random, an idea that was at odds with the scientist within her.

"Same array, time between change, holographic display," she said to the computer. The figures marched off the monitor screen, and started to dance around her head as the hologram formed. The time interval between each energy shift appeared alongside each energy reading, highlighted in red. This too appeared completely random. "It's hopeless," she said out loud. Surrounding herself with the holographic figures was a technique she used for the most difficult problems. She said it was as if the symbols and numbers became a part of her soul. She felt a strong kick in her tummy. She patted her bulging stomach. "Calm down in there, I don't need any kibitzing from the sidelines. I'm perfectly capable of being frustrated on my own."

She hit a button on the computer controls and the monitor switched to media reports. There were the usual stories about gang violence plaguing the casino districts, the latest on government efforts to provide guaranteed standards of living to all recognized citizens, an array of political announcements, interspersed with ads touting another successful joint venture between Diblonski Ltd., and the government. Nothing new under the sun she said to herself. She got up to get herself ready to go. She had rarely ventured outside her apartment since David had disappeared. Besides devoting her time to analyzing the mountain of data, she was reluctant to be too conspicuous, carrying an unsanctioned child. This was no time to stir up any more controversy. Government officials were already looking for any reason to close down the ITP program. The lead physicist carrying an unsanctioned child was enough, but the father being the primary ITP pilot would keep the media busy for weeks creating scandal where none existed. She put on her oversized coat, dark glasses, and big floppy hat, looked at herself in the mirror, and decided that she her attempt to be inconspicuous would only make her stand out. Better to dress as a pregnant woman, she thought. She put on a more sensible outfit, but kept the dark glasses.

She was heading towards the door, when the bell rang. She looked at the hallway monitor. Two men in dark suits with dark glasses were standing at the door. She opened the top half of the door. "May I help you?" she asked. "This is for you." They handed her an envelope with a message card inside. She pushed the card into the computer and the holographic message materialized. "GOVERNMENT SUBPOENA."

You are ordered to appear one month from today to testify before the Senate Interplanetary Committee regarding inconsistencies within the ITP program."

Adrian Leavitt, she thought, trying to make a name for himself. She forwarded the subpoena to her legal counsel and left to meet Joshua. I hope his good news is good, she thought as she called a taxi.

XXX. LIVING IN EDEN

DAVID WAS NEARLY BACK TO FULL STRENGTH. HE COULD RUN AND jump and do almost everything that he had done prior to his injury. He still became winded after exerting himself, but this was improving every day. He started a daily routine of running and weight lifting. He had fashioned various rocks and tree branches into makeshift barbells. He still wore his uniform and worked out in his shorts. He could not feel comfortable naked like the Edenites. They thought nothing of his being clothed and never questioned him, just as he didn't think twice about their nudity. Ruth, to her credit, joined him. She could run as fast as him and was just as adept at weight training. David thought she was remarkable. Elijah would watch them, but thought it all was pointless. "Why do all that work, sweating, exhausting yourself?," he would say. "It doesn't honor the Creator and it doesn't provide any new knowledge."

"You're probably right," David replied, "But, it makes me feel good when I'm finished."

"Why do you do it, Ruth?," Elijah asked.

"Because David does it and if we are to be together I need to be part of his life."

Ruth's words struck David like a sledge hammer. "Be together," meaning married. Is that what I want, he asked himself. She is beautiful, caring, devoted, intelligent, and she loved him. But, did he love her? Had he ever really loved another person? Joshua, Deborah, Little Bit? He did love Little Bit, but as human as he acted he was still a dog. Joshua was a good friend and David loved him like a brother. He had used Deborah to get what he wanted, but now he never stopped thinking about her; maybe that was love. He knew that she was probably frantically searching for a way to find him. Of course, David had no idea how difficult that search was proving to be. "Be together," he was starting to like the sound of those words. Yes, he thought to himself, we will be together.

"Let's take a new path," he called to Ruth. He started along a path that led to the center of Eden, a place he had not been before. They ran by trees laden with fruit, bushes ripe with manna, passed birds, rabbits, chipmunks, bears, and every other variety of beast and plant. David stopped suddenly and called to Ruth who had run ahead. "Look at that," he cried. Ruth came back and saw what had startled him. Two unicorns were prancing among the trees to their left. "I thought they were just myth," he said.

"Those are a special creation. Our Creator has given them beauty and grace greater than any other creature. They are highly revered by all the other creatures."

David watched them until they disappeared and then resumed his run. He could see a clearing up ahead and sprinted to make it there before Ruth. She joined in the game and the two raced side by side, reaching the clearing laughing and exhausted as they both fell to the soft grass to rest. David looked up to see a large tree in the middle of the clearing, filled with large red apples. He guessed what they were.

"This is the Tree of Knowledge, isn't it?" he asked.

"That is correct. If we eat from this tree we will surely die. As long as we stay away from it we will be kept safe. We try to stay away from here. It is best to avoid temptation."

There was a stream running in front of the tree and David bent down and took a drink. He lay back looking up at the sky as Ruth lay down beside him. "This is a beautiful place," he said, "and you are a beautiful woman. You have been much more than a nurse to me. You are my friend and confidant and I find you extremely attractive. I want to marry you. Do you think Abraham will so honor us?"

Ruth smiled and put her arms around him, "It is what we both have hoped for. We must go immediately to tell him and the others."

They started at a fast pace back to Abraham.

He was waiting for them when they arrived. "I am pleased to see you," he said as they approached. "Our Creator has told me of your choice and I am honored that you have come to me first with this wonderful news." The other Edenites all gathered around. "A wedding is a momentous event and fills all of us with great joy. This will be a special wedding for me as it will be the last I will perform. I am being called to join our Creator after living these many seasons. He has told me that after the two of you are joined in matrimony, I will be privileged to ascend into the Heavens and be permanently with our benevolent Creator."

David seemed to sense a hint of worry in his voice as he spoke. "I am doubly honored that my happiness will be your final act as the elder of these wonderful people. How soon can the wedding be performed?"

"There is no reason to delay. You may be married now if you wish."

David looked at Ruth and saw the love in her eyes. "Yes," he said, "Let's be married now."

They joined hands standing in front of Abraham. Sarah stood at Abraham's side and all the other people stood behind David and Ruth, solemnly watching as Abraham began the ceremony.

"Dear Creator," Abraham began, "we are all gathered here in your presence to join this man and woman together in sacred marriage, a sacrament that you instituted. The joining of two people, man and woman, will forever bind these two, David and Ruth, to each other. They have shown their love and devotion towards each other and they are prepared to face the coming days together with your help and guidance. David has come from far away and we have adopted him into our family. Ruth was created to fill David's life, to nurture him and love him. Now let us bring together for all time these two people who were made by your hand.

"Do you, David, take Ruth to be your wife, to love and cherish for all time?"

"I do," replied David.

"Do you, Ruth, take David to be your husband, to love and cherish for all time?"

"I do," said Ruth.

Abraham continued, "With all the love of our Creator that is showered upon us and has spread to these two people, I now pronounce you husband and wife. May our Creator's love continue to fill your lives and bless you forever." David kissed Ruth. "Now, we can all feast on the gifts that the Creator has given us."

The entire group moved into a sheltered area among the trees and was greeted by a feast the likes of which David had never seen in Eden before. There was fruit and Manna, but also vegetables and drink that David had not seen before. The drink was sweet, but also with some pungency, a sort of sweet wine. The vegetables were carrots, radishes, celery, peppers, and many others, raw, but beautifully prepared. Everyone gathered around and began to eat and drink. David and Ruth sat together, sharing their food and holding hands, lovingly. David understood why there was no delay in performing the marriage. He suspected a feast such as this was reserved for very special occasions. He wondered how they knew they had decided to wed and who had prepared everything.

As the people became full and satisfied they began to leave, each one offering congratulations to the happy couple. All of a sudden David and Ruth were alone. The night was clear and warm, with a bright full moon. In the moonlight David stared into Ruth's eyes and then wrapped his arms around her and gave her a long, tender kiss. He took her hand and the two retired to their usual place of rest.

David remembered his wedding night as never ending sublime pleasure. He had been with hundreds of different women, using every type of enhancement to heighten sexual experience, but they all paled in comparison to Ruth. David thought that his intense feeling was because he had been so sick, without any outlet for months, but Ruth also had the same feelings. Maybe it was love, or a gift from the Creator. Whatever it was David never wanted the wedding night to end. The two of them lay together and the pleasure that each felt in the other was never ending. There was nothing fancy or acrobatic, just pure love. Maybe that's what I've always lacked, David thought, as he stared at Ruth who was peacefully sleeping with her head on his chest. He kissed her as she slept, and then fell into a deep and peaceful sleep.

XXXI. SORINO

MAJOR ANTHONY SORINO HAD BEEN WORKING NONSTOP SINCE DAvid had disappeared. He was working with Scully on the new ITP vessel, designing new computer systems that could handle the fluctuating portal data, as well as trying to create an abort system that could respond instantaneously, as well as automatically if necessary. He also was training on the ITP simulator, sometimes for twelve hours a day. He wanted to be as ready as possible for the next flight and he wanted to return safely. Jessie didn't understand why he was doing so much to try to save someone who never had once done anything for anyone but himself. Anthony had said that if it was Jack the Ripper he would still try his best. He needed to be prepared for anything if he were to be successful.

The new ITP vessel required several modifications. Principal was the vibratory coating activation which now had to be much more flexible and compliant. This was necessary to enter a portal with a frequently changing energy output. Indeed it is possible that the vessel would have to change its vibration frequency as it traversed the portal, a very dangerous maneuver. Scully had equipped the new vessel with twenty-four activators, instead of the four found on the original. The computer and the sensors were accelerated so that new data was processed and received in nanoseconds, instead of milliseconds. Scully hoped this rapid response would be enough to prevent a potentially fatal power surge that theoretically could occur if a vessel, while traversing a portal, encountered a sudden change in energy output from the portal. The math predicted power levels such that the vessel would instantly disintegrate. Sorino and Scully hoped that instantly was measured in milliseconds, not nanoseconds.

The additional modification was the ability to carry two people. The original vessel had been designed to carry only one astropilot. All the calculations were based on a single pilot without a passenger and the engineering balanced for one person. This new vessel had to be outfitted to potentially carry two people if the rescue mission were successful.

Although most of the modifications were carried out by Scully and his team of engineers, Sorino found himself spending three to four hours every day reviewing the modifications with Scully and sometimes with General Moosewood. Sixteen hours a day left him with very little time for Jessie and the rest of his family. He would make his way home late each night, kiss his kids as they slept, eat a quick supper, and try to sleep. Jessie and he would talk for a period, before Sorino would fall into a fitful sleep.

He didn't know why, but his sleep had recently been invaded by vivid sometimes horrifying dreams. His friends and family, even Jessie, would appear as monstrous beings, always trying to rip him from the sky as he flew. At the last second he would wake up, drenched in sweat, almost screaming. The last time he had this dream he hadn't awakened immediately; as his ship was hurling towards the ground, Major Sanders intercepted him and carried him to safety. Sorino didn't have any faith in the predictive value of dreams, but the frequency of this recurring nightmare left him troubled. He took small comfort in the dream having Major Sanders being the one who saved him, since he was missing and possibly dead. He chalked the whole dream thing up to the stress of work and the fact that he probably would soon embark on a mission that some would call suicide.

Sorino hadn't heard anything about solving the current portal dilemma. He assumed the best astrophysicists and mathematicians were studying the data and trying to find an answer that would allow safe entry and return. Calls for more tests before another manned flight was attempted were dismissed. The longer the delay, the less likely Major Sanders would be rescued. Also, every precaution and exhaustive testing before Sanders flight had done nothing to ensure his safe return. Sorino, Moosewood, Tennyson, and the majority of the ITP committee agreed that the next ITP flight would be manned, with Major Sorino navigating. If he was not successful, if he were lost also, the entire ITP program would almost certainly be considered a failure and would be cancelled.

XXXII. JOSHUA AND DEBORAH

THE TAXI HAD DEBORAH AT MONMOUTH PARK IN FIVE MINUTES. SHE had never been to a racetrack before. She entered the clubhouse and purchased a disc containing information on the horses that were running that day. Joshua had told her to look as inconspicuous as possible; everyone else had purchased one of the discs, so she followed the crowd.

She took the high speed lift to the second floor and quickly found Bar#23. She had an hour before the first race was to go off; she figured it was too early for Joshua to arrive. She sat down and looked around him. The clubhouse was a huge cavernous structure. She walked towards a railing where she saw a large number of seats facing a large green oval. Everywhere she saw monitors flashing numbers, or replays of previously run races. People were intently scrutinizing the numbers or were mesmerized by the races being broadcast. Some wandered about looking bored, some anxious; nobody looked happy.

She made her way back to Bar #23 and waited. She put her little disc into a player and was treated to a hologram of horse's names and an array of numbers adjacent to each name. She clicked on one of the dates next to each horses name and a replay of that race appeared. She was able to zero in on any of the horses that were competing and she could watch the race from any angle. She thought it was interesting, but she couldn't see the point in confining your life to analyzing races like this.

"It's not much different from what you do everyday." She looked up to see Joshua standing next to her seat. He continued, "You spend your days analyzing data that is gathered from outer space. From this information you try to predict what will happen if a new variable is introduced. I'll admit your goal is somewhat loftier than trying to make a buck, but the techniques are similar. I take the wealth of information that is available for each horse, analyze it, and try to predict which one will be the fastest on this particular day."

Deborah answered, "I hear you are fairly successful. I guess there are some similarities." She did not want to argue the point. She was here for only one thing. She had no interest in the races or in the people who bet on them. "What can you tell me about David?" she asked.

"Straight to the point. You certainly aren't one for small talk. You really are showing, when is the due date, looks like six weeks, tops."

"That is not your concern. You said you had some information."

"Yes, I do. Let's go someplace quieter and less public." He led her through a door into an empty stairwell. "I've done a great deal of research into the philosophical implications of leaving the confines of time and space, which is what the ITP process really involves. The presumption that the interdimensional plane is an empty corridor leading from one place to another must be an error. Otherwise it would be impossible for any mishap to occur. If one assumes that there is something there, then that something must be responsible for David's misadventure. The question then arises: What is the something that would be found there? The logical answer is God or something akin to God," Joshua looked at his watch. "It's post time, I want to watch the first race."

"But, what about..." Deborah started to ask, but he was gone. She followed him and found him standing at the bar watching the race with a group of people, all of whom seemed to know him. Joshua watched silently, without any expression or emotion.

"Jackson's Lot leads by five as they approach the wire," she heard over the sound system. She looked at Joshua, his expression still hadn't changed. "I guess you lost," she said. "Oh no, I actually did quite well, thanks for asking," he replied. "Let's go talk some more. I don't have another bet until the fourth race."

He led her to another empty stairwell. "Where were we?"

"God," she answered.

"That's right. I believe that when David entered the interdimensional plane he encountered God or an angel or something like that. Whatever that encounter involved it threw him off course and we know he exited somewhere. I went to the most accurate resource I could think of and studied the nature of God. I'm sure that David is alive, but I'm also convinced that there is no way you can find him."

"That isn't much help. I've spent months studying the numbers and I know that I'll find the answer. As you can see I'm under some time constraint," as she patted her swollen belly. "I need to solve this problem within the next two months. The new ITP vessel will probably be ready to go in about five weeks. It was too much to hope that you would actually come up with something useful."

Joshua replied, "You asked me for my opinion. I went to a lot of trouble to research this for you. This is what I've come up with. I'm sorry that it's not the magic bullet you were wishing for. But, my advice is to wait. If David's going to return, it will be his or God's doing. Another attempt to send someone interdimensionally is guaranteed to be a failure and possibly dangerous."

"Well, this has been a useless trip. Thank you for your efforts. Oh, and bet on Savage Warrior in the next race. I'm leaving."

Deborah left the stairwell, left the track, and took a taxi home. Joshua was left bewildered by her response to his research. I did my best, he thought. Hm, Savage Warrior; he looked at the program. He hadn't planned on betting this race, but he decided to put an interest bet on Savage Warrior. Eighteen to one. Twenty bucks can't hurt. He walked up to the window.

XXXIII. BACK TO EDEN

DAVID AND RUTH SPENT EVERY MOMENT TOGETHER, AS IS EXPECTED of newlyweds. They continued their daily runs together. They joined the rest of the group for evening meal, which included homage to the Creator. They would usually enjoy a feast of fruit and manna, after which they would all join together and sing a cappella praises and devotion to the Creator. David was amazed at the sweet sound that came from the group as well as the complexity of the harmonies. His favorite was a psalm with a melody reminiscent of Bach:

Dear Creator, you are a joy to us
You have made us for Your pleasure
You are merciful and we adore You
We live in awe of Your majesty and power
And are humbled by Your Grace

Dear Creator we love You
Dear Creator we love You
Dear Creator we love You

Our Creator, You are good to us
We live to see Your face
We praise You with one voice
We love You and want to be with You
We are thankful for Your love

Dear Creator we love You
Dear Creator we love You

Dear Creator we love You

The song would be followed by prayers offered by the elder, followed by anyone else who wished to offer thanks or praise to the Creator. David never offered any prayers and still maintained a slight skepticism regarding the Creator. He had never seen or heard the Creator, while the others in Eden claimed to have daily encounters, walking and talking with him. David had questioned Abraham about this.

"Why is it that I have never seen the Creator?" he asked. Abraham's answer, "Why do you still wear your uniform?"

"I just don't feel right being naked in the company of everyone else that is here," he responded.

"Precisely," said Abraham. "You are born with the sin nature that is inherent to all beings on your world. When you crashed here you were badly injured. The Creator warned that you brought a great danger to our world, although, at that time, he was not very specific. The danger was the presence of sin, something totally unknown in Eden. The Creator offered to take you away, which would have protected us and probably would have been the end of your life, at least as it is now. He told us that we could try to bring you back to health and that in the process, with His help; we could try to purge you of your sin. We have been partially successful. I'm sure you've noticed some changes, which you attributed to your injuries. But, the manna that you have consumed and the healing of your body have washed most of your sins away. We have learned, however, that you can never be completely free from sin. Once man tastes the fruit of knowledge of good and evil, it can never be removed. We have accepted you, but we will always be wary. Ruth does not know all this. She is a part of you and will always see you as perfect, even if you were to fight the Creator himself, she will always be with you."

David was silent after hearing Abraham's words. He had never believed in any sort of God and he was beginning to think that the people of Eden were kept ignorant, almost in prison, to satisfy some perverse needs of this so called Creator. If the Creator was so powerful, why couldn't the sin that was ingrained be removed; why wasn't David allowed to see or talk with Him; why didn't He just send David back to Earth or just kill him. What was the point in David's being in this strange, wonderful place?

Abraham sensed what was going through David's head. "I'm sure that my words raise many questions. I'm afraid that I will not be able to answer them for you. With time, most of the answers will become obvious or the question will lose its meaning. Meanwhile, enjoy yourself, love your beautiful wife, we have welcomed you among us and we will treat you as one of us. Perhaps, in time, the Creator will choose to show Himself to you and your doubts will be washed away."

The dinner meeting ended and David and Ruth walked together to a secluded spot.

"Ruth, do you love me?" he asked.

"More than anything," she said.

"Would you do anything for me?" he asked again.

"Haven't I already?" she answered.

David thought to himself that, yes, she had done everything, nursing him when he was near death, cleaning him, seeing him in a condition that was totally foreign, and probably repulsive, to this perfect world. She had done it well and with never a word of complaint. The fact that another person could so lower themselves for a complete stranger was something that was impossible for David to completely understand. Whatever the reason, he was glad that she had chosen to, and he was grateful that she had become his wife.

He put his arm around her and kissed her. The two melted together in each other's arms.

The next morning Elijah came running to find David and Ruth. "Abraham is leaving," he said. "He is going to be with the Creator." The three of them ran to join the rest of the Edenites. They were all gathered together around Abraham and Sarah. David ran up to Abraham and hugged him. "You can't leave me now. I won't have anyone to argue with," David whispered in his ear. "My body is leaving, but what I have told you will always be with you. Isaac takes my place as elder. I hope the Creator is kind to you, somehow I feel you are destined to suffer, but also destined to achieve greatness. Ruth will take care of you and you would be wise to take care of her. Good-bye," he whispered back to David.

Abraham addressed the people around him. "My fellows, I have been with you for thousands of seasons. You have trusted my counsel as you trust the Creator. Sarah and I leave you to join Adam and Eve, Cain and Lilith, Enoch and Tasha, Abel and Rahab, all of them with our beloved Creator. Isaac is now Elder; I'm sure that he will be all that I have been to you and even more. I have aged and I look forward to a joyful eternity with our Creator. Good-bye."

"I always like short good-byes," David said to Elijah.

A bright light shot down from the sky and Abraham and Sarah were encircled by the light as if by a giant hand and slowly lifted up until they disappeared among the clouds. All the people stared until the last glimmer of light had vanished. Afterwards, everyone went about as if nothing had happened. David felt a great sense of loss and a slight sense of worry, although he wasn't sure why.

XXXIV. THE ANSWER

DEBORAH ARRIVED HOME TO FIND A DOZEN MESSAGES WAITING FOR her, all from the same person, Morrie Feldstein. "Hello, Deborah, this is Morrie, we need to talk... Deborah, call me...Deborah...Adrian Leavitt..."

That was it. Morrie had received the copy of the government subpoena. He must be even more nervous than usual, Deborah thought. Morrie was her personal attorney, assigned to her at birth. As best as she could determine his job was to do any worrying that might be necessary, with a little bit of legal advice thrown in. She was sure that the prospect of appearing before Adrian Leavitt was reducing him to a quivering bowl of jello. I better call him, she thought.

He appeared immediately. "Hello Morrie," she said.

"Hello Deborah."

She continued, "I see that you've read the subpoena. Make it go away. I don't have time for such nonsense."

"Deborah, I wish I could. This is Senator Adrian Leavitt, the devil himself. I can't make it go away, as much as I'd like to. You are going to have to appear; I'll do my best to help, but you'll have to be very careful. This man has destroyed more careers, usually good people, also."

Deborah was silent for a moment. "Can you delay it for about a month? I have some things going on that I just can't change."

"What could be more important?"

"Take a good look, Morrie." Deborah stood up and Morrie saw her full figure. He had to sit down.

"How long has this been going on?"

"About seven and half months. I need to delay any testimony until after I deliver. Adrian Leavitt would have a field day with this, even more if he were to find out the father's identity."

"It wouldn't happen to be a lost astropilot, would it?"

"I don't want to say, it could get you in trouble."

"We're already in trouble. I'll see what I can do, but Adrian Leavitt is not one to give up a chance at free publicity. You really need to keep me informed of such things. How can I help if you keep me in the dark?"

"I'm sorry, Morrie. I've been busy. Besides, I have not been in the mood for any lectures. I know this child is unsanctioned and I don't care. Now, I need to get back to intergalactic problems. Let me know how you make out with Senator Leavitt." She hung up and the screen returned to the long list of numbers she had been staring at for weeks.

What is the answer, she thought looking at the numbers. Each number was carried out to the sixth decimal; all were values greater than one million and less than one trillion. "Matrix by place value," she said and the numbers began to dance, rearranging themselves until all the values were properly arrayed. She stared at each matrix and something jumped out at her.

$6x^3 -4x^2+x-80$

Each value within each matrix corresponded to this formula. The value of x followed a definite progression of a-3, a+5, a-7 and so on where a was equal to odd integers starting with 333. She looked at each value again and mentally did the math for each matrix value. Every one was exact. She put up the most recent value measured from the portal; she calculated the predicted change and fed it into the computer. She would have to wait until the next reading came through, which could be one minute or two weeks.

She called General Moosewood. "I think I've found the solution. If I'm correct the next energy reading will be 4,550,012 joules. I am working on the exact formulation to feed into the computers and readjusting the protocol to compensate for the changes. I still can't predict the time between changes, but this will allow us to know the expected value sequence and plan accordingly. This will allow a new ITP flight to be made soon, probably as soon as the ship is ready."

"That's great news, Deborah. The new vessel is nearly finished. I will set up a briefing with the ITP committee for tomorrow at 10:00 A.M." The general signed off and Deborah went back to the monitor to continue with these new calculations. She thought about calling Joshua, but decided that he really didn't care about such things. He can hear about it from the media, she thought, as the baby gave her a hard kick.

XXXV. GENERAL MOOSEWOOD

AS SOON AS GENERAL MOOSEWOOD FINISHED TALKING TO DR. Tennyson, he called Major Sorino. "We've got an answer, I think. Dr. Tennyson just called and she's worked out the pattern, so that the energy values can be predicted. ...No... She's still working on the timing sequence... You're right, we can fly without the timing sequence, but that creates added risk... Yes, there is a time crunch... she says whenever you're ready. OK. Talk to you later." Sorino was in the simulator, requiring old-fashioned voice-only communications. The ITP vessel was in its final testing, weeks ahead of schedule, and would be ready for flight by next week. I hope I don't lose another astropilot, the general said to himself, as he started to call the rest of the ITP committee members.

General Moosewood had been one of the original astropilots fifty years ago, when they were still called astronauts. The original interplanetary vessels could travel at speeds up to .002c, too slow for frequent interplanetary travel, but fast enough to make regular visits every few months to the planets and moons of economic importance. He had distinguished himself as squadron leader, ridding the solar system of renegade astropirates. The initial mining and solar operations on neighboring planets had been plagued by these rogue pilots. General Moosewood led the unit that hunted and eliminated them, making it possible to safely develop neighboring planets. He had been the top astronaut for thirty years. Age gradually caught up with him. His reflexes slowed slightly making it impossible, at least in his commander's eyes, to pilot the newer faster interplanetary ships. He traded in his wings for a position on the ground, as director of the astropilots, and most recently acting as Chairman of the ITP Committee, coordinating all aspects of the program.

His work took all his time, but he preferred it this way. His wife had died unexpectedly ten years before the start of the ITP and they never had children. He had no remaining family. He always thought it ironic that the three leading characters of the ITP program had no family. It was better that way, however. The enormous amount of time required precluded any family life. He felt a close bond to Dr. Tennyson, regarding her as the daughter he had never had. And, even though he disapproved of his wanton lifestyle, the general felt a grudging admiration for Major Sanders. He had seen the major do the near impossible while flying around the solar system. He knew that if there were any way that the major could have survived, Sanders would have found it. Major Sanders was resourceful as well as talented. This was one of the reasons David Sanders had been chosen over Anthony Sorino. The general believed that Sanders inventiveness and creativity would play a big role if it became feasible to attempt a rescue mission.

The general was calling an ITP Committee meeting for tomorrow. He had sent automated messages to all committee members and his personal communicator showed that all the members would be in attendance. As he sat down to prepare the agenda an urgent message was received. An official printed document with the government seal appeared and the image of Senator Adrian Leavitt appeared. "Pending the result of an official inquiry by the Senate Interplanetary Committee all activities pertaining to the Interdimensional Transport Protocol are suspended. Such inquiry is to commence as soon as all pertinent parties have been contacted and are available to appear before the Committee... Signed, Senator Adrian Leavitt, Chairman, Senate Interplanetary Committee."

As soon as he finished reading a call came in from Major Sorino. "Sir, I don't believe what I've just received," came Sorino's voice. "I know," said the general, "I just received the same message. I don't know why Senator Leavitt would take it this far, especially with a man's life on the line." As he was talking another call was coming in, this one from Allan Steirs, his attorney. "Hold on a second, Major, let me get rid of this call... hello, Allan... yes, I got the message... no, you don't have to do anything... I'll call you if I need you... yes... good-bye." Lawyers are no better than vultures, he thought. "Major, I'm back; that was my lawyer making sure that he earned all that money that the government pays. Anyway, this could be bad. Senator Leavitt is no friend to the ITP and if he convinces the rest of the Senate committee that the program is too dangerous, we can forget about going after Major Sanders, or that interdimensional portals exist at all." Calls began coming in from all the other committee members. The general took them all as a conference call, but the bottom line was that nothing could be done until this inquiry was completed. The general was surprised that he had not received a call from Dr. Tennyson. He decide to call her himself.

XXXVI. TOGETHER IN EDEN

DAVID AND RUTH WERE ALWAYS TOGETHER. DAVID THOUGHT THAT Ruth still saw him as the near dead astropilot she had nursed back to join the living. He figured she never could picture him to be totally well and decided it was best if she kept her eye on him at all times. David didn't really mind. She was like a part of him, doing everything that he did, enjoying all the same things and thinking almost identical thoughts. They were deliriously happy together. David and Elijah also spent hours together. Elijah would teach David about Eden and David would tell Elijah about Earth. Elijah always said that he preferred Eden. Less to worry about.

Elijah enthusiastically pointed out the wonders of Eden. They would see polar bears walking with penguins, neither one concerned that it was eighty degrees or that they lived a world apart on Earth. Colorful parrots flew overhead and Elijah proudly named each one. Sometimes Elijah would spot something new and he would run ahead, studying it, and then reporting to David and Ruth. He would study a butterfly, which would sit on a branch and wait for a drop of water to fall into its mouth, or a bee flitting from one flower to another, all the time doing the Creator's work. The studying and recounting of details was good practice, because at night he would have to report to Isaac, which was almost like meeting with the Creator. Elijah told David that he had met the Creator, but he felt awed in his presence and much preferred the humbler company of Ruth and David.

This particular day was like so many others. David and Ruth had been running, had eaten breakfast and were now joined by Elijah as they strolled together along the stream that ran through Eden and emptied into a large lake. Very often the Edenites bathed in the protected coves of the lake. David had never seen them venture in to the main body of the lake. The lake was like blue glass that morning, a million diamonds sparkling as the sunlight reflected off its surface. Standing on the edge, fish could be seen swimming beneath the surface as ducks and swans swam on the surface. David held Ruth's hand as Elijah ran ahead calling out all the different plants and animals he saw.

"I see something new," he would yell, running ahead. David and Ruth sat down on the soft grass to wait. They knew that Elijah would get as close as he could to the new creature and watch it, sometimes for hours. One thing about Eden, David thought, one is never pressed for time. He took Ruth in his arms and lay down with her by the water, talking to her about nothing in particular. In a short time he dozed off, feeling Ruth's soft skin and hair pressed against his chest.

Ruth suddenly shook him. "David, get up, I heard a splash."

"Probably just a fish jumping."

"No, something's wrong. It was like a rock falling into the lake, but there are no cliffs near here. I don't see Elijah and he doesn't answer me. I think something terrible has happened."

David jumped to his feet. He saw a large tree with branches that extended over the lake. One of the branches was broken off and the water seemed disturbed beneath it. David ran along the lake to the tree, tore off his shirt and shoes, and dove into the water. As he swam out to look for Elijah, Ruth prayed.

David took a deep breath and dove under the water. Elijah was suspended lifelessly beneath the surface. David grabbed the boy by the waist and swam towards shore. Some of the other Edenites had started to gather. When David reached the shore, he first laid Elijah on his stomach as water drained from his lungs. The Edenites all watched, not one offering to help. Elijah wasn't breathing and David didn't feel a pulse. He pounded on the boy's chest, breathed into his mouth, as the Edenites stood by silently, never moving. After what seemed to be hours, David stopped. Elijah's lifeless body lay by the lake; the Edenites still did nothing, except talk between themselves and point at David as if he were the one who had died.

"What's wrong with you people? Don't you care? How can you do nothing?" David felt sickened, he ran away from the crowd, sprinting as fast as he could, screaming at the top of his lungs. Ruth gathered up his clothes as she ran after him, more bewildered than anything. She found him about a quarter of a mile away, breathing heavily and sobbing out loud. She lay his clothes down and lay at his feet. David looked at her with a wild look in his eyes. "I thought this was paradise, perfect, with your Creator totally in control. How could this happen? Where is your Creator?"

"David," Ruth started softly, "you must have faith. What you have seen is for the greater good. Our Creator has a purpose in everything he does, you must believe this."

"I don't know if I would believe it if Elijah walked up to me right now and said boo. I haven't seen this Creator. All I see is a bunch of people who don't care about anyone but themselves. If this is paradise, take me away, I don't want to be part of it."

Ruth sat at his feet silently. David sat down next to her and held her tightly. They stayed that way until nightfall. David had come to a decision and he hoped Ruth would agree. They walked backed to the lake which was deserted. Elijah's body had also disappeared. David was struck by a sense of irony. He remembered his biblical mythology. Elijah was taken up to heaven, never suffering death. Here, where people didn't die, but were all taken up to heaven, Elijah had become the only person that did suffer death. God had a warped sense of humor, he thought to himself, as he and Ruth drifted off to sleep together.

The next morning started like all the previous mornings. David and Ruth arose together, bathed, ate, and then walked along the lake. David hummed softly to himself, Beethoven's Ode to Joy. Ruth listened to the tune, one she always enjoyed. David had told her about symphonies and concertos and she wished she could actually hear such music performed by real musicians. David had an important matter to discuss with Isaac. As he approached, he saw something very surprising. There was Isaac, with Rebekah, but also he saw a very much alive Elijah. David ran to him, shouting his name, and wrapped his arms around the boy. "How can this be? I saw you, not a breath in your body," David said. Isaac answered, "You have lived with us all this time, but you have learned very little. This is not your fallen world. Our Creator is always with us. His perfect order is everywhere. We have purified your physical body, but the sin that fills your soul and clouds your thoughts, I'm afraid, can never be washed away. You are welcome to stay, but you will never be a part of us."

David sensed a change in Elijah. The boy was withdrawn, the love for the world around and the enthusiasm for every new bit of knowledge seemed gone.

Elijah spoke, "Isaac has told me of the pain that I caused you. I am sorry. I hope that I will be forgiven."

David started to protest, but Elijah merely turned and walked away, all sense of joy seemingly sucked out of him, leaving an empty shell where vibrant love of life used to dwell. David let him go and turned to speak with Isaac.

"You are right," he said to Isaac, "I am not a part of this world. Except for Ruth, who is so very special to me, the rest of you are alien, like another species. Even though we were given a great deal back on Earth, we still do a great deal for ourselves. If we had a creator, he abandoned us long ago. I can't stay here; I need to find a way to return to Earth."

"I'm sorry," Isaac replied, "You must remain here. It is impossible for you return to Earth."

Isaac and Rebekah turned and walked away.

David called out, "Where is my spacecraft? I know it is here somewhere."

"You are correct. Your spacecraft is here, but I don't know where," Isaac replied. "Abraham, Sarah, and the lion were the only ones that knew its location. Abraham and Sarah are gone now. You are welcome to ask the lion. But I don't think he will understand you or you him."

"You are telling me that none of you saw where I crashed and Abraham rescued me by himself?"

"No, the lion helped him, and yes, no one else saw where your ship landed. You certainly are welcome to look for it, and if it is our Creator's will, I'm sure you will find it."

David turned to look at Ruth and when he looked back, Isaac and Rebekah were gone.

"Do you have any idea where it is?" he asked Ruth.

"No," she answered, "I came to you when you were already in the place where you were healed."

"I wish I would have thought to ask Abraham about it while he was still here."

"Perhaps if we ask the Creator, He will tell you," Ruth suggested.

"Why would He tell me? He seems to want me here. I guess we'll just have to start looking. We'll start in the protected area where I recovered from my injuries. That must be fairly close to where I landed or at least there may be some clues." He started to run with Ruth at his side. From the bushes the lion watched and started to follow them, keeping a safe distance so as not to be discovered.

XXXVII. THE NEW ITP

DEBORAH WAS BESIDE HERSELF WITH JOY. THE ITP VALUES THAT SHE calculated were all perfect. All the changes fit exactly into her new formulation. Every portal that they were able to measure could now be safely predicted. The programming of the new ITP vessel computer was underway. She had never felt this excited. Now there was a chance to rescue David. She still had not worked out the timing of portal energy changes, but that seemed less important. The odds of an energy change occurring at the precise moment of entry were extremely low.

She sent a message to General Moosewood, summarizing her findings with attached detailed formulas which were to be distributed to the other ITP committee members for their verification. She also sent a message to Joshua, telling him he was wrong.

She lay down to relax, feeling very satisfied when she felt a sharp pain in her abdomen. It lasted for about two minutes and then went away. Three minutes later it started up again. What's happening? She looked at her swollen belly. Is it nine months already? Another contraction started. She hadn't thought to ever see a doctor and now she wasn't sure what to do. "Call Joshua," she said to her computer. It was night time so she was pretty sure he would be home.

"Hello, Doctor," he said as his image appeared beside her. "What can I do for you?"

"I need some help and I wasn't sure who to call. I started having these contractions. I think I'm in labor."

"Call for an ambulance and go to the hospital. They should be able to help you."

"I can't do that. You know that this is an unsanctioned pregnancy. I can't afford to have this in any public record. I thought, maybe, that you could help me deliver this baby, I mean if you're not too busy."

"It's almost midnight, what would I be doing? What makes you think that I can help you?"

"David told me that you went to medical school, that you were almost a doctor when you quit. You surely must have read the chapter on delivering babies."

"Well, you're right except all the babies that I ever delivered were in hospitals, with proper delivery equipment. All that I did was push a few buttons. I've only read about delivery the natural way."

"Can't you at least come over?"

"Why me? Surely there must be someone else you can call."

"You are the only person, besides David and my insipid lawyer, that knows that I'm pregnant. The fewer people that know, the better for me, David, and the baby."

"Alright, alright, I'll come over. At least I can hold your hand."

Joshua put on his coat and started out. It was about five miles from his apartment to Deborah's. Normally, he would walk, but the situation demanded he be as expeditious as possible, so he called a taxi. This delivered him to her doorstep in five minutes. She buzzed him in before he could ring and he ran up to her apartment with Little Bit leading the way. When he arrived at her door he found that it was open. The two of them walked in to find her sitting in her chair by the computer monitor, looking at an array of numbers.

"I don't think that you should have a baby sitting at your computer. Let's get you into bed and into some sort of gown that is more suitable to your condition." Joshua said.

"I need help moving to the bed," she replied. Joshua put his arm around her, but she couldn't even get herself up. He then put his arms under her legs and her back and picked her up, carried her into the bedroom and plopped her down on the bed. Little Bit hit a button on her central computer and tapped the screen and a pink gown appeared.

"That's a good choice," Joshua said. "It will hide any stains." I hope you're not too modest doctor, as he gently pulled off her clothes and dressed her in the gown. "I brought a few supplies and instruments that were gathering dust in my closet." He put on some sterile gloves. "You'll have to pardon me, but I need to see how far along you are. How often are you having contractions?"

"About every two minutes. Pretty intense."

"Raise your knees up. I need to check your cervix, to see how dilated you are. By the way I have some money for you, $360 to be exact. You probably don't remember, but Savage Warrior won, so the profit goes to you. Perhaps I'll use it to start a trust fund for David Jr. or is it Little Debbie. I guess we'll find out. It looks like you are dilated about six centimeters. I hope this isn't a big baby, you don't have the widest pelvis I've ever seen."

"You don't have to keep talking, I'm OK," whispered Deborah.

"That makes one of us. Do you need something for pain?"

"No, I'm alright."

"When did you start having contractions?"

"About two hours ago."

"You seem to be progressing fairly well; I'll check you again in about twenty minutes."

Joshua left her with Little Bit lying at her side. He looked through his bag of medical supplies. He had bought the emergency kit as a first year student, but had never really needed it until now. Inside were a vessel sealer, a few old fashioned instruments, such as clamps and scissors, tissue glue and sealant and instant bandages. He took out the vessel sealer, tissue glue and bandages. This ought to be sufficient, he thought. As an afterthought he also took out the clamps and scissors.

"Hot water, boiling," he said to the computer. "Please logon," the computer answered. "Never mind," he said. He went into the kitchen area and filled a large container with hot water from the tap.

He went back in to check on Deborah. "How are you doing?" he asked. Stupid question to ask a woman in labor he thought.

"That's a stupid question to ask a woman in labor," Deborah answered, with her usual hint of sarcasm.

"Let me check you again," he said gently. Thirty seconds later, "You're up to eight. I suspect we'll have this baby out before lunch time." It was 9:00 A.M. "I'm going to lay some towels around; it'll make the cleanup easier."

"I feel like a need to push," panted Deborah.

"Let me check again." He lifted the sheet. "I see a head. Go ahead and start pushing with each contraction." Joshua changed his gloves and laid out all the medical tools that he thought would be necessary. Deborah felt the next contraction, grabbed her knees and pushed as hard as she could. "It's coming, I see black hair," Joshua exhorted her. The contraction eased and Deborah relaxed. Little Bit kept running up on to the bed and then would jump off. "He seems more excited than either of us," Joshua observed.

Another contraction came. The head appeared and Joshua grasped it on the sides. "The head is out, the rest should be easy," he told her. "Hold on. The shoulder's stuck." Joshua pulled up and then down, but the baby wouldn't move. "We may have a problem." At that moment a call came in. General Moosewood the computer announced. "I can't let him know about this," Deborah gasped. Joshua didn't seem to hear her as he was confronting the much larger problem as the baby's shoulder was wedged against her pubic bone.

"Voice only," Deborah said as she took a deep breath. "Hello, General," she said in as natural and calm a voice as she could muster.

"Hello, Doctor. What's wrong with your imaging? Well, no matter. Have you seen the summons from Senator Leavitt?"

"Yes, a big nuisance. General, I'm in the middle of something, can I call you back?"

"OK, but don't forget, bye."

Deborah screamed in pain as Joshua reached his hand up inside to free the shoulder. He gave a strong downward pull, felt the shoulder pop out of joint and then it was free. The baby then easily slid out. The cord was wrapped around the neck and Joshua gently freed it. He took the two clamps and divided the umbilical cord, and then laid the baby on one of the towels. "It's a boy," he called out. Deborah smiled and then mercifully passed out.

The boy was pink, crying loudly. Joshua looked at his shoulder. He gently raised the baby's arm up and it popped back into place. The crying ceased immediately. Joshua wrapped the baby in the towel. "You watch him," he commanded Little Bit. He turned his attention back to Deborah.

She had a laceration and was bleeding profusely. He gave a gentle pull on the umbilical cord and the placenta was delivered intact. There was bleeding from within the vagina. He sprayed vessel sealant and tissue sealant and the bleeding was controlled. He repaired the laceration with a combination of tissue sealant and glue. "That should be good as new," he said softly, "I hope David appreciates it." He removed the soiled towels and covered Deborah with another blanket. He checked her vital signs and everything was normal. She continued to sleep, now more soundly. Joshua turned his attention back to the baby.

Little Bit had licked the baby clean and now was barking, playfully. "I don't think he's ready for games just yet." Joshua took out a tape. He measured the length at fifty centimeters. He carried the child into the bathroom and the baby weighed in at 3494 grams. The baby opened his eyes and smiled. Cute kid, Joshua thought, let's hope you have David's body and Deborah's brains. Joshua laid the boy on the floor and gave him a quick exam. Eyes, nose, mouth, heart, lungs, private parts, arms, and legs, everything seemed to be working properly. Even the shoulder that had been dislocated was moving without any sign of restriction or dysfunction. Joshua wrapped the boy up in a sheet and sat down, holding the boy across his chest, Little Bit curled up at his feet and Deborah sleeping on the bed. Before long all four were sound asleep.

XXXVIII. DAVID'S SEARCH

DAVID AND RUTH ARRIVED AT THE SPOT WHERE DAVID HAD RECOVered from his injuries. It seemed very different now. The area seemed less protected. The stream was still there, but he noticed that the plants growing manna were gone. The makeshift bed that Ruth had devised also had vanished. It looked like any other part of Eden now, not the sanctuary that David remembered. He looked at the trees and bushes, hoping to find any little thing that might lead him to his lost vessel.

"No blood, no broken branches, no displaced dirt, no remnants of my uniform. Your Creator does a good job of cleaning up. I guess we'll have to do this the hard way," he said, more to himself than to Ruth. Let's start this way. He pointed towards the east and the two started off at a slow trot, David's eyes scouring every tree and bush, looking for any trace. They had gone about seven kilometers without any success when David stopped to rest. "This could take months," he stated. We need to be able to see from higher ground." He looked around. There was a tall tree nearby. "Maybe I could see more from up there," as he pointed towards the treetop.

"It looks high," was all that Ruth could say.

David jumped to reach the lowest branch and pulled himself up. He started a slow ascent as Ruth patiently waited at the bottom. David realized that he would need to get pretty high to see anything other than the adjacent trees. This tree certainly looked like the tallest in the area. Along the way he passed colorful birds and lizards. Elijah would have loved this, he thought as he climbed higher and higher. He passed a black panther sleeping on a large branch. The big cat opened one eye, yawned, and then returned to it's dreams. David looked out to see that he was above most of the other trees. He no longer could see Ruth on the ground, but heard her call out.

"Are you OK?"

"I'm fine. I'm almost high enough."

David was about as high as he thought he could go. He crawled out onto a sturdy branch and what he saw took his breath away. He was probably sixty meters above the ground. Eden looked entirely different. He saw deep blue sky with an occasional cloud; on the ground was a mixture of different shades of green interspersed with brightly colored flowers. Birds of all sizes and colors flew beneath him and in the distant lake he could even see fish leaping out of the water. "This Creator knows his stuff," he whispered to himself. He looked as far as he could, but didn't see any breaks in the foliage or irregularity that would suggest something had crashed or was hidden. He looked for nearly an hour and was about to give up when a cloud passed and he saw a bright flash. It was from the north about six or eight kilometers away. Well, that will be a good place to look. He knew that there shouldn't be any mirrors or polished metal in Eden to account for such a flash of light. It must be from my ship, he thought as he started to climb down. He also wondered why he only saw it once. At least it gives me a place to start looking, he thought.

"Any luck?" Ruth asked as he jumped down from the tree.

"Maybe," he answered. "I saw a flash of light to the north. It could be a reflection from my ship. Let's eat and then we can investigate."

They sat down and enjoyed a repast of bananas, pineapple, and manna, washed down with coconut milk and water. They started off to the north, walking at first and then at a slow run, being careful not to miss anything. David had a pretty good idea of where he had seen the flash. There had been a clearing and then a cluster of large trees, after which dense forest resumed. They found the area and began to search. Nothing looked like a space ship, nor was there anything that could offer any reflection.

David sat down to think. The ITP vessel was completely black on the outside. Nothing from the hull should be reflective. However, inside there were numerous polished surfaces, which could have caused the flash. The ship, however, was designed to keep out any intruders if the crew was away. David was starting to think that what he had seen was his imagination, a mirage. He heard some rustling from the bushes. Like a cat, he darted towards the noise and grabbed hold of the lion's neck. There was a roar as the lion tried to shake free. David held on tightly, knowing that the beast was the only inhabitant of Eden that knew the ITP vessel's whereabouts.

The lion stopped struggling.

"Do you think that you can talk to him?" he asked Ruth. He continued to hold the lion's mane tightly.

"I can try," Ruth said.

Ruth came up to the lion and gently stroked its mane. The beast relaxed. "You may let go of him, he's promised not to run away," she said gently. David heard a low growling passing between the two. The lion seemed to shake his head and then a loud sharp growl came from Ruth, which startled David. The lion roared and then bounded away with Ruth in pursuit. David joined her in the chase.

"What's happening?" he asked.

"He's taking us to your ship. He says that he has been fond of you since he first found you and he feels badly about the way the others have been treating you. He wants to help."

The three of them ran as a team.

"How far away is it?" David asked.

"He's not good with distance. He just said to follow him. It could be 100 meters or 100 kilometers." David felt the adrenalin pumping as they raced through the lush foliage, birds taking flight as they passed, small animals scurrying for cover. David estimated that they had gone about twelve kilometers when the lion suddenly stopped. The ITP vessel was there amidst the underbrush, revealing a few obvious scratches, but otherwise no major structural damage to the outer hull.

"Thank you," he said as he turned to the lion and bowed. "You are a truly noble creature and I shall always be indebted to you, no matter what happens." The great animal shook his head, stood up and roared, seeming to have understood David's words. The lion bounded away, disappearing in an instant into the forest.

"Let's go in," he said to Ruth. They approached the doors which had remained tightly sealed while he was gone. David was instantly recognized and the doors automatically opened. Ruth clung tightly to his arm as the doors closed behind them. The ship had been in sleep mode. As soon as they walked inside everything immediately powered up.

"I'll need to run some tests on it to see if we can leave Eden safely," David said.

He started with the diagnostics computer.

"Complete scan," he spoke to the vessel. Immediately the panels, lights and gauges began to flash. David knew that it would take several minutes to complete. He sat down in his chair and motioned for Ruth to sit with him. She sat on his lap. He told her about traveling through space, about living on Earth, about life away from Eden.

She started to shake and a few tears rolled down her cheek.

"Don't you want to go with me?" He softly asked her.

"Nothing is more pleasing than being with you, except..."

"Except what?" he asked.

"Our Creator."

David understood her reluctance to leave. This was all she had ever known.

"I suspect that your Creator lives everywhere in the universe. If we leave Eden He will still be with you." David really didn't believe this, but it helped Ruth feel at ease. He held her silently for a few minutes until a voice announced:

"Scan complete, results are available on command monitor."

David turned his chair towards the command monitor and started to read:

Life Support is 100 % functional, atmospheric reserves are near capacity.

Food supply is 100% full and synthesizer is fully functional.

Medical system is partially disabled. Diagnostics are fully functional, therapeutics are not functional except for manual first aid.

Lift off is damaged but reparable.

Fuel supply is 40%. Scan of planet's surface reveals no acceptable fuel source within 250 kilometers.

Guidance is 100% functional.

Outer hull is slightly damaged. ITP coating can be regenerated to be safely activated.

ITP portal sensor is damaged and not operational. Repair may be possible. ITP computer monitor has the details necessary for repair.

Interplanetary sensors are 100% functional.

Autopilot is 100% functional.

Entertainment is 100% functional.

ITP activation and reentry system is 100% functional.

David thought that all in all the ship was in good shape. He reviewed what would be necessary to repair lift off and saw that it was a repair that he could easily perform. The ITP portal sensor was another story. This repair would require extensive rerouting of the ships sensors and computer systems and even then the computer estimated only a 33% chance of success.

"Let's get to work," he said to Ruth, "Only... wait a minute." He went to the ship's stores and removed a pair of mechanic's overalls. "Put this on. It will be safer for you and less distracting for me," he said. Ruth put the overalls on.

"It feels funny," she finally said as she squirmed a little. David didn't say anything as he pulled out the ship's emergency tools and handed them to Ruth.

"I know that you learn fast, so listen up. This is a circuit sealer. That is a pin driver and remover. These are circuit routers..." He went through the entire kit pointing out each tool. Ruth listened closely and committed each to memory. "When I need a specific tool I will ask and I want you to hand it to me like this." He showed her how to place it in his hand the way an old-fashioned surgical technician would pass instruments during an operation. "Let's get started."

XXXIX. A NEW BABY

DEBORAH WAS AWAKENED BY THE CRIES OF A BABY. SHE WAS CONfused at first, but then remembered everything that had happened. The baby was lying in a cradle next to her bed. She reached over and picked the boy up and held him against her chest. Little Bit came over and gave an approving bark. Deborah held her new son up and stared into his eyes. He had deep blue eyes and thick black hair. He stared back at her, almost like he was studying her and trying to decide if he approved of her as his mother. "Hello, David," she whispered into his ear. "Welcome to this world."

The sounds of Rachmaninoff played in the background as Deborah cradled the child in her arms.

She heard some stirring in the next room and Joshua came in.

"You make beautiful babies," he said. "How are you feeling?"

"Oh, I'm happy and a little sore."

"You should be good as new in a couple of days. The tissue sealant has a regenerative stimulant that will promote rapid healing. If you are feeling OK I'm going to leave you. I'll leave Little Bit here. He seems to have adopted the child as his own anyway. By the way, what's his name?"

"David, of course. Before you leave... thank you for coming. I know you didn't have to and I really put you on the spot."

"You're welcome. It was good to feel needed. It reminded me of why I almost became a doctor."

"Why did you quit? David told me that you were within two months of graduation."

"Let's just say that I could only stand so much hypocrisy. Being a doctor and caring for people used to be synonymous. Unfortunately, 'caring doctor' has become an oxymoron. It took me three and half years to learn this, but once it became obvious that physicians were only glorified button pushers, I quit."

"You certainly showed me that you have what it takes to be a caring doctor."

"Well, you see, that's the point. If you were at the hospital having the baby, you would be hooked up to the continuous fetal monitor, with continuous visual output via high resolution ultrasound and heat generated images that would provide the doctor, seated in another room at a computer console, with a visual representation of your labor and its progression. If your uterine contractions were weak, you would have received EUS, which is Endogenous Uterine Stimulator. If your pelvis were too small the computer and robot would apply the GPD or Gentle Pelvic Dilator. As a patient you may or may not actually see your doctor. I can't be just a technician. Maybe that type of medicine is better, but it wasn't for me. So, I left. I took what little I had and went to the track and I haven't left yet."

"David says you never make a mistake."

"That's a generous assessment. I manage to stay out of trouble, but I'm not perfect. The racetrack is a throwback to a different time. Years ago, attempts were made to make it more techno. These all failed. Horses need live jockeys. Having to deal with living beings adds an element of uncertainty that I use to my advantage. That's all. But, thank you for reminding me that there are times when it is right to care for other people and that healing can still be an art."

"I think that you would have been a great doctor. I must admit I didn't think much of you before. I always thought you were a very strange and insensitive person, but now you seem like the only normal person I know, while everyone else strikes me as artificial, like cheap plastic."

"Thank you for the compliment."

The music stopped and was replaced by the news. There was an announcement regarding the ITP program. Senator Adrian Leavitt was to commence hearings into the safety and effectiveness of the program.

"Did you know about this?" he asked.

"I received notification just a short time ago. I sent it on to my lawyer. It seems like a great nuisance to me."

"Be careful of any encounters with Adrian Leavitt. Of course, I don't know him personally, but I've followed his career. There is something that gives him inside information regarding subjects of his inquiries that ultimately leads to their destruction. I don't know how he does it."

"Well, that's not very reassuring. There is plenty that he can use against me. He wouldn't need to be very subtle."

"When are the hearings?"

"In about two weeks, I think."

"My advice is to bring your baby with you."

"What?"

"Bring David Jr. It may be the only way to preserve the ITP program."

"But that doesn't make any sense."

"That's exactly why you should do it, because it doesn't make any sense. Think about it. Call me if I can help." And he left.

Deborah did think about. He's crazy, she thought, and she picked up the baby as Little Bit maintained his watchful eye.

XL. A STORM BREWING

ISAAC HAD A FEELING THAT WAS TOTALLY NEW AND TROUBLING. HE had a sense of impending disaster hanging over Eden. Ostracizing David had been a difficult decision, but the risk of temptation was too great. He looked forward to the Creator's visit to provide some reassurance. He walked with Rebekah as a bright light appeared.

The Creator was clothed in bright white light that hid His body from view. All that was visible was His head. His eyes sparkled and the color seemed to change from blue to green to brown and back to blue.

"Tell me what has happened," He asked with a voice that sounded like muted thunder.

Isaac recounted Elijah's death and subsequent recovery, as well as what he had told David and how he thought it best if David remained separated from the rest of Eden's inhabitants.

"You are right to be careful," the Creator said as they walked together. "David is from a fallen world. Although he has tried to be good, the sin nature is deeply imbedded within his soul, he can never truly be a part of Eden. Prolonged contact will lead to great temptation which would be the end of all that Eden has become. You must remain obedient. As long as you obey what has been commanded, you will live your lives fully, and when your time comes, be brought to me for eternity."

"It will be difficult to eliminate all contact. Ruth is with him and they are often seen running throughout Eden," Isaac responded.

"Ruth is bound to him; she will go where he goes. She is protected from temptation. Now tell me what you have learned since my last visit."

Isaac recounted all that had been reported of new creatures and plants that had been discovered. The Creator was pleased. By this time many of the Edenites had joined Isaac and Rebekah, walking with the Creator.

"You have all been very observant. I am proud of the depths of your study of this world. I will leave you with this word of caution. Be faithful to all that I have shown and taught you. Do not be tempted by things outside of Eden. They are the work of the enemy and will lead to your doom."

With these words the light became brighter covering the Creator's face until it rapidly faded and He was gone.

Isaac turned to the company that was present. "You have heard the warning. David and Ruth are a grave threat. Stay away from them. Trust in the Creator. He has always been benevolent and always will be faithful to us." All those present murmured their agreement. Isaac continued, "Spread these words to all of Eden, every person, animal, and plant. This is a time of great danger, but I hope it will be a moment of ultimate triumph."

They all dispersed spreading their Creator's words to all corners of the garden. Isaac and Rebekah were left together.

"You still seem uneasy," she said.

"You know me too well," he answered, "I should have been comforted by our Creator's words, but I still have the sense that we are heading for a crisis. I will only be at ease when David has gone. I wish we could help him, but this would surely lead us into temptation. We've done all that we can. Now it is time to rest."

He and Rebekah gathered some food and then found a secluded area to lie down together. Rebekah slept peacefully, while Isaac remained with his eyes wide open, unable to sleep for the first time in his life.

David and Ruth had worked through the day, skipping the midday meal. With the computer guiding him, he had finished all of the repairs to the lift-off mechanism. A computer simulation had gone perfectly. "It looks like we can leave if we want. However, with only 40% fuel capacity we had better know where we're going."

They sat among some trees, having pineapple, grapes, and a type of bean for their supper. As soon as the work had finished, Ruth had shed the mechanics suit.

"That feels much better," she said as she sat down to dinner. David took her in his arms.

"I need to work up more of an appetite," he said as he kissed her. She laughed as they fell back together into the long, soft grass.

When they got up their dinner was waiting for them under the stars. After the meal they lay on their backs staring up into the night sky. "Somewhere up there is my home. I hope that we can find our way through the infinite galaxies, back to tiny, insignificant Earth. There's nothing like flying through space. Planets whiz by, the stars shine brightly. I could spend all my days going from one end of the universe to the other. Every day would bring something new and exciting; with you by my side, I couldn't ask for anything more."

"It sounds wonderful," she murmured as she drifted off to sleep with her head on his chest. He watched her as she slept, never before feeling as peaceful as he did at that moment.

XLI. TROUBLE?

DEBORAH LAY HER BABY DOWN ON HER BED SURROUNDED BY BLANkets and towels to keep him from falling off. "I guess we need to get you a crib," she said softly to him. "Shopping Channel on," she commanded the computer. Images instantly appeared on the monitor. "Baby furniture and clothes, newborn, boy." Images appeared instantly. She looked at all the different furniture and chose several to sample more closely. Holograms of each item appeared in her central room, allowing her to see actual size and true color, as well as special features each item may have had. She chose an automated crib that responded to voice command, had automated sensors and could produce a variety of toys and pacifiers to keep baby calm even in the most difficult or uncomfortable situation. The crib had built-in apnea sensors and auto rock. It would gently rock itself if the baby fussed or if its breathing became irregular. This was the latest in infant technology, guaranteed to keep any child safe and secure. She also ordered a high chair, some feeding utensils, baby bath, and changing center. She also ordered some formula, the latest formulation, called "Dr. Zebo's Perfect Formula." The entire order was scheduled to be shipped and to arrive by tomorrow.

When she finished she heard a cry from the bedroom, followed by a short bark. Little Bit was standing over the baby as it squirmed. He was starting to cry with a deep red face. She picked him up and held him.

"I'll bet you're hungry," she said, holding him close to her breast. He immediately tried to eat through her shirt. She hadn't planned to nurse him; that seemed so archaic. However, she didn't have any infant formula and he was getting hungry. I guess we can do it this one time. She opened her shirt and in an instant the boy was latched on, sucking with all his strength. "I see you got something from your father," she said. She was not nearly as disgusted by nursing as she thought she would have been. He finished on the right and she moved him to the left.

"I hope you don't starve," making light reference to her diminutive chest.

When he finished she realized that next he would need to be changed. Joshua had brought a few old style diapers for her. She cleaned him and sat down at her computer console, holding him in her arms. She looked at the numbers displayed, but she just couldn't think clearly. She remembered General Moosewood; she needed to return his call.

"General Moosewood," she said. His image quickly materialized beside her. "Hello, Deborah. I've been waiting for your call."

"I'm sorry, I was busy."

"Who's the baby, belong to a friend?"

"This is my son, David. That's why I've been busy. I wanted you to be one of the first to know."

The general was speechless, as the implications of what she was telling him started to sink in.

Deborah continued, "I know that it's a surprise and poses some potential problems, but at least I thought you would be happy for me."

"My dear, I am happy for you, but it just caught me off guard. Have you thought about what having such a baby could do to the ITP program? This could be used as an excuse to shut everything down, to question your morality and by extension, the morality of the whole ITP program."

"General, do you really believe that my actions are a reflection of the rest of the ITP committee?"

"It doesn't matter what I think. It's what Adrian Leavitt and the media think. They will have a field day with this; drag your name in the mud. Am I correct in assuming that the father was recently lost somewhere in space?"

"You know that's true."

"Oh great, favoritism, nepotism, unsanctioned babies to go along with the accusations of dereliction, incompetence, and wanton disregard for proper safety procedures. We'll be lucky if all they do is shut down the program."

"It won't be that bad. Have a little faith. What do you think of David Jr.?"

"All babies look alike to me."

"I hope you do like him because I want you to be his guardian if anything should happen to me. You've been so supportive of everything that I've tried to do. I know that you'll care for Junior here as well as you've cared for me."

"Of course I'll do this for you. I'm really happy for you; it's just one more complication to add to the list. Please, for me, don't mention this baby to Senator Leavitt. That wouldn't be good for the baby, you, me, or the ITP program."

"Thank you, I'll keep that in mind."

"We have an ITP committee meeting tomorrow. You can imagine we have a lot to discuss."

"I'll be there on conference."

"That's good enough. Good-bye," and his image disappeared.

I sounded confident anyway, she thought. In reality, she was terrified. Everything that they had worked for was hanging by the thinnest of threads. She could not afford the tiniest misstep. Still, she wondered why Joshua had said to bring her baby to the hearings. She made mental note to call him before the hearings commenced. General Moosewood made more sense. Keep David Jr.'s existence secret, away from the prying eyes of Adrian Leavitt. The baby was sleeping, so she decided to get some work done. She turned to her monitor, "data on," she said and her numbers came to life.

XLII. THE GOVERNMENT

POLICY FORMULATED BY GOVERNING BODIES BEGAN WITH THE UNITed Nations. Eighty years ago, a General Assembly of the United Nations voted to centralize all global policy and to standardize all laws. Freedoms and rights that were guaranteed to all global citizens were codified and approved by the United Nations. These were then distributed to each member nation for ratification. Once ratified, the enforcement became the responsibility of each nation. In the United States of America, the principal power to govern had shifted to the legislative branch, primarily the Senate. In 2075 scandals rocked the Executive Branch, as gross misuse of executive power had been exposed, causing the Senate to strip the presidency of most of its governing authority. This left the President little more than a figurehead without any significant power. The Justice Department and control of much of the military came under control of the Senate. In particular, as interplanetary travel and commerce became common, almost all of the regulation of these activities and anything remotely related came under the control of the Senate Interplanetary Committee, which was now chaired by Senator Adrian Leavitt. Under Senator Leavitt, this committee's influence had grown to the point where most major policy changes had to be approved by it. Senator Leavitt became much courted and even more feared.

The Judicial Branch retained some autonomy, but the selection process led to a make-up of justices that usually ruled favorably to Senate policy. Justice nominations came from a committee of senators and the president. The nominee then required approval by both the Judiciary committee and the Interplanetary Committee. Thus the courts were packed with judges sympathetic to the causes promoted by Senator Leavitt and his silent benefactor, Aaron Diblonski.

The partnership between government and industry had become a model for economic success and was exemplified by the large number of joint ventures between Diblonski Ltd. and the government. A majority of the casinos were managed jointly by these two entities. Media, entertainment, and a variety of commercial and manufacturing enterprises were jointly owned and managed by private corporations and the government.

The people didn't have any objections as they received all the necessities of life under the social net provided by these joint ventures.

The media was the purported watchdog for the people and media reporters and pundits were everywhere. It was very difficult for any politician to wipe his nose without media scrutiny. Every move a politician made had to keep the media's perception and probable presentation to the public in mind. Most politicians had their own media agents, supposedly to provide a balanced viewpoint to the voting public. The end result was that the variation in media viewpoints was endless and it was always possible to find a commentator who shared one's own opinion. However, most of the public paid close attention to the views as presented by the major media, ABC, IBS, FOX, and BST.

All in all the government was perceived as a benevolent representative body that guarded individual rights, maintained law and order and guaranteed that the social net was maintained. As a result, all properly sanctioned citizens were guaranteed food, housing, education, work and the basic necessities and luxuries that the times demanded. The people were generally content to live the life that was given to them. They had abundant leisure time, but still maintained their sense of self worth and the feeling that they were productive members of society. Almost universally, the media portrayed the government as benevolent. Although, individual members were often found to be corrupt, the "government" as a whole was good.

XLII. ANTHONY AND JESSIE

MAJOR SORINO LAY IN BED WITH JESSIE. HE WAS READING THROUGH performance reports from earlier in the day, measuring the ITP vessel's response time during simulated flight. He stared at the same graphs and tables over and over. The upcoming hearings had rattled him. He was never one for the public spotlight and, even though he was not the principal subject of the Senate Committee's investigation, the thought of testifying before a Senate committee with all the media attention was unnerving.

"Anthony, try to get some sleep. Worrying never solved anything," Jessie advised. She rubbed her face against his bare chest, but Anthony didn't move, oblivious to the invitation. Jessie persisted, putting her arm across his midsection. He got the hint and turned toward her.

"I know you're right," he answered, "I shouldn't let it worry me. That committee may be out for blood, but it's the blood of Dr. Tennyson. I feel sorry for her. She is the most brilliant astrophysicist I've ever met, but she seems so vulnerable. I'm afraid Adrian Leavitt is going to cut her up into little pieces, leaving the ITP program and planet Earth dead as a result. I just wish I could think of something to do to stop it."

Jessie yawned, "You're not a politician or lawyer. This is something that they should be able to handle. She has her assigned legal counsel, I'm sure he's doing all he can."

"You're right, as always. It's best left up to the lawyers," he said as he kissed her lovingly on her open lips. He wrapped his arms around her as the lights automatically dimmed. After a while, they both drifted off to sleep.

Sorino awoke with a start and sat up drenched in sweat. He was filled with a sense of terror. The recurring dream that had plagued him for years had returned, only with a new twist. This dream had always had him chasing a firefly, desperately trying to catch it and hold onto it. In the dream, he usually would be running after the little bug, its light flashing on and off and when he finally reaches out for it, it disappears. Tonight, as he reached it, suddenly the insect turned into Major Sanders and, just as he was about to reach him, he disappears. The message seemed clear, chasing the light or the lost Major was futile. Even so Sorino's terror was not because he feared what might be waiting for him in the interdimensional plane. No, his fear was that he would never be allowed to attempt the ITP, leaving him in some ways just as lost as Major Sanders.

A plan started to develop in his head, something that would remove Senate committees, directors, scientists and everyone else from the protocol. He would need the help of only one other person to pull off this wild scheme. If he were successful, he would save Major Sanders, save planet Earth and answer questions that had been gnawing at him for many years. If he failed he would end up with the same fate as Sanders, but his questions, he hoped, would still be answered. He needed to get help from Scully. The two of them knew every inch of the ITP vessel. He looked at the clock, 4:30 A.M. He's probably not up yet. Sorino tried to go back to sleep, but his heart was pounding and he was much too restless. He got out of bed and went to the bedroom monitor.

"Night mode, ITP portal chart and latest energy readings."

"Security Code," responded the computer.

"ITPAP 2," answered Sorino. The charts appeared on the monitor as ideas began to coalesce.

XLIII. DAVID AND RUTH

THE DAY STARTED IN THE USUAL WAY FOR DAVID AND RUTH. THE SUN came out and warmed them, they bathed and gathered breakfast. "We've got a lot to do today. We're going to try to repair the ITP portal sensor. That's most important if we are going to have any chance of making it home safely."

"Your home," Ruth said.

"Our home," David corrected her. "Do you want to run today?"

"Certainly," she responded.

They took off at a medium pace heading for the center of Eden. The run by the Tree of Knowledge was David's favorite route. He was fascinated by the majestic treestanding alone, like a king ruling over Eden. Secretly he had decided to take some of the fruit with him for the journey home.

Ruth picked up the pace and sped ahead as they passed the tree. This always made David speed up to try to catch her; leaving him less time to think about the tree. He quickly caught up with her, as a rabbit joined them, easily keeping pace with the two of them. Birds also flew overhead, racing ahead and doubling back. The same birds frequently followed them on their morning runs. They were a pair, one a bright green with red-tipped wings and a huge yellow beak, the other was deep purple with red patches and a black beak. David called them Isaac and Rebekah. The morning runs were David's favorite part of the day. He loved the closeness he felt to the animals that joined them, the beauty of Eden and the pleasure he always received from the physical exertion. Ruth even offered some real competition; usually they sprinted together at the end of each run, reaching the finish in a dead heat.

This particular day the flowers seemed especially brilliant and Ruth glowed with more beauty than ever. It will be hard to leave all of this, David thought. For a moment he considered giving up his plan to leave, but reason overtook sentiment and his resolve to depart returned.

"Enough fun and games," he called to Ruth, "We need to get back to work."

They headed back to the ITP vessel, Ruth put on her work suit and David laid out the tools. He activated the maintenance computer and brought up the ITP sensor schematic and instructions to repair the mechanism. It looked like it would be a tedious job that would take several days. He needed to scavenge components from systems that were nonessential to the immediate needs for space flight. These systems were food synthesizer, autopilot, entertainment and backup navigation. The components would be linked to the remaining functional portions of the ITP sensors.

This was a powerful probe that could scan into a large sector of space to detect and measure ITP portals location and energy output. The probe resembled a large telescope, but required a great deal of power. The depleted fuel supply would allow only one scan. Anything more than this would reduce the fuel supply to a level that would not allow both portal entry and exit. Luckily the vessels navigation computer had a complete record with star chart of David's exit and flight to Eden. This would give him the area that he would need to scan to find the ITP portal. He needed to determine the necessary coordinates and vector to approach the portal. He had hoped to have autopilot available for the journey, just in case his entry through the ITP portal was a repeat of his previous experience. He asked the maintenance computer for alternatives for ITP sensor repair, leaving autopilot intact. The answer was that there were none. He then asked if it would be possible to rebuild the autopilot from other components. Once again he was told that there were no alternatives.

David went to work, with Ruth handing him instruments as he asked for them. The ITP sensor housing was removed to reveal burned out computer drives and power supply. David removed each damaged component, carefully setting each aside so that he could inspect them later. It was possible that a part of each disabled component could be used at a later time. The work was very slow. Some of the ITP sensors were very delicate, housed within reinforced titanium alloy casings to shield them from damage. These had to be removed as they would require reconfiguration and calibration to the newly installed components. The day wore on. At times when David was engrossed in a one of the more difficult repairs, Ruth would sit back and listen to the different musical styles available on the entertainment system. David had removed the main computer components from this system, but there was a smaller portable system that contained all types of music from the last 500 years. She loved the classical music, thought that jazz was OK, liked some of the late 1900's rock and roll, hated rap, liked the neo-classical and hated the boomer music which David said was popular at present times. Ruth would lay back and closed her eyes, listening to Mozart or Beethoven, Bach, Vivaldi, Tchaikovsky, and many others. She learned many of the melodies and would hum along with them. Her thoughts would start to wander until David's voice would intrude asking for a panel remover or pin tightener. She would quickly get herself together and hand him the tool, ask him how things were progressing and then drift back to the music. David was amused, but also delighted that she loved the classical music as much as he did. David thought that she and Joshua would get along just fine, both sharing love for classical music. David felt a pang of homesickness as he thought about Joshua and then a sense of regret as the image of Deborah drifted through his mind. I can't worry about that now, he thought, and he went back to work.

Nighttime came and David stopped working. He realized they had missed lunch again and that he was famished.

"You must be starving," he said to Ruth. They left the ship and found food and water nearby, ate dinner, and lay down together under the stars. David was pleased with all that he had accomplished that day. Two more days and he would be done, barring any unforeseen complications. Ruth snuggled up to his chest.

"You were a great help to me," he said. "A few more days and she'll be ready to fly." They both quickly fell asleep, exhausted.

XLIV. ITP CONFERENCE

AT 9:00 A.M. GENERAL MOOSEWOOD CONVENED THE MEETING OF the ITP Committee. Everyone was there except Deborah, who was present via holography. Major Sorino walked in five minutes late, which was very uncharacteristic. He apologized and took his seat. The general addressed the Committee:

"You all know why we're here. The Senate Interplanetary Committee has called for hearings into the safety and efficacy of the ITP program. I'm sure you are all aware that this could lead to the end of the program and possibly doom planet Earth and all its inhabitants. The Committee, as you know, is chaired by Senator Adrian Leavitt. He has never openly acknowledged hostility towards the program, but he has never been a strong supporter, either. He does have a history of rendering prominent and seemingly irreplaceable people irrelevant. I am fearful that he will try to discredit the ITP by discrediting its principal architect, Dr. Deborah Tennyson. Dr. Tennyson has not been well recently, but she is with us today via holographic connection. Your comments, Doctor."

"Thank you, General," Deborah started. "The science and mathematics behind the Interdimensional Transport Protocol are sound. All the preliminary testing prior to the most recent flight was perfect. As we all know, there has been a major shift in the ITP portal properties since the flight by Major Sanders."

"Yes, we know all this," interrupted Dr. Combs.

"Let me finish," Deborah continued. "I have managed to determine the pattern of energy changes at the ITP portals. Therefore, it is now possible to send someone through the portal to look for Major Sanders. Theoretically, it may be possible to extrapolate the current energy value of the portal that the major exited. However, at this time we can only generate a list of possible values. The timing of portal changes has eluded us so far. That list of possible energy values is being generated as we speak."

"What about Senator Leavitt? He would like to see the whole program shut down, I fear." The question came from Dr. Drew Layton, always something of a worrier.

"I have no fear of Senator Leavitt," Deborah responded. "Although he has some knowledge of physics, he is no scientist. I'm sure that he can grasp the gravity of the situation facing our planet. It would take supreme shortsightedness to permanently shut down our only hope for the future just to score political points. I'm sure the Senator will be reasonable and understand that a setback like we've had is not unexpected, but that we all have confidence in the protocol; that it has been and will continue to be successful." Deborah sat down. She had sounded confident and forceful, but she knew that trouble was ahead. She also knew that the ITP Committee members would not be willing to fight a political battle with the likes of Adrian Leavitt. If he gave the slightest nudge the program would crash and even she wouldn't be able to find all the pieces. She hoped her words would instill some resolve into this Committee and help prepare them for a potential fight.

General Moosewood stood up. "Well said, Dr. Tennyson. I agree that the protocol is, in general, safe for our pilots and that the principal science is sound. These hearings are merely Senator Leavitt's attempt to score political points. I suggest that we continue working towards our next flight and that all the details that have not been addressed be attended to."

"Major Sorino, where are we on ITP vessel flight readiness?"

Sorino stood up. "The ship has been outfitted and updated. The newest, most powerful computers have been installed and the ITP sensors have been tweaked to provide faster response. Any changes in portal energy output will be discovered in nanoseconds and response will be nearly as rapid. The ITP vessel coating is more compliant to coincide with the more rapid response time. All flight simulations have been perfect. We are ready to fly at any time."

Dr. Layton spoke up again, "I don't think we have adequately discussed how we will handle the Senate committee inquiry. What should be said and what would best be kept confidential?"

"Now Drew," General Moosewood addressed Dr. Layton, "the best response to any question is the truth. We have always been completely open with the Interplanetary Committee and Senator Leavitt is only one member. If we present our case as transparently as possible, I'm sure the majority of the Committee members will agree with us." The general also tried to present an aura of confidence, but he also had his worries, which he thought best to keep to himself.

The remainder of the meeting was devoted to routine tasks, reviewing data collected from portals that could be monitored directly, approving personnel and duty assignments, subcommittee reports and a number of other mundane items that the bureaucracy required. Deborah tuned them out after about two minutes, leaving her hologram to be seen, truly present in body, but not mind or spirit. The meeting adjourned, having accomplished very little of substance. Both Deborah and General Moosewood hoped that their public displays of confidence would bolster the resolve of the rest of the Committee.

As they were preparing to leave, the general was handed a printed message:

To: ITP Committee Chairman
From: Adrian Leavitt, Chairman, Senate Interplanetary Committee

Hearings pertaining to the efficacy and safety of the Interdimensional Transport Protocol will commence November 27, 2156. Your presence is requested at 10:00 A.M. on that day. Thank you.

So it begins, thought General Moosewood. He looked up to see that each of the ITP committee members had received similar "requests."

XLV. JOSHUA

JOSHUA LEFT DEBORAH INTENDING TO FORGET ABOUT ITP, BABIES, and everything else that had anything to do with anything that did not have four legs and could run. He had neglected the races for too long. He flipped on his computer monitor and the following day's entries were displayed. There was the typical array of claiming and maiden races, a few allowances and the feature was the Demoiselle Stakes for two year old fillies. He was surprised, but also excited to see that Ruth Rising was entered, listed at one to five. He perused the remaining races, picking out a few horses that appeared to be promising betting opportunities.

Joshua decided to eat before he sat down to the business of seriously evaluating each of the races. "Bach," he said and the beautiful strains of a violin concerto filled his room. He found some fresh bread, an apple, some grapes and Muenster cheese. He washed all this down with some ice water. After dinner he poured a glass of white wine and sat down to review the next day's prospects more closely.

Horse racing, particularly, thoroughbred horse racing had changed very little over the years. Whereas, football, baseball, basketball and most of the sports involving people had given into technology, which rendered them safer, supposedly, and more competitive, attempts to modify horse racing had failed. Mechanical jockeys, although feasible and actually tested, never caught on. After their introduction it was soon discovered that the horses simply did not respond in the same way to a robot as they did to a live jockey. For a while the robotic jockeys were an option, but horses so equipped fared so poorly that the robots quickly faded from the scene. Considerable advances had been made in equine safety. Advances in body scanning allowed veterinarians to quickly and safely scan each horse and detect even the smallest injury at an early stage. Consequently, serious racetrack injuries fell dramatically. Another great advance was continuous competitive monitoring. Jockeys received continuous updates, during the running of the race, of the speed of their horse as well as the lead horse. Also, physiologic data was also transmitted, during the actual running, to the jockey and the veterinarian. This often allowed early detection of a horse in distress, resulting in the horse being pulled up and avoiding serious injury. For the racing audience, the improved safety made for more formful and competitive races.

As Joshua went through each race he picked the horse that he thought would win, as well as exactas and an occasional trifecta. Most of the races did not warrant a serious wager, he picked a horse only to place a small interest bet, to help pass the time. He came to the tenth race, which was the feature. Only four horses were challenging Ruth Rising. Joshua paused looking at the impressive performance line. Three starts, three wins, three track records at distances of five and half, six and seven furlongs. She had never been headed; every race was a series of ones with the lead increasing at every stage. She had demonstrated the speed to be Ruffian's successor; today she would be tested for stamina. Joshua waited for this race with great anticipation, the prospect of a spectacular performance overshadowing the betting prospects.

His thoughts drifted to David and Deborah. Joshua had no idea if David was alive. He was sure that if there were a physical God, he lived outside of the confines of time and space and Joshua had no doubt that, if he existed, he would be encountered during interdimensional travel. The God of the Bible was basically good, but his judgments could be interpreted as arbitrary and cruel. The death of Uzzah stood out in Joshua's mind. If David's flight was interpreted in light of Uzzah, then he was a billion disintegrated particles by now. Somehow, though, Joshua did not think this was the case.

mankind's aspiration to be God had led them to the brink of destruction. Joshua could not believe that God's plan was the destruction of His most precious creation. There must be some other purpose. One thing Joshua was sure about, if there were another purpose, it would become apparent when God was ready and not a moment sooner.

Deborah's trials were just beginning, Joshua was afraid. He was sure that Senator Leavitt was focusing on her during his "inquiry." Past events had clearly demonstrated that Senator Leavitt's inquiries were thinly veiled witch hunts and Deborah was his next target. Joshua had thought a great deal about her since he had delivered her baby. She was hard to figure out. She certainly was not typical of most people, who were concerned with their next "high," be it sexual, chemical, physical, or any of the other hedonistic rituals that the government and society provided. She seemed only interested in her work, David, General Moosewood, and now her baby. In public she presented herself as supremely confident, cocky really. Privately, she was vulnerable and unsure of herself. Joshua was definitely impressed by her genius. The ITP was the most imaginative and elegant piece of science he had ever seen. And, even though he didn't fully understand the math, the reasoning was like fine art, like a Bach concerto, a Shakespearean sonnet or a painting by Monet. Yet, despite all this talent, there was a sense of tragedy around her.

There was no way that she could weather the coming crisis unscathed. Adrian Leavitt had seemingly demonic forces guiding him, General Moosewood, although well meaning, was ultimately impotent and the remaining ITP committee members were no better than white mice. Joshua had given her advice that would save the ITP program, but probably would result in her removal from her current role as lead scientist and, in the end, public disgrace. From his encounters with her, he didn't believe negative publicity would concern her in the least. He also knew that she didn't understand his reasoning. He realized it made no sense to bring the baby, but that was exactly why she should bring him. She was facing a situation that could not be tempered by logic or reason. The answer, therefore, had to be something illogical and unreasonable. A newborn baby, especially one that was unsanctioned, was both of these and would provide the different perspective that was necessary. The presence of David Jr. would change the focus of the inquiry and give Deborah a chance against someone as cunning and calculating as Adrian Leavitt.

Joshua turned his thoughts back to the next day's races. "First race," he spoke and the computer monitor lit up and past performance data and footage of previous races appeared. He sat down and began his analysis of each of the races that he thought offered opportunity for success.

XLVI. SORINO PLANS

MAJOR SORINO LEFT THE ITP MEETING AND RETURNED TO THE ITP simulator. He had not stayed at the meeting long enough to receive his subpoena. He realized that he would have to work quickly, to be ready to launch at a moment's notice should the window of opportunity appear. He met Scully and was given the report of vessel readiness. He also had a copy of Dr. Tennyson's portal energy output figures, those from the recent past, current, and predicted values. He ran one more test run from the simulator, which proceeded flawlessly. Everything appeared in readiness. Now all he could do was waiting. This senate inquiry threatened to ruin everything. He originally had thought that being chosen as backup instead of primary ITP pilot had been a minor setback; he would eventually get his chance to tackle the ITP. However, now he could not stomach the possibility that the entire ITP program could be permanently shut down. Nearly his entire life had been spent preparing for such an opportunity. Now, a fellow astropilot's life also was at stake. He needed to be ready, with or without proper authorization.

The ITP vessel was fully operational. Although it was designed to launch from the lunar surface, Scully had modified the lift mechanism to allow for launch from the Earth's surface. The outer shell coating had been freshly applied and all tests confirmed uniformity of vibration at test levels from 100 to 6,000,000,000 vps. Sorino sat down at the control desk and pulled up the launch initiation codes. These were required to initiate any launch sequence. They were changed on a regular basis. Luckily, there were still codes in the computer, a detail overlooked by the Senate Committee. Sorino went to work. He accessed the launch codes and modified the program. In an emergency, he wanted to be able to override the usual codes and initiate a launch independently, without the usual ground crew. He also routed the launch to the ITP vessel computer, and stored a functional launch code within that computer, giving the pilot total control. As he finished General Moosewood came in. "Major, what are you doing in here? I thought you never strayed from the simulator."

"Hello, General. I was reviewing the launch codes."

"That's what I came to check. I received notice from the Interplanetary Committee to remove all launch code sequences from the ITP computer until their inquiry is completed. I guess they don't want any unauthorized flights. You really had no reason to review the launch codes as there won't be any launch for a while." The general sensed something wasn't right. He reviewed the codes and everything seemed to be in order. The computer use review showed nothing out of the ordinary. All use had been by properly authorized personnel and nothing had been altered. Still, it seemed unusual for Sorino to be there, reviewing launch codes that really were of no importance to a pilot.

"Major, I think you should be thinking about your testimony before the Senate Committee. We can't do anymore with the ITP until this is all resolved."

"Of course you're right, General. I was just trying to be prepared. Don't worry about me. I can answer anything that they can throw at me."

"That's good, because the circus begins in four days."

"That soon? I thought it would be a few more weeks. No matter, I think everything will work out for the best, just like Dr. Tennyson said. I'll talk to you later." And Major Sorino left.

The general thought Sorino seemed uneasy, which was unusual for a seasoned astropilot. He made a mental note to check on him later and returned to the monitor, finishing the removal of the launch codes.

As Sorino left he breathed a sigh of relief. He paused for a moment as the general removed the launch codes and checked the computer. Good, he thought, nothing out of the ordinary had been noted by the general. He could continue with his plans.

XLVII. TROUBLE IN EDEN

DAVID STARTED WORKING EARLY THE NEXT DAY, AS SOON AS THE SUN was up. Ruth was still asleep. He figured that it would take two more days to finish the repair. He was anxious to be off and cruising through space, away from Eden and headed home. He hoped that the change wouldn't be too much for Ruth. She had demonstrated great adaptability, seeming to adjust to any situation that they encountered with great ease.

He finished scavenging parts from other systems to be used for the repairs, lining them up carefully adjacent to the ITP computer and sensor mechanism. Next he started removing the damaged parts. Most were burned beyond recognition, a few were merely dented or cracked, but still inoperable for the necessary tasks. Ruth appeared at his side. "Why didn't you wake me?" she asked.

"I thought you could use the rest, you've been working so hard," he answered. "Anyway, I'm just about ready to start the rebuilding process." David lay on his back and pulled himself inside the shiny metallic cabinet that housed the computer and sensor mechanism. Ruth handed him each part or tool as before and the work progressed quickly. Each step in the repair was marked off as it was completed and by the end of the day they were nearly done. "A few more adjustments tomorrow and it will be ready to be tested," David announced.

As they finished the day's work, David hummed a new tune.

"I like that," Ruth said, as they gathered food for dinner.

"That was Hallelujah Chorus, by Handel."

Their dinner finished, they bathed and then walked under the moonlight, holding hands. David talked about space and home; Ruth listened in a dreamy sort of way. For a while they walked silently, various animals walking with them. They saw the majestic unicorns illuminated by the moon in an open field, but as they approached, the unicorns vanished. They walked back to the ITP vessel and lay down to rest.

"With any luck we will be on our way tomorrow," David said. He held her in his arms as they fell asleep.

Ruth shook David out of a deep sleep. "There's a problem," she said matter-of-factly. "Look!" She pointed to some large bright green birds. They were holding parts of the ITP sensor in their beaks, snapping them into smaller and smaller pieces. David raced inside the ship. Two of the main components were gone.

"How could they have gotten in? I know that I closed and locked the door," he lamented.

David sat down to think. "ITP Sensor Scan" he asked the diagnostic computer. ITP sensor inoperable, repair is not possible." David sat down and put his hands on the side of his head, feeling as if he had been buried under a truckload of bricks.

Ruth sat down next to him. "You'll think of something, I'm sure of it."

Nothing immediately came to mind. He was not smarter than the computer, particularly when it came to repairs. He thought about flying blind. The portal location and energy readings were recorded and it would be possible to reverse his course and enter the portal using data from his emergency exit. He also knew that this could end up being completely fruitless and dangerous. Energy readings from within the interdimensional plane did not necessarily correlate with energy output levels. They could find themselves wandering through space short of fuel looking for a compatible planet or be forced to return to Eden, which could turn out to be impossible. David thought that he needed a different alternative or that he needed to get much smarter in a hurry.

"Why don't you ask the Creator?" Ruth asked innocently. "He provides all things. Perhaps He would provide new components for the repair."

"I don't think the Creator would do much to help me," David respond-ed. But, David said to himself, perhaps He already has. A plan began to take shape, a longshot to be sure, but something certainly worth trying. Secret-ly, he wondered how those essential parts had found their way to those destructive birds. He kept his suspicions to himself, as there was nothing to do about it, anyway.

"I wish Scully was here," he said to Ruth. "If anyone could find a way to repair this thing, it would be him. I wish I could find a way to become an engineer, but I don't see that happening. It looks like we may be stuck here." Ruth tried to look disappointed, but David noticed a slight smile on her face.

He decided not to tell Ruth of his plan until the last possible moment. He was sure she would not approve.

"We can't do anything else today. We may as well enjoy ourselves. Let's go for a run."

"You're on," she replied as she took off almost at a sprint. David fol-lowed, quickly catching up and the two ran as a team; a grey wolf running alongside.

XLVIII. PRE HEARING

SENATOR LEAVITT PACED BACK AND FORTH IN HIS OFFICE, THE COLLAR of his white dress shirt drenched with sweat. The hearings were scheduled to begin in two days. Normally, he would have already received the topics he was to pursue, including the key question. I hope Diblonski hasn't for-gotten, he thought.

"Messages," he said to his monitor, but nothing new had appeared in the two minutes since he last checked. He looked around his office and saw an envelope on the floor by his door. Very unusual and dangerous, he thought as he opened it. There was a single sheet of paper inside. As he read it the paper started to dissolve and by the time he finished it was nothing but a small amount of ash and water. He had received instruc-tions like this before and committed the papers contents to memory as he read. A smile came to his face as he sat down at his monitor and plotted out his questioning strategy. He pulled up necessary data about the ITP program and its participants. He went through the expected answers to his questions. Like any good interrogator, he knew that it was best not to ask any question unless the answer was already known. He went through the history of each ITP Committee member. He paused briefly when he read

General Moosewood's biography, almost impressed. Majors Sanders and Sorino were only given a quick glance, as neither one was of much importance to this inquiry. He reviewed Dr. Tennyson. Very impressive was his first thought, brilliant. It will be a shame to destroy such a career. However, he was already savoring the thought of a new masterpiece added to his collection. There could be no other way; Dr. Tennyson would have to go. He sat back in his huge leather chair and a smile came to his face as he contemplated his future. Teaming up with Mr. Diblonski was bringing him to the pinnacle of power. Just a brief message from him was enough to strike fear into any adversary. He was already the most powerful member of the Senate and the UN chairmanship could be seen on the horizon, and ultimate power. Then there wouldn't be any need for help from Mr. Diblonski. He would be in control and nothing could hold him back. Still, he had to go through these formalities. He turned back to the monitor, making mental notes of any potential weakness that could be exploited.

XLIX. SORINO'S HOME

JESSIE SAT DOWN CLOSE TO ANTHONY. HE SEEMED TENSE AND HIS thoughts distant. "Are you OK?" she asked. He looked at her, startled, "Oh, yes, just nervous, this whole Senate investigation is unnerving."

"It seems to me that this doesn't involve you much at all," she answered. "You aren't responsible for safety, except at the final check and there was no problem with that. I'd worry more about the general and Dr. Tennyson."

"Of course, you're right. Still, there's just so much going on, I may never get a chance to fly the ITP," he said as he put his arm around her.

"Just have some faith, I'm sure it will be worked out and everything will be back on schedule."

As they were talking, Jason, their middle child came in. "Hey, Dad, I need some help. Would you look at this and see if you can get it to work?" Jason held out a matchbook sized device. Sorino looked up and saw the green dot on Jason's ear.

"When did you join the dot communicator mob?" Sorino asked. "I guess you need to keep in touch with somebody?" he added with a note of sarcasm.

"It's a gift from a friend," Jason replied. "It's cool. Really, I can call someone with only a brief word. If I'm talking nobody bothers me and I can keep up with all the latest media."

Jessie commented, "I think it's an instrument of destruction for civilization. It makes everything too easy and it takes you off into your own little world, away from your family, friends, everything. I'm sorry if I sound old-fashioned, but your family is important. Please, get rid of that thing."

"OK, Mom, at least for now. But I want to keep it for times when I'm out and about. You could even call me on it if you need to find me."

"You have a built in transponder, we can always find you," Major Sorino said.

"I guess you wouldn't be interested in the news then."

"Something about the latest teen hot spots? I wouldn't think that anything serious would be broadcast on the teen channels."

"It is serious and about you, sort of. There was a press conference by Senator Leavitt. He was going on about how the ITP program was a fraud, a complete waste of resources and he was determined to see it shut down. I guess you'll be back to escorting cargo vessels."

"So much for unbiased, open-minded hearings."

"I'm sorry to say, Dad, that he made a lot of sense. He talked about the lack of objective data, the hearsay voyage by that dog, 'Little Bit,' the convenient changing of ITP data. You've got to admit that it sounds pretty suspicious."

Sorino's face became red as he turned towards his son.

"You listen to me. We have busted our asses for years bringing interstellar space travel from mere fancy to reality. Our top astropilot is lost and probably dead, the Earth is being consumed by our insatiable appetite for more and more of everything. Don't you believe the lies of Adrian Leavitt. Politicians may speak of lofty, noble goals, but all they are interested in is their own power and wealth. If that's the rubbish that they broadcast as news, I'd rather have you listening to the latest reports extolling the virtues of teenage marriage."

Jason stared at his feet, "Sorry, Dad. Of course, I believe in your work and its importance."

"It's OK. Now go get ready to eat."

Sorino turned to Jessie. "I don't think the program stands much chance against such propaganda. I just wish there were some way to expose the Adrian Leavitt's of the world for the power hungry, greedy, low life's that they are.

"Don't worry," Jessie said, "there will be justice in the end."

"I wish I could be as sure of that as you. Perhaps in a few days I will be." He kissed her lightly on the cheek. "Let's go eat." And they joined their children for dinner as all the troubles and Adrian Leavitts of the world vanished with their mealtime prayer.

L. SABOTAGE

DAVID LOOKED AT RUTH IN A WAY THAT SHE HAD NEVER SEEN BEFORE. There was determination in his eyes and she sensed that he had made an important decision. She was almost afraid to ask him, but curiosity overwhelmed her.

"What are you thinking?" she asked.

He answered, "Someone from Eden must have sabotaged our vessel. The animals would never do that on their own."

"But, David," she pleaded, "no one native to Eden could ever do such a thing."

He realized that she was probably right It was not in the nature of the Edenites to resort to sabotage. Of course the ITP vessel was equipped with monitoring devices; any intruder should be seen on these recordings. David motioned for Ruth to follow him. They went inside the vessel and David activated the monitor.

"Surveillance last evening 1800 through 0800. The monitor lit up, but nothing unusual was seen. Fast forward," he said. The timer passed more rapidly. Nothing was seen for several hours and then a light came on. Someone was coming inside when, without apparent cause the light grew very dim and only a shadow of a figure could be seen. David could tell it was a woman, but that was all that he could tell. The women of Eden were all so perfect that there was no discriminating one from the other based on a silhouette. He could see her removing the essential components and leaving the vessel. The picture immediately brightened after the figure left.

"Odd that the image should do that. Someone must have altered the settings. It makes no sense that anyone from Eden would know how to manipulate such a thing, but you Edenites never cease to amaze me. You are remarkably advanced for a primitive people."

"Nevertheless, someone was in here. Somebody wants us to stay," he said to Ruth. She sat silently, at a loss for words. He put his arm around her bare shoulders. "It's alright, we'll find a way to escape." As he said this she started to cry. He held her closely, doing his best to console her as he scoured his brain for some other way to rebuild the disabled ITP sensor.

In a few minutes Ruth stopped crying and she looked up at David with a slight smile on her face.

"I'm OK," she said. "Let's go for a walk, perhaps the fresh air will help you figure out what to do." They got up and walked outside to meet the bright, warm sun. They were immediately joined by the unicorns.

"Perhaps we can help you," one of them said. Both David and Ruth were surprised. "You are talking to us?" David finally asked. "How is it that we can understand you?"

"The Creator has bestowed many gifts upon us. We would like to help."

"What can we do to return home?"

"The answer is in the tree. It could be dangerous for you, but it will bring you what you need to know. The knowledge that has eluded you. But be careful... if the others find out it will be the end of everything that is beautiful and good."

"Thank you," Ruth said. "We will be careful." The unicorns disappeared.

David and Ruth looked at each other. David assumed that "the tree" was the Tree of Knowledge. He was well aware of what had happened to Adam and Eve of biblical mythology when they ate from this tree. David had already considered eating the fruit. He had the thought that, perhaps, the knowledge obtained would provide some new insight and allows him to rebuild the ITP sensor.

"What do you think?" he asked Ruth.

"The Creator has told us that if we should eat from the Tree of Knowledge of Good and Evil, we will surely die," she answered.

"I know... on Earth our 'Bible' contains a similar story. But, Adam and Eve did not die immediately. They were forced to leave Eden and fend for themselves. We are already planning to leave Eden and we will be fending for ourselves. I think there will be no harm to us or to Eden if we do this. The unicorns are right, however, we would have to be certain that no one knows what we have done."

"We would be wise to wait until night; the darkness would provide cover for us."

David became very excited. He was sure that this idea, which had seemed like a longshot at first, would give them the necessary means to leave Eden and return to Earth. The unicorns were like angels, messengers from the Creator, their words had to be true.

It was midday now. Nothing could be done until later.

"Let's go for a run," he said and he sprinted away from Ruth. Laughing, Ruth took off after him, rabbits and a cheetah running with them.

LI. AT THE TRACK

JOSHUA STOOD AT BAR #23, HIS USUAL SPOT AT THE TRACK. SOME

of the usual faces were there, Edna, Harry, Obadiah, among others. They were a group that shared one thing: serious commitment to the track. They had all dropped out of mainstream society, and now spent their days chasing the perfect wager. Most barely survived. They enjoyed each other's company, sharing their triumphs and their more frequent failures. David had met Joshua at Bar #23. Of course, David had not been a "regular" when they met. It was purely by chance that David had stopped there for a drink and struck up a conversation with the usually reticent Joshua. They discovered a mutual love for classical music, and David became fascinated with Joshua as they became friends. They would meet at the track, rarely getting together outside its friendly confines. Joshua almost never talked of anything other than horses or music. David often talked of flying or his excessive lifestyle. Joshua became very interested in the ITP program, listening carefully, absorbing each fact, but never asking any questions.

Today, Joshua had come to the track for two reasons: Maria Isabel and Ruth Rising. Maria Isabel was running in the fourth race and was one of the best betting opportunities Joshua had seen in months. On paper, she was a full second faster than her competitors, she had just run a decent race in a higher class five days before and the pace setup seemed perfect for her running style. There was also a filly named Lester's Babe that was being touted as a future stakes competitor by its connections. Joshua hoped that this would bring the odds down on Lester's Babe and allow Maria Isabel to be at least three to one.

Joshua made some small interest wagers on the first three races, even winning a few dollars on the third race. When the wagering opened on the fourth Maria Isabel opened at six to one, while Lester's Babe was three to five. This looks good Joshua thought, as he made his way to the paddock to watch the horses prepare for the race. Both looked calm and cool as they were saddled. The odds on Maria Isabel dropped as the horses paraded on to the track. Joshua decided that Lester's Babe was terribly overrated and decided to wager with the assumption that she would finish out of the money. Maria Isabel was now seven to two with three minutes to post. Joshua made a large wager to win and several exactas and trifectas keying Maria Isabel.

He made his way to his seat as post time approached. It was seven furlongs. He expected Maria Isabel to be three or four lengths off the lead and then move to the front at the top of the stretch. As the race unfolded everything was going as predicted. Lester's Babe opened a clear lead through a first quarter of twenty-two flat; Maria Isabel was sitting fourth on the rail. As they reached the top of the stretch Lester's Babe still had a three length lead as the third choice Angie Baby started to close the gap. Maria Isabel was still fourth trapped along the rail, but making up a little ground. As they approached the eighth pole, Angie Baby put her nose in front of Lester's Babe. Maria Isabel finally shook loose and took off as if she had been shot from a cannon. She made up a three-length deficit in four strides and blasted into the lead at the sixteenth pole, pulling away to a three-length win, with Angie Baby second.

Joshua's hand shook slightly as he headed to the wagering kiosk to run his winning tickets. He had made enough money to stay solvent for another few months. Several of the other regulars had made good money on the race and they all celebrated. Joshua leaned quietly against the counter, sipping club soda, silently reflecting on his success. Edna, a young blonde in her forties, sat silently at the table next to the counter. She had her face buried in her hands and he thought he heard her crying. He went to sit by her. "Don't be upset, it's just a horse race. There's always another one coming up."

She looked up at him, tears having stained her makeup, "It's not the race," and she started to cry again, "Look at this," and she played a holographic message.

A gray headed man appeared and started talking "Edna, I hope you remember me, it's been a long time. I want you to come home, your mother is dying." The image of an emaciated, wrinkled old woman, lying in bed appeared. She lay there silently, staring straight ahead, expressionless. The message ended with only reply information remaining.

"Your parents," Joshua said matter-of-factly. "It must be a long time since you've seen them."

"Thirty years, damn these transponders. Why did they have to find me," she said more as statement than question.

"What happened?" Joshua asked as gently as possible. "Two minutes to post," announced the PA system.

"You're going to miss the race," she said.

"I don't care about this race. Go ahead."

"We had been happy once. Typical family, nice home, all the basics and a few luxuries. Then there was an accident; I was never told the details. But afterwards, Mother was always in bed. She could talk for a while, but that stopped after about one and a half years and then she just lay there. My father became bitter and angry. I was only ten, but he seemed to hate me. I looked almost exactly like my mother; it was like he thought I was her. He hurt me, maybe like he hurt her. At fifteen I went out to buy some food and I never looked back. I managed to find odd jobs, supported myself as well as I could. One thing about society today, you always have the basics. I've been happy living my life on the fringe with the rest of you misfits and now this comes along and stirs up everything that I thought had been buried years ago. Look at her, she looks 140, but she's only eighty. She used to be so beautiful. He did it to her; I'll always hate him for what he did to her... and me."

"Maybe he's changed."

"He'll never change and I wouldn't care if he were the one dying. She's been dead for years. He should be dead for all that he has done. Look, the race is going off."

They both stopped to watch the race, although neither had any real interest in its outcome.

Joshua started up again, "Call your father, you won't regret it. I think you'll find him a different person and he really wants to have some peace in his life before he is gone. You see, you're right, he is dying. You don't have to believe me, but it is true."

"How can you know this? Just by looking at that message?"

"That's right, just from that message. If you are going to do it, do it soon. I don't think he has much time."

"You're no doctor and even if you were, there was no computer physiologic data. You can't tell just by looking at a hologram, nobody could."

"You're correct. I'm no doctor. But I can tell and I am right about this. Now let me get you something to drink." Joshua went over to the counter and returned with an ice water and a large napkin. She dried her eyes and took a sip.

"Thank you," she whispered. "I would like to talk to you more, get to know you better."

"I'd like that, perhaps supper after the tenth race, my treat."

"OK," she said as she turned her attention to the upcoming race and, for the moment, her troubles faded into the background.

The races leading up to the feature were forgettable with no worthwhile wagering opportunities. Joshua did make a few interest bets and won a small amount of money. He stayed with Edna, talking about nothing in particular, reliving past betting triumphs and failures. The others joined in as everyone had stories of their big wins and near misses. Joshua always liked to tell the story of his near perfect day at one of the upstate tracks in New York. He had won five races in a row and had one more wager that he thought was worthwhile. He was not able to make large bets in those days, as he was a student with very little money. That day, however, he had started with forty dollars in his pocket. He had won the initial Double and his next three wagers. He reached the seventh race $3,000 ahead. He thought Whispering Nicki an outstanding prospect. He took $2,000 of his winnings and bet her to win and in various exacta combinations. She was six to one and he stood to make more money than he had ever seen. The race had gone as planned until the turn for home when Whispering Nicki started to make her move. As she moved into fourth the two horses immediately in front of her veered in and out closing off the hole she was trying to sneak through. Pinched back, she had to move around the leaders in front of her and gallantly raced after the leader, but missed the win by ½ length. Joshua was forced to go back to school, $1,000 richer for the day, but he always remembered what could have been.

As the stories ended the horses came on to the track for the featured race, the Demoiselle Stakes. One and one eighth miles for two-year-old fillies. Four horses were challenging Ruth Rising who was one to ten on the board. She was a large, black filly, except for the white blaze on her face. She danced on her toes as if to say, "Look at how pretty I am." The other entries looked almost sheepish, as if they didn't even deserve to be her stable pony. Everyone waited for the start, anticipating great things from the rising star.

As the field approached the gate, she stood quietly, calmly entering the gate when led by the assistant starter. "It's post time!" blared over the loudspeaker. They were all in the gate. ...And they're off. Ruth Rising quickly takes the lead... past the quarter in twenty-two flat... Ruth Rising leads by eight as they approach the top of the stretch, three quarters in 1:09... past the eighth pole and she is cruising by eighteen lengths, under the wire it's all Ruth Rising winning by twenty lengths, final time 1:44 flat.

Everyone looked at each other speechless. Harry, who was never at a loss for words, was the first to speak.

"Mark your calendars boys and girls, today you have seen greatness that is found only once a generation." Everyone started to talk at once as superlatives flowed out like champagne after a World Series victory.

Joshua sat down next to Edna. Even she had a big smile on her face. He took her by the hand. "Shall we go?" he asked.

"By all means," she answered and they left together.

LII. MEETING IN EDEN

ALL THE EDENITES MET TOGETHER AT THE REQUEST OF ISAAC. THERE were about two hundred of them, men, women and children. The Creator had asked Isaac to call them together, and was to join them as they discussed the danger that was posed by the presence of David. Isaac started with a prayer of homage to the Creator. The Creator then suddenly appeared, dressed, as always, in bright white light.

The Creator spoke: "I brought David among you as a way to keep him among the living. You have been gracious and generous in all that you have done for him. However, the sin that is inherent within him cannot be removed. He has been trying to find a way to leave Eden, but his efforts have unfortunately been thwarted. He will try much more drastic measures to make his escape and there will be dangerous consequences for all of you. For you to avoid this and remain safe, remember to be obedient to your Creator. If you remember and obey all that I have commanded of you, then you will be safe." And He departed.

Isaac stood up and addressed the assembly. "You have all heard it directly from our beloved Creator. Be obedient and He will keep us safe. Miriam has been watching David and she is ready to report to us."

Miriam stood up. She was young looking, appearing to be about fifteen, but, of course, really much older. She had jet black hair and the perfect features seen in all the Edenites. Her eyes were piercing, dark, probing and she was known to be one who noticed and remembered everything that she saw and heard. She had been given a special gift that allowed her vision when others would be blind. She addressed the congregation:

"My fellows, I have observed David and Ruth these last few days. It is true he is making all plans and haste to leave our garden and Ruth, of course, is to go with him. He has been working within a strange black structure, what he calls his ITP vessel, named the Falcon. During the day they have spent hours inside, Ruth being forced to cover her body while they work. I endeavored to look inside and was able to do this for a moment when they had stepped out to eat. There were numerous lights and a strange noise that sounded like singing without words, but most pleasing to the ear. David seemed happy until just yesterday when he became very concerned and disheartened. Their work stopped and they spent their time running as they tend to do; I don't know why. The animals seem to favor them as there are always different ones running or walking with them. Even the unicorns stopped to talk with them; I could not hear their conversation, however. The lion has befriended David on several occasions; he was the one that showed him the location of this ITP vessel. They have run past the Tree of Knowledge on several occasions, but never take any unusual interest in its content. Today, David seemed much happier, almost joyful. I think that he is planning to leave Eden very soon. Isaac has asked me to continue to watch and I will be diligent and keep all of you informed."

Isaac stood up. "Thank you, Miriam, for that very informative report. All of you have heard our Creator's words. Continue to be obedient and all will be well."

Isaac stopped Miriam as she was leaving. He spoke softly to her, "You must continue your vigilance. We must be kept safe from this danger. As you learn of his plans, that knowledge will be vital to our safety and maintaining our way of life, living in harmony with our Creator."

She answered, "I know what to do. I believe that whatever he is planning it will be carried out very soon. I am returning to their resting place now. Please send a messenger to the area near the Tree of Knowledge tomorrow just before sundown. I will have more information then."

They said a short prayer together: "Our dear Creator, please keep us safe and whole and protect us in these troubled times, that we may serve you always." And she left.

LIII. DAVID AND RUTH

DAVID WOKE RUTH. SHE HAD BEEN SLEEPING ONLY A SHORT TIME; HE had not been able to sleep at all. "We must go now," he said. They quietly stood up and looked around. There was no sign of any other people. There were bats flying overhead and a black panther had come to join them, along with a tiny antelope. Ruth told them that they were to be their eyes and to warn them of any other people nearby. They started off at a slow trot with the panther in the lead, his eyes glowing in the pale moonlight. They moved through the dense forest silently, even David did not make a sound.

They arrived after a short time at their destination, the tree standing majestically by itself. Ruth grew fearful, clinging tightly to David's shoulder. He could feel her shaking. He put his arm around her as if to say we are in this together and will always be together. When they arrived the lion and the unicorns were waiting.

The unicorns spoke, "We have searched the entire area. There is no one close by. Please be quick." He looked around, nervously. "We cannot stay here while this deed is done." All the animals left silently, leaving David and Ruth standing alone at the foot of the tree, bathed by the light of the full moon. The lion was the last to leave, shaking his great mane as he turned away, a forlorn look on his regal face.

"Hurry," David said quietly. He ran up to the tree, plucked two shiny red apples and returned to Ruth. "Shall we dine?" he asked facetiously. "I am so afraid," she answered. "We have no choice; remember the words of the unicorns." He raised the fruit to his mouth. Ruth did the same and together they each took a bite. The fruit was sweet and rich and was consumed quickly, leaving no part behind.

"I don't feel any different," Ruth said after several minutes.

"Nor do I, but I must say that it was the best fruit in the garden." He ran up to the tree and took four more of the apples. "We must leave now." They ran at a faster pace, back to the Falcon, there way lit by the moonlight.

Miriam sat down, feeling very confused. She had seen them take the fruit, eat it, and yet they did not die. Was the Creator wrong? She put her hands on either side of her head, burying her face, not knowing what to do. A unicorn appeared next to her.

"You looked troubled," it spoke to her.

"I have just seen something that has left me bewildered and troubled. I am left doubting my Creator."

"Tell me child, what troubles you?" asked the unicorn.

"We have been told that on the day we eat from the Tree of Knowledge we will surely die. But, I have just seen two people eat this fruit and nothing happened. Our Creator has always been true to us, why has He been untruthful now?"

"The Creator knows that if we were to eat this fruit we would have all of His knowledge and we would be like Him, all knowing and powerful. He keeps us to be his servants when we should be His equal. That is what David and Ruth have learned. They have not died and even now they are making plans to leave this place and join Our Creator in the sky as His equal, no longer being held in servitude."

"I am afraid. I think I should ask Isaac what should be done."

"Did not Isaac give this task to you? He trusted you to do what is right. Surely, he would be very disappointed if you were to lay this burden on his shoulders. You have seen that there is no danger; you have seen that this is the way to be like our beloved Creator. You must realize that our Creator wants you to be bold enough to think for yourself to prove that you are worthy to be with Him forever."

"Your words are frightening, but also contain a great deal of wisdom. Let me go and pick the fruit from the tree." She went to the tree and reached up and plucked one of the bright red apples and held it tightly in her hand. She stared into it and her face stared back from its shiny surface, illuminated by the moonlight. She felt like the apple was speaking to her, begging her to take a bite and set herself free. She raised the fruit to her lips and bit into it. It was good for eating. She ate the whole apple. I don't feel any different, she thought, except she felt a cold breeze and she felt a shiver run through her. "This is truly marvelous fruit, the best I've ever tasted. I must share it with the others."

"We will help you," said the unicorns. She gathered a large number of the apples and the unicorns helped her carry them to the meeting place.

Even though it was night and very dark she called all the Edenites to join her. "My friends, I must tell you what I have learned." She recounted all that she had seen and had learned. She told them that she had eaten the fruit and she had not died. David and Ruth had also eaten and they ran away unencumbered. All who were present were impressed as Miriam passed out the fruit to them. Shouldn't we wait for Isaac and Rebekah, who had not yet arrived?

The unicorn spoke, "You can see very well that there are no ill effects, this fruit will give you the Knowledge of your Creator; you will be like Him." There were murmurs of assent through the group. Each one had an apple; almost as one, they each took a bite, and then devoured the fruit completely. At this moment, Isaac and Rebekah appeared.

"Look what I have brought you," Miriam cried.

"Where did you get this?" Isaac asked.

She told him the same story as she had previously told the others. "How could you do such a thing? We will all surely die," he spoke forcefully.

"We have all eaten this fruit and we have not fallen ill. This fruit is very good for eating, sweet and flavorful. It was not right for the Creator to keep it from us."

Isaac looked at the fruit and felt like it was calling to him. He handed an apple to Rebekah and the two ate together. Now all of Eden had eaten save one. Elijah was not there and he was nowhere to be found. It was late and they all felt tired. "Let us sleep now and tomorrow we will bring this fruit to Elijah so that he may be allowed to enjoy its goodness." And they all quickly fell asleep.

LIV. THE ITP VESSEL

DAVID AND RUTH ARRIVED BACK AT THE ITP VESSEL, DAVID ANXIOUS to see if he could now find a way to make repairs. He did not feel any different, but he also remembered his Bible mythology. When Adam and Eve ate the apple, they realized that they were naked and God discovered their sin. They were kicked out of the Garden of Eden, forced to toil for their survival and were never to return to the garden. Of course the story was mere myth. So far it seemed like nothing had happened to David or Ruth.

It was still night and they were very tired. "Let's sleep and we can start to work first thing in the morning." David's watch said 2:00 A.M. As they lay down, David thought about the repairs that needed to be made. He had not had any new revelation since eating the apple. Perhaps it takes awhile he thought as he drifted off to sleep.

The next morning David awoke with a feeling of disappointment. He had no new ideas for making repairs. The unicorns had been wrong. David looked at Ruth with a puzzled look on his face.

"Something is not right. The unicorns are the Creator's messengers, aren't they? A message from them should be the same as hearing it straight from the horse's mouth. How could they be wrong?"

Ruth thought for a while, "We've always considered the unicorns to have some special favor from our Creator, this has been tradition, but I don't know how this tradition started. Are you saying that they lied to us?"

"That's exactly what I'm saying. And, if they can lie, which is a sin, then they are not your Creator's messengers. We could be in big trouble. I think there may be something else afoot besides our leaving Eden. Anyway, to be on the safe side, I'm going to make sure that we are functional for takeoff, even if we can't utilize the ITP."

David ran through the preflight checklist and found all systems were ready and liftoff could be initiated with less than three minutes preparation. He left the ship with all preflight checks and preliminaries completed. All that was necessary was to enter the flight initiation code and they could be off.

"Remember these numbers and letters," he said to Ruth. "If anything should happen to me you can get us out of here by entering this sequence this way." He showed her how to input the sequence. "Then all you have to do is push this blue button when it starts to blink and the vessel will lift-off. It will head to the ITP portal I exited and will even go through an automated program to initiate portal entry based on the stored information. Hit the green button when it starts to blink and the portal will be engaged. That's as much as can be done to automate the ship. There's nothing more that I can do now. So, let's take a break."

They left the ITP vessel and took a leisurely walk along the lake's edge; they saw the lion in the distance. David had become quite fond of the stately lion. His natural fear of the "King of Beasts" had dissipated, replaced by love and respect. After all, of all the inhabitants of Eden, save Ruth, it was the lion that had been most helpful. He had been the first to find David when he had crashed in Eden and he had also revealed the location of the ITP vessel. They had spent hours walking and running together. Even though David couldn't communicate with him the way Ruth or the other Edenites could, they did seem to understand each other. David regarded the lion the same way he regarded Little Bit back home, with respect and as a trusted friend.

The lion saw them as they walked, but did not approach. There was a small deer up ahead, which darted into the bushes as they approached. The lion saw the deer, also, and ran after it. Something's wrong, David thought. David noticed that none of the animals joined them, which was unusual. He looked up; the sky suddenly grew dark with a black cloud. Looks like a thunderstorm is heading this way, he thought, something he had not previously seen in Eden.

"Let's head back to the ship, it looks like there's going to be a storm," David said. Ruth looked terrified as they turned around and started to run slowly back to the ship. They arrived at the safety of the ITP vessel as the first flash of lightning and boom of thunder hit, followed by high winds and heavy rain that almost came down horizontally.

"David, this is scary, I've never seen a storm like this before. What have we done? The Creator must be angry."

"Hold on, we'll be OK. I've been through much worse than this." He turned on Prokoviev and held her as the storm outside pelted the ship with heavy rain.

LV. EDNA

JOSHUA AND EDNA LEFT THE TRACK TOGETHER AND WENT TO DO-minique's for dinner. This restaurant prided itself on the freshest food available, some truly fresh and some freshly synthesized. Edna had been dressed in tight jeans with a short jacket at the track. When they arrived at the restaurant, she removed the jacket, revealing a very low cut and nearly transparent top.

"That's quite an outfit," Joshua said.

"I have to work this evening. Those days when I don't win I have to earn some money, or else I can't bet the next day."

"What do you do for a living, if you don't mind my asking?"

"I work evenings and nights, sort of public relations. I meet people and show them the best places to go out; sometimes I can make $2,000 in one night."

Joshua was beginning to get a better idea of just what sort of relations she was involved with, but didn't pursue it anymore. They ordered dinner and Edna asked, "How can you tell my father's sick, just by looking at that hologram?"

"He has the appearance of someone with untreated cancer. His cheeks are sunken in and he has a yellowish pallor that I've only seen in people with advanced cancer. It's hard to say what type it is, but I would guess it is his esophagus. I noticed some saliva buildup in his mouth, which suggests that he is having difficulty swallowing."

"You are remarkably perceptive."

"I can tell you that untreated esophageal cancer will leave him dead inside six months."

"Serves him right, the way he treated my mother and me."

"Perhaps you're right. It's best that you stay out of his life, let him die in peace. You'll be much happier living here, with your "public relations" and days at the track. I can tell that you are deliriously happy," Joshua said, somewhat facetiously.

Edna was starting to squirm and felt uneasy. Her voice grew louder as she said, "What do you know? You're as much dropout from society as the rest of us, acting so smug and high and mighty, like your some big authority on human nature. I live the life that I want, do what I want to do and I am my own boss. I don't need to listen to you, my father or anyone." She was screaming at the top her lungs by this time. She looked around. "I don't care if the whole world hears me," she shouted. "I'm nobody's fool, but my own." She started to calm down and took her seat.

"I'm sorry," Joshua said. "I know that you've had a tough life and you're doing the best that you can. I just don't want you to look at yourself in five years and regret that you missed this opportunity."

At this point their food arrived and they started to eat. They were both quiet during dinner; afterwards Joshua walked Edna to her apartment, which was less than two kilometers away.

"Would you like to see my home?" she asked.

"Certainly, lead the way."

The building was old and badly in need of fresh paint. They walked up two flights of stairs to her apartment, two rooms at the top of the stairs. There were old and worn chairs and a sofa, the walls were bare and there were only a few modern conveniences, a computer, an old food synthesizer, and an automated hygiene center.

"Let me change my clothes," She said. She went into the other room as Joshua quickly pulled up some information from the computer. Edna returned, now dressed in a completely see through outfit that left nothing to the imagination. Joshua stared at her and handed her the information he had just obtained.

"I'm sorry to disappoint you, but I must be leaving. This is the transport schedule for buses to Cleveland. I hope that you'll take the next one and go to your Father. You won't regret it."

Edna looked embarrassed and started to cry. "I'm sorry; I don't know what I was thinking." Joshua took a blanket off the sofa and wrapped it around her. He held her and dried her tears.

"It's OK. You'll be fine. This life here is not for you. Go back to Cleveland. Go back to your Father. I promise everything will be OK. And, if you have any problem, call me." He gave her a card with his number along with an envelope. He put his hand on the side of her face and left.

When he had been gone for about fifteen minutes, she sat down and opened the envelope. Inside was a bus ticket, $5,000 and a disc. She put the disc into the computer and the image of her father as a young man appeared. She saw him playing with her and her mother, everyone looked happy. She saw him leave for work one day and her mother sitting on the bed crying. Edna figured that she was about two years old at the time. What she next frightened her; her mother filled the bathtub and then tied a heavy weight onto Edna. Her mother took a hand full of pills and then put Edna into the tub. She saw her mother pass out on the bed and she saw herself struggling under the water, drowning. At that moment, her father burst into the room. He rescued both of them. Afterwards, nothing was ever the same. Edna began to cry as she packed her few belongings for the trip to Cleveland.

LVI. HEARINGS

THE SENATE INTERPLANETARY COMMITTEE WAS SEATED IN THE HEARing chamber. The Committee was composed of nine members: Senator Angelina Torres of Texas, Senator Oscar Bulovar of New York, Senator Mary Phillips of Ohio, Senator Gregorio Pietro of Puerto Rico, Senator James Bowdin of Florida, Senator Dennis McCally of Iowa, Senator Adrian Leavitt of California, Chairman, Senator Arthur Fitzpatrick of Washington and Senator Eloise Gump of Rhode Island.

"The hearing is now called into session, the Honorable Senator Adrian Leavitt presiding," announced the attendant. The senators were all dressed in standard senate issue, black suits with white shirts and red tie or scarf depending on gender and preference.

The hearing room was filled with representatives of the media, as well as interested scientists, representatives of the judiciary and the president's staff and other visiting officials. All the observers were behind a glass partition. Any comments that they may made were shielded from the senators and the witnesses, to prevent any undue influence on the testimony. There was a desk before the senators where the witness and his lawyer sat. The witness was connected to a finger probe which monitored a number of physiologic functions. These were pulse, blood pressure, respiratory rate, blood oxygenation, carbon dioxide production, electrical brain wave output, body sweat production and composition, kidney output and composition and generalized heat production. These values were collated by the physiologic monitor and used to determine if the witness was being truthful. The studies of these monitoring techniques had demonstrated 99.97% accuracy. The unfortunate execution of Randy Calhoun, which was the result, exclusively, of a faulty physiologic monitor was a rare aberration and was not to be taken as an indictment of the entire judicial process. It had later been determined that a worn cable was responsible for making the determination that Mr. Calhoun was lying, not the monitoring process per se. When the monitors determined that his testimony was false, the court found him guilty and he was executed. Later, the true guilty party had been apprehended and properly executed; this after only two more victims had been identified.

"Will the attendant call the first witness?" Senator Leavitt said.

"General Justin Moosewood is called to the stand."

General Moosewood walked down the aisle and took his seat at the desk. He was alone. "General, do you not have counsel with you?" Senator Leavitt asked.

"I'll answer any of your questions. I don't need any shyster telling me what to say or not say. I want the committee to clearly see that I am totally cooperative and supportive of this inquiry. I see it as an information gathering session and in no way an attempt to undermine the importance of our work."

"Well said, general," Leavitt replied. "General, would you please state your name and current position for the record."

"General Justin Moosewood, Chairman ITP Committee." The general looked impressive in his perfectly clean, creased uniform displaying his numerous medals and decorations.

"General, I think we can dispense with the usual overview of the ITP program. All the Interplanetary Committee members are familiar with the work you have claimed to accomplish and the basic fundamentals of the ITP. However, would you please recount the events involving your lead ITP pilot, Major David Sanders, the evening before his ill-fated flight?"

The general remained calm as he answered, "Major Sanders was involved in a minor altercation with some would be assailants. He had been out to dinner with a friend when they were accosted. The Major defended himself as any individual would, his attackers were arrested and the major suffered no ill effects."

Senator Leavitt followed up, "Would you say that spending the evening in a casino was proper preflight preparation for such a historic and important mission?"

"Major Sanders was evaluated completely prior to his lift-off. All mental and physical parameters were at optimal levels. There was no indication of any bodily impairment, mental or physical."

Senator Bulovar jumped in, "Could you summarize the safety precautions that are taken to prevent such a mishap as has occurred?"

"Certainly," the general answered. "The ITP vessel is inspected completely, going through an exhaustive checklist prior to flight. The preflight check is made by the Chief Engineer, Dr. Robert Scully, and the backup pilot, Major Anthony Sorino. The checklist is then inspected and confirmed by the lead pilot, in this case, Major Sanders. The ITP portal is continuously monitored for any change in energy output that could alter the entrance into the interdimensional plane. Deep space conditions are also continuously monitored and any changes passed to the ITP pilot and Committee members. You can see that every aspect of the flight was monitored for any possible alteration to the flight plan that could have any potential to pose a danger to the pilot."

Senator Bulovar continued, "With all these safety precautions in place, how do you account for the actual events?"

"Senator, with all due respect, everything you are asking is on the public record and, as a matter of fact, summarized in the ITP brief that Senator Leavitt has previously said did not need to be reviewed. I believe that if you look on page three, paragraph three, your question will be answered."

Senator Bulovar's face turned red and he appeared flustered at the general's response. Senator Leavitt chuckled softly to himself. What a fool you are Senator, he thought as he interjected a question, "General, given your initial data on the ITP portal, contrasted with the current available data, would you say that the initial data was in error?"

"I would say that there has been a change. We cannot account for this change, but we have been studying it and we are now very close to understanding this change, which will enable us to launch a follow-up ITP flight."

"But, general, given the dismal failure of your first manned ITP flight, how can you justify sacrificing another of our top, nearly indispensable, astropilots, on a flight into oblivion?"

"Senator, I assure you that every precaution will be taken to insure the safety of Major Sorino. He is more than willing to chance another ITP flight."

"General, I'm afraid that you have only raised more doubts. Even referring to the next flight as chance suggests that you really don't know what to expect. All you have is more of the same, which has left our finest pilot missing and probably dead."

Behind the glass partition a loud murmur ran through the spectators as members of the media spoke rapidly into their recorders or pounded vigorously on their nanopods. The headlines and banners were already being written: "General calls ITP 'CHANCE.'" It didn't matter what else he said or what he really meant, that word was all that anyone would remember.

General Moosewood's testimony continued for a few more hours. He tried, in vain, to refocus the Senate Committee on the importance of their work, but any mention of overpopulation, expanding potential resources or providing easy access to suitable planets for colonization were lost in the word "chance." As the general finished his testimony and left the witness stand, he caught a glimpse of Senator Leavitt displaying a look of triumph and superiority. The general silently fumed as he left the hearing chamber.

LVII. EDEN?

ISAAC HAD SOME DIFFICULTY STANDING UP AS HE WAS AWAKENED BY the warmth of the morning sun, his back and legs were stiff. He had never felt this way before. He also felt a pressure feeling in his lower abdomen. He looked around at his sleeping companions and felt a sense of shame. They were all uncovered, exposed to each other and he felt ashamed. What has happened? He gently shook Rebekah to arouse her from sleep.

"We need to leave," he said. She got up with him and they silently left together. Isaac felt no shame with Rebekah, but he felt the need to hide from the others. Rebekah had identical feelings.

"We should cover ourselves," she said and they pulled down some of the large leaves that they used as blankets and fashioned them into very crude clothing.

As the others arose they had similar feelings, each couple going off to find some form of cover for their naked bodies. As they walked they notice that the ground was rough and hurt their feet. The animals, which were usually underfoot, but almost always ignored were nowhere to be seen. There was still fruit on the trees, but they did not find any manna, only withered bushes where the manna had previously grown. Each of them felt uncomfortable as organs that had long been kept dormant by the Creator began to function. They all felt the need to urinate as their bodies, no longer pure, began to generate the waste products that the Creator had previously removed.

"What have we done?" Isaac said to Rebekah. "When the Creator comes he will destroy us." He put his arms around Rebekah and cried.

Rebekah shook him, "Stop it, what is done is done. We must be ready to talk to the Creator, to tell him how we were tricked. He is good, he will forgive us. But, to win his favor, we must punish the responsible person. Miriam did this; she brought the fruit to us and she must pay for her sin. Come we must find the others."

They walked back to the meeting place. They gradually found the other Edenites. They had all fashioned some sort of clothing. Isaac, as elder, stood before them, "My friends, we have been tricked by one of our own. Miriam must be punished, along with David. We must find them and, when we do, we must each take a large stone and cast it at them. Our Creator would want us to do this. We must bring justice and then we will be forgiven and return to our old ways.

The Edenites separated and began searching for Miriam, their hearts filled with anger and hatred. As they started their search the thunderstorm hit. Each pair of Edenites cowered under the fierce storm, huddling together at the base of one of the tall sturdy trees, not knowing if the storm would ever pass. As the storm strengthened and their fear increased, so did their anger. The names Miriam and David were cursed out loud and the Creator was forgotten.

The storm did pass and David and Ruth emerged from the ITP vessel unharmed by the storm. They also had noticed that they needed more frequent bathroom breaks. Previously, David had only needed to urinate about once a week and his bowels moved even less frequently. Ruth had only gone about once a month. David noticed that his bodily functions were back to normal. Ruth also noticed the change. David explained that it was probably a consequence of their actions, that it was no big concern and it was just something to get used to. Ruth didn't give it a second thought. She also quickly accepted the storm, even coming to enjoy the thunder and lightning, as long as she was safe within the ITP vessel.

The air seemed different to David, heavy and thick with a slight smell of decay. "Something has happened, Eden seems worn and tired, no longer paradise. I think that we should check on the others, but we need to be careful."

Ruth took a few steps, "David, the ground is rough. I can't walk very well."

"Let me get something to help," he said. David went back into the ship. He returned with Ruth's work suit and a pair of slippers, with solid hard soles. "Put these on," he said, "They'll protect your feet and shouldn't be too uncomfortable for you." The slippers conformed perfectly to her tiny feet. They walked on. The air was silent and gloomy, as if Eden had been drugged and put to sleep. An eerie fog covered the ground as they walked. There was nothing about, no animals, no people, just the soft thud of their own footsteps.

David saw something that troubled him. Up ahead he saw some flies flitting about. There had never been any insects of any type, except bees and butterflies, in Eden. They reached the spot and found what had attracted the flies, an Alpaca; or rather its remains lay on the ground, its body mutilated, apparently eaten. The flies were dining on the carcass. David looked up to see vultures circling overhead. Paradise Lost, he thought to himself.

"Oh David, what has happened?" Ruth asked with a trembling voice.

"Death has come to Paradise and probably is now a permanent resident." David looked ahead and saw a familiar figure. "Look up ahead, there's the lion," he said. As they approached the lion turned its head towards them. David and Ruth stopped; its mouth was covered in blood. When it saw them coming near it growled and bounded away. David caught a glimpse of sadness in its face before it turned away.

"We need to be careful," he whispered to Ruth. "Eden has become a very dangerous place. The Edenites will not look kindly upon us when they realize that we are responsible for this. It may be best for us to return to the ship and prepare to leave." They turned around and started to head back when Ruth said that she heard voices. Two of the Edenites, Jacob and Rachel, were approaching. "We'd better hide," David said. They ducked into the brush as Jacob and Rachel passed by, talking to each other, carrying large stones, with very angry expressions on their faces. After they passed, Ruth turned to David, "They're looking for Miriam; they said she's responsible for these events. David, Miriam has a special gift of vision. It's possible she had been watching us and saw us eat the fruit. She may have thought that nothing would happen and tried it herself. She's in danger because of us; we need to find her."

"If that's true, then you're probably right. Do you have any idea where she would be? If she's smart she's hiding somewhere. It's too bad we can't get the birds to help us. It seems the animals don't trust us anymore." David thought for a moment. "We should head back to the ITP vessel."

"But, what about Miriam?" Ruth protested.

"If we're going to find her the ship is the best place to start looking and we need to go now."

Ruth had not heard David speak so forcefully and she sensed it was not the time to argue. They turned back towards the ship and took off at a brisk pace. Along the way they were shocked to see animals running in fear, wolves chasing deer, swarms of insects descending upon the carcasses of dead animals, plants withered and dying and then they saw something that made them stop. Lightning had struck one of the tall trees, which seemingly burst into flames and then crashed to the ground. Lying beneath it were two Edenites, Daniel and Esther, crushed. David approached them, but saw that they were dead.

"They're gone. We can't do anything for them. Perhaps the Creator will be merciful." Secretly, David thought that He may have already them shown his mercy, but he kept this thought from Ruth. As they approached the ship, a black panther jumped into their path.

"We don't have time for this," he said out loud. He picked up a large rock and threw it, striking the big cat squarely on the nose. It let out a loud yelp and jumped into the nearby tree. David and Ruth ran up the ramp into the ITP vessel and sealed the door behind them.

They sat down to catch their breath. "How is being at the ship going to help us find Miriam?" she asked.

"Don't worry, I think Miriam is quite safe. Aren't you, Miriam? You may come out from wherever it is you are hiding."

Somewhat sheepishly, Miriam came out from the supply closet. She seemed embarrassed, probably for several reasons. She was still naked, now being aware of her nakedness, along with the fact that she had been discovered so easily.

David handed her an extra jumpsuit. "Put this on, you'll feel less self conscious." She quickly donned the suit. "Now," David said to her, "tell us what has happened.

Miriam started at the beginning, from the moment she started watching them until the morning after they had all eaten the fruit. "It was the unicorns; they made me take the fruit. They tempted me. Why, why did I listen to them?"

"On Earth it was the serpent, here it was the unicorns....Satan's messengers." David sat silently for a few moments.

"Did everyone eat the fruit?" He asked.

Miriam thought for a moment. "Everyone was there… but Elijah. He's been going off by himself a lot recently. He was not with the group."

David jumped up suddenly, "Darn…We need to find him. When the others realize that he has not fallen, they'll feel threatened. And if there's one thing that I know about human nature, it's that people don't want anyone to be different, particularly if they think someone is superior. They'll go looking for him, just as they have been looking for us. If they find him before us it will not be a pretty sight. Miriam, do you know where Elijah might be?"

"I can show you where."

"No, just tell me. We need to hurry and I don't think that you can keep up with us. Stay here where you'll be safe."

Miriam told them of the place, on a hill looking over the center of Eden, surrounded on three sides by tall trees and thick brush. She said that Elijah spent hours there looking out over the garden, at the Tree of Knowledge and staring at the sky. She thought he was contemplating being with the Creator and she had guessed that his return from the death somehow made him long to be with the Creator always. He seemed sad that he would have to spend so many seasons "trapped" in Eden until he could one day join the Creator for all time. She felt sad for him; he said that he regretted being brought back to the living. He knew that it was wrong, but he wished that he would be dead, because then he would be with the Creator always.

"If we don't hurry, he'll get his wish. It's too bad there aren't any weapons on this ship. We'll have to rely on our wits."

"We're in big trouble," Ruth quipped. "Let's go."

LVIII. TESTIMONY

THE SENATE HEARINGS CONTINUED WITH MAJOR SORINO SET TO TESTIFY. He was not considered an important figure by the Senate Committee, but each member of the ITP committee was to testify. Sorino was dressed in his flight suit, no dress uniform or display of medals. He looked a little shaky as he took the witness stand and was connected to the usual monitors. He was accompanied by his lawyer, Arthur Pendercost, a high profile attorney known for his verbosity. Senator Leavitt addressed Major Sorino, "State your name for the record."

"Major Anthony Sorino."

"Relax, major, we will try to make this as informal as possible. Your physiologic parameters seem very high for a solar pilot who is known to be cool under the most trying conditions."

"I'm sorry, Sir. Flying is one thing, but sitting in front of all you bigshots without a parachute is a completely different story." Senator Leavitt had no idea the real reason for Sorino's agitation and the major was happy to have the Senator believe what he wanted.

The first question came from Senator Pietro, "Major, could you explain your role in the ITP flight of Major David Sanders?"

Sorino looked at Pendercost, who sat silent and still as a marble statue and then answered, his voice wavering slightly, "I was the backup pilot for that mission. I was prepared to assume lead pilot role if Major Sanders had become incapacitated for any reason. I also was responsible for the preflight checklist, along with the lead engineer, Mr. Scully. We assess all ship's functions and systems and then provide the checklist to the lead pilot for his final inspection prior to lift off. As can be seen this was performed per protocol and final check by Major Sanders is noted by his signature at the bottom."

"Thank you, I have no other questions," said Senator Pietro. Sorino started to step down when he was stopped.

"The rest of the Committee may have questions for you." Senator Leavitt said. Sorino muttered inaudibly as he sat down.

Senator Gump coughed. "The eloquent Senator from Rhode Island wishes to be heard," Senator Leavitt announced.

Senator Gump, with her usual nasal voice, started, "Major Sorvino..."

"Sorino, ma'am," the major corrected.

"Yes, Major Sorino, would you say that the ITP is potentially more dangerous than the average interplanetary flight?"

Sorino tried hard to keep a straight face, "Senator, judging by the outcome of our only manned ITP flight, I would have to answer yes."

"Yes, I know that it seems obvious, but could you characterize the additional dangers that one faces on such a mission?"

"Senator, it is the danger of the unknown. The ITP pilot enters a black box of unknown size, having only his faith in the numbers generated by a computer and our astrophysicists to, hopefully, guide him out. For an astropilot used to depending only on himself and his skills, I would say that is the greatest danger."

"Then you would agree that the ITP is dangerous."

"Of course... but isn't mankind's willingness to accept danger in the hope of bettering himself, isn't that the stuff that brought us to where we are today? From the first man to walk upright and crawl out of the slime, we have lived with danger. Now our sociologically correct society runs from any hint of danger and leaves us at the brink of extinction. Does that answer your question, Senator?" Pendercost turned his head towards the major, but continued to be silent.

It was Senator Gump's turn to fume as she quietly answered, "Thank you, Major."

What fools these mortals be, Senator Leavitt thought. "I have a question for you, major," Senator Leavitt stated. "What was your purpose in joining the ITP program? You have a family and have been one of our most successful astropilots. Why would you risk such, in your own words, such danger?"

"Senator, I truly believe that we are here on this planet to help one another. The Earth faces potential disaster, slow, agonizing destruction. If my humble services can be of any help in brightening mankind's dismal future, then I would be grossly negligent to shirk such responsibility."

There was loud spontaneous applause in the spectator room at the major's strong response. Senator Leavitt looked at the physiologic meter, there was some fluctuation and a few numbers even strayed into the unacceptable range, but the major parameters remained acceptable. Major Sorino looked more relaxed as the senators seemed satisfied with his responses and there was no indication that any of his responses were judged to be untrue.

"One more question, major," Senator Leavitt asked, "is it true that you believe in God?"

Major Sorino hesitated momentarily, stared at his "lawyer" and then answered. "Senator, science has shown that we are here as a result of natural phenomenon. I am a man of science and I believe that it is scientific pursuit that will save this planet, not any apathetic deity. You may draw your own conclusion as to my beliefs."

Senator Leavitt smiled slightly at this response, and, after a few moments thought decided not to ask any more questions. "Thank you, major, I have no more questions for you."

There were a few more queries from other members of the committee, most of which demonstrated their profound ignorance and did nothing to provide any more insight into the ITP program or its safety.

Sorino was happy to be finished. Scully was to testify next. Sorino quickly left the chamber so that he could be ready as soon as Scully was finished. He felt a little shaky, which was normal after taking Sympathocide. The pharmacist had been correct. The drug allowed him to give false answers with little change in the physiologic monitors. It had been worth the money. He hoped the shakiness and feeling of unease would wear off soon.

LIX. SEARCH IN EDEN

ISAAC AND REBEKAH TRIED TO BRUSH THE GRIME AND DUST FROM their makeshift garments. They had encountered so many new things that left them frightened and confused. Tiny flying animals attacked them, biting them and leaving painful sores. The ground seemed to reach up and pinch their feet, which ached and swelled. They had cried to the Creator and were answered with silence. The search continued, however, the evil had to be purged. David and Miriam had to be removed from Eden. The elimination of this evil from Eden would appease the Creator and return them to the blessed state coexisting with Him.

David and Ruth ran on, a little slower than usual as Ruth was not used to running wearing shoes. She led the way to Elijah's place of solitude. He had spent a great deal of time alone since the accident. As they ran on they did their best to avoid detection by any Edenites. No animals joined them and Eden continued to be eerily quiet and gloomy. As they left the cover of the trees and entered a large grassy area, two of the Edenites, Judah and Tamar, spied them running through the grass. They let out a cry to the other Edenites to join them in their pursuit of David and Ruth.

Isaac and Rebekah had also heard the shout and emerged from the wooded area. The mob of Edenites was angry and determined. David looked at Ruth, "We might be in trouble," he said, "how much farther?"

"If we pick it up we can leave them behind and reach the spot in about ten minutes," Ruth answered. She threw off the shoes and picked up pace. David kept up, but kept himself between Ruth and their pursuers. The Edenite men tried to keep up as the women stopped, tiring and giving up. The men continued on, losing ground, but still keeping David and Ruth in their sights.

Isaac called to the others, "They are looking for Elijah; I'm sure of it. Follow me; I know a shorter way to him." The Edenite men turned to the west, following Isaac.

Ruth and David looked back. There was nobody in pursuit. "I wonder what happened, where did they go?" Ruth asked.

"I don't think we've outrun them already." David replied. "We'd better hurry, anyway." They raced through the grass towards the woods and hills ahead.

"Elijah will be on the largest hill up ahead," Ruth said. They picked up speed. David knew that once they found him, they would need extra time to get him back to the ITP vessel. Elijah was not a runner and in his present state may even need to be carried.

As they reached the woods, Ruth followed a twisting path through the trees to reach the bottom of the hill.

"Elijah will be in that cave at the top of the hill, but we need to hurry. Isaac also knows about this place and I'm sure he is leading the Edenite men here."

As they race up the hill, David called out Elijah's name. No one emerged from the cave. "I don't think he's in there," David cried.

"No, I'm sure he's there," answered Ruth.

They reached the mouth of the cave and raced inside, calling Elijah's name. They saw a figure laying on the floor of the cave, curled up into a ball.

"Elijah, get up. It's David and Ruth." They ran up to him and shook him.

"Leave me alone. Let me die. Let me return to the Creator," he whispered, his voice barely audible. He looked thin and pale, and felt cold.

"Let me carry him," David said, as he scooped him into his arms. They raced out of the cave to see the Edenites ascending the hill. David, carrying Elijah, and Ruth turned and ran up the hill. They reached the top to see the Edenites closing the gap. David noticed a large number of loose rocks along the side of the hill and he had an idea. He gently lay Elijah down at the top of the hill and called to Ruth. "Come help me loosen this large boulder; perhaps if we get it rolling down the hill it will stop them.

Ruth and David dug at the bottom of the rock and pushed it, rocking it back and forth and gradually loosening it, as the angry mob moved closer.

"Almost," David yelled and with a final push the boulder started to roll down the hill. Much to David's chagrin the rock rolled harmlessly to their side and no other rocks followed. The Edenites were almost at the top as David and Ruth started back to Elijah.

At that moment they heard a loud booming crash, like thunder. A light shot out of the sky and, to David's amazement, a chariot ringed in fire rapidly descended from the clouds to Elijah. A man with long dark flowing hair, a dark beard and mustache, and dark olive skin reached out of the flaming chariot and effortlessly picked up Elijah with one arm, placed him at his side in the chariot and turned and raced back into the clouds. David saw Elijah standing at the man's side, tall and straight, with a broad smile on his face. David and Ruth and all the Edenites stared, immobile, until he was out of sight.

As soon as Elijah had disappeared, David turned towards the mob of Edenite men, each carrying a large stone and starting to move closer.

David called to them, "men of Eden, you come to us with malice in your hearts, blaming us for the calamity that has befallen you. I say to you that it is part of your Creator's plan that you should be freed from his domination to live a life apart from Him. This happened on my world and it has been your destiny to be free. You can never return to your old ways. Destroying us or Miriam will not return you to any favored status with your Creator. Please join me and I will help you to live on your own, free and independent."

The Edenites stopped and Isaac turned to the other men speaking softly. David turned to Ruth and whispered, "They're thinking about what I've said. You need to get away. Quickly, run back to the ship and stay there with Miriam until I can get away."

Ruth looked surprised, "but, what you said to them, about helping, didn't you mean what you said."

"Please believe me they will never trust me to help them. I said those things to buy some time. They will always blame me and Miriam for their fall from grace. At this moment, they may be considering what I've said, but we could never really be safe. Now, while you have the chance, leave and I'll join you as soon as I can."

Ruth thought for a moment and then turned and started back to the ITP vessel, running as fast as she could. "It was a lie," Isaac said, as he saw Ruth racing down the hill. The Edenite men turned once again to approach David.

Once he was sure that Ruth was safely away David called to the Edenites once again. "You hide behind those stones, not one of you is man enough to meet me face to face. I have no weapons and there are many of you. Come on, fight like men."

The Edenite men threw down their stones and surrounded David. In their faces David saw anger, but also fear. Those closest to him suddenly lunged and were met with a sharp kick in the teeth, followed by a whirlwind of arms, hands, legs and feet as David fought off every attack, leaving the Edenite men beaten and bloody on the ground. They have a lot to learn he thought shaking his head as he turned and ran away. As he was running a large rock flew past his right ear and another grazed his left leg. They learn fast, he thought, as he sprinted away, out of range of their stones.

LX. BIG DAY

MEDIA REPORTS OF THE SENATE HEARINGS FILLED EVERY OUTLET. THE latest reports of General Moosewood's testimony were broadcast everywhere with variations of the word "chance." The Daily Blog's lead story started with "General Admits ITP takes a Big "Chance." The Times, being more dignified reported "Moosewood Takes a Big ITP "Chance." CBS news ran in depth commentary on the potential liability of taking chances with human lives, featuring General Moosewood's personal attorney, Allan Stiers. This blue ribbon panel concluded that risking human lives, even for the noble cause of saving the planet and humanity was never worth the risk. Such a foolhardy endeavor could lay the groundwork for the return of global wars, pollution of our precious water supply and widespread food shortage.

General Moosewood was shocked at the response to what he had thought a very simple explanation. He found much of the commentary unfair, unduly sensationalized, but also amusing. He had called Deborah after the initial reports had come out. She had not seen his testimony, having been busy with David Jr. and working on the new ITP timing.

He sent her a holographic record of the testimony along with a sample of the memedia response. "This will show what we are up against, and, remember, we are testifying in front of politicians. They don't care about right or wrong or the potential for catastrophe 100 years from now. They care about public opinion and getting re-elected. I forgot that the truth and relevance are unimportant. Simple words and sound bites are all that matters to them and to the media. We shouldn't count on any help from the few thoughtful politicians and media personnel who actually care about the importance of our work."

Deborah seemed preoccupied, but responded, "General, all this shows is that we don't stand a chance against Senator Leavitt. He has already decided to eliminate the ITP program and I'm sure the media is working for him, playing up every little negative comment to bring public opinion against us. Maybe I'm wasting my time trying to figure out the final piece to this ITP puzzle."

The general answered, gently, "You have a new baby, you're young and brilliant. The ITP is only the first great success you will have and, no matter what Senator Leavitt or the media say, we all know that it has been a great success and that ITP travel is the future of mankind."

"That's what needs to be said, general. I just hope that I get the chance to say it." She stopped speaking for a moment. "Sorry, general I have to go. I hear a baby crying. Good-bye." She turned off the phone and picked up David Jr. "What's the matter little one?" She sniffed, "Oh, that's it. Let's put you in the changer." She laid him down in the GE baby changer. There was a light whir and a smile on the baby's face. When she took him out he had a new diaper and his bottom had been cleaned and sanitized. The dirty diaper was collected in the waste bin, where it would dissolve and be recycled into a new diaper. The waste material was separated and processed down to ash, water and CO_2 gas.

Deborah thought about her testimony, which was scheduled for the next day. Today, minor members of the ITP committee were going before the Senate Committee. No one was paying them much attention. She was the big one and she was afraid that Senator Leavitt was out to get her on a personal, as well as a professional level. That's just silly she thought. He doesn't know me and certainly couldn't care about me except for the ITP. Still, the idea wouldn't leave her head. I wonder what Joshua would think about this. As soon as this thought popped into her head she realized that it was exactly what David said before his ill-fated flight. She decided to give Joshua a call.

She pushed the phone button, "Joshua Smith, voice only," she said. It was only ten in the morning, so she figured he would be at home.

"Hello, doctor," came his voice. "What can I do for you?"

"I wanted to get your opinion on something. Would you let me buy you lunch? I don't want to talk over the phone."

"Who's going to watch the baby? I know you don't like to take him out."

"I'll bring him with me... and Little Bit. Do you know where Buddie's is?"

"I can find it. Can we meet at about eleven thirty?"

"That's fine with me. I'll see you then."

That gave her plenty of time to get ready. She called Little Bit. "We're going out to see Joshua," she said to the little dog, treating him like a person, "I'll need you to watch the baby for me." Little Bit barked and jumped up on his hind legs. Going out always made him excited. Deborah gathered the baby's things and changed him into a new outfit and fed him. He fell asleep as she put him into the astro-stroller. This was the finest stroller available, fully mechanized, high end shock absorbers, climate and light entry controlled. Nothing but the best for my child she always said. As they prepared to leave she picked up the baby and Little Bit jumped into the stroller for the short walk over to Buddie's. "Spoiled dog," she said as Little Bit put his feet on the edge of the stroller and looked out as they walked. Deborah had on her big floppy hat and her dark glasses, once again looking very conspicuous in her attempt to be inconspicuous. It was a beautiful sunny day; a cool gentle breeze blew as they took the leisurely stroll to Buddies.

Joshua was waiting with an outside table as they arrived. He stood up as they arrived. "Hello, doctor... Hello, baby...Hello, Little Bit." he greeted them. Little Bit gave an excited bark and jumped into Joshua's lap as soon as he sat down. "This little dog sure is a good judge of character," he said as his face was licked.

"I'm inclined to agree with you," Deborah replied. "Have you ever eaten here?" she asked. "This is your kind of place. All the food is fresh, non-synthesized, and home grown; just don't count on it being very healthy."

"I'm sure that I can find something," he said as he perused the menu. He ordered the garden salad and she ordered the Monster burger with jumbo fries. The waiter brought freshly baked bread and butter after taking their order.

As they waited Deborah started, "What did you mean when you said that I should bring the baby with me when I testify?"

"It was sort of a joke," he answered. "I've looked over the testimony from previous hearings that Senator Leavitt has conducted. He usually starts out with fairly innocuous questions and puts the witness at ease and then a question will come that inevitably leads the witness to 'hang himself'. It is uncanny how he does this. It's like the devil has delivered the question to him, one that is precisely worded to give the poor victim just enough rope."

"But, why bring the baby?" Joshua was silent. Finally, Deborah's face lit up. "I get it. It will distract him; perhaps rattle him enough to make him veer away from his set plan. I'd be surprised if it would work."

Joshua replied, "Adrian Leavitt does not strike me as the type of person who is comfortable around babies or dogs or anything that has an air of innocence. I'd suggest that you bring Little Bit, but I doubt that he'd be allowed to testify, even though he has more firsthand knowledge of the ITP than anyone or anything else. Besides, I'm going to need Little Bit for something else, something that could get Senator Leavitt off your back permanently."

"What could you do that could help and why would you do such a thing? You know, I don't trust that man. Even more, I think that he is dangerous. I have no doubt that he would eliminate anyone that got in his way as easily as we would squash a bug,"

"There is something that I've discovered that may explain a great deal about this whole affair. Have you ever heard of Diblonski Ltd.?"

"I've heard the name. It's some big industrial conglomerate, correct?"

"You're close. It's an industrial, media, mining, entertainment and everything else conglomerate that is involved in everything, including politics. Look at this..." He took a printed page from his pocket and handed it to Deborah. She turned it over and over inspecting it from all angles.

"I'm sorry." she said, "I can't read it. Don't ask me to explain why."

Joshua thought for a moment. "I'm sorry. I shouldn't have been so insensitive. I'll read it for you."

"Thank you," she said, "Although, sometimes I consider my 'disability' a blessing. I think that I have been given a unique perspective, which has allowed me to see things in a way others cannot. It certainly has made me a better scientist and mathematician. In a way, we wouldn't be where we are today if I didn't have my reading disorder. Of course, given recent events, maybe that would have been a good thing. Anyway, what does the paper say?"

"This is the printout of news reports that appeared after Senator Leavitt's first committee hearing. You probably don't remember, but it concerned mining rights on other planets and the bidding process for obtaining government contracts. This is all pretty mundane stuff, but the upshot is that the head of Berry Inc., a leading mineral processing company was shown to have had questionable dealings with criminal elements in the past. He was discredited, his company went bankrupt and the bidding process became very difficult for any small company. Berry Incorporated's stock plummeted after that hearing, even before it had any financial difficulty. At the same time, a different article appeared, just one paragraph, which reported that Diblonski Ltd. Stock jumped up twenty-two points or 30% in one day. It just so happens that the committee ruling was very favorable to Diblonski. This was about twenty years ago. Since then, Senator Leavitt has held hearings once or twice a year. Each one resulted in the discrediting of one or more individuals, very often over some obscure event in the past that was not really relevant. Coincidentally, Diblonski Ltd., benefited every time, their stock value jumping 10-50 % with each hearing." Joshua paused for a moment.

"What does all this have to do me?" Deborah asked.

Joshua answered, "I think that Senator Leavitt and Diblonski are somehow related. Really, I think that Senator Leavitt is Diblonski's puppet. They pull his strings to get what they want."

"That just doesn't add up. Senator Leavitt is probably the most powerful man in the government. Why should he have to be anyone's puppet?"

"If you think about it, he had to get his power somehow. I've heard Adrian Leavitt speak and I found some of his writings archived at the library. He is not the most dynamic person in the universe. As a matter of fact, I'd be surprised if he's ever had an original thought. I'm sure that there is some system in place that feeds him the information necessary to subvert his adversary. That's why you need to watch out. Diblonski wants the ITP shut down and that means shutting you down. They've always done such things by discrediting lead personnel, which is a very clever approach. Think about it. Suppose they eliminated you by paying someone to poison your salad. You'd be gone, but the program would remain, crippled, but not mortally wounded. However, if you and your work were completely discredited, your fall would bring the ITP down also. I'm sure they will try to show that the entire ITP has been a total fraud. The problem now is how to beat them at their own game. I know that you are more resourceful than most people realize, but you'll be up against the entire Diblonski corporation which has awfully long arms."

Deborah wondered, "Before, when you told me to bring my baby...do you really think that would work?"

"Maybe, I don't know, I was just thinking that with you having an unsanctioned child, it would distract the Committee from the real issues, perhaps create a media wave that would overshadow the ITP hearings.

"Perhaps, it could buy some time, but we would need something more to put a halt to Senator Leavitt's plan."

"I have had another thought, but it is even crazier."

"What's that?"

"Discredit Senator Leavitt. Prove that he is Diblonski's lackey, find his Achilles heel and bring him down with a properly placed arrow. Of course, I've researched him through all the available databases and there is nothing publicly available that is in any way damaging."

"What about privately?"

"Well, that's always a possibility. But, digging up any dirt in two days is not going to be easy. I think that I'd have to get into his private office and see what I could find. I guess the future of the entire planet is worth the risk of me going to jail. There is someone I've met that is pretty good at getting into places he doesn't belong. So, here's the plan ..." And Joshua spelled out to Deborah exactly what he was going to try and what she could do to help.

When they finished Joshua saw Deborah push a button on her watch. She noticed his interest. "You don't miss a thing, do you? This is a scrambler. Anyone who tried to intercept our discussion will receive only gibberish. It's my own invention, modified from the old style wrist phones. It is completely undetectable, makes the one eavesdropping think the problem is with their receiver."

Joshua looked surprised, "You continue to amaze me. You're not the innocent naïve person that David believes you to be."

"Oh, I'm still innocent, but there isn't any harm in being careful."

LXI. EDEN

RUTH SAFELY RETURNED TO THE ITP VESSEL. MIRIAM REMAINED IN-side and Ruth closed the door behind her, turned on the outside surveil-lance and waited. Miriam asked what had happened and Ruth recounted the entire story. "This is my fault," Miriam said.

"We all ate the fruit, Miriam. We were all deceived. Even the most beautiful creature can be evil, it seems," Ruth said. "What's important now is to escape from the Edenites." Ruth continued to stare at the monitors, searching for David among the trees and bushes. The day was clear and sunny and she could see a long way in all directions, but there was no sign of David.

David was running back as fast as he could. He didn't bother to look behind as he ran. He had given the Edenite men quite a beating and it would take them sometime to recover. He hoped to be long gone by then, off in space, on his way home or at least to a new, safer world. He smiled to himself. There are worse things than starting a new life with two beautiful women. If it came to that he would have to make the best of it. Of course he really wanted to make it home, he missed rare steaks, synthesized or real, ice cream and his friends. He was getting closer to the ship. I should be visible to the surveillance cameras by now, he thought. Sure enough, Ruth could see him on the monitor, even though he was still about one mile away.

David picked up the pace knowing that he was in the home stretch. Suddenly, he stopped. What's wrong, keep going Ruth thought.

"David's stopped," she said to Miriam, who came over to look at the monitor.

"Look at that," Miriam said and she point to brown object. "That's the lion, but something is wrong."

David had seen the same thing. He was a little apprehensive as he ap-proached, not knowing how he would be received. The lion lay on his side. David saw a large wooden spike protruding from his shoulder. The lion opened his eyes as David approached and let out a weak growl. David felt uneasy as he knelt down to examine the lion's wound. He gently pulled on the spike and loosened it. It seemed to be away from any major arteries, although he was worried that it could have penetrated the lion's chest. Gradually he was able to loosen the spike and remove it. Blood started welling up from the bottom of the wound. David ripped off his shirt and stuffed it into the wound and held pressure, stemming the tide of blood.

Ruth watched, nervously, from the ITP vessel. Hurry up, she murmured, the lion will be OK. She recognized where he was, only about 200 yards from the ship. "Stay here, Miriam. I'm going to see if I can help. She picked up a medical bag as she ran out. Miriam moved into the seat staring at the monitor.

Ruth arrived at the cleared area and stopped at the edge of the woods, about fifty yards from David and the lion. "Is everything OK," she called out, "I brought some bandages."

"Stay where you are. Something isn't right," David yelled. As he said this a volley of stones flew out from the bushes surrounding the clearing. "Get up lion," he shouted.

The lion opened its eyes and started to stand. Stones struck David on the shoulder and back coming from all directions. Ruth watched with great alarm as the stones rained down on David. She bolted out of the woods into the clearing as fast as she could, screaming "Stop...stop." She watched in horror as a stone struck David on the back of the head and he crumpled to the ground. She reached his side and threw herself over him as the stones continued to fly; now striking her as she lay over the now unconscious David. Stones pelted her back and legs as she too was struck on the back of the head. Blood spurted from her scalp.

The lion had struggled to his feet, away from the still bodies of Ruth and David. His first thought was to run away, but something held him. He had a vague remembrance of the unconscious man and woman. He turned to see the stones flying from the trees and bushes and charged into the barrage, roaring and growling. He found one of the women of Eden and picked her up in his powerful jaws and in a quick motion snapped off her right arm. Screams resounded from the other women as they turned and ran from the fierce beast. The Edenite woman fell to the ground as blood gushed from the open socket of her shoulder. The lion walked over to the motionless bodies, gently pushed Ruth off David and lay down beside them. A tear rolled down from its eye.

Miriam had watched the entire spectacle from the ship, horrified. She raced out to the clearing as soon as the Edenite women had left, being careful to close the ship and make it safe from intruders. As she approached the lion growled at her, seeing her as one of the Edenite women. She looked at the great fangs and decided to keep her distance for now. She watched for what seemed to be hours, the lion never budging. David suddenly rolled over and slowly stood up, rubbing the back of his head. He saw the lion lying down. "What happened, big fella," he said quietly. The lion lay stationary as a statue and stared at Ruth. David then saw her, lying in a pool of blood. "No," he screamed as he knelt down. There was no breath from the lifeless lips, no heart pumping beneath her motionless breasts. David saw the Edenite woman lying on the ground, her severed arm beside her, still with a stone in its hand. He picked up the stone and turned to the Edenite, raised his arm and brought the stone crashing to the ground next to her. He knelt down next to Ruth as tears welled up in his eyes. He picked up her lifeless body as Miriam joined him and they silently walked back to the ship.

He laid her body on the seat, covering her with a light sheet. The lion stood at the door as Miriam dressed his wound. When she had finished she went inside to see David preparing the ship for departure. "It's time to go," he said, sadly. "There's nothing left for me here."

"But, David," Miriam started to say, "the Creator..."

"The Creator did this," he interrupted angrily. "There is no good in your Creator to take a life such as hers. If this is what God gives then I'm happy to be from a world rid of such cruelty.

"I cannot believe that. The Creator did not cause this. We did. me and you and Ruth and all of Eden. It's just as happened on your world. We disobey and now we pay the price. Don't you see? Your coming here was no random event. We Edenites had always expected a third and final temptation. Most of us even suspected that your arrival was that temptation. Even with this knowledge we failed. You gave us a glimpse of a new life and, unfortunately, we rejected our Creator to become like you. Even before the fruit was plucked from the tree we had sinned. Eating the fruit was only the final nail in a coffin that we started to build the moment you crashed. Satan has won and now we will spend the rest of eternity trying to find our way back into harmony with our Creator. All I can do is ask his forgiveness."

"Miriam, if I remember my Bible stories, your Creator will not abandon you as long as there is faith. My world has buried any faith far underground. If the people of Eden are wise they will remember their Creator, even in dark times as these. As for me, I will never forget your Creator, nor can I forgive Him for the hurt he has caused."

"What will you do?"

"We must leave now. I will leave the Edenites to themselves. The anger and hatred that was directed at me and they will turn on themselves. Soon the name Eden will fade into myth as your world sinks into war and disease and the people will beg for death to release them from the evil that will fill the world. I may have given them a glimpse of a new life, but the reality that they will live with will not be pretty. You should be happy that you won't have to be a part of it."

"That's where you're wrong. I'm staying here. This is my world; I'm as much of an Edenite as they are. I can't leave."

"But, you are in such danger here. The Edenites won't let you rest. You'll be hunted like a wild beast until you are caught and destroyed."

"Perhaps, but I believe in our Creator. He will protect me. I won't believe that we have been sustained for thousands of seasons to be completely abandoned. The Creator has loved us and he will continue to love us. I have to believe this or else I may as well throw myself off the high cliff."

"I guess there is faith left on this world. I wish you luck and I hope that the Creator will watch over you and all of Eden. But, I have to leave. Perhaps there is still hope for Ruth if I can get help soon. Travel through the interdimensional portal could bring me home in a few minutes. Maybe on Earth something can be done to save her." They were both silent for a minute. "I guess this is good-bye," David said. "At least you won't be alone. Look out there. The lion is waiting for you. Maybe, the two of you can restore some sense to Eden. Anyway, good luck."

Miriam walked out of the ship and was met by the lion. She was wearing dark blue overalls and had a pair of running shoes on her feet. The lion started to growl, but upon seeing the familiar figure the growl became a purr. He walked up to Miriam and rubbed his large muzzle against her shoulder. All the instincts that told him to be fearful and to fight against humans melted as she put her arm around him, more of a pussycat than a fierce beast. The two walked together, unafraid, as David watched them until they were out of sight. I hope they find happiness, he thought, I hope their Creator has not abandoned them. He returned to readying the Falcon for departure.

LXII. CONFRONTATION

DEBORAH WAS REMARKABLY CALM. CONSIDERING THAT SHE WAS scheduled to testify before the Senate Committee today and that her career could be over she seemed complacent. She looked at David Jr., reminding herself of what was truly important. She also was filled with the confidence that comes from knowing one is in the right and that in a just world no amount of lying or distortion of the facts could prevent the truth from being known.

She looked at her wardrobe, a mixture of drab and drabbier. For once in her life she thought that she needed to make an impression. Normally, she would wear a sensible shirt and sensible pants covered by a white coat. That would do for press conferences and committee meetings, but today she needed to stand up to the scrutiny of the entire media world, as well as the Senate Committee. Unfortunately, she was clueless as to how to begin and she didn't even know who to call for advice. Her friends were scientists and mathematicians, most of whom wouldn't know a camisole from cummerbund. She looked at the clock, 8:30 P.M. Her testimony was scheduled to start at 11:00 A.M., not much time to transform herself. A quick search may help and she sat down at the monitor and asked for current fashion. What popped up on the screen left her appalled. The popular clothing was designed to reveal every body part, short of leaving the person naked. She modified the search to current business fashion. A variety of men's clothes appeared. One more modification: Current women's business fashion. A wide range of outfits appeared, ranging from sensible pants suits to outrageous, flamboyant skirts and tops. She picked out a neat, pink dress which was described as guaranteed to win over clients and leave everyone with a positive outlook. She went through the computerized sizing and purchase and then called General Moosewood. "Hello, general," she started. "Can you do me a big favor before you pick me up?"

"Certainly, Deborah, what is it?"

"Could you stop by the Clothier and pick up my new outfit. I thought I needed something new and bright to make a good impression. It's a pink dress. It's already paid for."

"Certainly, my dear. I'll be there by nine fifteen."

"Well, at least that's taken care of." She looked again at David Jr. What am I going to do with you, she thought. Joshua and Little Bit were busy. I guess the general can baby-sit for a little while. She picked the baby up, changed him and dressed him.

I'm ready, she thought, as she sat there in her underwear, waiting for the general.

The bell rang and she saw the general with her dress. She put on her robe and opened the door. "Thank you so much, general, for picking this up." The dress was white, but she was sure that it was pink when she ordered it. "I thought this was a pink dress."

"I know that's what you said when you called me. I asked the saleslady, but she just gave me a funny look. It is a very attractive dress. You'd better get ready or you'll be late," the general replied.

"Here, hold little David."

General Moosewood held the baby with one hand, cradled between his arm and his chest, like a running back holding a football. He swung the child up and down and the baby squealed with delight. "There's a lot of the father in this child," he said. "With any luck he'll have his mother's brains."

Deborah came out in her new dress, which now was pink. "Odd," she said, "the dress is pink now. I guess it was the lighting. Let's go. I have to meet Morrie by ten thirty."

"If you're smart you'll give Morrie the heave ho. Lawyers are only in it for the money and to try to score points with the politicians and bureaucrats. He won't do anything but get in the way."

They walked to the general's car. The day was damp and cool, typical of November and a harsh wind swirled the few fallen leaves around the street. The general drove a four seat Mustang 4, although he left the car on fully automatic. He keyed in the destination and they all sat back to enjoy the quick ride to the senate building.

When they arrived they left the car for the attendant to park. Morrie was pacing back and forth in front of the senate building. Despite the cool day he was flushed and sweating. "Look at the time," he said pointing nervously at his watch. You said you'd be here by ten. It's after ten-thirty and you're supposed to be on the stand at eleven sharp. How can you do this to me and what is this child doing here. We can't have any baby here. Whose baby is this anyway? A fine time to decide to baby-sit."

"Calm down, Morrie," Deborah said. "I'm here and I'm ready to testify. Don't worry about the baby; he won't be in the way. Let's go inside, out of the cold."

"You need to be more serious. This is a Senate Committee, not your Garden Club. You'll make a bad impression."

General Moosewood grabbed Morrie's arm. "Morrie, do you really want to be helpful? Make yourself really useful and stay out here and watch the baby. Deborah, don't you think that Morrie would be more helpful that way?"

"I think you're right. Here's his bag and diaper changer. There are some toys. He's sleeping now so he probably won't be any trouble. Look, they even have a nursery room. You stay here with David and I'll check on both of you when I get a break." Her dress had turned a harlequin color while talking with Morrie.

Before Morrie could raise any objections, Deborah and General Moosewood were gone and he found himself holding the sleeping child. He looked around, somewhat sheepishly, and sat down, gently cradling the sleeping child and, overall, feeling greatly relieved.

Deborah turned to the general as they quickly walked away. "I think that's best for everyone, except, maybe David Jr."

"Don't worry your pretty little head. I'll check in on them. You get in there and show Adrian Leavitt what you're really made of." Deborah's dress now was white.

LXIII. JOSHUA'S PLAN

JOSHUA LEFT DR. Tennyson AND RETURNED TO HIS APARTMENT. ALL his planning was done and it would soon be time to get to work. If he was correct, and his plan was successful, Dr. Tennyson would be safe, there would be a major shakeup in the Senate and it was possible that the current state of society would be permanently altered. If he were wrong he could end up incarcerated, Dr. Tennyson disgraced and David permanently lost somewhere in the universe. Of course, he could just as easily forget the whole thing and go back to the track. That would leave Deborah to fend for herself against Adrian Leavitt, something of which she was certainly capable.

He lay down on the bed, as Chopin floated gently through the air. Little Bit lay beside him, sleeping. The tentacles of Diblonski Ltd., reached far and wide, touching every corner of the world. It would be a very tricky task to pierce its seemingly impenetrable protective shell and expose Adrian Leavitt and possibly Diblonski himself for the demons Joshua knew them to be.

The doubts began to dissolve as his plan began to take shape. He needed to get into Senator Leavitt's office. He was sure that he would find something linking Leavitt to Diblonski, something that would expose the vast corruption that emanated from Diblonski Ltd. Joshua laughed out loud as he pictured himself, standing on an old plastic crate preaching the evils of the corporate world to a population continuously fed a steady stream of drugs, sex and a promise of happiness fueled by the generosity of our government and Aaron Diblonski. No, he would do this job as neatly as possible then high tail it back to the track as quickly as possible.

His room lightened as nighttime turned into morning. Almost time, he thought. With this thought, Little Bit popped up his head and jumped off the bed. He took a long drink of water and then jumped into Joshua's lap, licked his face as if saying that it's time to go. Joshua got up, went to the bathroom and put on a dark shirt and dark pants as he prepared to leave. He opened the Bible and looked at the stamp on the inside cover.

He popped a green dot inside his ear and one inside Little Bit's collar. The two stopped a taxi and took the short ride to the outside of town. The first order of business was to find Richard Cosby and Jameson.

LXIV. MORE TESTIMONY

DEBORAH WAITED IN THE CORRIDOR WHILE THE SENATE INTERPLAN-etary Committee members, media personnel and visitors filled the hearing chamber. A record number of media passes had been issued for her testimony, over 1,800, nearly as many as for the Super Bowl. General Moosewood waited with her. He tried to make some light conversation. "Your baby seems to be growing fast. He looks just like you... Don't worry about your testimony. I've probably already ruined the program anyway."

Deborah looked up at him, "You don't need to make small talk. I know what to expect. It isn't the program that Senator Leavitt is after, it's me. The program will continue in some capacity, with safeguards put in place by Adrian Leavitt to guarantee that it is never successful, but also never-ending. That way the politicians can point to it and say, 'See, we're doing all that we can. In the meantime, could you use our casinos and buy our synthesized food?' That's what they want. You are right about one thing. No matter what I say, the outcome has already been decided."

A uniformed attendant came out of the hearing chamber. Deborah's dress which had looked white a moment before, now was pink. "Dr. Tennyson they are ready for you," the attendant said.

"Thank you," she replied.

"Good luck, Deborah," said the general. He let her go in first with the attendant and then quietly went in and sat in the back of the chamber.

Deborah felt like a lamb heading for slaughter as she walked to the front of the room. She felt a billion eyes upon her. As she reached her seat her demeanor started to change. A bright light shined on her as she walked between the spectators. The image of the lamb faded, replaced by that of a heavyweight contender, entering the ring to challenge the perennial champ. Her dress returned to white.

She sat down in her seat and was connected to the monitoring devices. Her dress remained bright white. As the light illuminated her from above, the media commented that she looked angelic. The image faded as the lights displaying the committee members came on.

"The Senate Interplanetary Committee is now in official session. The item on the agenda is the safety and efficacy of the Interdimensional Transport Protocol. Deborah Tennyson P.h.D. to provide testimony."

Get on with it, Deborah thought. The attendant turned to her, "Do you swear that your testimony will be the whole truth?"

"I do," she replied.

"State your name for the record."

"Dr. Deborah Tennyson."

Senator Leavitt started the hearing, "Dr. Tennyson, I notice that you, too, are not represented by counsel."

She stared into his eyes, "My lawyer has been called away to more important matters. I am perfectly capable of answering any questions that the Committee has." Her words echoed those of General Moosewood a few days earlier

"Very well, doctor. Senator McCally, you have the floor."

"Thank you, Senator Leavitt," Sen. McCally began. He was only in his first term and was one of the youngest members of the Senate at age thirty five. He had gone to Las Vegas University and had made a name for himself in the business world before selling his clothing business to Diblonski Ltd. After this he entered politics, starting as a state Senator in Iowa. After one term he was elected to the national Senate. He was bright and ambitious and greatly indebted to Diblonski Ltd., for helping him advance so quickly in the political world. Senator Leavitt was aware of this and was keeping a very close eye on the junior senator from Iowa.

He started his questions, "Dr. Tennyson, I'm Senator McCally. I've never been much for science. Could you explain to me the practical basis for the ITP and what data you may have demonstrating the efficacy of the program?" He felt very pleased with this initial question; it went straight to the heart of the matter and there was no grandstanding on his part.

Deborah's dress turned the same harlequin pattern that it had been when she met Morrie. "Certainly, Senator, although it has all been detailed by those who previously testified and it is clearly outlined in the simplest of terms in the briefing manual that was sent to all the Interplanetary Committee members."

McCally's face turned red as she answered. Deborah continued, "The ITP was born of mathematics which predicted that there are innumerable, if not infinite, dimensions that coexist with the one that we occupy. Derivation and balancing of the equations predicts that these dimensions have intersections and that there exists a plane outside any dimension. The ITP Committee was able to locate the intersections which are present throughout the universe, we call them portals, and mathematically determine how to pass out of and back into our dimension. A series of tests confirmed our theories, which ultimately led to our current situation. Would you like me to go into greater detail?"

McCally sheepishly said that he had no further questions and her explanation was more than adequate.

"Thank you, Senator," said Senator Leavitt. Another witless fool, he thought. Leavitt took note that Dr. Tennyson was not to be taken lightly. She was going to be a very formidable adversary. "Senator Fitzpatrick," he said.

Arthur Fitzpatrick was middle aged, eighty years old, and usually tried to avoid any controversy. He stayed with the party line but was careful to bring plenty of government resources back to Washington state.

"Professor Tennyson. This Committee is concerned with the safety of the ITP program. You've lost one invaluable pilot and we don't want to lose anymore. Can you tell me what happened to Major David Sanders?"

Her dress turned blue, "He's lost sir."

"I know he's lost, young lady. Why is he lost?"

"I don't know, sir."

"How do you intend to find out?"

"The only thing that I can think of is to send another ship through the portal to get more firsthand knowledge of what occurs when we leave our dimension."

"Isn't that dangerous?"

"Apparently so."

"Why should anyone want to do this then?"

"The ITP Committee was charged by this august Senate committee to find a way to expand humanity's reach outside the confines of our solar system and into the entire universe. I believe the risks were fully weighed by our Committee, your Committee and all the astropilots that are part of the program. We have done this to try to advance and preserve mankind."

"So, you are of the opinion that risking valuable human life is completely justified to better mankind as a whole, that the value of one life is expendable to serve the larger body of humanity?"

"Senator, with all due respect, I don't believe that any life, human, animal or otherwise is expendable. Our Committee has no intention of sending another astropilot to be lost. We have worked diligently to make improvements in ITP vessel safety. Major Sorino has been tireless in his efforts to prepare for an ITP flight that will be safe and, hopefully, successful in returning both he and Major Sanders home in one piece."

"Do you expect me to believe that Major Sanders is still alive?"

"I have not given up hope, Senator. If you examine Major Sanders' record, you will find that he is intelligent, resourceful and extremely capable of overcoming any difficulty that may arise. I believe, I have to believe, that even though he is lost, he is alive and is at this very minute trying to find a way back. Furthermore, the transmission that we did receive as a result of Major Sanders' flight, the one that was sent back through the interdimensional plane, detailed how Major Sanders exited. We know that he did exit." Deborah's eyes started to fill with tears as she said this, one rolled down her cheek as her dress turned deep blue and then black. She dabbed her eyes, composed herself and her dress became a neutral brown.

"I am sorry that I upset you, doctor. I have only one more question, actually more of an observation. Sending our finest pilots one by one into an unknown abyss to be eliminated one by one seems like the height of folly. If this program is to continue and be successful, the next flight would best be served by a fleet of well armed astropilots and soldiers, equipped to deal with any dangers that may be encountered. What is your opinion, doctor?"

General Moosewood was watching and saw Deborah's face become flushed and her eyes narrow slightly. He had seen that look before when she was angry. He knew that there were some fireworks forthcoming.

Deborah replied, "Senator Fitzpatrick that is the most inane suggestion that I have ever heard." Her dress alternated between harlequin and bright red. "There are a dozen reasons why what you suggest would be the greatest act of stupidity in the history of space travel. I will leave it to the media to analyze my response, but I will not dignify such stupidity with any sort of explanation."

The Senator answered, "I am sorry that you have such an attitude, for you have surely lost a supporter today. I have no further questions."

Senator Leavitt interjected, "I think this is a good time to break. We will return in two hours.

During the lunch break media reports poured out. Quickly drawn cartoons portraying Deborah as a Queen dressed in a kaleidoscopic dress surrounded by senators dressed in harlequin outfits with a caption that read, "The Queen with Her Court Jesters." Other cartoons depicted Deborah as Joan of Arc, leading the ITP Committee to victory.

Barney Felder, one of the leading political analysts filed this report: "Today, Dr. Deborah Tennyson, the bespectacled lead physicist and developer of the Interdimensional Transport Protocol testified before the Senate Interplanetary Committee. This Senate Committee has been beating up on the scientific community for years and the last few days have been no exception. But, today, Dr. Tennyson, like an avenging angel, swooped into the testimony seat and may have pulled the ITP program from the ashes back to the land of the living. With a combination of wit, sarcasm and a dress that reflected her every feeling, she has proven to this reporter that the politicians should leave science to the scientists and leave the fate of our world in the hands of people who are actually capable of accomplishing and completing a given task. Dr. Tennyson strikes me as just such a person. Petite in stature, but with a mind that surpasses Einstein, with her large tortoise shell glasses she appears to be another weak pseudo intellectual, but when she speaks the knowledge, intellect and passion for her work shine through..." He went on to explain details of the ITP and the day's events. Similar stories filled every media outlet.

Chaunce Edwards also gave his perspective: "Dr. Deborah Tennyson, the shining star of the ITP program lit up the Senate Interplanetary Committee today with a unique blend of wit and charm. The ITP program had been a jewel in the scientific communities crown until the catastrophic error of sending Major David Sanders on its maiden manned flight. Had the committee the foresight to choose the more levelheaded Major Anthony Sorino, they would not find themselves in the pickle they face today. I doubt that even such an intellectual colossus as Dr. Tennyson will be able to salvage the wreckage wrought by Major Sanders..." and so it went, the usual diatribe railing against David Sanders, but with back handed admiration for Dr. Tennyson.

Senator Leavitt, who had not even questioned her, quickly left the hearing chamber, refusing to answer any questions. This can't be, he thought, this little girl was supposed to be an easy mark. By the time I get to her it may be too late. He knew that he would not be able to find any intellectual weakness, he would have to attack her personally, an area where she was much more vulnerable.

He went back to his office to plan for the next day and to see if there were any messages that required his attention. Thankfully, there were none. He did notice that there was a light flashing on the security system that safeguarded his office. He called one of his aides, "Could you please attend to this, one of the sensors is out." The aide replied, "Yes, sir, I noticed that earlier and I've already called the Senate Security agency. They'll have someone out tomorrow morning. The sensor that is out is the floor level motion and heat probe. The office should be OK, unless someone six inches tall plans to break in."

"I suppose it can wait," Senator Leavitt said. He turned his thoughts to the hearings. He decided that the line of questioning that he had planned (provided by Mr. Diblonski) would still be adequate to accomplish his objective. Dr. Tennyson may have her brief moment in the spotlight. By this time tomorrow her momentary triumph would be a distant memory. He ordered some lunch and made his way back to the hearing chamber.

The afternoon session was uneventful. The remaining senators were hesitant to ask any serious questions and the day's session ended early. Deborah was grateful for the break. She left quickly, picked up David Jr. and disappeared home. She ignored all requests for interviews and shut off all media outlets at her home. Tomorrow's events would make or break the ITP and she wanted to be able to think without any distractions. She had enough insight to realize that Senator Leavitt would not be able to challenge her on the science of the ITP. She had already addressed safety concerns and the importance of the program. No, it would be personal. Although she had always kept her personal life private it was, in general, very difficult in this day and age to keep private matters private. She reasoned that she would be questioned about her relationship with David and their baby. As she thought more and more about it, she realized that Joshua had been right... again. Her shield would be David Jr.

She picked him up and cradled him to her breast. He looked up at her with his sharp, dark eyes with a very serious look (for an infant) on his face. "It seems like you know what's happening," she said softly. With these words, he yawned and fell asleep. Deborah fixed herself a simple meal and tried to get some rest. She wished that David were there with her. She knew that he was a bit of a scoundrel, but he could always find the perfect way to allow her to relax and unwind. Lying around here is not going to help. She changed her clothes; put David Jr. into his cart and she went out. She returned about an hour later, tired, but much less anxious. She lay down with the baby and they both fell asleep.

The next morning she and David Jr. were up just after sunrise. She fed him and got herself some fruit, bread and juice for breakfast and put on one of her older dresses. General Moosewood picked her up at 9:30 A.M.and drove her to the hearing chamber. As she got out, carrying the baby, the general stayed in the car.

"Aren't you coming?" she asked.

"I'll be back in a little while. I have some business to attend to at my office. Good luck." And he drove away.

Deborah was surrounded by memedia types as she made her way to the chamber. "Are you worried? Do you think Senator Leavitt is worried? Whose baby is that? Do you think the Senate Committee is a farce?" Questions came rapid fire. She ignored them all as she entered the chamber lobby and was ushered into the hearing chamber.

The Senate Committee was already seated, except for Senator Leavitt, who entered almost simultaneously. Like boxers of old they briefly stared at each as each took their seat. Deborah was still holding David Jr. People whispered to each other as the usual murmur of the crowd rose to a higher level.

"Dr. Tennyson, is that a baby you are holding?" Senator Leavitt asked.

"Yes, it is, Senator. You're very observant. You could be a doctor," she replied, facetiously. A snicker ran through the crowd.

"Of course I can see that it is a baby. Why is it here?"

"I couldn't find a sitter, so I decided to bring him. You don't mind, do you?"

"I have nothing against babies, but I don't think a Senate hearing is the proper place for such a young child."

"Well, I had no choice. Like I said, I couldn't find a sitter."

"Whose child is that?"

"Why, it's mine of course. You don't think that I would bring just any baby with me do you?"

Senator Leavitt did not like the way the questioning was going. But, he thought, perhaps I can use this to my advantage. He decided to change his planned questioning to one that he thought would be more fruitful. "Is that child a properly sanctioned baby?" He knew that it wasn't and was sure that he had her in the noose.

"Certainly not. I know that I should have ended the pregnancy when I could have like a good little citizen, but when I saw his little heart beating I just knew that he was meant to come into the world."

Another loud murmur came from the crowd. Such an important public figure ignoring all the laws and regulations, what a scandal. The memedia were all salivating at the prospective stories and commentary germinating in their minds.

Deborah continued, "Oh, I thought about doing the right thing, but, when David. I mean Major Sanders was lost; I just had to keep him. It's like a part of his father is still here and I just couldn't flush him down the toilet."

Senator Leavitt, for a moment, was speechless and then he felt a sense of relief. Everything would work out better than he had planned. This sense of elation was short-lived. "You are telling this Committee that Major David Sanders is the father of this unsanctioned child?"

"Exactly right, senator. You really are perceptive. Major Sanders and I started our relationship before he was selected to be the lead pilot. I guess

I was careless and David Jr. here is the result. To his credit, Major Sanders did want me to terminate the pregnancy, and probably thinks that I did, but I figured that I could raise him, even if the government won't help. Why, if one thinks about it, should the government be telling me when and where I can reproduce? Shouldn't it be my choice to bring a child into this world?"

Senator Leavitt looked flustered and his face was turning a bright red. "But, such rules are put into place for a reason. We have limited resources and the population is exploding. It is every individual's responsibility to do their part to safeguard the future of this planet." There was a smattering of applause as the Senator finished reciting the standard government propaganda.

Deborah responded, "Of course, you're right, but what's one more child in this world. Besides, you've forgotten who I am. I designed the ITP and, despite this Committee's misgivings, I know that it will be the path that will provide the resources that will sustain the human race no matter how the population grows. I think it is a woman's right to choose to bring life into this world. How do we know how many Plato's, Lincoln's, Curie's or Einstein's have been lost? And this child, why, he should have all the rights of anyone, although, if you want to forego assigning him a lawyer I'll bet he will be grateful in the years to come. Oh, and one other thing. You've just stated that we have limited resources and the population is exploding. The ITP is intended to help mankind deal with those issues, to open up an infinite number of possibilities for expansion and resources. Yet here you are holding hearings into the ITP's safety, which is really a veiled attempt to shut down the program and protect your and these other politician's personal interests. Believe me I am more upset than anyone that Major Sanders has been lost, but this program represents such a giant leap forward for mankind that the dangers or 'chances' we must take pale in comparison to the potential benefits."

A roar of laughter and applause came from the assembly and even a couple of senators joined in the ovation. At this point David Jr. started crying and all sense of order was lost. Senator Leavitt looked beaten as security personnel vainly tried to restore order. Reluctantly, Senator Leavitt adjourned the hearing for the day.

Senator Leavitt quickly exited to his house, well away from the hearing chamber and the media's questions. There were no messages waiting for him. He felt a little uneasy, not sure if it meant he was doing a good job or if Mr. Diblonski had lost all confidence. He hoped that tomorrow's testimony would bring him back into Diblonski's favor.

Deborah was swamped by the media as she left the chamber, carrying David Jr. She had no choice but to make a statement:

"Today's events were a milestone for the downtrodden members of our society. Those wanted, but unrecognized children are humans with the same inalienable rights bestowed upon them as any person properly sanctioned by our 'benevolent' government. We are given so much candy that we grow fat and complacent, accepting any edicts with a shrug as we take another pill, spend another night at the casino in self-indulgent pleasure, all with our government's approval. It's time for all of us to take a good look at why we are here on this planet. We should pull together to solve the problems that we will face in the future. Burying our heads in the sand and blindly following a government that has its self preservation as its sole motivation will surely lead to our ultimate destruction. The answer is not in destroying our children; rather it is in allowing our children the freedom to imagine and to reach for the stars. I hope that what I showed today will be the start of a new perspective that will foster the talents and imaginations of all the people, not just for our immediate pleasure, but also for the future well-being of all of mankind and the planet Earth. Thank you. I will have more to say tomorrow."

She made her way to her apartment, put David Jr. to bed and fell on her bed, exhausted. Her words sounded strong and confident, but at that moment she felt weak and alone. She worried that her audacious comments would not be seen very favorably by the powerful people behind the government. She didn't want to disappear and she worried about David Jr.

LXV. THE GREEN DOT

THE "GREEN DOT" WAS DEVELOPED BY PICOTECHNOLOGIES, THE CULmination of fifteen years of research into picophysics and processors. The technology used charged matrices on a molecular and atomic level to store information and transmit data.

The result was an extremely powerful personal information device that was the size of an old fashioned penny. The device was usually placed in front of or behind the ear. Minimal power, provided by body heat and local electrical variances, as well as sunlight allowed the Green Dot to receive and transmit voice and image data, store audio and images, personal data, health information and almost everything else from within its memory cells or via telemetry from a home information resource center.

The device became ubiquitous, initially being seen on all the important people, but eventually making its way to the general population. Initially,

The Green Dot was manufactured by Picotechnologies and distributed by Diblonski Ltd. As demand increased, Picotechnologies production capacity was strained to the limit and the company was forced to merge with its distributor. Diblonski Ltd., then partnered with various governments and made the "Dot" available to anyone that wished to own one. The "Dot" became indispensable to the general population, keeping families linked and allowing for continuous flow of information and news.

The device could store almost infinite data and when coupled with a small amplifier could project holographic images and provide continuous linkage to other people or computers.

Everywhere, people could be seen sporting their Green Dots. As time passed and the technology improved, the Dot became smaller and no longer had to be green. Even though it became available in millions of colors, even flesh tones that allowed it to be almost invisible, green remained the most popular color.

It became a common sight to see people sitting serenely as the Green Dot played their music, showed their videos and cinema, sheltering them from or connecting them to the world outside. A faint glow arose from the Dot while it was active. Therefore, anyone passing by would know that the individual was occupied and not to be disturbed.

The Dot was responsive to changes in body physiology. It could sense fear, anger, love, contentment and a multitude of other bodily states. These were sensed via transcutaneous and EEG monitors, sensing hormonal and electrophysiologic alterations. The Dot could then implement preprogrammed responses to the physiologic change. For example, if an individual felt a strong attraction to another person, the Dot would sense this and provide suggestions that helped lead to a connection. One Dot could even contact another to see if there was a mutual attraction.

The Dot became an essential component to many routine daily activities, increasing efficiency and productivity. Initial fears that unscrupulous people could use the Dot to illegally acquire personal information were quickly dispelled. Every individual had his personal "cell" number programmed into the Dot with security codes that were required before information on the Dot could be accessed. Each individual's unique EEG sequence also was needed for access. The Green Dot was not only efficient, but also very safe. It truly was good for everything but cooking breakfast as the numerous advertisements claimed.

LXVI. AFTER THE FALL

DAVID STOOD AT THE ITP VESSEL ENTRANCE AS MIRIAM LEFT WITH the lion. "Good luck," he called out as the two disappeared into the dense forest. He went inside, closing and locking the entry door behind him. He activated the security perimeter, an added precaution against unwanted guests.

Miriam and the lion were a long way from the Edenite camp. She looked with sadness at Eden. Once bright and beautiful flowers and fruit lay rotting on the ground. Insects of all types crawled and flew about, feasting on the decay that Eden had become. A thick mist rose from a swamp that had been a rushing river only a short time ago.

Miriam walked despondently, silently. Finally, she and the lion reached the Edenite camp. They stayed hidden in the dense bushes that surrounded the clearing where the Edenites had constructed makeshift shelters. She waited with the lion until mealtime. This would be the best time to approach, she thought. They would all be together and there would be less opportunity for surprises.

It was late afternoon when she saw the women gathering food. When they had all reclined to eat, Miriam and the lion walked into to camp.

"Isaac, Rebekah, I have returned," she called out. The Edenites stood up almost as one, each looking around for a stone to throw. The lion roared loudly and started to charge. The Edenites froze with fear.

"My fellow people of Eden. I am not here to bring destruction, rather words of peace and reconciliation."

Isaac replied, "If you are being truthful, then send the lion away and we will talk."

Miriam stood silently and whispered in the lion's ear. The great beast withdrew into the forest, leaving Miriam alone, unarmed and completely vulnerable.

Isaac's eyes were filled with hate and anger as he picked up a large stone. The others quickly followed, approaching Miriam, preparing to cast their stones and kill her. As Isaac drew back his arm, there was a crash like thunder, a bright light appeared and the stones disintegrated into dust.

The booming voice of the Creator rang out, "People of Eden, what have you done?"

Fearful, The Edenites fell to the ground. Isaac, his eyes closed and his head held tightly to the ground responded with a wavering voice, "Creator, we are avenging your name. The woman, Miriam, brought us fruit to eat and now our world is filled with woe."

"Did you also eat the fruit? Are you any less guilty than she? Judgment is reserved for me," the Creator replied with anger in his voice. "Satan has deceived you. The true agents of his evil approach us even now." The unicorns appeared from the edge of the clearing.

The Creator turned to them, the light surrounding Him shining more brightly. "You were my favorites, exalted above all the other creations and you chose the evil of Satan," declared the Creator as he stared at the beautiful beasts.

One of the unicorns replied, "You have loved us unconditionally. Surely, you can forgive us our transgression. We were deceived by the Evil One." There was no remorse in his voice.

The Creator answered, "Even now there is no repentance of the evil you have brought. You deserve death. But, you will live, forever to be a reminded of the sin that you brought into the world."

A bright light flashed and there was rumble that started softly, but grew stronger until it was a loud roar. The unicorns stood proudly, their heads held high and their bright eyes staring defiantly at their Creator. The polished horn in the middle of their head began to grow dull, the bright eyes became small and dark, the smooth white coat became gray and coarse, and the long graceful legs short and thick. The quick, bright minds became dull and fearful.

The people fell back, frightened by the sight as the unicorns lumbered away, confused and frightened by this transformation.

Miriam started to approach the Creator, but before she could take a second step she was stopped by His booming voice, as He addressed her:

"You had the choice to stop this evil, but even after all the lessons and teaching about temptation you were weak. However, only you have remained faithful to me, only you have repented and asked forgiveness. You will live, but your life will be separate from all people. Only the beasts and plants shall you have for companions."

He turned to the remaining Edenites, "People of Eden, you have made a mockery of all that I have created; all that was good has been made unclean by your sin. Now you will leave the Paradise that I created for you. You will work to live and live with the pain that your sin has brought into the world, and you will know death. This evil will live from generation to generation, never leaving until I decide that you are ready to return to me.

With these final words the sky darkened, there was a loud crash, followed by a bolt of lightning. The ground opened up, creating a wide, bottomless chasm between Miriam and the rest of the Edenites. Miriam turned and ran into the forest, joined by the lion. The Edenites cowered on the ground, frightened and confused, afraid to look at their Creator or each other.

When they were sure that the Creator had departed, they stood up. Jacob, who was second eldest, pointed at Isaac, "You have led us to our doom. It was you who insisted upon vengeance." He picked up a large stone and hurled it at Isaac. The rest of the Edenites hurried to join the execution. Rebekah ran to her stricken mate. Stones rained down upon them until their bloody, lifeless bodies lay motionless and the Edenite mob was exhausted of both strength and stones.

The anguished mob looked at the fruit of its work, then scattered, as vultures circled overhead and flies descended upon the bloody bodies of Isaac and Rebekah.

Miriam stopped to rest once she was well into the forest, her heart full of fear. The grass was cool as she sat down, the lion staying at her side. There was a clear stream running through the woods and she stooped to take a drink. When she looked up she saw the bright reflection of a man in the water, cloaked in light, only his head visible to her.

The man spoke with a gentle voice, "Miriam, Miriam you have committed a great sin, but your faith is also great. Although it is your destiny to live your life apart, with only the beasts and plants for companions, I will always be with you. If you despair or weary of your solitary life you need only look up and call and I will come to you."

Miriam stared at the man's face. He had dark, olive skin and black hair. She felt as if his dark eyes pierced her soul. The voice, although gentle, was powerful, as if the rocks would start to dance if commanded by that voice. She looked away for a brief moment; when she looked back, he was gone.

She put her arm around the lion's broad shoulders. The wound miraculously was completely healed without any scar. The fear in her heart had also healed. Together, she and the lion walked slowly through the forest; not knowing what challenges lay ahead, but confident that God would always be at their side.

LXVII. ESCAPE FROM EDEN

DAVID LOOKED AROUND HIS SHIP. RUTH WAS LYING IN A PORTABLE chair, wrapped in a blanket. Everything was stowed away, very neatly. Miriam's doing, he thought.

He sat down at the console and ran a final check on each system. All systems were functioning within acceptable levels, save medical Therapeutics. He looked with anguish at the large INOPERABLE flashing on the monitor.

medical Diagnostics listed Ruth's injuries: fractured skull, subdural hematoma with herniation, fractured ribs one to ten on the right and four to ten on the left, bilateral pulmonary contusion, cardiac contusion, lacerated spleen, lacerated liver, renal contusion, bilateral fractures of the tibia and fibula. Five flatlines running across the monitor indicated death.

David had run a quick diagnostic on himself, revealing fractured ribs seven to ten on the right, right pulmonary contusion and laceration of the liver. He felt only mild discomfort as he prepared the ITP vessel for take-off. Fuel calculations suggested that he had adequate reserves to get to the ITP portal and to pass through. Once inside the interdimensional plane it would be guesswork as far as getting home. His previous experience left him doubting that he would find his way back to Earth. However, he could not stay in Eden and there was a chance that if he could find his way back to Earth's solar system quickly enough Ruth could be restored She had been dead about forty minutes. Restoration of life function within 180 minutes could allow her to return to her normal self, without permanent damage.

Ships sensors and calculators indicated that the portal could be reached in less than thirty minutes, from there passage through the one-dimensional plane should take eight minutes, return to Earth would take several hours, but if an astroplane with functioning medical Therapeutics was nearby, it was possible she could be saved.

It was time to leave. The automated, computer guided lift-off was initiated. The ship lifted straight up, above the trees, rose to a safe level and suddenly activated. The Edenites saw a flash of light which was followed by a loud boom, mistaking the ship for thunder as it blasted into space. Miriam looked up and softly said, "God be with you, David," as the lion roared.

David followed the trail he had left months before, picking up speed as he approached the portal. The ITP sensor was inoperable. He knew from the ships flight data the exact location of the portal and the velocity and vibration values that had allowed his exit from the interdimensional plane. He put these numbers into the ITP activation sequence. The ship approached 0.19c and he started the vibration activator. Computer models indicated perfect escalation of vibration levels as the extrapolation suggested that vibration would match portal energy output. As the ship reached the portal location velocity was 0.2c, vibration hit 2.975×10 sixth.

In an instant he was through the portal. He had strapped Ruth and himself in and taken all precautions to prevent a repeat of his previous experience. This time, however it was completely different. The cabin filled with bright white light. There was no sudden force slamming into him. As quickly as the light had filled the cabin, the ship came to a complete stop, all power readings went to zero and everything went pitch black. Reserve power came on for a brief moment, before it, too, blacked out.

David lay there, outside time and space, his ship dead and the clock ticking for Ruth. He was starting to think that he should have just taken his chances in Eden.

LXVIII. BREAK IN

JOSHUA AND LITTLE BIT LEFT JUST AS THE SUN WAS RISING. DEBOR-ah's testimony was to start later in the day and he needed to finish this task before Senator Leavitt finished questioning her. If patterns of past hearings held true, Leavitt would allow the other committee members to start the hearing, while he studied his adversary. Deborah would probably testify for two or three days; Joshua figured that he would have all of this day to complete the job.

He and Little Bit headed to the outskirts of the city. He had found Richard Cosby easily before; he hoped that he would be just as successful this time. He carried the Bible that Cosby had given him, hoping that it would be both a shield and a passport, allowing him to find Cosby quickly. They started in the area where they had encountered the old sentinel, but found the area deserted without any signs of life. This could be bad, he thought. His plan would never work without the kind of help that Cosby and his gang could provide.

"Come on, Little Bit, let's walk a further. We'll check out those old buildings." Joshua pointed to a group of rundown brick buildings, the few windows blown out and a large brick wall with barbed wire along the top, surrounding them, and acting as a never tiring guard against unwanted guests. This looks like either an old prison or school," Joshua said, "Not that there's much difference between the two. Either way, it looks like a good place to hide out." Little Bit ran ahead and disappeared through an open gate. Joshua arrived a minute later, walking into a courtyard between the buildings. The grass had long ago been choked by weeds, the ground was littered with fallen bricks and broken glass. Little Bit was already there, sniffing around the tall weeds. As they walked along an old gravel path, the gate clanged shut and they found themselves surrounded by at least a dozen youths, each brandishing the latest in high powered assault weaponry.

"Not what I'd hoped for," Joshua said softly to Little Bit. "Lie down," Joshua said. The little Westie immediately lay down at Joshua's feet. Joshua sat down, pulled out his Bible and started to read out loud. "The Lord is my Shepherd, I shall not want..." Twenty-Third Psalm is as good as anything, he thought.

His would be assailants came closer, lowering their weapons. Little Bit let out a low growl as they approached. "Quiet," Joshua whispered.

"We have never heard such words," one of the young men stated.

"Do you know a Richard Cosby?" Joshua asked, ignoring the young man's words.

"Please, sir, would you read us more from your book."

"If you help me, I will read as much as you care to hear. Perhaps I will find one that you may keep for your own. Now, I ask you again, do you know Richard Cosby?"

The one that seemed to be the leader answered, "Of course, he's here, in that building over there. Follow me; I'll take you to him."

"Thank you," Joshua replied. Something struck him as strange, something about these young men wasn't right. I'll figure it out later he thought, as he tried to focus on the more urgent task at hand.

Inside one of the old buildings, Joshua was brought to Cosby and Jameson. "I brought your Bible back," he said, holding the book out to Cosby, "it's a little worn."

"It's yours to keep," Cosby said, "I know that you haven't gone to all this trouble just to return a book. What do you really want?"

"OK, OK...I need your help. I need to get into a Senator's office, specifically, Senator Adrian Leavitt's. There's something in there I need to find. Something that, I hope, will be of great help to a friend of mine who's in trouble."

"Who's your friend?"

"Deborah Tennyson. This is critical for her to allow her to continue her work. What she is doing is of the greatest importance to everyone, even those that have been displaced by society."

Cosby sat down. "That's a tall order. Senate offices are well protected. There are all sorts of alarms and security devices."

"I know that, but if you can get me inside the building and up to his office, I think I can find a way to get past the security system.

Cosby scratched his head and thought for a moment. "I think that I can help you. A simple diversion should get us into the building and past the guards. Let me talk to Aldous and his boys outside." Cosby left the room to speak to the gang; Jameson sat silently staring at Joshua and Little Bit. She didn't trust outsiders.

She had been traveling down a path towards self destruction until Richard Cosby found her. She had been cast out of her home at a young age;

her genetic manipulations had been unsuccessful, leaving her flawed, with a personality prone to violent, uncontrollable outbursts. As she grew, she became more dangerous. She was huge and muscular, and even though she was "only a girl," she was capable of causing serious injury or killing with only her powerful hands. She had been arrested by "government" authorities, interrogated about a matter she had no knowledge of, which resulted in her losing most of her tongue. She was surviving in the streets when Cosby had found her and showed her that there was a way that could free her from the violent life she had lived, truth that could remove the hatred and anger that had festered inside her head for so many years. Cosby's teaching had left her with only love for a spiritual world that she knew was all around. Now, she would only do what Cosby instructed, protecting him at all costs. Her imposing size was usually all that was necessary to keep her benefactor safe from any would be assailants. It was rare that Cosby actually asked her to truly harm another person.

Cosby returned. "It's all set, but we'll need to wait until nightfall. The boys out there will get some of their friends, enough to create a diversion spectacular enough to draw the attention of most of the security forces. This should give us the opportunity to get into the building. You'll still need to deactivate all the security devices in the office."

"I've got a plan for that," Joshua said. "I guess we have nothing to do but wait until it gets dark."

"You wait here; Jameson and I will get some food and water. We'll be back in a minute."

When Cosby got Jameson into the next room he whispered, "We need to be careful, I'm not sure I trust this guy. You need to be ready if we need to do something." Jameson nodded. The two loaded up a tray with a variety of food and bottles of water and brought them in for Joshua and Little Bit.

LXIX. FINAL PLANS

MAJOR SORINO WAITED UNTIL DEBORAH WAS TO START HER TESTImony. The ITP hearings, particularly the testimony of the diminutive lead scientist, had become a major media circus and people were riveted to their varied media devices, awaiting the inevitable verbal battle between the doctor and Senator Leavitt.

Sorino met Scully in the ITP Committee room. They made no attempt to hide themselves from the security monitors. Nothing could be more natural than the current lead pilot for the ITP meeting with its chief engineer.

"Everything is ready for liftoff from here rather than the lunar surface. As soon as the word is given you're ready to go. This new ITP vessel has a safe liftoff mode that will allow it to take off even from populated areas. Once you are airborne and clear of any hazards, sublight drive can be engaged to get you into space. From there you are on your own," Scully explained.

"Excellent," Sorino replied, "But, I'm leaving today."

Scully looked confused. "You can't do that. There aren't any support personnel, and there is the little matter of the Senate committee ban. You know that there will be Senate security forces around the vessel. Look at the latest memedia reports." Scully hit a button and the image of Monica Reynaldo appeared, Senator Leavitt's media aide. She was blonde with perfect face and body, typical of Senator Leavitt's staff. She was standing in front of a camera, holding a microphone.

"Rumors are circling around the ITP compound that there will be attempts at unauthorized ITP flights as the Senate hearings reach their climax today with the testimony of Dr. Deborah Tennyson. These rumors have compelled the Senate committee to increase surveillance and security around the only functional ITP vessel and its associated launch computers. All launch sequences have now been removed from the launch computers. There are armed security forces around all launch controls and the ITP vessel around the clock. Any unauthorized persons approaching either will immediately be disabled."

Sorino smiled. "This may be better than I'd hoped. I don't need the launch computer, just the ships computer. All I need to do is get past the guard in the hangar deck. There's probably only one guard, two at the most. Of course they'll be equipped with the latest anti-intruder technology. I think that we can use that to our advantage."

Scully did not look happy. "I think you're crazy."

"Maybe so, but, I have to go before the Senate hearings are finished. Once they're done and the decision is made to shut down the ITP program the ship will immediately be disassembled. Now's the time for you to make a choice. You can help me, in which case you may become a big hero for playing a role in finding an important ITP pilot, proving that the ITP is not a failure, or you can go home, in which case I will go on alone. As for me, there is no option but to do this now or else give up completely on Major Sanders and the ITP program."

Scully saw a look on Sorino's face that he had never seen before. The usual calm demeanor had been replaced by wild desperation. This can't all be for Major Sanders, he thought. Those two barely tolerated each other.

He looked into Sorino's eyes. "Just tell me what's going on. It must be more than Major Sanders."

"You're right," Sorino answered, looking calmer. "You know that the ITP is of vital importance to the continuation of humanity on Earth. Unless we are able to find new inhabitable worlds, life on Earth is doomed. The Senate refuses to acknowledge the big picture, aiming to scuttle the program for their own, petty short term gain."

Scully had heard the ITP party line before. "OK, I'll help you, major. But at the first sign of trouble, I'm gone. Just tell me the truth; what's the real reason?"

Sorino looked at the ground, "I have to go, I have to find out what's out there. If I don't I'll go crazy or worse."

Scully put his arm around the major, "OK...OK, let's do it, then."

LXX. INTERDIMENSIONAL VOID

DAVID SAT IN THE BLACK STILLNESS NOT SURE HOW TO PROCEED. Even the slight luminescence from his watch was black. He put his hands directly in front of his eyes and saw nothing. He had never felt such complete helplessness. This is definitely the end he thought. He reached out to feel Ruth's body. He felt the blanket that had been covering her, and the lifeless body. If we have to die together in this black void, then so be it, he said to himself.

He sat there in the darkness for hours, perhaps days, he had no idea. It was strange; he never felt hungry or thirsty, never had the urge to urinate. He knew that he was still breathing, but more out of habit than necessity. He even tried a test. He held his breath to see if all his bodily functions had stopped. He held his breath for what seemed to be an hour. Nothing happened. He felt his pulse and there was nothing.

This is very strange, he thought. No need to breath, drink, eat, pee or poop. I must be dead, although this is certainly not my idea of heaven. A black box devoid of sight, smell or taste definitely was not heaven. He could still feel, however, although there was nothing but lifeless glass and metal consoles and switches around him. In the darkness, he thought about all that he had left behind, his carefree lifestyle, Deborah, Little Bit, Joshua and the words of Fyodor came back to haunt him. Well, I've had a taste of joy and suffered great sorrow. What's next?

Well, at least I'm with Ruth, even if she's dead. He eased out of his chair and carefully felt his way through the blackness towards her chair. He only banged his knee once as he reached her. He felt the blankets that were covering her, but when he reached underneath, she was wasn't there.

Now, David was worried. He climbed into Ruth's chair and lay in the darkness. He slowly came to realize that he was alone, lost and there was nothing that he could do. He had always managed to find his way out of any fix, either by his wits or physical prowess, but now he truly was helpless. He was suspended in time, without hope, not even the hope that death could release him. He lost all sense of time, laying there for what may have been two hours or two months...

Then, he felt a slight cool breeze. He thought he heard a faint whirring sound and an occasional knock. He looked up to see a single light in the blackness. The light very gradually grew brighter, the whirring became louder and the knocking more frequent. The breeze grew stronger and within it there was a slight scent of what he was sure was freshly baked cookies.

The light continued to brighten, the noises louder, as the wind whirled around. David strapped himself into the chair and pulled the blanket over his head. The light became intense, blinding just as the noise became painfully loud, deafening. An even louder boom followed and the light disappeared, the wind stopped and the noise replaced by silence. He could still smell cookies. David opened his eyes to see that the solitary light had been replaced by innumerable tiny lights twinkling in what looked like a clear night sky, although David did not recognize any star patterns. The lights slowly rotated.

David felt a slight sense of movement. He felt like he was moving closer to one of the lights. The light grew larger until he could clearly see that it was a galaxy, one he recognized as his own Milky Way. He accelerated, moving at what seemed to be faster than light speed, as he entered the galaxy, zooming towards one of the stars. As he approached the star, he slowed down, coming to rest above a planet that he was sure was the Earth.

He watched as it rotated, relieved that he was home. However, something wasn't quite right. The continents were shifted, the oceans were different. He felt a sense of movement again and came to rest on the planet's surface. The ground was hard, rocky, without plants and only darkness filled the sky. He heard a rumbling voice, "Let there be light." Suddenly, he could clearly see the world that was around, harsh, devoid of life.

David watched as creation unfolded before his eyes, Day and Night, plants, dinosaurs, birds and fish all appeared. He circled the globe as different plants and animals came into existence. He came to rest in a lush jungle, which he immediately recognized as Eden, filled with the familiar plants, trees and animals he had come to know in the past few months. A strong wind came up, swirling the dust. "Let us make man in our own image," he heard. The dust began to take shape and David saw Adam. He saw God take him by the hand and lead him into the garden and he saw Adam eat the food that God provided. Adam paused at each new plant and animal, studied it and gave it a name. David saw God, cloaked in bright light, walk with Adam. The face of God revealed love and kindness, just what one would expect from a loving Father.

Adam spent days, months, years walking through the garden, studying and naming each new plant and animal.

David heard God's voice again, "It is not right for man to be alone." Adam fell asleep, David saw God approach, open his right side and take a portion of a rib from Adam's right side. From this God fashioned the most beautiful, perfect woman that David had ever seen. David remembered the pain he had felt in his right side and a tear came to his eye as he thought about Ruth.

Adam awoke, looked into her eyes, took her hand and the two walked away together hand in hand. She was named Eve.

David watched them live happily together, always together, in the garden. Then the serpent approached. "Get away," David yelled, but they couldn't hear. David cried as he saw Adam and Eve live through the pain of their fall from grace, driven from the garden to toil in the wild, dangerous world. In the garden they had been shielded, but now they were separated from God and his protection.

Adam was a loving husband, tireless worker and Eve a devoted wife. She reminded David of Ruth and he felt tears well up in his eyes again. She gave him many children. David saw Cain murder Abel as all of Biblical history unfolded before his eyes.

Noah, the flood, Abraham, Joseph, enslavement all played out as real as anything David had ever seen before.

He marveled at Moses, battling Pharaoh in a test of wills, as the Israelites were freed from bondage. He felt sorry for Pharaoh's soldiers and horses as they vanished into the Red Sea. He watched Moses prod and cajole and scold his people through forty years of wandering through the desert, suffering through every second with them.

Finally, the Promised Land; David felt sad for Moses as he was allowed to only see the end of his long quest from a distance, but not be a part of the journey's end. He thought of Joshua Smith as Joshua of the Bible lead the Israelites across the Jordan River, into the Promised Land. He cheered as the walls of Jericho tumbled down. He watched Deborah triumph, seeming so unlike the Deborah that he knew. Judges gave way to kings, the madness of Saul, the great faith and greater sin of King David fascinated him. The series of faithless kings saddened him as the Israelites turned away from God.

He felt Job's pain, heard David singing Psalms, saw Solomon teaching the people. He even blushed at the Song of Solomon.

He wept uncontrollably as Ruth appeared, so beautiful, the same Ruth he had known and loved, but different, like an actress playing a role.

The prophets frightened him as the people defied God and were taken into exile. He watched empires rise and fall, Babylon, Persia, Greece and finally Rome.

He felt great peace as Jesus was born. And, as Jesus started his ministry, David began to understand, finally, that God was always there, watching, helping, until he finally came Himself, to tell all the people, once and for all, His ways.

It was clear to David that Jesus, in every way, had God's complete purpose and power. This is God's final triumph, David thought. But, no, there was Jesus betrayed, beaten and given up to die a horrible death. David agonized as he saw Jesus' bloody body nailed to the cross. David screamed in terror as he saw the Roman soldier driving the stake through Jesus' hand. Jesus was silent. The soldier looked directly at David. It was David's own face staring back at him, then turning to drive the huge nail through Jesus' feet, blood splattering everywhere.

As Jesus hung on the cross, the light around his head faded. Demons of every type tormented Jesus as all the sins of the world were heaped upon his head. Jesus spoke and then He was dead. David saw Jesus' lifeless body in the tomb; then He rose and descended into the land of the dead, ministering to all those who had passed away, giving them hope.

David cried uncontrollably and wished that he could die, unable to get the image of himself nailing Jesus to the Cross. But the light appeared, the tomb was found empty and Jesus lived. And, with Jesus rising, David also rose out of the depths of his own despair.

The rest of history raced by. The letters of Paul, the Revelation of Jesus, the growth of the church, Augustine, Mohammed, Aquinas, Luther, philosophers, inventors, war and all of human progress came and went. All through post Biblical history David saw the Prophets and Saints watching, hopefully, from Heaven.

He saw Satan, loose upon the Earth, repeatedly bringing death and pain, but always; ultimately, his attacks were repelled by God. But Satan found a new trick. God is responsible for your woe; trust in yourself, there is no God. Science is God. Slowly, these words became the new gospel, spread by Satan and his minions.

Mankind rejected God and David saw Satan smile. One by one the Saints and the Prophets turned away. He was sure that he saw Fyodor among the prophets; even he turned away. History reached the present and David saw himself lifting off on his historic flight. He looked into Heaven and there was only one left watching: Jesus, with his arms outstretched, waiting to welcome anyone who asked to be with Him. David saw a tear in Jesus' eye as no one accepted the generous offer. David screamed out loud, "Please take me with you," and he closed his eyes and wept as the room went black.

He wasn't sure how long he sat in the darkness; he really didn't care. He saw a faint light appear and he heard footsteps quickly approaching. It was a lone man dressed in a bright white robe. The man started to run as he got closer to David. "Quickly, we're late, we need to clean you up. Get out of those old clothes. Hurry, there isn't much time," the man said. David started to question him, but the man put his hand to David's mouth. "No time," he said, "the king is coming."

David pulled off his flight uniform. "The underwear, too," the man said. Out of thin air a warm shower rained down on David as thousands of years of grime washed away. "That's better," the man said. He handed David some new clothes, a T-shirt and sweatpants. "Put these on. The king won't mind you wearing them, it will tell him that you're on my team. David put on the shirt which had a picture of a lamb on the front and number two on the back, surprised that it fit him perfectly. The pants also had the number two with the lamb symbol on the hip. The man was had similar clothes except his had the number one.

"Wait here," the man said, "They'll be here soon. The man disappeared and everything was dark again, except for a glow which came from the new uniform David was wearing. Something about the whole scenario with the man and changing clothes seemed very familiar to David. He remembered a similar episode in the historical images he had viewed. If he was correct, then he was about to meet the real "King," God the Father.

Without warning, a bright light appeared and the room was filled with white-robed angels, as well as elderly men, also dressed in white. Fyodor was among them. David felt small and inadequate. He walked forward as he heard the angels and the elders singing: "Holy, Holy, Holy is the Lord God Almighty. The whole universe is filled with his glory." As David came forward he was struck by a sight so wonderful and glorious that he thought that he would die. He fell to the ground, feeling worthless and ashamed as a bright light revealed all of David's numerous past transgressions.

As David lay prostrate before God, he was able to muster the strength to say two words, "Forgive me."

He felt a hand take his own. "Get up," a familiar voice whispered. The man, now wearing his old flight suit, was standing next to him, gently helping David to his feet. The man addressed God, "I present to you Major David Sanders of the United States Astropilot Corps. He comes to you as one who belongs to me."

David heard a voice like thunder, "You have been chosen to carry my message to a dead world, one that has rejected me and has joined forces with the Evil One."

David answered, "Lord, I am not worthy of such a task. I am the worst of all sinners. Do not charge me with such overwhelming responsibility."

The Lord replied, "You were chosen for this task before you were born. It is for this purpose that you have lived your life. It is time for you to return to your Earth and teach the people about me. Do not be afraid, for the Spirit will always be with you and My words will flow from your mouth like water over a waterfall and Hope will return to your world."

God, his Glory, all the heavenly host receded, and David was left alone with only the man. "Who are you?" David asked.

"You know me as surely as I know you," the man replied. "Look closely."

David stared into the man's eyes, studied his face and realized that, yes, he did know this man.

The two walked away together. "We need to get you ready to go home," the man said. David saw the ITP vessel, looking good as new.

"Wait," David paused before getting into the vessel. "I need to know something, about someone. Is she here?" A faint smile came to the man's lips and his eyes twinkled like stars. "Yes she is among us," he answered.

"I have to see her, at least one last time."

"It isn't right, not for her."

"You're sending me to be a lone sheep surrounded by wolves, battling Satan in his own backyard. Can't you grant me this one request? I need to know that she is OK. I know that you have the power. Please let me see her."

The man was silent for a time. "Very well." He disappeared in the darkness and David found himself standing next to Ruth. She was beautiful, dressed in a light pink robe. He put his arm around her and they held each other tightly, saying nothing as tears filled their eyes. Finally, David spoke, "I was so afraid, so afraid that I'd never see you again." He kissed her. "I know," she said, "I have missed you so much. It is so good to hear your voice, to touch you, to look at you. Yet it will be so hard to see you leave."

"How can I leave you, now that I have found you?" David asked. "You must come with me, I can't go alone." He kissed her again. She leaned her head against his shoulder. "You have been given a wonderful and holy task. You must trust God to do what is right for all of us."

"I can never be happy without you. At least, tell me, in the end, won't we be together?"

"I will always be part of you. And, if you look and listen carefully you will find me in your world."

They walked slowly together, holding each other. David talked about all that he had seen and they talked about the days in Eden. Finally the man appeared. "It is time to go." David kissed Ruth one last time, holding her tightly. He let her go and she was gone. David found himself standing next to the ITP vessel. He went inside.

LXXI. SURVEILLANCE AND SECURITY

FOR OVER 150 YEARS, SINCE THE EARLY TWENTY-FIRST CENTURY, THE development of adequate security has been a primary goal of public and private institutions. Initially, increasingly prevalent video and audio monitoring provided security, thwarting many potential terrorist and criminal aggressions. The use of DNA to identify suspected perpetrators greatly improved the accuracy of criminal and security investigations. As technology improved, particularly computer-generated imaging, security limited to audio and visual modalities became less and less reliable. The development of accurate and rapid physiologic monitors revolutionized the security industry.

These monitors allowed a surveillance beam to quickly determine cardiac activity, body temperature, respirations, perspiration, and, in the most advanced models, CNS electrical activity. The latest models also had a rapid DNA scanner that provided a DNA profile from a light beam trans-illuminating an individual's skin. The scanners used in such security monitors prevented an individual from deceiving the antiquated AV cameras; something that was all too easy with the high quality holographic images that could be generated.

Attempts had been made to elude the physiologic monitors, but none were completely successful. It had not been possible to accurately replicate all the physiologic parameters that were assessed by the powerful surveillance devices that were now routinely used. As a result, the incidence of serious criminal activity was greatly reduced. The security monitoring was everywhere, the collected information stored in huge databases; criminal investigation was greatly facilitated, while the initiation of criminal activity was greatly retarded.

LXXII. ESCAPE

MAJOR SORINO CALLED SCULLY. "I'M READY TO GO, NOW. ATTENTION is on Dr. Tennyson, we should be able to get in with minimal fuss."

"I'm with you, major. We'll need to hurry. I just spoke with a friend who works at the Senate. Senator Leavitt is sending his own security forces over to guard the whole ITP complex. For some reason he thinks that some fool-hardy ITP Committee member will try to take off before he has finished his hearings. He said he doesn't trust the usual military security personnel."

Sorino answered, "We'd better hurry, then."

They met about thirty minutes later, about a half kilometer from the entrance. Scully activated his surveillance monitor to check the entrance to the complex. Nothing happened. "We may be too late, major. If Senator Leavitt's security forces are already in place, the first thing they would do is change all the security codes. That's the only reason for this blank screen."

"It doesn't matter. We're both senior members of the ITP Committee. They'll have to let us in," Sorino said. Scully thought he sounded more than just nervous, sensing desperation in his voice.

The two men reached the entrance to the complex and, as expected, security forces dressed in the dark blue uniforms of the Senate were at the entrance. There were four guards at the entrance and they saw at least eight more patrolling the perimeter.

"This is hopeless, major. If they have four men just at the entrance, just imagine what they've put inside."

"It doesn't matter. We have perfectly legitimate reasons to be here. Let's go."

The two walked casually towards the entrance. "Stop," said one of the guards, as all four aimed their weapons at Scully and Sorino. Sorino spoke, "Now, boys, just calm down. I'm Major Anthony Sorino and this is Chief Engineer Scully." They each flashed their ID badges. Both had "white" clearance levels which should have allowed entrance anywhere in the complex.

"I'm sorry, sir, but we have strict orders from Senator Leavitt, No ITP personnel are allowed in. Not until the hearings are finished."

Sorino replied, without missing a beat, "Well, I don't want to get you in trouble. It's because of the hearing that we are here. We both have to testify and there are important files that we need. You are more than welcome to escort us."

The guards looked at each other, "We'll have to clear it with our commander."

"Go ahead," Sorino said, "We don't want to get you in trouble."

The guard walked away and could be seen speaking into his communicator. After a few minutes he returned. "Commander Richards said no at first, but when I told him your names, he said it would be OK, as long as you're accompanied by two of us. But, you are only to get the files that you need and then immediately leave."

Sorino smiled at his good fortune. Ned Richards was an old friend. He was really going out on a limb to let them in, directly defying orders of Senator Leavitt. "Of course, sergeant. We don't want to get anyone in trouble."

They walked through the entrance scanners, confirming their identities and that they were not carrying any illegal devices. Scully and Sorino walked side by side, with guards in front of them and behind them.

Sorino said, "The files will be on the main launch computer in the ITP control room." The control room was adjacent to the hangar dock where the ITP vessel was kept. Sorino studied the surveillance monitors. There appeared to be four security guards in the hangar. Everything was going as planned.

"Let's get these computers going," Sorino said, "Then we can copy the files we need and be out of your way."

Scully went first, copied two files while the guards stood at the entry door and at the door that led into the hangar. Sorino than copied his files, a total of four. After he had finished the first three he put them on them on the counter. One slipped off and fell under the computer. "Excuse me, guys." He had to lay nearly flat to reach under the computer and retrieve the lost disc. He got up, finished the last file and the four men left. Once again, Scully and Sorino were side by side, and the guards in front and behind.

The four engaged in small talk as they walked towards the entrance. As they walked down the corridor about twenty meters from the door, Scully seemed to lose his balance and fell into the guard that was in front. As soon as Scully started to stumble, Sorino took off down the hall as fast as he could. The rearguard calmly pulled his weapon, "Stop or I'll shoot." Sorino kept going at what seemed impossibly fast speed. The guard fired just as Sorino was turning the corner, heading away from the entrance. "I know I hit him" the guard said as he ran ahead. He got to the next corridor, but when he turned the corner, no one was there. He sounded the alarm.

"Surveillance, intruder alert."

"Retrieve Physiologic data." The data from the entry scan was transmitted into the guards wrist monitors. "Attention, the intruder, Major Anthony Sorino, is in Building D, East end. Confinement and Recovery crew respond."

"We're on it." The security forces gathered outside Building D which was at the opposite end of the complex, a kilometer away. "You watch him," the ranking guard said to his subordinate, pointing at Scully. "I'm going to help apprehend our other guest." He took off on foot towards Building D.

Back in the Main Control Room, a panel at the base of the computer housing was kicked out and a man, dressed in a gray mechanics uniform, with a gray hood, emerged. His body was completely encased in this very special suit made of a silicon lead polymer that had one very special property. It served to totally shield its wearer from all physiologic security monitors.

The real Major Sorino had stashed the suit in the computer console weeks before and had managed to wriggle himself into the suit while hiding in the small space. The actual security cameras were disabled by the program he had activated while pretending to retrieve data from the computer. He knew that as long as the physiologic surveillance was active, security personnel would not fret over the loss of a video security monitor, which had always been much easier to fool than the more sensitive physiologic monitors.

As he had planned, the majority of the security forces were at the other end of the complex, trying to capture a ghost. He hoped Scully was OK, as he looked at the screen above his head, which revealed only two guards remaining to guard the ITP Vessel. He activated another program at the computer console, one that opened the hangar doors, while releasing a silent hypersonic wave that would disable the two guards.

He figured that he would have twenty minutes at most before his diversion was discovered. If all went as planned he would be off in space in half that time. He went into the hangar. Both guards were lying on the ground next to the vessel. He moved the first into the control room.

"These guards are well fed," he said out loud, as he struggled to drag the unconscious man into the adjacent room. One hypersonic wave would keep them out for about two hours.

He went back into the hangar and started to drag the second guard when he felt something grab his arm and pull him to the ground. The guard stood up and kicked Sorino in the side. Sorino grabbed the guards ankle, gave it a sharp twist as he jumped to his feet. The guard struck him with a sharp blow to the chest. Sorino countered with a shot to the side of the guards head.

As the two struggled Sorino started to get the upper hand. He felt several ribs crack beneath several blows that landed on the guard's chest. Blood spurted out of the guard's mouth and nose as he crumbled to the ground. "I don't have time for this," Sorino mumbled, as he pulled the guard into the control room. As he stepped over the beaten man's body, an arm shot upward and a razor sharp knife plunged into Sorino's inner thigh and was pulled down to knee level, opening a long gash. Blood spurted out as the guard passed out. Sorino pulled the knife from his thigh and grabbed the guard's jacket, stuffing it into the wound to try to stop the bleeding. He hobbled into the hangar. Twelve minutes had passed. He needed to hurry. He hobbled to the ITP vessel and managed to climb inside, leaving a dark pool of blood on the hangar floor.

The other security personnel that had been pursuing Major Sorino, surrounded Building D. They called for Sorino to come out. There was no response. The commander studied the surveillance data from within the building. Something wasn't right. Even though the monitors confirmed that it was Major Sorino, there was no change in heart rate or sweat production, despite Sorino having sprinted from one end of the complex to the other.

"Something's wrong," he said. "Send in the assault team." The heavily armored assault team stormed the building through every available door and window. Inside they found some tables, chairs, old computers and a small solid green box, which turned out to be source of all the data that they had been receiving.

Across the compound, Sorino powered up the ship, activated the computer and the launch code. Luckily, the vessel accepted the code. His course was already laid in. The ship started forward, picking up speed. He saw the hangar door warning lights come on. They've discovered my little ruse, he thought. The hangar doors would snap closed in thirty seconds, just enough time to get through. As he cleared the doors, he heard the clang as they closed. He was on his way to fulfill the destiny he had been pursuing for the last thirty years.

His head was spinning and he saw patches of white as the ITP vessel lifted off the ground, moving forward in anticipation of lift-off. Hold on for a few more minutes, he thought. He hoped that he would have at least an hour's head start on the pursuit that he knew was inevitable.

The time to reach the portal would be three hours and thirty-nine minutes. It would be close, but his calculations showed that he would be through the portal before he could be intercepted. Once through the portal, he was sure that his injury wouldn't matter. He strapped himself into the pilot seat, activated the ship's computer and started the launch. Getting out of the Earth's atmosphere would require a little finesse. He had to be careful not to accelerate too quickly or else the outer vibratory coating would be damaged; at the same time he had to reach a high enough speed to escape the Earth's gravity and atmosphere. He was lucky that this new vessel had a repair mechanism for the outer coating, so that small defects could be corrected while in flight, once he was in space. He eased the ship's accelerator, gradually increasing velocity, always watching the hull temperature. As the speed increased the temperature also increased, but very slowly. Altitude increased and hull temp was holding steady. The sleek design of the vessel actually was making it easy and his fears that the ship would be damaged by takeoff proved to be unfounded.

The security commander was calling for additional forces to secure the ITP Vessel when he looked up to see the black ship shoot into the sky, quickly becoming only a blip in the sky that rapidly disappeared.

LXXII. MOOSEWOOD RESPONDS

GENERAL MOOSEWOOD WAS IN HIS OFFICE, ADJACENT TO THE ITP control Center away from Senate Security forces. He shuffled some papers, distracted, reflecting on the day's events. He chuckled to himself as he thought about Deborah and her "testimony." She had certainly taken the wind out of Adrian Leavitt's sails, creating an entirely new focal point for the media.

He was quickly brought back to the present as a siren blared from ITP control and a call came in accompanied by a red flashing light. Some VIP was calling...it was Adrian Leavitt.

The image of the senator appeared. "General, one of your ITP astropilots has broken into the ITP Control Center, assaulted two Senate Security guards and stolen the ITP vessel. I'm sure that you had nothing to do with this, but I thought that you should know that I've spoken with General Abraham. The Astropilot patrol is being mobilized to intercept the ITP vessel and escort it back to Earth. If there is a hint of resistance or if Major Sorino should make an attempt to pass through the interdimensional portal he will be blasted into the next galaxy."

General Moosewood tried to keep cool. "That seems rather drastic, senator. Let me try to call him."

"He is currently moving at .12c and accelerating. A radio message will take some time to reach him. Your entire committee was ordered to stand down until the senate hearings were completed. You know that I have the authority to order him intercepted, returned or annihilated as a national, global and interplanetary imperative."

"You do have that right, Senator, but I think that I can take care of this without blasting Major Sorino into the next dimension."

"You have my permission to do as you see fit, but, I will not change my orders."

The general jumped out of his chair, ran down the stairs, and crossed the street to the ITP Control Center. He flashed his ID badge and ran to the main control room.

He found medical personnel tending to the two injured guards. They both were going to be OK, but the one with the broken ribs had internal injuries and was receiving ventilator assistance. Still, he was expected to make a complete recovery.

There was a trail of blood that led into the hangar, with the large pool of blood adjacent to the spot where the ITP vessel had stood.

"The blood is Major Sorino's, sir," one of the medical attendants said. "The guard says he slashed his leg pretty good. He thinks he got his femoral artery."

Without another word General Moosewood ran into the hangar and then placed a call to the flight deck. "What have you got that's fast and ready to go?" He asked that day's flight officer, Captain Williams.

"Sir, the best we have is an X-71 level five, capable of .312c."

"Is it flight ready?"

"Yes, sir. Fully fueled and fully checked this morning. Who will be flying?"

"I will, captain. I'm in the ITP hangar. I'll be there in two minutes. Have it warmed up and ready to go."

"Excuse me, sir, but, with all due respect, do you have proper clearance and are you authorized to fly this class of aircraft?"

"Don't argue with me, son. Lives are at stake. I was flying around this solar system before you were separated from your mother's breast. Just have it ready."

The general ran across the compound. The X-71 was revved up and ready for takeoff as he had ordered. This space vessel was fully equipped: tracking device, full weaponry and energy shield. Its specifications called for maximum velocity of .312c, but the general knew of pilots that had reached sustained speeds of .331. The ITP vessel was not designed for high sustained speed. Although it easily cruised at .18c, it could only reach higher velocities for short distances, as may have been necessary to pass through a portal. The general figured that at maximum velocity he could overtake Major Sorino's head start and intercept him before he reached the ITP portal.

The general climbed into the cockpit, assisted by Captain Williams. "Thanks, captain."

Williams replied, "You can trust me to help anyway that I can, but what's it all about."

"Oh, nothing important really, just the future of mankind, senate politics, maybe God and the devil," the general said facetiously. "Ask me again when I return. There is one thing that may help. Can you keep a continuous radio beam on me and on Major Sorino?"

"Already in place, sir, and one on the major also, as a matter of standard protocol. Your beam will activate as soon as you takeoff."

"Very good, captain," the general said. "Oh, and captain, keep this military."

"Certainly, sir." Williams knew that meant to try to keep the Senate Security forces away. He left the runway and returned to the control tower. As soon as the general was safely in the air he called his radio man, Lieutenant Gleason. The radio beam light came on as soon as the X-71 was airborne. "Looking good, general. At top speed you should intercept Major Sorino in less than four hours. Good luck."

"Thanks, captain. As soon as you can cross link the two radio beams."

"Already done, sir, you can communicate with Major Sorino, but at your current separation and velocities the delay will be eighty-six minutes." The delay was due to the differences in the space vessels velocities and the velocity of the radio beam which was equal to the 1.0c.

"Thank you, captain."

The general looked at his gauges. Velocity was .17c and accelerating. The space craft responded smoothly to every course alteration. The general felt like he was thirty years old again. He opened a channel to Major Sorino, "Major, this is General Moosewood. I know that you are injured. Please respond with your status. I'm sure that you are aware that the senate has absolutely forbidden further ITP engagements. The Astropilot Corps has been mobilized against you, and is authorized to use any and all necessary force. Please respond. At present rate I will reach you in three hours and forty-six minutes. You should receive this message well before that time."

I've done all that I can, the general thought. His speed passed .19c, eventually reaching .312c. He sat back to enjoy the ride. He had forgotten how much fun it was to rocket through open space and made a mental note to do this more often. He looked at the monitor and saw that Sorino was traveling at a higher velocity than he had thought possible, which altered his calculations. He also saw something a little more concerning, a third vessel, also on an intercept course with Major Sorino. The computer model predicted that he and the presumed astropilot would reach the major almost simultaneously and, because of his increased velocity, which this would be very close to Sorino's arrival at the ITP portal.

Maybe I can squeeze a little more juice from this lemon, the general thought. "Thrust and velocity configuration," he said. The power train diagrams came up on the monitor. The general followed each step on the diagram, from power generation to transmission to implementation. There was one coupling which siphoned power away to weapons. Bypassing that coupling would increase power transmission and provide a little boost. He saw no need for weapons, at least not now, so he shut the coupling off. His velocity increased to.3129c, just enough to get him to Sorino before he reached the portal and ahead of the other pilot.

LXXIII. ANOTHER PILOT

CAPTAIN BART JOHNSTON WAS NEW TO THE ASTROPILOT CORPS. HE had recently graduated from the Air Force Academy, where he had matriculated after his father made a very sizable donation allowing a new athletic center to be built. Captain Johnston had graduated in the lower half of his class, but had managed to be selected to the elite Astropilot Corps. However, the glamorous life that he had anticipated turned out to be everything but that; it was best described as mundane.

He had spent the last three months escorting huge freighters traveling at speeds below 0.1c. They originated at such exciting venues as the moon, Mars or the asteroid field. The most action he had seen was a loose cable on one of the freighters sending sparks into open space. No pirates, no smugglers, no call for anything other than routine patrol and escort services.

I guess I should be thankful that everything's been quiet, he thought. Still, the promise of defending the Earth and its agents against the criminal element, which had enticed him to join the Corps, had never developed and he found his job an incredible bore.

It was against this background that the call came in. A rogue pilot, the most valuable, sophisticated new space vessel stolen, intercept and subdue using all necessary means. This was what Captain Johnston was waiting for. He didn't care who or what he was going after, he just knew that it was finally time for some action.

After he received the message and looked at the current positions of the rest of the Astropilot Corps, he realized that he was the only astropilot in flight with any chance to intercept the stolen spacecraft. He plotted the course, switched on maximum sensors and maximum weaponry. The orders included details of the ITP vessel, its characteristics, such as top cruising velocity, anticipated course, on board weaponry and a profile of Major Sorino. Johnston saw that he could intercept him at the end destination point. He looked at his star charts and saw no reason for anyone to travel to an empty area deep in space. But, orders are orders. He plotted his course, put his foot on the gas, so to speak and quickly climbed to a speed of .312c. He anticipated intercept in about three and a half hours, Earth stationary time.

LXXIV. TO THE PORTAL

ONCE SAFELY IN FLIGHT AND AWAY FROM THE EARTH, MAJOR SORINO checked to see if there was any pursuit. The monitor was clear. He turned his attention to the gash in his thigh. The bleeding had slowed considerably, but at the same time he felt weak and lightheaded. Don't pass out now, he thought.

"Diagnostics on,"he whispered weakly. He activated his pilot's seat to run through the medical diagnostics computer. After about fifteen seconds, the computer gave audio and visual summary of the injury. "Laceration to the right thigh skin, sartorius muscle, superficial femoral artery, saphenous vein, and vastus medialis muscle. Estimated total body blood loss, 40%, Right lower extremity perfusion, 15%, sensory nerve deficit, motor nerve deficit, superficial invasion of tissues with normal skin flora." He couldn't feel his foot or move his toes.

"Medical therapeutics," he whispered, barely audible. The therapeutics center came on. The ITP vessel was equipped with only a basic therapeutic system and Sorino wasn't sure that it was capable of repairing such an extensive injury.

The therapeutic system started to move. There was a faint whirring noise as it moved towards his seat and descended onto his thigh. The partially numb leg became numb from groin to toes. The whirring grew louder. After about two minutes the system moved away and what Sorino saw was amazing. The long gash was sealed; closed in a neat, straight line. The sensation was returning to his leg and he could move his toes as if nothing had happened. He still felt weak, but he no longer was lightheaded or worried that he would lose consciousness. Once finished, the therapeutics machine summarized the repaired organs: repair Superficial Femoral Artery with restoration of normal blood flow, repair Sartorius Muscle with synthetic actin myosin complex, repair vastus medialis with synthetic actin myosin complex, repair saphenous vein, repair and seal skin, sterilize with high density subcellular bacterial inhibitor, seal wound with neocellular activator, infuse blood substitute restoring circulating volume to 90%. Remarkable, Sorino thought. It should be smooth sailing from here. He looked at the monitor. There was a radio beam tracking him and several attempts had been made to try to establish contact. They can call all they want, he said to himself. He kept his eyes on the monitor. Three hours twenty minutes to go.

LXXV. SENATOR LEAVITT'S OFFICE

JOSHUA, COSBY, JAMESON AND LITTLE BIT QUIETLY APPROACHED THE service entrance of the senate office building. Even this rear entry was brightly lit with very conspicuous surveillance systems. Joshua balked at the security, but Cosby was well prepared. "Put these on," he said, to Joshua and Jameson. All three donned the gray uniforms that announced that they were with Star Maintenance, the service company for the Senate. The uniforms were complete with ID badges, which were actually small chips sewn into the sleeve.

"What about Little Bit, I'll need him inside," Joshua asked.

"It's all been arranged," Cosby replied. He produced a heavy leather bag, large enough to hold the little dog. The bag was labeled "cleaning supplies" and looked like a regular supply bag. It was lined with a lead, silicon, and carbon alloy that shielded the contents from detection, but also gave a false reading that was entirely consistent with the most common cleaning agents.

"This bag has been designed to evade all types of surveillance," Cosby explained. Little Bit will be inside, but all that the monitors will see is a bag filled with standard cleaning supplies. Oh, and one other thing, ditch the Green Dot." Cosby pointed to the tiny device in Joshua's ear. "We won't be able to get that past security. Any attempt to use such a device inside will set of all sorts of alarms, so just leave it here." Joshua took it off and left it outside the building.

"OK, let's get going," Joshua said. Come on, Little Bit." The little Westie jumped into the bag. Cosby touched a few buttons inside the bag and then shut it and sealed it closed.

"He'll be able to breathe OK, won't he?" Joshua asked.

"The bag has built in ventilation. Those buttons send out data for the security system that will give all the readings of cleaning supplies."

They backed a truck up to the service entrance and breezed through security without any questions. So far, so good, Joshua thought. They picked up a large maintenance cart from the service closet. The cart was rolled down each hallway and the trash from each office was automatically deposited inside to eventually be emptied down a chute for final processing and disposal. Normally one man was enough to monitor the work, but there was a monthly quality control run. This allowed the three of them to enter together. No one questioned why they were a day ahead of schedule.

They took the service elevator. "Forty," Cosby said and they zoomed to the fortieth floor in seconds. Senator Leavitt's office occupied half of the fortieth floor. Joshua looked at his watch, an antique mechanical named De Bethune, 10:40 P.M. So far, no problems.

Joshua had found the original plans to the building in an old architectural journal. He knew that over the years the interior would have been modified. He only hoped that the anteroom, just inside the front door, was still there. This room was about three meters square on the plans, large enough to allow them to get out of the hall and bypass the security system undetected, but too small, he hoped, to have monitoring of its own.

Outside the senator's office they could see the glass doors and the anteroom. Joshua was disappointed to see that, despite its small size, there was surveillance in place. The security system had been designed by Bolton Security. Their systems were very sophisticated, providing video, audio and physiologic monitoring of anything within the systems purview. Although it was not public record, Joshua assumed that the senator would have the latest, newest, most complex system available. As soon as he looked through the glass he saw this to be true. He started to ask Cosby how he planned to get in when he saw him take a clear plastic sheet from the bag he was carrying. Joshua also saw a thin metal frame. In less than one minute the frame and sheet were assembled into a tent, large enough for all of them to fit, but small enough to fit in the anteroom.

"This will shield us from the surveillance, at least in the anteroom. We'll be able to work undetected." Cosby looked at the locked entrance, took a metal tool from his pocket and inserted it into the locking mechanism. "This will be a minor annoyance," he said. The door popped open.

"Hurry," he said, "we've got about forty-five seconds to get in and closes the door. The three men and dog pushed the tent through the door, abutting the door to the main office. They scooted into the tent as the hallway entrance slammed shut.

Joshua said, "You've done very well to get us this far. However, getting into the main office, past the security system will be trickier. The alarm and surveillance system has monitoring beams that run horizontally from the ceiling to ten centimeters above the floor. There are vertical beams running in a grid pattern every fifteen centimeters. This leaves a 10 x 15 cm corridor along the floor that can be used to evade the surveillance beams. We're lucky. The floor weight sensor is set for 10 kg. Little Bit will be able to get in without detection. On the desk is the control grid. The manufacturer's specs indicate that it will look like this." Joshua held up a diagram. "This switch on the right shuts down the system. However, as soon as it's down, the security guard is signaled. So, we need to shut it down without anyone noticing. Once it is down we can bypass these three circuits within the control grid. Once that is done the signal to the security guard will say that the system is active. I'll need about three minutes to bypass these circuits."

"My people outside are ready," Cosby said. "They're just waiting for my signal."

Joshua had a look of worry on his face. "I hope the signal is not anything electronic or any sort of electromagnetic wave that will alert the security guards. Oh and how do we get Little Bit into the office without being detected?"

"Relax, it's taken care of." Cosby produced a device that looked like an old fashioned compass, with suction cups. "Where's the safe corridor?"

Joshua put on some rose colored glasses and pushed a button on the side. He had picked them up from a shop that sold old security supplies. They were the sort of things that used to be used by repairman to check that the light beams, which were essential to all alarms and security systems, were working properly. Of course, these days, the systems were continually self monitoring, so there was rarely a need for such apparatus. Joshua stared through the glasses into the main office. There was a tight grid of light beams. He saw a safe corridor that ran adjacent to the desk, with the space that would allow Little Bit to jump on the desk and disable the system. "The safe corridor is here," he said and he pointed to a spot on the glass door. Cosby started to cut a hole there, whistling nonchalantly as he worked. Through all this, Jameson sat by, staring at Joshua, never saying a word. She's probably thinking that she should have cut my throat when she had the chance, Joshua thought. He hoped that Jameson would not have a second opportunity. While Cosby was cutting through the door, Joshua whispered in Little Bit's ear. The little dog listened closely.

"Do you really think that dog understands what you're saying?" Cosby asked.

"You better hope that he does, or all this will be for nothing."

"OK," we're ready for him to do his stuff."

"Good," Joshua said. "It's time Little Bit. Time to show us what you're made of."

Cosby pulled out the cut circle of glass from the door. The cutting device stayed in place, making the door think that it was still intact. Joshua hung a small gray box on the opening and pushed a button on its side. The surveillance beams became visible and the path to the desk could be seen between the tight grid of green lights.

Little Bit crouched down and inched his way along the floor. Joshua had greased the dog's hair and patted it down, making Little Bit's body as narrow as possible. The Westie inched his way along the narrow path with surprising ease. Reaching the desk in about two minutes. Now came the tricky part. Joshua told Cosby to signal his men. Cosby pushed a button on his wrist watch.

"Give it about one minute," he said. Alarms went off, as expected and some guards ran down the corridor outside Senator Leavitt's office. The three burglars were safely hidden within the tent, invisible to anyone in the hallway.

"Now, Little Bit," Joshua said.

The dog jumped straight up onto the desk and hit the switch. The door opened and the three men hurried into the room. Joshua went to the control panel, quickly pulled off the front cover and pulled out three modules. He replaced them with three that he had brought. "We should be OK now," he said.

Joshua checked the control panel again. All the lights were off except the light indicating data being fed to the security guard. Perfect, he thought. "We're in, let's look around.

The office looked pretty ordinary. There were the usual monitors and computer controls, all blank at the moment. The desk was locked and there was nothing incriminating. There was another door, which led to the inner office. The inner office would be Senator Leavitt's private domain. They scanned for additional surveillance; none was detected and the door was unlocked. Inside, Joshua took a quick survey of the room. Something was not quite right. He wasn't sure, but there was an artificial quality. He had a feeling that this office was only for show and that anything of importance would be found elsewhere. There was a lone monitor on the desk.

Cosby looked at the computer. "It will take me a while to get into this computer," he said.

"I wouldn't bother," Joshua replied, seeming distracted.

Little Bit kept sniffing around the wall opposite the window. All this time Jameson stood silently, awaiting directions from Cosby. Little Bit started scratching at the base of a built-in bookshelf. Joshua walked across the room to see what the little dog had found. "Look at this. The wall looks like it should open." Indeed, there was an opening around the entire bookcase. "There should be a switch or latch or something around here somewhere."

"Maybe this will help." Cosby pulled a small device from his pocket. This displays circuitry and systems. It should show us how to open the door. He peered into the tiny screen; then pulled out one of the books, an outdated copy of congressional rules and procedures. The bookcase swung open and a large room was revealed.

"Would you look at this?" Joshua said, staring at a very impressive art collection. "Amazing," Cosby remarked as he walked into the room, glancing from side to side at the artwork adorning the walls. These must be worth billions. Joshua saw something else, which he did not mention. He did say, "How can someone like Adrian Leavitt, a senator of humble origins, afford such an art collection? I know that senators are well paid, but...look at this. I've heard about this painting, read about it. It was stolen ten years ago. There's definitely something unsavory about this whole thing. I think the senator will have a lot of explaining to do. This will certainly be of help to Dr. Tennyson." He turned towards Cosby.

"Now, Jameson," Cosby said quietly. Cosby's powerful assistant grabbed Joshua around the waist and before Joshua could say a word he found himself completely disabled, immobilized and silenced. Cosby pointed his hand held device at Little Bit, who was about to attack, there was a flash and the brave Westie was knocked out.

A few minutes later, when Joshua came to he found himself shackled with magnetic hand cuffs, in the large chair behind Senator Leavitt's desk. He was alone with Cosby, who had directed Jameson to stay in the outer office, watching Little Bit.

"I guess you've gotten all that you need," Joshua said. "Of course it was all too easy, getting into the office and all. Senator Leavitt has good help."

Cosby sneered. "You think that I work for that hopeless clown, my boss is much more important."

"Oh, so you report directly to Mr. Diblonski," Joshua surmised. "My, but you are a big shot. You definitely are a vital cog in the machinery of today's society, providing an enemy for the population to fear, a threat... something to give our benevolent government purpose."

"Something like that. Let's just say that Mr. Diblonski knows how to maintain order, at least the kind of order that he wants."

"And poor Ms. Jameson, you use her to maintain this order?" Jameson was standing silently in the doorway. Cosby was facing Joshua, with his back to the doorway.

"No, I take care of her and hundreds more like her. I teach them what they need to know."

"You teach them enough to keep them in their place."

"Say what you like, but it is a better place for them. These unfortunate souls would be destroyed by mainstream society."

"But, what you teach them. Do good deeds and God will reward you. The Lord helps those who help themselves. God wants only what is best for them, as long as they are obedient to Mr. Cosby and in the end Mr. Diblonski. It may sound good, but it has nothing to do with the Bible or God. You really should read the books that you pretend to preach."

"What I teach them is sound theology."

"It may be somebody's theology, but it certainly does not come from the Bible, at least not from the Bible you gave to me."

"They don't need to know such drivel."

"This 'drivel' is supposed to be good news. You speak endless, worthless platitudes and ignore the true message of God's faithfulness to his creation and his gift of salvation for all men."

Jameson came into the room. "What is he saying, Mr. Cosby?" Jameson asked with her very slurred speech.

"He's trying to trick you, Jameson. You know me. You know that you can trust me."

"Don't listen to him, Miss Jameson," Joshua interjected. "He's been lying to you. Look closely at him. You'll know that I am right."

Cosby looked angry, his face growing red. "Silence him once and for all, Jameson. Listen to me...do what I say. I'm the one that cares about you. I'm the one that pulled you out of the gutter and looked out for you."

"Do you hear that?" Joshua calmly asked Jameson. "No mention of God, no mention of salvation through faith, only I did this and I did that, only himself."

Jameson stared at Cosby and what she saw was shocking and terrified her. Cosby's face was deep red, the eyes were a darker red with black pupils and ringed with black, his teeth were yellowed and his voice had become a snakelike hiss.

"Don't be afraid, Jameson," Joshua continued gently. "Look at him for what he really is."

Jameson saw the demon figure and her fear was replaced by anger. She grabbed Cosby around the chest, slowly crushing the life out of him. Flames shot out and the sickening smell of burning flesh filled the room. Jameson held tightly as the flames died away leaving the huge woman clutching a gray skeleton that quickly faded to dust as she collapsed to the floor. Little Bit had come to and he came into the room, found the magnetic key in the pile of dust and freed Joshua, who ran to Jameson. Joshua held the simple, powerful woman to his chest. Her breathing was labored and Joshua felt only a weak pulse.

Jameson spoke, her voice barely audible, but remarkably clear, "Tell me the truth about God."

Joshua held her as he recounted all that he had recently read in the Bible; he spoke of God's creation and man's great sin. He recounted the Gospel of God's Son and God's grace and mercy and the Kingdom of Heaven. Jameson's breathing became shallower, her pulse faded and she was gone. But, in that last moment Joshua saw a smile cross her lips and Joshua knew that in the end the poor misguided girl understood... understood about faith, hope and salvation in a way that most people could never really grasp. In the end Jameson had learned the truth and Joshua knew that she truly believed. He envied her.

"Come on, Little Bit," Joshua said. "We'll need to send all this to Deborah." They hurried out of the building and Joshua loosened Little Bit's collar. He took the Green Dot and put it in front of Little Bit's left ear and activated the amplifier in the dog's collar. The dot had recorded all that he had found in Senator Leavitt's office: the art collection and evidence that it was all pay-off for a career of dirty deeds, which Joshua had discovered with the paintings. He was disappointed that there was no evidence linking Senator Leavitt directly to Diblonski, but he was sure that it would be enough to bring down the powerful Senator and, hopefully, keep Dr. Tennyson and the ITP program going. "OK, Little Bit, you know what to do." The little dog took off, a white streak racing into town.

LXXVI. ENTRY AND EXIT

MAJOR SORINO FINISHED THE MEDICAL THERAPY. THE BLEEDING HAD stopped and his leg felt almost normal. Although he felt weak and drained, overall he was content, confident that he would reach the portal safely. He still had about three and a half hours to go. The course was charted, all monitors were functioning and ITP values, based on current portal energy readings had been entered. The vessel was ready for portal entry. Now's a good time to get some rest, he thought. He lay back and fell asleep.

His sleep did not last long. An alarm sounded and Sorino awoke and looked at the control panel. The radio beam was tracking him, which did not surprise him, but there were two ships in pursuit. He could see that both ships were astrofighters, the fastest in the fleet. Both were capable of overtaking him, even with his head start. His current speed was .21c. At this rate they'll catch me long before I reach the portal, he said to himself. He increased his speed to maximum, climbing to .30c. At this higher velocity it would be close. He also saw that one of the fighters had linked to the radio beam that was tracking him. He anticipated receiving a radio message soon.

The brief nap had renewed his strength and he was ready for whatever they might fire at him. The ITP vessel, unfortunately, had minimal weaponry. It was, however, extremely maneuverable, equal to the best astrofighter. He looked at his flight plan, still two hours until portal intercept. He decided his only chance was to make it to the portal before he was caught. His weapons were virtually useless against these astroplanes. He diverted weapons power to his propulsion, boosting his speed to .31c. The monitor showed that now he should easily reach the portal before he was overtaken by his pursuers. Sorino hoped that they were already at maximum. At this point there was nothing to do but wait. He reclined his seat, but stayed awake, keeping his eyes on the monitors, watching for any surprises.

Time passed very slowly. He tried to relax, but all he could do was stare at the monitors and the clock. The two fighters chasing him were closing. Current calculations revealed they had narrowed the gap a little. At the present rate they would intercept him just as he reached the portal. He looked at the clock, thirty-five minutes to go.

A blue light blinked on the control panel as the computer announced, "Incoming message."

"Review message, audio only," Sorino said. A familiar voice came over the speaker.

"Anthony, this is General Moosewood. I don't know everything that has happened or what you are going through, but you need to know that orders have been given to stop you from passing through the portal using any and all necessary force. You know what that means. Any pilot that is in pursuit has the green light to blast you into oblivion. Senator Leavitt has authority over the Astrocorps and he does not want you utilizing the ITP. If you are doing this for Major Sanders, I ask you to rethink your position. I cannot afford to lose a second valuable pilot. If Major Sanders is alive somewhere out in space he is very capable of taking care of himself. I don't need you flying off helter-skelter on a misguided search for a needle in a haystack. You are needed at home, by the ITP program and by your family. Our radio beams are locked so I'll receive your response fairly quickly. See you soon." And the message was over.

The general means well, Sorino thought, but he doesn't understand. He thought about Jessie and the kids and tears came to his eyes. But, childhood memories of overwhelming joy returned and all doubts vanished. As he continued to careen through space towards the portal he thought about his pursuers. He felt lucky that one of them was General Moosewood. The general was a friend and would never try to shoot him down, even if it meant his career. Still, he worried about the other astropilot. He needed something to tip the scales in his favor. What do I have that he lacks? An idea came into his head; he reached for the controls and made a slight alteration in his course. This will give me the edge I need. He smiled as he felt able to relax again.

Captain Johnston noted the change in Sorino's course. He altered his course to intercept. According to his flight computer he would catch him in twenty-eight minutes. General Moosewood also noticed the change and he was confused. The slight alteration would cause Sorino to miss intersecting the ITP portal. The general decide to maintain his course. After all he really did not care if Sorino flew off someplace else, as long as he did not pass through the ITP portal.

Meanwhile, Sorino saw that the pursuing astropilot had matched his course alteration, just as he had planned. He looked at his flight computer and ITP sensor. This is perfect he thought; twenty-five minutes to go.

Captain Johnston locked his tracking sensor on Sorino's ship. He activated his radio beam to intercept and sent a message, "Major Anthony Sorino, this is Captain Bart Johnston of the Interplanetary Astropilot Corps. I have orders to intercept you utilizing all available and necessary means. I do not wish to fire upon you, but I will carry out my mission. You should receive this message five minutes before I reach intercept point. If you do not acknowledge this message and reverse your course, I will fire upon you." The message sent; Captain Johnston armed his weapons. At the high velocity that they were traveling, the only effective weapon was the concentrated laser photon. This weapon was released at light speed to intercept and detonate at a fixed point. From the point of detonation a blast would emanate and cover an area with a radius of 400 kilometers in all directions. Anything at the center would be immediately vaporized, with lessening degrees of destruction as the distance from the blast center point increased. Captain Johnston's astroplane was equipped with full weaponry and was capable of releasing ten laser photons every thirty seconds, thus he could decimate a very large area in a very short time. Surely this renegade pilot was aware of the firepower he was up against and would back off. Johnston was aware that there was a second astroplane chasing Major Sorino. He activated a second radio beam, this one aimed at the general's astroplane. "To unidentified astroplane. This is Captain Bart Johnston of the Interplanetary Astropilot Corps. I am on an intercept course with Major Anthony Sorino, who is wanted by the Senate Interplanetary Committee of the United States for theft of a space vessel and unauthorized spaceflight. I will use all available means to carry out my mission. If Major Sorino does not halt his flight and surrender I intend to respond with laser photons at full dispersal. The center point will be at the anticipated intercept point, which is accompanying this message. I advise you to take any and all necessary precautions."

General Moosewood received Johnston's message about twelve minutes later. The general's course intercepting with the ITP portal was about ten thousand kilometers from Johnston and Sorino's anticipated intercept point, plenty of distance from any laser photon blast. He sent a warning message to Major Sorino, as a precaution. However, Captain Johnston would have also sent a warning, which was standard procedure in a situation like this. The general also had an idea of Sorino's plan and, if he were correct, it would be best to wait close to the ITP portal. The general suspected (correctly) that Captain Johnston did not know the exact position of the ITP portal. Only the ITP vessels and the main control centers on the Earth and the moon were equipped with ITP sensors. The general had the portal locations fed into his flight computer prior to his departure, so that he would know exactly where Sorino was heading. Johnston's lack of this crucial information gave a little edge to Sorino. The general maintained his course to intercept at the portal, ETA fourteen minutes.

Sorino looked at his weapons monitor. He was counting on Captain Johnston following the optimum attack plan as determined by the weapons computer. This would be laser photons at maximum dispersal, fired at maximum rate over two minutes. A total of forty laser photons would be released in a grid pattern to cover an area of 1.3 billion cubic kilometers. Sorino's plan required very precise timing, but would get him safely to the portal and leave Captain Johnston thinking his mission had been a success.

Captain Johnston watched as Sorino approached the intercept point. His message had been received and no response had been dispatched and there was no alteration in course or speed. You can run but you can't hide, Johnston thought. With the firing sequence entered, he activated the weapons and bursts of laser photons were released, traveling at light speed, they formed a cubical pattern as they traversed empty space.

Sorino's weapons computer revealed the attack, with the pitiful response of impending destruction and no successful countermeasure. Sorino smiled as he impatiently waited for the onslaught to reach optimum range. At that moment he activated his weapons and released his lone weapon, a laser torpedo, slow and not nearly as powerful as a laser photon, but adequate for Sorino's purpose.

As soon as he released his torpedo, Sorino slowed and altered his course. He released decoys on his previous trajectory and prepared for what was to be a wild ride.

Captain Johnston released his last cache of laser photons. He also slowed to maintain a safe distance from the blast. He saw the decoys released, but easily kept his sights on the original target. As he followed Sorino's ship on the monitor there was a blast, followed by a chain reaction of blasts from the laser photons. He lost sight of Sorino on his monitor and, simultaneously, he was gripped by fear. The blast, which he thought would be thousands of kilometers from his location, was heading back towards his ship. He slowed his progress and quickly reversed course, trying to outrun the energy wave that was approaching.

At the same time, Sorino also waited for the energy wave, increasing his velocity to stay at the edge of the wave. As the wave hit, his velocity reached .319c. He was four minutes from the ITP portal. Portal energy output was unchanged, calculations were set and hull vibration was ready to be activated. Like a Malibu surfer, he rode the wave of the blast racing to the portal.

Captain Johnston managed to outrun the blast, which took him in the direction opposite the ITP portal. He saw Sorino's new course.

"Blast it," he said. He altered his course to catch the major, but he had lost a great deal of distance. "He won't get away with this." Johnston calculated a new intercept point and reactivated his weapons. He still was not aware of the ITP portal. As he was preparing his new course a directive from Astro Corps control came in over his communications system. Apparently, this directive had been following him and only now had reached the astroplane. It provided details about the ITP and gave the coordinates of the portal that Sorino was trying to reach. This information was automatically transmitted to the weapons system and it immediately determined that Sorino would reach the ITP portal at least twenty seconds ahead of any weapons fired from optimum distance. At this point Johnston realized that he would have to make a long range shot aimed at the ITP portal to prevent any entrance. The weapons computer showed that he had to fire immediately to have any chance of stopping Sorino before he entered the portal. He activated and launched his plasma photons, concentrating them at the portal entrance. He slowed as he awaited the blast. With the detonation point so far away the plasma photon was the only weapon capable of maintaining destructive energy.

General Moosewood saw what was happening. There was no possibility that he would reach Sorino before the major entered the portal. He also saw that it was unlikely that the plasma photons that had just been launched would reach their target in time. With nothing left to do, he sent a message, "Anthony, I can't stop you. I am asking you to reconsider this foolish stunt. I can't replace you, the ITP program needs you. Please turn around while you still can. Whatever you decide, good luck. I'll be waiting for your return."

The message was sent; Sorino would receive it 21.5 seconds before he hit the portal. Sorino activated the ITP. At that very moment he received the general's message He released a solar flare as acknowledgement as the ITP vessel's outer hull began to vibrate. Sorino watched the ITP Monitor. Portal energy output remained constant. The incoming plasma photon was still well away, although Sorino's monitors had not picked up its release, being shielded by the energy from the previous blast. The major felt a wave of tranquility and contentment envelope him as he reached the portal. A lifetime of doubts and questions that had gnawed at his soul were about to answered. For the first time in years he felt at peace. As he was passing through the portal, his gauges revealed an energy surge, a bright white light started to fill his ship. He felt the same feeling of elation he had experienced years ago and finally felt at peace. As these feelings came over him, there was a sudden lurch and then intense shaking as the ship began to break up. The light grew stronger as the ship disintegrated and Sorino was gone.

The general watched from a safe distance as Sorino reached the portal and with a bright flash the ITP vessel disappeared. The general moved his ship away from the portal to be a safe distance from the incoming photon blast. Seconds before the expected blast he saw a second flash emanate from the portal. He looked at his monitor. It was anITP vessel. The major came to his senses, the general thought, I hope he knows to get his ass out of there. However, the ITP vessel was heading straight into the path of the incoming plasma photon. "Get out, Anthony," the general screamed into his radio. The general saw the vessel make an abrupt change in course, but too late. The blast was imminent. The ITP vessel was moving away at

.32c, not fast enough to be safe. The general saw the bright flash and the energy wave of the blast overtaking the helpless ship, which had abruptly slowed. The general's monitors picked up an increase in the ITP vessel's shield power. Yes, maybe that will be enough to save you, the thought. The blast reached the ship and it disappeared from the general's monitor.

Major Sanders passed from the interdimensional plane back into time and space. He no longer felt like the brash astropilot. He finally understood the evil that had engulfed the Earth, trapping all of mankind in the endless hell of separation from God. In his mind he carried the vivid images of mankind's disobedience as well as God's message of hope to a lost world.

As he passed through the ITP portal, these thoughts filled his head as he watched his monitors, by rote, with little concentration; feeling that God would keep him safe to deliver his message. Everything seemed perfect. He had noticed a slight energy fluctuation as he entered the portal, but this had quickly passed and now all readings were right on the money. He emerged from the portal into open space anxious to get home. The moment he left the portal every light, bell and whistle in the ship lit up, chimed and sang out. He saw two words and a time: Plasma Photon and five seconds. The ship immediately accelerated away from the blast center. It would take a few seconds to reach maximum velocity and Sanders quickly realized that he would not be able to outrun it.

A plasma photon blast would move at light speed after detonation and would encompass a sphere with a diameter of 60,000 kilometers. He would never get far enough away. He looked at his flight data and the blast data which were displayed side by side. The plasma photon was detonating; he was 28,000 kilometers away, but not moving fast enough to be safe. For a fleeting moment he thought about God and his new role as messenger. Surely he won't let me die after everything I've been through. But, he also decided that this was not the time to put God to the test.

There was one chance. He abruptly stopped his ship and turned it to face the blast. He diverted 100 percent of his power to the stronger forward shield. As soon as he completed this maneuver the blast hit, passing around the ship like a roaring river around a large boulder. Sanders felt the ship shaking violently as the energy blast passed around it. As the plasma force passed the shield started to buckle, the shaking and the vibrations increased and the ship began to break up. As the ship fell apart, Sanders was encased inside an escape pod, which automatically enveloped him when sensors indicated irreversible destruction. The blast completely passed and he found himself within the one meter by two point five meter pod, surrounded by debris. Sanders surmised that the blast must have come from an astropilot. If standard protocol was followed the pilot would soon be searching for survivors. A beacon would automatically be activated after three minutes, which would facilitate his rescue. So, he relaxed and waited.

General Moosewood saw the blast and the ITP vessel destroyed. He assumed it was Major Sorino. He radioed Captain Johnston that the ITP vessel was destroyed and that Major Sorino was presumably dead, but that he would search for survivors, as he was closer. Captain Johnston acknowledged this and held his position. The general was not expecting to find Sorino alive. He quickly moved into the blast zone and surveyed the debris. His monitor picked up an egg shaped object, two and a half meters long and symmetrical. That seems to be an escape pod, the general thought. He quickly moved in and snatched up the pod before the beacon was activated. He radioed Johnston that there were no survivors.

Johnston had mixed feelings. He was pleased with himself for having successfully launched a very difficult shot, but he felt a twinge of sadness at having destroyed a fellow pilot, even one that was a fugitive. He turned his ship around and started for his usual patrol, sending a message to Astropilot Control Center detailing all the events, emphasizing the superior skills that led to the fatal weapons hit.

The general put his ship on autopilot and went down to the cargo hold. The scan of the escape pod revealed that the occupant was alive and that there was nothing harmful either on the pod or inside. He opened the escape hatch and received a shock when Major Sanders popped out.

"Hello, general," Sanders said, "You look like you've seen a ghost."

The general was completely dumbfounded, first reaching out his hand and then wrapping both his arms tightly around the wayward major. "Where have you been...what happened?"

Before Sanders could answer Captain Johnston's voice came over the communication system, "General, this is Captain Johnston. Just confirming that there are no survivors." David put his finger to his mouth and shook his head.

"No, captain. No sign of survivors."

Johnston replied, "Well, that was quite a shot wouldn't you say?"

"Yes, captain. Quite a shot. You will report to your headquarters, won't you?" the general asked.

"Already done, general, as per standard protocol."

"Very well, captain. I'll return to Earth. You may resume your usual patrol duties." The general and David watched as Johnston took off at high speed. "Stupid... incompetent," the general muttered. He smiled and turned back to David. "OK, tell me all about it."

David proceeded to tell his tale, the general listening attentively, completely fascinated, as they headed back to Earth. Once David had finished, the general related all that had been happening and what Dr. Tennyson was going through.

"We've got to get back," David said. "I think I can help our pretty, young doctor. Let me drive general, with all due respect, you drive like an old woman."

The general smiled as David took over the controls. Some things never change, he thought, as he pondered everything that the major had told him.

During the flight back to Earth, the general filled David in on all that had happened. Major Sorino's rather unusual, obsessive behavior and actions were confusing. David had always thought Sorino to be 100 percent by the book, following rules and regulations no matter what the situation. He had always considered this one of Sorino's strengths, but it was also a weakness. It certainly was uncharacteristic of him to disobey orders, assault guards, and steal an aircraft, particularly to go looking for someone that he really didn't care for...hated really. But, Sorino was gone now and David knew that if he returned it would not be due to anything that he or any astropilot would do. David silently prayed that Sorino was safe, confident that whatever was meant to be had transpired.

The general asked, "Why keep your return secret? If we send a message that you are safe that has to be beneficial to Dr. Tennyson and the ITP program. That stupid Captain Johnston certainly doesn't know and the escape pod beacon never activated and I see that your subcutaneous transponder has been deactivated."

David replied, "I think a surprise appearance by the supposed dead ITP pilot would be best. It may shake up the Senate and the memedia and help me get started on what is sure to be a very difficult job. I think my first stop will be the Senate hearing chamber. I'm sure that I'll be able to rescue Dr. Tennyson from the hot seat."

LXXVII. TESTIMONY RESUMES

DEBORAH WAS BACK IN FRONT OF THE SENATE COMMITTEE. THE PREvious days' events and aborted testimony had left Senator Leavitt angry and embarrassed. He was determined to expose Dr. Tennyson for the fraud he believed her to be. There was a sense of desperation in his voice as he resumed his questioning. He clutched a piece of paper in his hand, a message that he had received the previous night:

"Senator, I am not happy. I will be very disappointed if you allow this insignificant woman to show you up. AD."

Senator Leavitt had no desire to find out what happened to people that caused Mr. Diblonski to be unhappy and disappointed. He hadn't been able to stomach looking at any of the media reports, knowing that he had been portrayed as a fool or worse.

He started questioning Deborah, "Good morning Dr. Tennyson. I trust that we can proceed today without any theatrics."

"Of course, Senator. I am sorry for everything that happened yesterday," she lied.

Senator Leavitt continued, "I would like to ask you to provide definitive evidence that any of these so-called ITP flights actually went anyplace other than out of our immediate sight. What can you produce that we, the members of the Senate Interplanetary Committee, can examine or question to convince us that the ITP is not some scheme to defraud our government of valuable resources and that it is truly safe for our brave astropilots?"

"Senator Leavitt, with all due respect," Deborah answered. "We have data mapping the energy output from all scannable portals. Transmissions have been received from Alpha Base One in minutes, rather than years, and our record of Little Bit going through the portal and safely returning."

"Yes, all very impressive and so easily fabricated," Senator Leavitt said with a tone of dismissal. "Do you have anything definitive?"

"I can provide that," a voice shouted from the back of the chamber. "I am about as definitive as any evidence could be."

A loud murmur ran through the packed room as Major Sanders slowly walked to the front of the hearing chamber.

Senator Leavitt stood up. "Who are you to provide such proof?"

"Why, senator, I am disappointed that after all that you've said and how deeply involved you are in the ITP that you don't recognize me. I'm sure that almost all the people here know me." Senator Fitzpatrick leaned over and whispered into Senator Leavitt's ear. Leavitt's face turned white like snow and then bright red. He tried to compose himself, as the murmur running through the crowd grew into a roar that was loud enough to penetrate the partition separating the spectators from the hearing chamber.

Senator Leavitt brought his gavel down hard on the table, "Quiet, please, everyone will be quiet or you will be removed from this chamber." He was desperately trying to salvage what he realized was a near hopeless situation. He addressed David, "Major Sanders, certainly, I am pleased to see that you have returned safely from wherever you have been hiding. It is rather convenient that you show up at just this moment."

"It was one hundred percent intentional, senator," Sanders said, "I thought I should make a memorable entrance. With the committee's permission I would be more than happy to testify and tell you the truth about the ITP. I've returned from a remarkable journey to tell you that the ITP is a complete success and a total failure. Dr. Deborah Tennyson is the most brilliant mathematician and scientist of our time and all of her work has been perfect. However, the ITP is completely unusable and cannot, in any way, be utilized to secure the future of mankind. I am requesting that this august committee accept my testimony as it pertains to the Interdimensional Transport Protocol; accept it as definitive proof that Dr. Deborah Tennyson is in no way a fraud. However, I will testify only if the Committee allows me to present my story completely and without interruption, except for questions."

Senator Leavitt was drenched in sweat and his hair was now tousled. He was seething with fear and anger at this disruption to his plan of attack. "I don't think that the c ommittee is under any obligation to hear unsubstantiated testimony," he said, grasping for any excuse that would prevent Sanders from speaking.

The other committee members, unanimously, objected. They all wanted to hear what the major had to say. "OK, major, you have the floor," Leavitt said. "Please take Dr. Tennyson's chair."

"Thank you, senator, but I prefer to stand. And you won't need any of those physiologic monitors. You must accept, by faith, that what I tell you is the whole truth or may God strike me dead."

"An unusual request," Senator Leavitt said, actually feeling somewhat relieved, "But, it is acceptable to me, as long as the other committee members don't object." He turned to the rest of the senators. They were silent. "Apparently, the Committee agrees to your request. You may proceed, major."

"Thank you, senator. Let me start by telling all of you that the Interdimensional Transport Protocol performed flawlessly, carrying me through the portal exactly as all the science, math and testing predicted. Once through the portal, inside the interdimensional plane, the proverbial black box, my adventure really started. I was met by a powerful blast, which caused me serious injury and, due to my own lack of confidence and fear, sent me out of the interdimensional plane to an unknown planet. The ship's very efficient sensors carried me to a garden on this planet, populated by humans who were lovingly cared for by their benevolent Creator. He provided them with all their wants and needs. When I landed I was badly injured, one step from death, really. One of the inhabitants of this garden nursed me back to health." David paused for a moment, took a deep breath and resumed his testimony. "As I regained my strength, I learned about the people and their world and they learned about me." David went on to recount the entire story, leaving out his marriage, but recounting Abraham's ascension, Elijah's death and resurrection, the fall, and his escape. "...I left Eden and was able to re-enter the interdimensional plane. Once inside, however, time stopped. I was held there for what seemed to be thousands of years, without the passage of time. I was privileged to witness the entire classic Bible played out before me like a live cinema. I was brought into the presence of God, our Creator, where I finally realized how insignificant and worthless I truly am." At the mention of God a snicker and stifled laughter could be heard. David continued undeterred.

"God has not abandoned our world, although we are more than happy to keep him buried in the backyard or locked in the basement. After all, who needs God when we have our government and benevolent industries giving us everything that they decide we need, telling us what to eat, what to do, what we can and cannot believe as well as when we can have children. We are told that it is all for the good of the world and mankind. Do what you like, as long as it feels good and nobody gets hurt. Meanwhile, so many of us drift through life without any sense of meaning or purpose, hoping for a brief thrill to make us feel alive for a day, all the time longing for the freedom that death will bring. That's the cruel joke, however. Medical Science now prolongs our misery, keeping us alive longer and longer, allowing us to thoroughly enjoy the emptiness that is our existence. And, if something isn't right, if our minds start to weaken or die, it doesn't matter, because the body lives on. But, not to worry, that body will be locked away from the rest of productive society, to be fed and watered like a plant until death mercifully takes it away forever.

"Yet, we should envy those lost souls living on in mindless bodies. They are spared the daily misery that all of us face each day; days of utter hopelessness, because they have no awareness of the despondency that fills our world. But, I am here to tell you that there is hope. God is in our world and because of this statement of fact there is hope. His holy spirit is all around us and he wants us to know that he is here and that he loves us. Like the Prodigal son we have left our home, squandered our fortune and now we have nothing. But our father, God, has not lost hope and waits with open arms, ready to kill the fatted calf and rejoice at our return."

"The ITP took me into God's presence, outside time and space. I was shown, repeatedly, mankind's folly, ugliness, and sinfulness. Before my journey, I was the worst of all sinners, living a life of wanton hedonism, filled with self indulgence; indulgence and selfishness second to no one. Selfishness that led me to seduce our brilliant Dr. Tennyson, all for a few brief moments of fame. But, here I stand, now, before you, humbled and shamed. I beg all of you to start to change the evil ways of the world, to have faith in God, to believe that He is here and loves us and that he will care for us in His own special way. And, if just one person that hears these words believes and offers the tiniest word of thanks to our benevolent, omnipotent, omniscient God, then I will have accomplished my task." David paused for a moment, "Does the committee have any questions?"

The room and the Senate Committee sat silently. After what seemed to be hours, Senator Leavitt spoke, "Major, you preach with great eloquence, more than I would expect from an astropilot, but, why should any of us believe one word that you have spoken? You refuse the very monitors that would allow us to determine the veracity of your word. I don't see a shred of physical evidence proving that you made a journey of any kind. Please, I want to believe you, but give me some proof."

David smiled, "Spoken like a true skeptic, senator. I offer only myself, senator. I was lost, mostly dead, but God, our Creator, took pity on me. He sent an angel to heal my body and cleanse my soul. I am sorry, senator, but that is the only proof that I have. Now... it is only a question of faith, yours and mine."

Deborah had been sitting silently, pondering every word she had heard. The beauty and truth of what David had said filled her heart and, as she thought of her work and God, she realized that everything that she believed about science, all she had observed in this universe made perfect sense in the context of an omnipotent God. She rose from her chair and stood by David's side.

She started to speak, "Senator, as one who has spent her life trusting in the order and perfection of a mathematical equation, I tell you now that no truer, more perfect words have ever been spoken. These hearings are moot, the ITP is irrelevant and we should give up the ITP folly and trust in God."

Senator Leavitt smiled. This may turn out better than I'd hoped, he thought. He started to speak when a holographic image appeared. No one could determine its source. There, for the entire world to see was the clear image of Senator Leavitt's office and his art collection. There was a female body lying on the floor surrounded by blood and a pile of dust; apparently she was dead. The time stamp showed the images were only few hours old. Senator Leavitt did not recognize the body, but he turned ashen as the holograph focused in on each of the paintings, each with its title, date of acquisition and the deed for which payment had been rendered. There was an empty spot with a note that read Dr. Deborah Tennyson with today's date.

"Shut this off," Senator Leavitt screamed, but it was too late. Each of the committee members was taking great interest and members of the media quickly copied the hologram. General Moosewood called the Senate Security forces, who were immediately dispatched, along with the local police, to Senator Leavitt's office to investigate.

As pandemonium erupted, no one noticed the little white dog that was in the back of the chamber. Little Bit scooted out the back door as soon as it opened and the images disappeared. Deborah smiled as she stood by David. "You were right about Joshua," she whispered to him. She thought that Joshua had proven to be very resourceful and she felt like she owed her life to him.

The next several hours were filled with endless media reports. The response to David's testimony ranged from guarded acceptance (rare) to venomous denouncement (common). The few truly thoughtful analyses weighed the wisdom of his words against the realities of the world. Conspicuous by its absence was a report from Chaunce Edwards of the IBS network.

No matter what anyone believed the ITP was dead, at least for now. The government would be forced to consider other resources and potential solutions to the problems the planet was facing.

In the days following his testimony David was kept isolated at the ITP compound while he was completely examined and debriefed by the ITP and astropilot investigators. The exam revealed him to be in perfect health with no evidence of any injuries, except the absence of his right tenth rib. The absence of any evidence of healed fractures or old injuries to internal organs gave credence to the reports that David's entire ordeal had been a fantasy. David chalked it up to the excellent nursing that he had received from Ruth and her Creator. After this was completed, he asked for and was granted discharge from the ITP program and from the Astropilot Corps. He had a new commission from God. His next role would be his most important and probably would finally bring him lasting fame, albeit a different fame from what he had anticipated before he started his adventure. He went home to his apartment, taking some time to reflect on all that had happened and to make plans for the days to come. There was a mountain of requests for interviews from all the usual media outlets, all politely refused.

After about a week of solitude he thought about calling Deborah. Each time he started to call, he would stop, unable to complete the call.

Deborah's week had been filled with everything but solitude. With David being unavailable, Deborah became the new media darling. She received thousands of requests for interviews. There were offers of book deals, video broadcasts, and personal appearances of every type. Overwhelmed, she retreated to her apartment, activating and maintaining a security system she had never previously needed. She wasn't sure whether David's words left her vindicated or disgraced, but she also knew that it did not matter. The media, being just as confused, was in a state of bliss. Confusion, and controversy, these were what the media always craved. Viewpoints ranged all across the spectrum, all presented as plausible, factual, and with an air of certainty. In the end they all were completely pointless. The mainstream outlets, controlled by Diblonski Ltd., presented David as having been drugged and hallucinating or crazy, certainly consistent with his past behavior; the ITP was called a complete fraud and Deborah was portrayed as its devious mastermind.

Paul Samuels, subbing for Chaunce Edwards, summed up the general consensus in his nightly commentary:

"In a stunning turn of events, Major David Sanders made a surprise and surprisingly timely re-appearance at the Senate ITP hearings today. At the point where Senator Adrian Leavitt was to begin serious questioning of Dr. Deborah Tennyson, Major Sanders conveniently showed up to offer his testimony. And what testimony it was. The apparently demented Major spewed forth the most foul swill I have ever heard. He appeared disheveled and ranted on about God and Eden, proving to this reporter that he is what we've always claimed, unfit for duty in any capacity. Now, more than ever, we must question our leadership for entrusting the safety of our planet and solar system to a man as unstable as Major Sanders. Of course the responsibility for this sham rests squarely on the shoulders of Dr. Deborah Tennyson, who it has been shown, relied only on selfish nepotism and personal feelings to choose Major Sanders for this vital mission. It is the opinion of the IBS network that they both should be banned from future involvement in interplanetary and interstellar research and a criminal investigation should commence into the entire ITP program...."

LXXVIII. FALLOUT

THE OFFICIAL GOVERNMENT POSITION WAS THAT THE ITP, IN GENERAL, was successful, but Major Sanders had suffered a mental breakdown.

Future ITP missions were put on permanent hold. It was also the official viewpoint that Major Sorino had been stopped and destroyed while trying to steal military property, deliberately disobeying direct orders of a superior. He was posthumously stripped of rank and dishonorably discharged from the Astrocorps. Captain Johnston, meanwhile, was given a Gold Star for his bravery and performance in stopping the renegade Major Sorino. General Moosewood felt more than uneasy at the vilification of one of his pilots, but did not publicly object.

General Moosewood and Deborah, as chief administrator and lead scientist for the ITP Committee, issued an official statement, corroborating the government position, calling the ITP successful and potentially useful to solve the many problems that planet Earth faced, but with too many potential dangers to make it plausible to utilize at this time. They made the recommendation that the ITP continue to be studied, but all work be done with unmanned probes. As a result, the ITP as a means of opening up and expanding space travel was effectively dead.

After issuing this statement, Deborah appeared in a few interviews from her apartment. As a practical matter, she agreed to write a series of articles about the technical aspects of the ITP process and the committee workings from its inception to the present. After about a week the media hype abated somewhat and she had some time to herself. She decided to make a record of her entire ITP experience, perhaps write a book. She fielded numerous queries from the Birthright Freedom League, a group that promoted reproductive freedom for women. Her public testimony had emboldened their cause and they wanted her to be their new spokeswoman. She respectfully declined. She thought about David and tried to call him, but he did not respond. She had lunch with General Moosewood. He recounted his pursuit of Major Sorino and they reminisced about the ITP and speculated on the future of the human race. They parted, wishing each other well, each hoping that they would stay in touch.

Deborah thought for a few moments about Joshua. She had this overwhelming sense of gratitude, but didn't feel it was right to try to contact him.

Adrian Leavitt was immediately stripped of his chairmanship, pending the results of a senate inquiry. His entire art collection had been confiscated and, it turned out, many of the paintings had been stolen, some as long as 250 years ago. A criminal investigation also was underway. Leavitt had no way to explain how the paintings came to be in his possession. He didn't dare reveal his connection to Mr. Diblonski. As the investigation quickly progressed it became apparent that Leavitt would be facing a considerable jail time. Not one of his fellow senators offered any support. As he sat alone in his office, staring at empty walls and blank spaces that had been adorned with his precious collection, he received a message, "Do the right thing." He looked around the room, terrified, feeling completely alone, without hope. The room was illuminated by only the faint glow from a solitary light at the entrance, which now grew brighter with a reddish hue. The smell of burning sulphur filled the room. There was a rope hanging over a chair. It hadn't been there an hour ago. The red glow became deeper. The rope was tied in a peculiar way. Filled with anguish, he threw the rope over the exposed ceiling beam. Crying, he tied it to a hook in the wall, stood on a tall chair, put the rope around his neck and kicked the chair away. As he dangled and his life faded away, the light returned to normal. He was found the following morning. The media reported that justice had been done.

Joshua, amazingly, had gone through his whole adventure without any recognition, or even any record that he was in any way involved. This pleased him, greatly. He was delighted that David had returned safely and made a mental note to call him for dinner once all the excitement had passed. Tracking down violent gang members, delivering unsanctioned babies, breaking and entering, battling demons was not for him. He decided it was time to return to the track. Ruth Rising was running down south next month and he planned to be there. As he planned his return to his old life, he decided to make a few detours. As he walked towards his apartment, he buzzed David. Little Bit was still with Joshua and when the little dog heard David's voice he started barking and racing around with great joy. When they arrived at David's apartment Little Bit race ahead, up the stairs to find David waiting at the top. The little dog jumped into David's arms, licking his face over and over. When they had finished their hello, David asked, "Where's Joshua?" They both looked down the stairs and then ran down to find Joshua, but he was gone. "I'll catch up with him later," David thought, as Little Bit yelped and continued to lick David nonstop. David put him down and the two raced up the stairs and into his apartment.

Joshua walked up the stairs to his apartment. He had decided that David and Little Bit deserved some time to themselves. He flipped on his computer monitor, planning to study the next day's races. He sat down at the monitor with a glass of water, but felt distracted. He picked up the book from the table and started to read randomly "...this is my beloved son with whom I am well pleased..." He had read it before, but the words remained fresh. The races can wait for a little while, he thought, as he slowly, thoughtfully read through the Gospel of Matthew.

Aaron Diblonski sat in his huge, plush office, a fire blazing away in the huge fireplace. The events of the past several days had been unexpected, but the outcome had been satisfactory. For all practical purposes, the ITP had been halted and his vast empire remained soundly in place and for the most part undisturbed. Senator Leavitt had finally reached the end of his usefulness and had been efficiently dispatched without any troubling questions being asked. The loss of Richard Cosby was a much bigger problem. It had taken years to get him set up in that position and now he'd have to start over. Diblonski had no idea why Cosby had gone to Leavitt's office. There must have been a good reason, he thought. Whatever it was it had died with Cosby. Diblonski had no idea of Joshua's involvement with Cosby, which was fortunate for Joshua.

Diblonski gave a brief consideration to Major Sanders and his tale. He knew that it was all true, but was confident that Sanders would have his thirty seconds of fame and then fade away. People won't care about God and salvation. They want what I give them, pleasure for a brief moment, a prelude to an eternity of pain, suffering and despair. No, he thought, I can always count on human nature, as he sat close to the huge fire to face another in an eternity of sleepless nights. He opened an old leather bound book and started to read, his smooth bony fingers delicately turning each page.

LXXIX. JOSHUA AND JESSIE

WITH ALL THE EXCITEMENT FINALLY SUBSIDING, THERE WAS ONE more visit Joshua felt compelled to make. He hadn't really known Major Sorino, having met him, briefly, one time. But, he had learned of the events leading up to Sorino's ITP flight and there were a number of unanswered questions that kept gnawing at him. He went, uninvited and unannounced, to the Sorino's house to speak with Jessie. He knocked on the door and Jessie's voice came through the intercom, "May I help you?"

Joshua answered, "Mrs. Sorino, my name is Joshua Smith. I was wondering if I might talk to you about your husband."

The door opened and Jessie was standing in the entrance, dressed in a long black dress, her eyes red and swollen. "Do I know you?" she asked.

"No, I met your husband once, but I'm really a friend of Major Sanders," Joshua said. Jessie started to close the door. "I don't think I want to talk to you," she said.

"Please, Mrs. Sorino," Joshua pleaded as he put his foot in the door. "I have questions that only you can answer and I may have some information that will help ease your grief and suffering."

Jessie stared at him for a moment. She saw kindness in his eyes, but also sensed some desperation. "Very well, come in."

She brought him into the small sitting room. Joshua saw the automated home cleaner scooting back and forth, busily picking numerous wads of crumpled tissue paper. He saw a blanket on the couch and a tear stained pillow.

"Please sit down Mr. Smith."

"Thank you, but call me Joshua."

"How can I help you? You know I don't think I should be so friendly with any acquaintance of Major Sanders. After all, he's the reason that Anthony is gone."

"Perhaps," Joshua replied, "But I think there was more to your husband's flight than rescuing Major Sanders. I suspect that you do, too. Do you know much about the accident Major Sorino suffered as a child?"

"Just what he told me. He turned over a three wheeler and nearly died. The doctors didn't think he'd survive and he drifted towards death until they all thought that he was gone. But, he made a miraculous recovery, baffling all of them. His mother told me that after this accident and recovery he had a sense of purpose that had been missing from his life. He improved in school, never misbehaved again and decided as he grew up that he was going to be an astropilot; not just any astropilot, but the best astropilot. And, with the possible exception of Major Sanders, he was."

"All that makes perfect sense, Mrs. Sorino. What can you tell me about how he viewed the ITP?"

"That program gave him a new life, really. Before the start of the ITP he was becoming depressed. I never knew why. I think the life of an astropilot can be mundane and boring, which was a disappointment to him. But, the ITP re-energized him. The idea that he could do some good that would help the entire planet was very appealing to both of us. I hadn't seen him with such enthusiasm for his work in years. After Major Sanders was lost, Anthony became obsessed, working nonstop to try to get the ITP back up and running to find him. Just the thought that the program would be shut down terrified him."

"Was he terrified because Major Sanders would remain lost or because he wouldn't get the opportunity to traverse an ITP portal and leave the confines of time and space?"

"I'm sure that he was worried about Major Sanders. Although they weren't really friends, there is a camaraderie among pilots that binds them together. Major Sanders was so many things that Anthony was not. Anthony was a loving husband and father, a good sober man. David Sanders is a hedonistic, selfish man who cares only about his own pleasure and personal fame. It did seem a little strange that Anthony worked so diligently to try to rescue Major Sanders."

"What you're saying makes a great deal of sense. May I tell you what I think?"

"Please."

"The ITP provides a passage to a place outside of time and space. If there is a God, although he is everywhere, the Bible clearly shows that he and his glory are most clearly found in heaven, outside the limited confines of our existence. This had been my theory even before Major Sanders returned. I think that your husband had the same idea. He had more than just theory to base this on, however. His childhood injury, near death experience and miraculous recovery suggest that he had some sort of supernatural encounter, perhaps with God. After this he spent the rest of his life trying to get physically close to God, trying to find his way back to God, but in a way that would be acceptable to God. Certainly dying is one way, but God has never accepted suicide and he would know if your husband engineered his own death, even if it appeared to be an accident. His joining the Astropilot Corps was an attempt to get close to God, trying to get back to what he must have experienced as a child. I think that he was disappointed by the Astropilot Corps. Flying around the solar system did not bring him any closer to God. That would explain the sense of apathy that you described, until the ITP came along. This was his chance to drive right into God's living room. I'm sure that he was disappointed that he was not selected to go on the initial mission, but I'm also sure that he was confident that he would get his opportunity on the second manned ITP flight. He had waited years, so a few more weeks or months would be tolerable. However, Major Sanders' flight went awry and the Senate was threatening to dismantle the ITP program. He was left with no choice but to take matters into his own hands or his lifelong pursuit would have been for naught. Do you think that I'm right?"

Jessie was crying, wiping her eyes with an endless stream of tissues, throwing them on the floor, keeping the little robot busy. "You're right about Anthony's obsession with God. We both know that God exists and is part of our lives, but it was different for Anthony. It was incredibly personal for him. He would kneel for hours sometimes, anguished, pleading with God through prayers. When I would ask him if he was OK he would give me a little smile and say 'it's just me and God kid' and then he would be fine. There was always urgency to his prayers, like he had to be perfect in what he prayed to win God's favor."

"That certainly jibes with my thoughts. But, I want you to think about what has happened to him, because, no matter what did happen he has to be with God now. Admittedly, he sinned repeatedly in stealing the ITP vessel and going off on his unauthorized flight. As long as he was repentant God would be forgiving. Going through the ITP portal was definitely not a suicide mission. If he made it through he would be in God's domain and have achieved his life's goal. If he died passing through the portal he would be taken to heaven to be with God and also would have found his happiness. And there can be no question that he is now with God. The Bible reveals that faith such as his is the key to getting to heaven. He demonstrated more faith, to give up a loving family, and risk his death, all to be with God. I know that you miss him, but you can be sure that he is happy and is making a place for eternity with you and with the God that you both love."

Jessie was still crying, but now the tears were those of joy rather than grief. "Thank you, thank you so much for your thoughts. I know that what you've said is the truth. It just makes too much sense with everything I used to see in Anthony."

The two talked for a while longer about nothing in particular, until Joshua said that it was time for him to leave. Jessie had some parting words, "Thank you so much for coming." She had stopped crying. "You have brought me out of the depths of despair, I am truly grateful and I hope to see you again. I also think that you should listen to your own words and believe some of what you have convinced me is true. Perhaps, then, you will find your own peace with God."

Joshua was silent as he left, starting the long walk back to his home.

LXXX. DINNER WITH DAVID

WHEN JOSHUA REACHED HIS HOME THERE WAS A MESSAGE FROM David waiting for him. They had seen and spoken to each other only briefly since David's return. David wanted to get together with him, inviting Joshua to dinner at his apartment. There was some anxiety in David's voice, as Joshua called to accept the invitation.

Joshua walked to David's apartment. He stopped at the market on the way and picked up some fresh vegetables, fruit and bread. He assumed, correctly, that David would only have computer synthesized fare. Joshua thought that this dinner should be special, a celebration. David saw Joshua coming and met him at the building's entrance. He embraced his friend, almost knocking the bags of food to the ground. "Fresh food," David said. "It will be like a taste of Eden." Little Bit was with him and jumped up on

Joshua before running ahead to the apartment entrance.

"It was the least that I could do," Joshua replied. When they reached the apartment, David put the food away and got Joshua a glass of ice water. They sat in silence for a moment, until Joshua spoke, "I guess I was wrong."

"What?" David asked, "Wrong about what?"

"You don't remember. I said that you would return as a perfect English gentleman, but I was wrong. You've returned as the new messiah."

Joshua saw David's eyes flash briefly. "Definitely not the messiah. He'll come later. More akin to John the Baptist. A lone voice crying in the wilderness."

"I guess you're right, although I'm not in the mood for locust and honey tonight."

"You surprise me, as always, with your knowledge."

"Well, while you were out flitting about the universe and God knows where else, I took a crash course in the Bible."

"I didn't know that. I did receive a message from Dr. Tennyson and she said that you'd been a great help, but she didn't give me any details. Just as well, to keep you safe."

"'Oh, yeah, I did have some excitement. Let's see. I delivered your son, I nearly got my throat slit, I broke into a senator's office and exposed his corruption and I've become an expert in Biblical history and space time philosophy. And, Ruth's Rising is still undefeated and unheaded."

David winced and a tear came to his eye at the mention of the filly's name. Joshua noticed the change immediately. "Surely you're not feeling sentimental over a horse... that's my job."

David composed himself. "No, the name Ruth...that was my wife's name."

Joshua looked surprised. He was silent for a minute. "That wasn't in any media reports."

"No and it won't ever be. She was the most beautiful, perfect woman. I've never known such happiness. A part of me that had been empty became filled until it overflowed. She saved my life, but I couldn't save her. My only consolation is that I will be with her again, when my time here is over."

"That explains it, then."

"Explains what?"

"Why you haven't done anything to contact Deborah."

"Don't you think that I've tried? I've prepared messages, started to call a hundred times, but I just can't; I'm so afraid of hurting her."

"And what are you doing with your silence? She needs to be told something. She deserves to know the truth. And, you have a son."

"I know. And I will contact them, but I don't think I can right now. I don't know how I would explain it to her."

Joshua thought about continuing to fight for Deborah, but he sensed the anguish in David's voice. If he had learned anything from this whole ordeal it was that there were some things that were out of our control. If David and Deborah were destined to be together it would happen at the proper time. Joshua changed the subject, "Was there music in Eden?"

"The people there sang the most beautiful a cappella psalms, with wonderful, sweet sounding harmonies. I gave them a taste of our music, they seemed very impressed. Ruth loved the classical music that I played from the Falcon's computer. Since I've returned I seem to be playing more Bach and Vivaldi. But, enough about me, what about you? I never would have thought a simple horseplayer, especially someone as brilliant as you, would get tied up in such a sordid affair."

"Well, it's all your fault. After all, if you hadn't gotten lost none of this would have happened and if you hadn't told Deborah to ask for my opinions I would have gone through the whole of it in perfect anonymous bliss."

"Any repercussions?"

"Nothing so far. I am still looking over my shoulder a lot, though. How I ended up in such a situation, I don't know. I managed to use one of Aaron Diblonski's main operatives to expose a corrupt senator, also working for Diblonski, somehow both of them ending up dead, yet managing to stay completely anonymous and out of the picture. Oh, and Little Bit was a huge help with everything. I would probably be dead if this little dog had not been with me. All things considered, I'm glad it's over and I'm glad that you're safe. I feel sorry for Major Sorino's family. I went to see his wife, Jessie. She was devastated. I told her some things that made her feel better."

"That seems very noble on your part, since you never knew him or her."

"I learned some things about her husband that I thought she should know and would be a comfort to her. I think they were."

"I'm sure that you helped. You have a way about you that puts people at ease, a way of helping them realize that their problems may not be so insurmountable after all. You have a great many gifts, I don't think you are aware of. It's a shame that they are wasted on something as trivial as horses."

"You're right, no doubt, but I'll stay at the track until something better comes along. What about you? You're certainly not staying with the Astropilot Corps."

"Oh, no...no way. I've already resigned my commission and been discharged. They practically insisted. They don't want anyone as unstable as me in the Corps. Besides, I have a much more important job. I lived through thousands of years of history, saw things that other people only dream about and received a charge directly from the Lord God Almighty. I have only one job left in my life, to prepare this world for God's return. I will be that lone voice crying in the wilderness."

"When will you start?"

"I'm giving myself time to prepare, to find the words and the courage to go out into a hostile world, to stand up to scorn and ridicule, and speak the truth."

"If anyone can do such a thing, it's you. You're the one who jumped out of a plane at 38,000 meters, flew at near light speed through an asteroid field, single handedly took on an entire hostile population in Eden. You've lived through every challenge this universe has to offer. We both know what you'll be up against, but just remember, you've got the best material ever written on your side. And, you're only the messenger; one thing made clear in the Bible is that God does all the work. He takes the most unlikely individuals and raises them up to do his work and to glorify him. By the way, do you have a Bible?"

"Strangely enough, there was one waiting for me in my apartment. I guess a gift from God."

"Well, there are millions of disaffected people out there looking for a glimmer of hope.All you have to do is find them. I can tell you where to start. On the outside of the city there are a group of people, lost souls really, looking for the type of guidance that you have to offer. They were being misled, straight to hell, but you can set them back on the right course. They will listen to you without any ridicule or derision. Little Bit knows how to find them."

"Thank you. We'll do our best to find these people and show them the truth. Could you do one thing for me? Tell Deborah I'm sorry and keep an eye on my son. For some reason, out of all the people I know, you're the only one that I trust."

"I certainly will do what I can."

They sat together for some time longer, mostly in silence, while Bach and Vivaldi filled the room. Joshua left, leaving David in solitude, except for Little Bit who continued to be David's constant companion. Not another word was heard about David Sanders for nearly six weeks until Joshua received a brief message. "It starts today....DS."

That day at 1:00 P.M. David and Little Bit ventured into a rundown building at the edge of town. There had been only word of mouth advertising as David didn't want to bring too much attention to himself at the start. There was a gathering of about three dozen people, men and women, the desperate and disheveled. These were his audience, the downtrodden looking for an alternative to the artificial world that shunned them. David pitied them and hoped that he could bring some hope into their lives. He recognized a small group of media types in the crowd. He pitied them too.

David stood on a small platform, dressed in a plain white shirt and gray pants. He started, "May the blessings of peace from our Lord, God be upon you. My name is David Sanders. Some of you may have heard of me. God sends his love, but also his disappointment. From the beginning, when he formed you ...out of dust, he loved you. In the beginning God..."

And so he preached with a passion and conviction for God that filled the hearts of everyone in that room, bringing tears to the audience's eyes. Afterwards, he personally greeted everyone in attendance. They all thanked him, even the members of the media, who had gotten more of a story than they had bargained for. One member of the media made a special point to meet David afterwards. A distinguished looking man with white hair and a deep voice that seemed familiar approached David. He addressed David very cordially, "Major Sanders, I don't think you recognize me. My name is Chaunce Edwards. I want to tell you how much I enjoyed the message that you brought to us today. I know that you have every right to be angry and have nothing to do with me, but I just want you to know that the words I've heard from you since your return have brought me hope and peace that I thought impossible to ever realize. I hope that you will continue this work no matter what the media, government or the Diblonskis of the world say or do. You have one convert, at least, although one whose voice has been removed. I am sorry to say that the IBS network relieved me of my duties as soon as they learned that I intended to file a favorable report about you after your return. "

David thought that Fyodor would have been very pleased and replied, "Mr. Edwards, thank you for your kind words. However, thanks should be given to God. The words that you have heard come from him. I am only his woefully inadequate messenger. Your support is greatly appreciated and you are more than welcome to travel with me on the difficult journey that I am embarking upon."

"Thank you," Edwards answered. "I certainly shall and if a new outlet for my voice can be found you can be certain that your message will be carried to the ends of the solar system."

Many others in attendance asked him when and where he would speak again and many promised to bring their friends. David felt that perhaps this little ripple he had started would grow to be a tidal wave. Wishful thinking, he thought.

After most everyone had left and he was preparing to leave, Little Bit started to bark with great excitement. A woman in a gray suit wearing a ridiculously large floppy hat was slowly approaching. She was carrying a package, which when she got closer, David recognized as a baby. His heart leapt a bit, but then fear and anxiety took over.

"Hello, David," Deborah said. "I thought that you should meet your son."

David stood there, motionless, not sure what she expected. But, he ran to her and embraced her and the baby. Tears rolled down Deborah's cheeks as David gave her a long kiss. Little Bit barked and ran around, jumping up and then barked some more.

"I was afraid to see you," David said. "In Eden I had a wife and I could never see someone taking her place."

"I know," Deborah cried. "Joshua told me."

"He always knows the right thing to do. Let's sit down, let me see my son." David stared into the baby's eyes. "He's beautiful, like his mother."

Deborah told him all about what had happened and how she had, at least for now, become something of a celebrity. She was finished with the ITP and she hadn't decided on any new position, although she had numerous offers. For the present she was busy as the latest media darling; the fallout from her electrifying senate testimony.

"You know," she said. "I've found that all this attention is very draining. I've taken up a new hobby to help me relax."

"Really," David said. "Tell me about it."

"Well, when I get really stressed and need to get away, I put David Jr. in his little cart and go for a run. Usually eight or ten kilometers. It's relaxing and takes me away from all the unwanted attention."

"That's amazing," David replied. He put his hand under her chin and lifted her face and stared into her eyes. He saw a look that he thought he had lost forever. "Thank you," he said softly.

"What?" Deborah asked.

"Oh nothing," he answered. "I think that's great. It's something that I've done for years."

"Well," Deborah said, "we could go for a run now."

"I'd like that. I can see how good you are. We can change here and run home."

Little Bit's tail wagged back and forth as he barked his approval.

LXXXI. AFTERWARDS

AFTER THE ITP HEARINGS, GENERAL MOOSEWOOD RESIGNED HIS commission. He had come to realize that spaceflight was all he ever really wanted to do. The whole affair with Sorino, Sanders and Captain Johnston made him want to get away from the Earth and bureaucrats. He traded them for the endless expanse of space. He joined up with Scully, bought an old astroplane and fixed it up so that it was space worthy. Scully, who had managed to get through the whole affair with only a slap on the wrist, made several propulsion modifications that allowed the old space vessel to achieve .38c and maintain that speed for extended periods of time with ease. The general also found one of the latest navigation computers to complement the souped up astroplane. The two men formed "Solo Transport Corporation," an interplanetary messenger, transport and escort company. They worked in direct competition with the Astropilot Corps, providing many of the same services, but without the bureaucracy. The general was happy to be free, selling his skills to anyone willing to pay with no questions asked. He did maintain contact with Deborah and monitored the development and growth of his "grandson," but never again set foot on Earth. Living his life from planet to planet and space station to space station, he had not felt this happy since his wife had passed away.

Captain Johnston was decorated by the senate for his courage and skill in thwarting Major Sorino. After this he told anyone who would listen of his exploits on this mission. The tale grew, taking on numerous embellishments, but always ending with the "Great Shot."

His fellow astropilots grew tired of the story, giving him the nickname "One Shot" Johnston. He never advanced in rank and mostly was assigned escort duty along slow freighters carrying mining waste into space to be dumped. One day, after one such dump, as the freighter turned to go back to its mining base, Johnston kept right on going out into space. He was never heard from again.

Joshua Smith went back to the track. He rejoined the regular gang at Bar #23. He never told any of them where he had been or what he had been doing. No one ever asked. Edna never returned to the track. Joshua received a hologram from her several months later. She had taken care of her parents until they both died within two weeks of each other. She was at school, learning how to be an elementary school teacher. She said that she would never forget him and wished him well. Joshua sent her some old style grade school textbooks to help her get started in her news career. He promised to visit if he was ever in Cleveland.

He read about David and Deborah every so often, but he did not see them again for quite some time. Years later he read that Jessie Sorino had remarried, a home cleaner repairman of all things.

Ruth Rising continued her dominance of the racing scene. She swept through all the stakes races for fillies, remaining undefeated and unheaded with track records established in all six of her races. She stepped up to compete against the boys, and remained just as much a powerhouse. She retired after her four year old season, undefeated and never headed in fifteen career starts. Joshua finally felt that he had seen the second coming of the great Ruffian.

Aaron Diblonski always knew that there had been someone else involved with Richard Cosby and the break in at Senator Leavitt's office. Despite every effort and all his numerous contacts it remained a mystery that gnawed at Diblonski for years until, under much more dire circumstances, their paths crossed again.

www.ingramcontent.com/pod-product-compliance
Lightning Source LLC
Chambersburg PA
CBHW050506260626
47157CB00004B/1211